Praise for the Darkwing Chronicles
by Savannah Russe

"Exciting, fast-paced. . . . It has everything: humor, action, mystery, and romance."   —Huntress Book Reviews

"Savannah Russe [lets] us know that there is more than one way to tell a good vamp's story."
                —Victoria Laurie, author of *Crime Seen*

"Superior supernatural suspense."   —The Best Reviews

IN THE BLOOD

THE DARKWING CHRONICLES
BOOK FOUR

SAVANNAH RUSSE

A SIGNET ECLIPSE BOOK

SIGNET ECLIPSE

Published by New American Library, a division of
Penguin Group (USA) Inc., 375 Hudson Street,
New York, New York 10014, USA
Penguin Group (Canada), 90 Eglinton Avenue East, Suite 700, Toronto,
Ontario M4P 2Y3, Canada (a division of Pearson Penguin Canada Inc.)
Penguin Books Ltd., 80 Strand, London WC2R 0RL, England
Penguin Ireland, 25 St. Stephen's Green, Dublin 2,
Ireland (a division of Penguin Books Ltd.)
Penguin Group (Australia), 250 Camberwell Road, Camberwell, Victoria 3124,
Australia (a division of Pearson Australia Group Pty. Ltd.)
Penguin Books India Pvt. Ltd., 11 Community Centre, Panchsheel Park,
New Delhi - 110 017, India
Penguin Group (NZ), 67 Apollo Drive, Rosedale, North Shore 0632,
New Zealand (a division of Pearson New Zealand Ltd.)
Penguin Books (South Africa) (Pty.) Ltd., 24 Sturdee Avenue,
Rosebank, Johannesburg 2196, South Africa

Penguin Books Ltd., Registered Offices:
80 Strand, London WC2R 0RL, England

First published by Signet Eclipse, an imprint of New American Library,
a division of Penguin Group (USA) Inc.

First Printing, November 2007
10 9 8 7 6 5 4 3 2 1

Scripture quotation on p. 129 taken from the Amplified® Bible. Copyright © 1954, 1958,
1962, 1964, 1965, 1987 by The Lockman Foundation. Used by permission.
(www.Lockman.org)

SIGNET ECLIPSE and logo are trademarks of Penguin Group (USA) Inc.

Printed in the United States of America

To my agent and friend
John Talbot.
You led the way.

INTRODUCTION

Should a vampire such as myself wear white to walk down the aisle? White is traditional, but seems inappropriate. My soul is anything but pure as driven snow. In point of fact, a rich, dark vermilion is my favorite color, and coal black would suit me quite well, being both symbolic of my sins and eminently more practical. Practical? Oh, yes. You see, my clothes often become stained by my victims' blood—a blot difficult to launder out. Personally, I don't dare send garments with that kind of soiling to the dry cleaner's. It raises too many questions.

I don't want attention, of course. I prefer to stay under the radar, to remain an anonymous creature who roams Manhattan's streets at night. Secrecy is my forte. Deception is my game. Both skills have kept me alive for over four hundred years. Coincidentally, they now make me very good at my job.

Let me introduce myself. My name is Daphne Urban. I work for the United States government. In these times of turmoil and terror, I protect and serve . . . in my own way.

I am a member of Team Darkwing. I am a vampire. And I am a spy.

CHAPTER 1

Coitus Interruptus

I wanted to sink my teeth into the young man lying next to me. To bite or not to bite, that was the question. Biting was, after all, what vampires did. But I aspired to something different: I was struggling to become a moral, principled vampire, of a better class than the run-of-the-mill bloodsuckers out there in the world. Well, chalk up another victory for vain self-delusion. I was making a balls-up mess of it.

The white sheet slipped down to my waist as I sat up in the bed, twisting away from the muscular hand that had been caressing my right breast. Through the plate-glass windows of the modern apartment building, the weak light of the illuminated city revealed my body. It was as ghostly pale as the sheet. I was hungry for blood, and anemic from lacking it.

"Something wrong?" The voice of St. Julien Fitzmaurice, my lover, was husky with desire.

I turned my head to look at him. Lying prone, Fitz had propped himself up on one arm. His long, lithe body was naked except for the bandage still covering the nearly healed stomach wound where he had been shot not long ago. His eyes were heavy-lidded, his hands were now stroking my back, and it was obvious how much he wanted to make love to me—while I, on the other hand, wanted to dine on him.

"I'm not in the mood," I answered, lying artlessly. I learned to lie centuries ago in order to save my life. Since then, I've done it often, and I do it well. If I told the truth, I'd have to say I was very much in the mood, but any further arousal would make it impossible for me to resist what all my instincts were pushing me to do.

Quickly I slid my eyes away from Fitz. I realized I had been staring—not at his sensual lips, not at his lean body, not even at his stiff member, so clearly ready for love. I had been staring at the carotid artery steadily beating in his neck. I imagined I could hear the blood rushing through it. And with my animal senses, perhaps I could.

Not good. Oh, not good at all. Annoyed with myself, I threw the sheet aside and stood up. Cool air embraced my body. I shivered. This wasn't my apartment. I kept the thermostat at my place cranked up to eighty.

Tonight, however, I was at Fitz's new apartment, three rooms with a terrace over on the East Side of Manhattan. He had money, old money from his family's bootlegging business back in the 1920s, so he could afford the astonishing rent for rooms not much bigger than closets.

My money was far older than his. I could afford a much larger place even in this neighborhood. However, I found the Upper East Side too conspicuously affluent and conventional. Rich I was, but hardly conventional, so I lived in the area bordered by the Columbia students who rented sublets near the university, the psychiatrists who clustered their practices along West End Avenue, and the working mommies-with-nannies who pushed strollers along Central Park West near the Museum of Natural History. The West Side of Manhattan had more funk and more secrets. It did, after all, have me.

"I don't understand you," Fitz said.

"I never expected you to. Let's not go there. We'll only end up fighting again." I gazed through the window at the murky sky above the East River. I once overheard Samuel Johnson call second marriages "the triumph of hope over experience." The same thing went for rebound romances. That was what Fitz and I had. We had both been left betrayed and embittered. I didn't think our relationship had a snowball's chance in hell of surviving, even without the complication that Fitz was human and I . . . I was not.

I picked up Fitz's sports coat off a chair and slipped it on in lieu of a bathrobe. The silk lining was icy and smooth against my skin. Something hard in the inside pocket knocked against my ribs. It was Fitz's gun. He was in the Secret Service. A very secret part of the Secret Service. I worked for . . . oh, who the hell did I work for? Some other intelligence agency. The CIA? NSA? USAMI? I can only fathom a guess.

My all-vampire spy group, the Darkwings, operated in deep black. In other words, we were a covert operation that didn't exist on paper, wasn't overseen by Congress, and probably wasn't even known to the president himself. He wasn't part of the permanent government—the people in Washington who really ran things, like J. Edgar Hoover back in his day. And if the president were told about us, he'd never believe it. He'd have to accept that vampires really do exist, and I have a feeling that wouldn't be politically correct.

But Fitz, whom I now heard stirring on the other side of the room, was a frank and honest man. I mistrust those qualities in anyone, but everything he had ever told me turned out to be the truth. That made him far too good for me. I suppose we ended up together because we were both lost, each in our own way.

A lamp with a low-wattage lightbulb came on next to Fitz's side of the bed. I heard a cap being unscrewed and liquid being poured into a glass. I knew without glancing over that Fitz was pouring himself a Jameson, straight up, no ice. I wasn't as much surprised as disappointed. He had promised to stop drinking. It was a promise he couldn't seem to keep for long. Fitz wasn't a drunk by any means. He held his liquor well, but he sometimes drank until his demons disappeared.

I was in no position to criticize. There were worse vices.

Just then strong arms encircled me from behind and soft lips nuzzled my ear. Fitz turned me around to face him. He kissed me. I tasted the whiskey on his mouth; its sharp taste bit into my tongue.

"Don't," I managed to say, turning my head away.

"Ah, Daphne, darlin', you know you want me," he said.

I did want him, and I was rapidly losing control. I had started out the evening with good intentions—to enjoy being in Fitz's arms and do no more than that—but my base desires were making a mockery of my efforts at morality.

Fitz kissed me again, and this time I didn't resist. My humanity receded and the beast within me crept forth. My incisors lengthened, my nails extended, my breath quickened. I was hungry—terribly, urgently hungry for blood.

Unaware of the changes occurring within me, Fitz lifted me up and carried me back to the bed. Focused on his own desire for intimacy, he noticed nothing. Blindness to reality is always dangerous. I never let my guard down, which is why I've stayed alive for more than four hundred years.

Even now, with the urgency to drink Fitz's blood growing exponentially by the second, I detected a police siren in the distance increasing in volume as the squad car raced up East End Avenue toward Gracie Mansion; I heard the hum of the refrigerator in the tiny galley kitchen clicking on. I smelled the Jameson mixed with Fitz's salty sweat, the odor of a dog in a nearby apartment, and the lingering traces of my own perfume. I was aware of those things in the back of my consciousness and ready, if I sensed anything amiss, to escape or fight in an instant.

But confident that nothing threatening was near, I ravenously watched Fitz's young, strong body poised above me. His breathing was coming hard. He ran his hand down my body, causing a flutter inside me as his fingers caressed my belly. I closed my eyes and enjoyed the sensations pouring over me like warm honey. He used his knee to part my thighs and he knelt between my legs, using one hand to spread my nether lips.

Then he stopped.

"What a liar you are." Fitz broke the silence with a stern voice. My eyes flew open. He was looking down at me. Anxiety swept through me. Did he suspect my intention? "Do you know how wet you are? You are very much in the mood."

"Hush, hush," I said, and put a finger on his lips. "Don't stop; don't stop." I let out a long, low sigh as I reached up, gripping his shoulders with my strong fingers, preparing myself to rise up and sink my teeth into his flesh the moment his shaft entered me. My body trembled. My thighs began to quiver. I pushed against his probing fingers.

Desperate to feed, I cared nothing about the effect my pernicious act would have on Fitz. I didn't care that after one bite, he would be addicted to a craving to repeat the experience. Nor did I care that if I bit him a second time, I could make him my sex slave—and if I were judicious in my drinking from his veins, I could keep him in that state indefinitely. I didn't even care, at that instant, that if I became too greedy and drank too long or too deeply, I would either kill him *or* make him a vampire, one of those creatures called undead, although we are obviously vital and alive.

And I especially cared nothing for the promise I gave Fitz: that I would not bite him without his consent. He shouldn't have believed me. As I said, I prevaricate often and expertly.

Now my eyes glittered like those of a raptor about to swoop down on its prey. I could barely contain my impatience, but I hadn't long to wait. I began to moan as the velvet helmet of Fitz's hard shaft rubbed tantalizingly against me, and then I cried out in pleasure as he shoved hard inside me, igniting a fire that would explode into ecstasy the moment I tasted his blood.

Holding on to his shoulders, I lifted myself, pretending I was about to kiss his mouth, but planning to move like a snake to strike that sweet spot on his neck. My lips pulled back, my teeth were razor sharp, and I was excited beyond thought, knowing I was about to be sated with the blood of the man who said he loved me, and whom I was about to betray in a terrible way.

At that moment, the phone on the bed table shrieked jarringly.

"Fu-uck!" Fitz yelled, rolling away from me and pulling out of my body with a cruel abruptness.

I gasped, then snapped my mouth shut. Fitz looked over his shoulder at me. "Sorry. I have to answer it. It's my work line." Then he took the receiver from its cradle.

If I had been a better person, I would have felt relief at the narrow escape for us both. Instead I turned facedown, punching the pillow with my fist, and audibly groaned.

I heard Fitz say, "Hello? What? Yes, I understand." Then he turned to me. "It's for you."

I sat up then, shaking my head to get my long hair off my face and regain my composure. I pulled the sheet under my arms, wrapping it around my breasts. Despite that cover, a chill racked my entire body. I took the receiver from Fitz with a hand cold as ice. I felt confused, thinking, *Why would someone be calling me on Fitz's line? I have a cell phone with me. What the hell is this?*

"Hello?" I said cautiously.

My mother's voice responded without identifying herself. "Daphne. We have a situation. Get to the office as fast as you can."

When my mother said, *Jump,* she expected me to ask, *How high?* I didn't. I snapped, "Why did you call me at this number?"

Not answering the more obvious question—how she knew exactly where I was—she snapped back, "It's a more secure line. And your cell phone seems to be turned off. Is there a problem?"

"Yeah. I'm in the middle of something."

"Drop it. This is urgent."

"Pardon me, but it's always urgent for *you.* It's not always urgent for *me.*"

"Obviously I got you at a bad time—"

"You don't know how bad," I broke in. "Look, I'm supposed to be on R and R."

"Be that as it may, the Darkwings have been called back early. Meet J at oh-three-hundred hours. You know where."

I didn't answer. My cold fingers tightened on the phone. My flesh was all goose bumps. And I was starving for blood.

"Daphne? That is a direct order." Besides being my mother, Marozia Urban was a power in America's intelligence community. I didn't know what title she held, but much to my dismay, she was my boss. Actually she was my boss J's boss. It was a double whammy no matter how I looked at it. I had spent over four hundred years trying to get away from the steel fist in Mar-Mar's velvet glove, only to end back under her thumb when I was recruited to be a spy. My stomach churned at the thought.

"Did . . . you . . . hear . . . me?" she asked, hitting each word hard.

"I heard you," I spit out. Chronologically I was an old soul and wise in the ways of the world. Physically and emotionally I was a teenager, no more mature than I had been the day a rakish young Gypsy king had seduced, bitten, and transformed me into a vampire. I had rebelled against my mother's control ever since.

"Daphne, don't push me right now. I said we have a situation. You have an hour to get to Twenty-third Street." She slammed down the phone.

"Shit," I said, and handed the phone back to Fitz. I didn't look at him. I couldn't bear to. I climbed out of bed shivering and started searching for my panties, which I had dropped somewhere on the floor.

"I have to leave. Something's going down," I said with my back to my lover. I could feel his eyes watching me. Finding my black silk thong, I hopped around on one foot putting it on, stepped into my jeans, pulled on a sweater. I tugged on my heavy Frye boots, then straightened up.

My denim jacket was in the hall closet. I walked out of the bedroom to get it. It was April, the cruelest month, and near freezing after sundown.

Fitz followed me, wrestling a T-shirt on over his head. "Give me a minute to get dressed. I'll see you home. It's after two in the morning."

I didn't slow my progress toward the closet, where I grabbed my jacket off a hanger. I put it on without turning around. "Fitz, that's very gentlemanly of you, but I don't need protection from the bogeyman. In case you've forgotten, I *am* the bogeyman. The thing that goes bump in the night. The reason people should fear the dark."

"You're pissed off."

"To put it mildly." I grabbed my backpack off a chair.

"I'll make it up to you later. Give me a call when you're done."

I looked at Fitz then, my body stiff and distant from him. "Forget about it. Like I said, I wasn't in the mood anyway. Besides if the meeting runs long, I may barely get home before sunrise."

"In that case, do you want me to walk Jade?"

His thoughtfulness about taking care of my dog brought me up short. Fitz really was much too good for me. My voice softened. "Thanks. That would be a big help." Then against my better judgment I added, "You can wait at my apartment until I get back, if you want to. Maybe, you know, I'll be in the mood later."

Fitz came over and kissed me, pulling me close. He was naked from the waist down, and I could feel the hardness of him press against my crotch. I moaned and squeezed my eyes shut, burying my face in his shoulder.

"You're sexy when you're angry," he said, holding me tight.

No, I'm dangerous, I thought. But as my desire welled up again, I whispered, "You're sexy all the time. And if you keep doing what you're doing right now with that thing of yours, I won't leave. My mother will be sending out the cavalry to find me. Look, I gotta go." I gathered my resolve and pushed him away.

Fitz let his arms fall. I gave him a quick kiss on the cheek. "Later," I promised, and winked before I went through the door. Once I was outside, my face set in hard lines and I didn't look back.

I burst through the door of my apartment as if the devil were after me. My malamute, Jade, bounced around in excitement, and my white rat, Gunther, squeaked in his cage. I ignored them both, making a beeline for the refrigerator and my bags of blood-bank blood. I pulled one out of the meat drawer and rushed, all thumbs, to get it open. Normally I'd pour the ruby fluid into a beautiful Waterford crystal glass, put on classical music, and sip it like fine wine. Now I poured the blood directly into my mouth, gulping it down crudely.

Rivulets of red ran out of the corners of my mouth and left dark, ugly stains on my jean jacket. I wiped my mouth with the back of my hand. Blood dripped onto the kitchen counter. My fingers were sticky with it. I licked them clean. Blood gave me a rush more intense than any shot of liquor, snort of cocaine, or hit of crystal meth. It lifted me body and soul from near death to euphoria.

I opened up the refrigerator and reached in for a second bag. This pint I drank more slowly, but still straight from the pouch. With each swallow, warmth spread through my icy limbs. The weakness left my arms. The light-headedness that began to overtake me during the cab ride across town receded. Only when I had finished did I lean both hands on the counter; only then did I hang my head down. Only then did I regret what I had almost done.

I was terrified of what I was becoming. I had been steadily losing control of my behavior for the past month, since the day I had first stepped foot in a posh vampire club on Irving Place. I had experienced an unfortunate incident there. A gorgeous young satyr hoping to achieve immortal life had seduced me and tricked me into biting him. He was a fool to try to outsmart a vampire. He died for his mistake.

But afterward I started to dream of warm blood, fresh blood, blood directly from the veins of willing young men, preferably during the act of intercourse. The dreams horrified me. For well over a hundred years, after taking stock of my life and the harm I had done—accidentally killing the love of my life, Lord Byron, topped the list—I had restricted myself in both the arenas of blood drinking and sex. In fact, I had remained celibate from 1824 until earlier this year, when I fell and fell hard for a vampire hunter–turned-vampire named Darius della Chiesa. The bastard.

Evidently once Pandora's box had been opened, I could not close it again. The years of denial and repression had created a nearly insatiable thirst in me for sexual pleasure, and I felt ashamed because of it. Worse, since biting a human to suck his blood was by its very nature an intimate act, my going around all hot to trot had resulted in a renewal of my worst fears—that I would never again be sated by the sterile bags of blood I purchased and kept cold in my refrigerator.

As much as I'd like to deny it, I had to face facts: I was a monster. I had come within a hairbreadth of biting Fitz. I'd stopped only because the phone rang. I hated the dark side that could drive me to do such things. Fitz was a lover I cherished, who was only good to me, who didn't deserve a vampire for a girlfriend.

I had warned him. That's all I can say in my defense. And he'd said, to my amazement, that he'd consider becoming a vampire if we were committed to each other, if he knew we wanted to be together forever. The problem was, I couldn't make that commitment to him. There was something lacking in me that I didn't have a wild, breathless, I'd-die-for-you feeling for such a good man. But hell, he did turn me on. Maybe love—that kind of love—would happen one day, like a lightning strike that could change everything.

Sure, it could happen. And there is a Santa Claus. I was just a fuckup when it came to men. I had to face it.

But not right now. I was late, late, late. I scribbled a quick note to Fitz to give Gunther a piece of banana and feed Jade four cups of Science Diet. I peeled off my soiled jean jacket and dropped it in the laundry. I rushed into the bathroom to clean my face. When I approached the sink, I saw my reflection in the mirror behind it. My mouth was surrounded with gore, as if I were a wild beast who had been feeding on a carcass. I picked up the soap dish and flung it with all my might against the glass, shattering it. Jade barked crazily at the crash. Shards fell in shiny pieces onto the vanity and into the sink.

Avoiding the broken glass, I walked to the shower. I turned on the hot water, wet a washcloth, and wiped my face clean. But I couldn't clean my soul.

CHAPTER 2

Those who'll play with cats must expect to be scratched.

—*Don Quixote* (III, 8) by Cervantes

I showed up at the Flatiron Building twenty minutes past the hour.

It wasn't my fault, I thought. New York City has thirteen thousand taxis, but finding a single cab on my block in the middle of the night proved an impossibility. In order to flag one down, I'd walked all the way over to Broadway, where traffic never stopped no matter what the hour.

Besides that inconvenience, I was in a lousy mood. I wasn't dressed warmly enough either: I had put on only a thin leather jacket over my sweater. And despite the fact that it was technically spring, a chilling drizzle had soon saturated both the night air and me. The wet of the pavement seeped right through the soles of my boots. I felt shivery, my teeth beginning to chatter. I was uncomfortable in my body and in my mind.

If J himself had called me I'd feel different about being summoned to work in the wee hours. But my mother's intrusion into my life, once again, had dampened my enthusiasm for this meeting. I tried to shake off my agitation, reminding myself that there might be a terrorist threat looming.

Millions of lives might be dependent on me and my friends—although I'm sure nobody in this city would sleep well if they knew how fragile their security truly was.

With my cold hands sunk deep into my jacket pockets to warm them, I shouldered my way through the glass doors of the lobby and, bypassing the elevators, climbed the two flights of stairs to the offices of "ABC Media Inc." on the third floor. The phony publishing company was merely a front for Darkwing headquarters, unlike St. Martin's Press, the legitimate publisher that occupied the top floors of this old landmark structure.

I pulled a hand from my pocket, turned the knob, and pushed the door open so forcefully that it hit the wall with a bang. Surprised faces within the room turned and stared at me. I deliberately made an entrance. My modus operandi has always been: *Never slink in with your tail between your legs. Always brazen it out.*

With my chin held high, I stepped into the shadowy room. The overhead fluorescent bulbs were dimmed in deference to a vampire's preference for low light. The resulting gloom disguised the office's discolored walls and uneven linoleum tile floor. I noticed that the air smelled of stale cigarettes and burned coffee. It crossed my mind that our spymaster, J, might be a smoker. He was a master of secrets, and kept everything personal about himself, even his name, hidden from us.

Tonight J sat in his army dress uniform at the head of the conference table that occupied most of the space in the room. He was all spit and polish. His face was clean shaven; his hair was buzzed short. Despite the late hour, J was clearly wide-awake and ready for business. He raised his hard blue eyes to mine and gave me a curt nod. His demeanor was as starchy as his shirt.

Benjamina Polycarp and Cormac O'Reilly, my two

vampire teammates, occupied chairs on opposite sides of the table. Benny's bloodshot and unfocused eyes sought out mine. Her mascara had smudged into black rings, giving her a raccoonlike mask. Her pink cardigan had been buttoned wrong. Her blond Southern-girl "big hair" looked like a rat's nest.

My other colleague, Cormac, a Broadway dancer when he wasn't a spy, appeared to be in only marginally better shape. Long, dark hair needing a good wash fell in strands around his pale face. His collarbones and shoulderblades were visibly outlined under his black turtleneck. He had become cadaver-thin since I saw him last. I wondered what he had been ingesting in lieu of food or blood. Meth? Coke? Alcohol?

With Cormac I never knew. He kept his life nearly as secretive as J did while he immersed himself in a series of love affairs or haunted New York's vampire underworld. Cormac and I met in Regency England nearly two hundred years ago. We had squabbled often over the decades. Currently, we were on cordial terms. His mouth curved up in a smile when I walked in. I smiled back.

That was it. Just the three of us. Team Darkwing had recently lost two of its members: The first, Bubba Lee, a vampire from Kentucky, had been murdered by a silver bullet. The second, Tallmadge, a secret operative for centuries, had rebelled, disobeying our prime directive—to serve or die. He had chosen to run. The team was now shorthanded, and, like me, I suspected Benny and Cormac were emotionally wiped out, our last mission having ended not much over a week ago.

If we had to jump back into action, it would help to have some new bodies to join us. Since I saw no other vampires at this meeting, I assumed the agency had not been looking for replacements for our missing teammates. What happened to the government's prioritizing the War on Terror? National security concerns seemed to have slipped to the bottom of the current administration's to-do list.

J's sharp voice interrupted my mental woolgathering. "Late as usual, Agent Urban. Sit down and join us, won't you?"

"I'm fine, thanks for asking," I said, shooting him a dirty look. J and I had "a history," so he got an extra dose of my pique. I winked at Benny, though, when I sat my butt on the chair next to hers. I slipped my backpack off my shoulder and dumped it on the floor. I leaned toward her and whispered, "You look hungover."

"Hungover? The hell I am. I'm drunker than Cooter Brown," she whispered back, then hiccuped. She covered her mouth with her hand, but another hiccup erupted. "Commode-huggin' drunk," she said between her fingers, and groaned. "I was entertaining. You know what I mean. I weren't planning on attending to any business this evening."

J cleared his throat loudly. "Let's get started."

We looked at him and waited.

"First off, make a note of this: We will be in contact at six thirty p.m. daily until the mission is completed—either here at a meeting or through contact with an intermediary. You should either be available by cell phone or check your messages frequently for updates. Now, to impress upon you the seriousness of the current situation, you need to see this." J stood up and removed a plastic bag from a white Styrofoam cooler. He put it gently on the table in front of us three.

Within the clear bag lay a human ear: a delicate ear with a diamond stud in the lobe and two smaller diamonds embellishing two higher piercings.

"Euuccch," Benny said, turning a shade of green. "Whose is it?"

"It belongs to a seventeen-year-old female named Nicoletta Morris," J said.

"Obviously she's been kidnapped," Cormac said.

"How do you know that? The incident is top-secret," J barked.

Cormac, always the drama queen, rolled his eyes at J. "Oh, for Pete's sake, J. Remember John Paul Getty the Third, kidnapped in Italy in 1973? His billionaire grandfather refused to pay up until one of the boy's ears was sent to a newspaper. Rich kids get snatched a lot. Let's see," he said, counting on his fingers, "there was Eric Peugeot, son of the automobile magnate. Also Victor Li, heir to a Hong Kong billionaire's fortune—a record-high ransom was paid to get *him* back. Don't forget the Lindbergh baby." He nodded at the plastic bag on the table. "I see a lopped-off ear, what else is it going to mean?"

My eyes widened. Cormac's rattling off those facts impressed me. I had assumed he bothered to remember only upcoming auditions listed in *Variety*.

J nodded. "You're correct, of course. We are dealing with a kidnapping."

So a rich kid was kidnapped, I thought. *Where's the national security threat?* "Okay, J," I broke in. "The ear got my attention. What's the whole story? Why the big rush that we had to show up on an hour's notice? This isn't about weapons of mass destruction. How is this a Code Red situation? What's the threat?"

"Agents Urban. O'Reilly. Polycarp." J looked at each of us in turn. "The country's safety is very much at stake here. Let me give you some background—"

Benny broke in. "I'm not meaning to be out of line. But I ain't doing real well. I'm a-needing to get back home."

J held up his hand to tell her to hang on a moment and began to speak: "I'll be as brief as possible. Yes, you've been brought in because of a kidnapping. And I know what you're thinking: Kidnappings are an FBI matter. Usually they are.

But we're in this because of *who* kidnapped young Nicoletta Morris—and the *nine* other girls." J scanned each of our faces again, looking at us intently.

"Look, I understand none of you expected to be here tonight. You expected some R and R. But you are here because there *is* urgency and there *is* a threat to national security.

"You must understand that since September eleventh, 2001, terrorist activity has not abated. In fact, it has heightened. British MI5 recently uncovered at least thirty plots originating in the U.K. Our own intelligence agencies have been tracking twice that number here in the U.S. The threat we're facing right here, right now, doesn't involve a bomb, bioterrorism, or poison gas in the subway. But it's heinous and especially cold-blooded. To save some time, I'd like you to read this." He stood and handed a sheet of paper to each of us.

I glanced down at a copy of a memo from a United States agency, but the name of the agency, the sender, and the recipient had been blacked out. I began to read.

DEPARTMENT OF XXXXXXXXXXX

Intradepartmental Correspondence

From: XXXXXXXX

To: XXXXXXXX

Classification: Top Secret
Subject: Abduction, Westchester
Sleepy Hollow, NY. At approximately eighteen hundred hours on Sunday, April 9, six agents from the Manhattan office of XXXXXXXXXX entered the landmark residence called Kykuit on the Rockefeller estate at Pocantico, New York.

Upon entering the mansion through the front door,
agents noted a wide smear of blood across the black-
and-white marble of the building's entrance hall. A
male, probably of Spanish descent and dressed in liv-
ery, lay dead with bullet wounds to the chest, at the
opening of a hallway leading to a room in the rear of
the mansion. This room was later identified by
Roberto Asciola, a member of the Rockefellers' private security force, as a music room.

Inside the music room the agents witnessed signs
of a struggle, noting the following:

The white upholstery of an overturned armchair
bore the outline of a boot print.

Gift boxes, some still wrapped in festive paper,
were scattered on the couch and coffee table, covered
by a spray of blood.

A small green handbag, later determined to belong
to Nicoletta Morris, had fallen onto the rug, its con-
tents spilling out.

Overturned drinking glasses, a smashed birthday
cake, and discarded cell phones were also noted and
photographed.

Another casualty, a middle-aged woman shot in the
head, sat slumped in an armchair.

According to information received from Roberto
Asciola, twelve to fourteen gunmen riding in a convoy
of white-and-black police cars and two ambulances
had gained access to the 250-acre grounds of Kykuit.
A guard, Michael Paterno, had been discovered, shot
down at the estate's entrance gate.

Paterno became the third confirmed casualty found
at the site.

Asciola further reported that the gunmen wore ski
masks and carried semiautomatic rifles. He had ascer-

tained that the armed men entered the mansion by forcing their way past the butler, a longtime employee of the Rockefeller family. The intruders rushed into the music room, which had been leased for a catered afternoon tea being held for Nicoletta Morris and nine of her guests to celebrate her seventeenth birthday and acceptance to the Sorbonne.

One of the intruders gunned down the chauffeur, who ran into the mansion, evidently having seen the gunmen enter. The woman in the chair, later identified as Nicoletta's aunt, started screaming and had also been summarily shot. Members of the catering staff were rounded up and locked into a closet. A perpetrator held a gun to the butler's head but allowed him to remain in the music room.

The butler told Asciola that the ten girls were ordered to hold out their hands, which were then bound with duct tape. None of the girls resisted but several were crying. A hood was put over each girl's head.

At this point, agents on the scene asked to speak to the butler, who was awaiting transport to a hospital. He was identified as Clarence Roberts, a British national, age forty-five. Although suffering from facial injuries, he relayed the following information:

The leader of the assailants identified himself as a member of Al Qaeda. His face was hidden by a ski mask, but he appeared to be in his twenties, approximately five feet, six inches in height, and slight of build. He spoke English without an accent.

The Al Qaeda leader ordered Mr. Roberts to contact Ms. Morris's parents. He warned that if the butler reported the incident to police authorities, the group would execute one of the girls and send him the body.

The abductor left the butler with an envelope of

instructions to be given to the Morrises. He then smashed the butler in the face with the butt of his rifle, resulting in lacerations and possibly a fractured cheekbone.

The young women who were abducted have been positively identified as:

Jemina Livingston, age eighteen
Antoinette Duke, age fifteen
Ann Armbruster Ford, age seventeen
Martha Brown-Ives, age seventeen
Teresa "Sunny" Harriman, age seventeen
Elizabeth Beatrice Campbell, age sixteen
Penny Philpse, age sixteen
Catherine Putnam, age seventeen
Alice Roosevelt, age eighteen
Nicoletta Biddle Morris, age seventeen

As the first kidnapping by Al Qaeda in North America, this incident is of the highest security concern. It is believed that the ten girls, one as young as fifteen and all from America's wealthiest and most influential families, were abducted by a cell of Al Qaeda as part of a larger terrorist offensive plan.

The account ended abruptly. The "larger terrorist offensive plan" may have followed the description of the incident, but it was not included. I looked up after I finished reading. When Cormac and Benny were also finished, J continued the narrative.

"The kidnapping occurred on Sunday. I'll get back to what occurred on Monday in a minute. But on Tuesday morning, which is technically yesterday, it now being after midnight, a video of the missing girls was delivered to the

Morris home via a FedEx package. The package had been shipped from a Kinko's in Manhattan.

"The videos were graphic, showing each girl naked, in a humiliating pose mimicking the Abu Ghraib abuse photos. Some of their faces were covered, but each girl spoke on tape, pleading with her parents to save her life. But as far as we know the girls are still alive."

"And yet the ransom demand hasn't been met," Cormac observed.

"That's right," J answered him.

"Well, I can't understand that." Cormac shook his head. "I'm sure the families are willing to pay. The police would even advise it. In fact, I'm surprised the families called the police. They had been warned not to, and a lot of people in that situation don't bring in the cops."

"They didn't call the police," J said. "They followed their instructions to the letter."

"So who in Hannah did they call?" Benny, looking visibly ill, broke in.

"The Morrises went straight to the president. Of the United States. The short of it is, Al Qaeda members have these girls. Their ransom demands are one billion dollars in diamonds and a Buffalo."

"What the hell? A buffalo? That makes no kinda sense." Benny pressed her temples with her fingers and squeezed her eyes shut. "I can't handle riddles tonight. I don't feel so hot."

J was silent for a moment. His face was grave. "We have a situation on our hands that is much worse than it appears— and it already appears to be extremely serious. We not only have an Al Qaeda kidnapping on U.S. soil, but we now know that security experts bungled badly when they analyzed certain facts. We've had information for years that Al Qaeda had obtained ambulances. It was assumed they would be used to get a dirty nuclear bomb into a populated area. We were wrong, dead wrong. They were part of this operation, and their purpose was to transport these girls.

"As for the Buffalo . . . we feel without a shadow of a doubt that obtaining the Buffalo is Al Qaeda's motive behind the kidnapping. The diamonds are simply a subterfuge. With the Buffalo—which is, Agent Polycarp, a nearly unstoppable assault vehicle—these people pose a credible threat right here in New York. We think these people intend to use the Buffalo to destroy a symbolic target, and right now the thinking is that they are after another building such as the UN."

CHAPTER 3

"Alas, how dreadful to have wisdom where it profits not the wise."

—Sophocles, *Oedipus Rex* (trans. by Sir Richard C. Jubb)

My stomach clenched. I shut my eyes for a moment, remembering how the situation had gone down to the wire when a nuclear device had been smuggled into Port Newark in a ship container. New York City had been within hours of being annihilated. I had a feeling that the terrible pressure was about to start all over again. If we didn't measure up, if we couldn't stop this, the consequences would be catastrophic.

J's voice broke into my musings once again. He explained further that a Buffalo was an advanced type of armored vehicle manufactured here in the United States by a company in South Carolina. Faster and more maneuverable than a tank, it could withstand rocket-propelled grenades (RPGs) and roadside bombs. These machines were so good that not a single American life had ever been lost in one. The insurgents fighting in Iraq and Afghanistan had made several attempts to capture a Buffalo or its smaller model, the Cougar. Now the company that produced the Buffalo had a prototype for a newer adaptation, one protected with advanced armor and fitted with laser weaponry that could level an apartment building.

"A Buffalo, and specifically the new model, is what Al Qaeda wants," J finished up. "They're willing to kill ten innocent young women, each in a horrible way—or so they threaten—to force us to turn one over."

"Turn it over? What are they going to do with it? Drive it to Iraq?" I said, my mouth dry as sand.

"Not quite. They want it delivered to a place of their choosing—and they obviously plan to use it here, not in Iraq."

"Do they honestly think they can succeed in this?" I said, incredulous.

Normally as impassive as stone, J let his emotions show for a brief moment. He rubbed his hand over his eyes. His shoulders slumped the slightest bit. I sensed a deep weariness in him. When he spoke again, his throat was tight and his voice strained. "Have you read any of the speeches or written tracts put out by bin Laden or his number two man— the man who may be the real brains of the organization—al-Zawahiri?" he asked.

"No," I answered. "I saw a bin Laden videotape for about thirty seconds on CNN. That's about it."

"Same here," Cormac said, while Benny shook her head.

"Okay, I didn't really expect you had. The statements haven't been publicized in the West, but a lot of them have been broadcast on Al Jazeera television in the Arab world. I've provided you with a few things to look at in a dossier, but to sum it up, with Al Qaeda we're dealing with fanatics, not professional criminals. They have taken hostages many times in the Mideast, but as far as a sophisticated kidnapping like this goes, they don't know their ass from their elbows, and that's the truth. Their backgrounds are mainly in the sciences and engineering. They're not stupid people, but they're not streetwise. Besides that they are totally blinded by their beliefs, which are pretty far out there."

"What do you mean, 'pretty far out there'?" I asked.

"You need to read Al Qaeda's own proclamations, in particular a document called 'Loyalty and Enmity' by al-Zawahiri. It's in the file I have for you. But meanwhile, I can give you a few examples," J answered.

"First of all, they consider any and all men, women, and children who are not radical Muslims to be infidels, and it's not merely okay to kill them; it's Al Qaeda's duty to kill them. Frankly, to me, it means the kidnapped girls are as good as dead—or they will be as soon as their purpose is served.

"Second, while the Koran instructs Muslims to tell the truth, bin Laden and al-Zawahiri believe the rule doesn't apply when they're dealing with non-Muslims. So remember, no matter what they promise, we cannot believe anything they say.

"Third, they hold the West in contempt. They believe we Americans in particular are immoral and corrupt. They have stated outright that their mission is to destroy the United States, period. They call us the Great Satan. And because they believe they are right and we are wrong, they're arrogant. They do think we're stupid—and yes, they do believe, I'm sure, that we'll give them a Buffalo in exchange for the girls."

"Why would they believe that? What leverage do they think they have?" I asked.

"They hold some very high cards. Every family affected by the kidnapping has access to the highest circles in Washington. When the Morrises were instructed to contact the president, they were able to simply pick up the phone and call him. The kidnappers knew that. They did their homework well. The families were talking directly to the White House by Sunday night.

"As you must be aware, the government's official position

to any hostage situation is: 'We don't cooperate with terrorists.' What really happened was this: The president immediately called in the heads of all the intelligence services. He instructed them to put an assault team together and get the girls back. Plans for a rescue were already in the works by Monday, the same day negotiations started with the kidnappers via a phone call to the Morrises.

"Then earlier this evening, maybe seven or eight hours after the tapes that came via FedEx, a messenger from a local twenty-four/seven delivery service showed up at the Morris residence with another package—holding Nicoletta's ear. The family panicked. They got the president out of bed—he turns in at eight thirty—and yeah, they have that kind of access. The president brought the agency heads to the White House immediately and tore them each a new asshole. One of them—it doesn't matter which one—contacted Daphne's mother a few hours ago. She called you in. Now this is in your laps."

"We're supposed to get them back?" Cormac asked.

"Somebody thinks so," J responded, implying that he didn't agree with that opinion.

I had been listening quietly. I immediately understood why we were called in to handle the situation. The Darkwings had an advantage over any other kind of assault team. We could come in by air and come in fast. Since our appearance when in vampire-bat form struck terror into anyone seeing us, it was unlikely any of the captors would have the presence of mind to pick up a gun and start shooting the hostages.

Okay, so I got it. If anybody could get the girls out alive, we could. But it didn't bear thinking about what was happening to the girls in the meantime, and a doubt, small yet persistent, said that with as many as fourteen terrorists, ten victims, and only three of us, we were asking for some major fuckup to jump off. I did the math. We needed a bare minimum of five team members to even carry out the girls from any location—if we could each handle two. Without some help, this looked like a mission impossible.

Pushing these thoughts aside, I broke the silence that had descended on the room and asked, "Do you have information on the whereabouts of the girls? You said rescue teams had been assembled. Where were they headed?"

"The girls are here in New York City," J said. "We're reasonably sure of that."

"Reasonably? Why only 'reasonably'?" I began to get the sense that there was more than one fly in the ointment.

J explained that analysts studying the videotapes Al Qaeda had made of the girls had identified the background as an abandoned sanatorium out on North Brother Island. He added that North Brother Island was in the East River between Manhattan and Brooklyn, in deference to Benny, who was from Branson, Missouri, and had been in the city only a few months. "But . . ." he said.

"But?" I asked.

"They're no longer there. We have determined that," J said.

Cormac wrinkled his nose and looked disgusted. "So where does that leave us? With no leads? With the vague possibility the girls might still be here?"

"We have *something*." J was clearly getting agitated. "We have linked a cell phone communication to one of the terrorists. We know the girls are still in New York City."

"And so are eight million other people," I said. "You have any place specific in mind?"

"Probably in Manhattan. All routes out of the city are being monitored."

"Every van? Truck? Bus? Car trunk? It can't be done. The city would shut down." I shook my head.

"They're being *monitored*, I said." J's voice showed his annoyance. "Videotaping—by *our* people. Stepped-up searches. Alerts about anything suspicious. We know what we're doing," J shot back.

Sure you do, I thought, but kept silent.

"How much time do we have?" Cormac asked.

"Until Saturday, maybe Sunday if we can get the kidnappers to agree to an extra day. They have been assured that the diamonds are being procured. They were initially given a no on the Buffalo, of course. But they insist it's not negotiable. They've set a deadline right now of Saturday night. If the deadline passes, the kidnappers threaten to start beheading the girls. After they rape them. They promise to provide each family with a videotape of it."

"I'm going to be sick," Benny said, and jumped up, bolting for the door.

"Those bastards. It's going to be a pleasure to rip their throats out," I growled.

Cormac looked at me. "I thought you had a no-kill rule. You had a change of heart?"

"There are exceptions to every rule. This is one of them. Let's stop wasting time gabbing, J. You've got a report for us in that pile, right?" I nodded toward the stack of manila folders in front of J. I knew the drill. It would contain what they wanted us to know and nothing more, even if it turned out to be important to the mission. "Give us everything you've got so far, so we can get out of here."

J was staring at me. He never liked me challenging his authority. Maybe he was surprised at my show of anger or my willingness to expose my emotions. The cruelty of this crime repelled me, and the helplessness of those young girls touched my heart. I might be a bloodsucking, amoral vampire, but I did not now and never had preyed on innocence. My "victims" had either been paid well or volunteered, tonight's near miss with Fitz being an exception. But Fitz knew he was playing with fire, so to speak. He was with me by choice.

But I had once been innocent myself. I had been abducted, and my innocence had been stolen from me. It may have been centuries ago, but I didn't forget. I didn't forgive. If I had it in my power to bring the wrath of God down on these kidnappers' heads, I would do it without hesitation, without conscience, without mercy.

Benny reentered the room, her skin a fish-belly white. She remained standing on shaky legs while J handed out the folders. I stood up too as soon as I had one. Cormac followed suit. We didn't have to talk to communicate what each of us knew: We needed to speak privately, out of J's earshot.

"What are we supposed to be doing until your people locate the victims?" Cormac dared to ask.

J was silent a beat too long. Then he said, "Somebody thinks you can find them before anybody else does. Go prove them right."

None of us spoke. We looked at one another. Of the three of us, Cormac had the best relationship with J, and that was somewhere between stiff politeness and guarded admiration, so he ventured, "It's two hours to dawn. If you're done with us . . . ?"

I heard J mutter under his breath, "I only wish I were," before he said louder, "Yes. Ms. Urban. Ms. Polycarp. Agent O'Reilly will liaison with me tomorrow after sundown. He'll bring you up-to-date on any new information. Dismissed."

We three exited out of the office into the hall. One of the historic building's antiquated elevators stood waiting, its doors open. We got in. The car started its slow journey downward.

"You okay?" I asked Benny.

"I had a bit of a spell, that's all. I'll live." At that moment she swayed, and Cormac slipped his arm around her waist to hold her steady. It wasn't a sexual gesture, but it sure was familiar. I raised an eyebrow.

Cormac spoke. "The way I look at it, even if we hadn't been ordered to start hunting for the girls, we couldn't wait for J and the analysts for this one. There are probably other rescue teams out there looking. I hope they don't screw things up. I have a bad feeling about it."

"Ditto," I said.

"Me too," Benny said, "but Macky—"

Macky? I never heard *anyone* call Cormac that before. I knew he and Benny had been spending time together. Had they been intimate?

The thoughts raced through my brain. Benny and Cormac screwing? It didn't bear thinking about. Benny wouldn't do that, would she? It wasn't that Cormac was bad-looking. He was almost pretty with his pouty lips, fine features, and long dark lashes over midnight black eyes. But he was—and it was no secret to anyone who knew him—a total whore. He'd fuck a duck. An inflated doll. Anyone willing, male or female. He had humped his way through Europe's ballet companies for two hundred years before landing a part via the casting couch in *A Chorus Line* on Broadway.

I looked at the two of them again. I didn't get a vibe that they were a couple. Benny's affectionate nickname for Cormac was probably her being, well, Southern, I guessed. Oh, God, I hoped so.

Unaware of my inner dialogue about her, Benny continued, "We're gonna need some help. There's only three of us, a passel of them, and we're going to be busier than a cat trying to cover shit on the linoleum."

"Yeah, I think so too," Cormac agreed.

A suspicion wormed into my gut. "Where are you suggesting we get some help? The only other vampire in the spy business whom I know is Darius. You aren't suggesting I contact *him*, are you, Cormac?" Tiny flecks of spit flew from my lips as I spoke.

Benny opened her eyes wide. "But it's a great idea! Darius is a professional; he is good at what he does."

I turned on her, feeling a burst of anger. "No! Forget it. I can't work with him. You know I can't. Besides, he's on tour with his band in Europe, doing some kind of undercover crap for his agency."

Cormac's voice was low and soothing when he spoke again. "Actually, I wasn't even thinking about Darius. I have a different idea."

"Well, what?" I admit, I was surprised at Cormac's stepping out in front on this.

"I believe we three agree that it's unlikely we can succeed against these terrorists alone. We do need to do some recruiting ourselves and get some fresh blood, I mean new vampires for the team."

"Huh? You know somebody?" I said, surprised.

"No. I was thinking we go out and interview some locals. Vampires who are really into New York. Tough enough to handle themselves in a rough spot. It would be ideal if they associate with the city's criminal element and have some connections. You know, they hear things about stuff jumping off. That kind of thing."

Suddenly I knew where Cormac was going with this. I wasn't happy about it. "And where were you thinking of finding these 'locals'?"

Cormac slid his eyes away from mine. "Oh, you know. Here and there. In the scene."

Benny's whole face brightened. She had perked up instantly, intrigued enough to forget she was sick. "The scene? What are you talking about, Macky?"

"The vampire clubs, the bars, that kind of thing," Cormac murmured, and began inspecting his fingernails as if he were deciding whether he needed a manicure.

My face was getting red. Steam was likely to start coming out of my ears. I gave Cormac the evil eye, which was why he was avoiding mine. "Benny, Cormac is talking about the meeting grounds for the underground vampire community in New York. And Cormac, the answer is no. Absolutely not. I'm not going there."

The overhead light fixture blinked in the elevator as the car stopped at the ground floor and gave a few small bounces. With a slowness that was excruciating to impatient New Yorkers, the doors laboriously opened.

We all stepped out in the dark, empty lobby. Benny kept her arm wrapped around Cormac's and peered at me as if I were an adversary. "But why not, Daph?" she asked. "Won't we find lots of vampires?"

"Hundreds!" I said, my body stiffening as I worked myself up for a diatribe. "And every one of them a stone-cold degenerate. And don't get any notions that the scene is like Tallmadge's club. It's not refined. It's crude. It's every kind of vampire from under every kind of rock. People teaming up and screwing in threesomes, foursomes. Cocaine, marijuana, meth, heroin, and enough alcohol to float a battleship. Anything goes. The idea is to hook up, period. And then, whenever possible, go looking for blood, if nobody has dragged along a willing donor to the party, that is—"

"Really?" Benny's eyes were positively glowing. "I mean, you mentioned a New York vampire scene, I remember. When I first got to New York. But I had no idea."

I began to turn on her, anger about to spew forth. Then I stopped and just sighed. I was a Puritan among libertines. We shoved through the glass lobby doors and went out onto the street. I looked at Cormac's face illuminated red by a storefront neon sign. "You know this is not a good idea, don't you? What kind of vampire are we going to find in those places? One who's ready to die for his country? *We* had to be forced to be spies. How are you going to make one of these party animals give up all the fun?"

Cormac stared at me, shaking his head a little. "You sell us and them short. There are some good folks out there. Your problem, Daphne Urban, is that you're afraid. You're afraid of your passions and you're afraid to be tempted. It might be a good idea to give yourself permission to let loose in a place like a vampire club. You might not be so bitchy all the time."

"I'm not bitchy."

"Yes, you are. You seem mad at the world. You're edgy. Your voice sounds like a buzz saw. You act like you're not getting laid, or not getting laid enough, if I may be blunt."

"That's rude."

"But it's true, isn't it? You're with a human. That's your first mistake—"

"Mistake! Fitz may be human, but you'd stoop to screwing a pumpkin. And I'll have you know—"

"Hold up a minute, you two," Benny broke in. "This isn't about you, Daphne. Or Macky. It's about saving the lives of ten young women. And if Macky says we can find some kickass vampire spies in the scene, then we go there. Soon as we all get up tonight."

I shut my mouth. Was I that obvious? Cormac made me feel transparent. Benny made me feel selfish and small-minded. A real snob. I blinked hard. My eyes were wet, but it couldn't be tears.

CHAPTER 4

Blond waitress to patron: "Would you like a beer?"
"What are my choices?" the guy asked.
"Yes or no."

Life, at its most basic, is less complicated than we think it is. As I took a cab from the Flatiron Building, returning to my apartment an hour before dawn, I sat in the musty backseat not thinking about national security or about the kidnappers and their victims. Like most of us, I was the center of my own universe, and I was taking stock of what I most cared about: my love life.

It was simple, really. My relationship with Darius della Chiesa, former vampire hunter, now a vampire himself—and a cheating SOB—was now history. Over with, done, kaput. Fitz and I were on rocky ground. But with this nice and decent guy, I had to either shit or get off the pot. I could stay with Fitz, or I could leave. I would bite him, or I wouldn't. If I had sex with him, I would probably bite him. I aimed to be virtuous, but hell's bells, I was a vampire. I had my limits.

I also knew that if I had sex with Fitz and bit him without his consent, he would never forgive me—if he were still alive. Yet the only way not to have sex with him would be for us both to agree to abstain from intimacy, which I didn't think possible, or to end it between us.

End it? I didn't relish being lonely. I enjoyed having a

lover. Beyond that, this relationship, for the first time in my long life, seemed nearly normal. Fitz wanted commitment. He was willing to compromise. He believed in our being a "couple" and wanted both families' approval, or at least their awareness, of our union. He'd be happy if we lived together; he'd be happier if we got married—despite the problems such a marriage faced. How could I just throw a relationship like this away? And I cared about Fitz—a lot. I might even love him, if one can love without knowing for sure whether one did.

I didn't have to be a brain surgeon to figure out my options. It was making the choice that was so damned hard.

And sometimes fate, or circumstance, makes our choices for us.

I returned to my apartment a little after five a.m. A low-wattage bulb burned in a table lamp in the living room. Fitz, stretched out on the sofa, was *Endymion Asleep*. With his dark hair and sharply etched features, his eyes closed like two pale wings, the beauty of his face made my breath catch in my throat. As for his nude body—in my overheated apartment, he needed no clothes or covers—despite the bandage on his stomach, its perfection stirred my blood.

I let my backpack slide quietly to the floor. I crossed the room and knelt down next to his slumbering form. I could feel the faint stirring of air made by his breath. His head was flung back, his throat exposed. My skin tingled with the nearness of him as a frisson of sexual excitement spread through me from head to toe.

I reached out and with cool fingers stroked his cheek. Love crossed the island of space between him and me. A terrible grief, watered with unshed tears, began to grow as I was inexorably drawn to him, for my passion was neither still nor patient. My desire was a lunatic carousel whirling my thoughts around and around, faster and faster, spinning me toward a point of no return.

Fitz moved in his sleep but didn't awaken. I slipped off my jacket, then my sweater so that my breasts were bare. I twisted my long hair into a rope. As I leaned down, I gently slipped it behind Fitz's neck so that as my left hand tugged, my face was pulled down toward the pale skin of his throat. My incisors were lengthening and growing sharp even as my lips softly kissed the sweet spot there.

Fitz stirred, moaning, but not awakening. My breasts brushed his chest, and I very carefully laid myself down beside him, all rational thought gone. I intended to feed upon him. Feed deeply until I was sated, fulfilling my needs and my fantasies in the same moment when I damned him, and myself, with my barbaric bite.

Yet I stopped. It seemed as if the walls themselves were weeping, for didn't I hear a low sob from somewhere? It could not have been me who cried, for I had no conscience. Fitz's skin was so tender under my lips. I tasted its saltiness with my tongue. My veil of hair hid my eyes, and my own hand entangled in my hair held me fast against him.

In one small movement the deed would be done. Sex and pain would mingle as his blood filled my mouth. We would be joined, perhaps forever, with that profane communion. I could barely breathe with my hunger for it.

And yet I did not bite. My fist opened and released my hair. I moved my body away from Fitz and pulled free. I stood, unsatisfied and bereft. Blue frost ran through my veins. I picked up my sweater and jacket. Turning away from what I desperately wanted, I walked into the hall and opened the door to my secret room. Entering it, I crossed to my coffin and climbed inside. In its pink satin depths I fell into darkness, cold tears a small comfort for doing the right thing.

* * *

When I awoke, the violet dusk of the April evening was a smudge outside the windows. Fitz's note sat propped against my coffee cup on the kitchen counter.

> Lady Daphne,
>   Sorry I fell asleep. It seems I'm always breaking my promises to you. Don't stop believing in me. Like Domino's Pizza, I do deliver! But I've been called into work today. First time since I got shot. Be back at my apartment around six tonight. Call me when you get up. Love you.
>   St. Fitz

I glanced up at the microwave readout to see the time. It was only five thirty. *Good*, I thought. *It will be easier if I get his machine when I call.*

And that was what happened. I left a rambling message about how it was okay that he fell asleep last night, and anyway my team had a new assignment, so I'd be out all night. And he shouldn't call me and he shouldn't worry and I'd call whenever I could. Then I paused for a long moment before adding that I'd check whether or not we were still on for dinner with my mother tomorrow night.

Meeting Mar-Mar was Fitz's idea, and to my surprise my mother not only agreed; she seemed delighted with the prospect. I had already met Fitz's family on our very first date. The meeting was okay; the aftermath was a total disaster. A few days after our meet and greet, the truth had come out that the Fitzmaurice cousins had been involved in a drug cartel, Fitz's Washington-VIP uncle tried to engineer Fitz's murder, and Fitz's mother, as ruthless a lady as I ever met, shot his uncle to death—*her brother*—in retaliation. With that kind of a black mark against his family, Fitz believed that my relatives couldn't possibly be worse. He had another think coming; that was for sure.

Now, my new mission gave me the perfect excuse to cancel our cozy get-together with Mar-Mar, and I was about to tell him that. But at the last moment it occurred to me that meeting my mother might be more than even Fitz could handle, and I wouldn't have to make any decisions. He'd walk away from our relationship *before* I did anything irrevocable, like marrying him . . . or biting him.

Then too, if Fitz met Mar-Mar and didn't turn tail and run, maybe he'd understand what a dilemma I had and consider his own transformation. I had never tried to convince him to become a vampire. I saw how totally soul-destroying it had been for Darius. The upshot was that Darius had hated me for biting him. But Fitz and I couldn't go on much longer as a half-human, half-vampire couple. One way or another it had to end, for better or for far, far worse.

Before I terminated the phone call, I didn't say I loved Fitz. I told him to be careful and to have sweet dreams, my voice sincere but noncommittal. Okay, I admit I was staying on the fence. My rational mind wanted to take the high road with Fitz. But my body, my aching, yearning flesh, had an insatiable hunger for his touch—and his blood—and that was the bottom line.

Before heading out that night, I settled into the plush velvet cushions of my living room sofa with my pet rat on my shoulder and my dog at my feet. I opened the manila folder I had picked up last night from J and went through the information each of us had been given on the abduction. In sum total it wasn't much:

Re: The police cars used in the kidnapping. Ford Crown Victorias professionally painted to look like highway patrol vehicles. No information on where they had been painted.

Re: The ambulances used in the kidnapping. Bought on eBay. The buyer was traced to an apartment house in the Bronx; he moved out—four years ago. I concluded from this that a kidnapping of some sort had been among Al Qaeda's plans for years.

Re: Al Qaeda in the U.S. The kidnappers were believed to be affiliated with a cell of Al Qaeda operating out of Lackawanna, New York, a small town near Buffalo. Six Yemeni men there had been arrested and convicted for terrorist activities back in 2002, and intelligence agents were currently questioning them. Quite frankly, I didn't think that sounded like a very promising direction.

Re: Inside information used in the kidnapping. Knowledge of the date, time, and place, plus the guest list, for Nicoletta's party could have been obtained only from an inside source. Staff and workers at the Rockefeller estate had been questioned. Members and associates of the girls' families were being questioned. Among the completed interviews were:

Clarence Roberts, butler. The principal eyewitness at the Rockefeller mansion, he was a longtime employee of the Rockefeller family. He had no link to Nicoletta Morris or her guests. He confirmed that this abduction involved fourteen men. They wore ski masks. Only the man identifying himself as the leader spoke to him. The butler felt he would be unable to identify any of the abductors.

All members of the catering staff had been questioned. They had been brought in for that particular occasion; they were not on the payroll of the Rockefellers. None of them had any ongoing relationship with the Morrises. None could be linked with the crime.

From the Morris household, however, four people were under scrutiny: a limousine driver, a cleaning lady, a personal trainer, and a gardener. Transcripts were being prepared and were to be available from J tonight.

I also quickly read through the short transcript of the interview with the counterperson at Kinko's. Charise Robinson said the store had been busy on Monday. The sender paid cash, which was a little unusual, but it happened a couple of times a day. She remembered that he looked to be in his early twenties, and she thought he was maybe Italian. He could have been Arabic, "But he didn't wear a towel on his head or anything." He was sort of short, maybe five-seven. He was very polite. She found the store copy of the mailing form. It indicated that the sender was Ray Medina, and the address turned out to be a dry cleaner's on Avenue A in the East Village.

The Tuxedo Park courier service gave a similar description of the young man who'd brought in the package.

Another sheet of paper gave the medical examiner's report. The ear had been severed from Nicoletta using a medical scalpel, and the incision had been made with professional skill. Also, from the blood extant in the ear, he discovered that the sedative Valium and lidocaine had been administered to the girl before her ear was cut off. That had been done perhaps out of a sense of humaneness, or more likely to make the victim more docile and the mutilation easier for the kidnappers. In any event, it was now thought that at least one of the perpetrators had some medical training.

Also included, as J had promised, were primary materials from Al Qaeda. I scanned a printout of the al-Zawahiri tract "Loyalty and Enmity" and quickly read through a short transcript of the bin Laden videotape aired on Al Jazeera about a month after the terrorist attacks of September 11. My eyes were drawn to an underlined passage at the end of his address:

> *I have these words for America and its people: I swear by Allah that neither America nor anyone living there will ever be safe.*

I sat back against the sofa cushions and stared unseeing into the shadowy room. We had next to nothing to help us find the ten young women, and it was already Wednesday. How were we supposed to come up with a rescue with so little to go on? A great sense of sadness settled upon me. It was terrible that a young girl had already been disfigured, but I thought that was not the worst that could happen. I honestly didn't think any of the victims would be found alive.

An hour later, the 1 train, of the Broadway–Seventh Avenue line, carried me like a hell-blasted chariot down to Christopher Street in the Village. I stepped out onto the subway platform, where the white-tiled walls were too bright for my sensitive eyes.

I looked around me. Without a doubt, here ended the known world. A drag queen, hands on hips, screamed at some guy in leather that "Shit happens! I can't be held responsible, you hear me! I'm not responsible." An old lady, toothless, her gray hair hanging like cobwebs, dragged a green garbage bag up the stairs and mumbled something about Jesus. A small dark man playing a Peruvian flute sat cross-legged on the filthy floor, a hat upside down in front of him where people could toss coins.

I remembered a tragic poem and tried to forget where I was going.

No such luck. Benny and Cormac, their arms linked, waited for me on the sidewalk as I emerged from the subway stairs into the mauve-colored evening. I told myself to lighten up, that I was working, not about to embark on a pub crawl into the vampire underworld for pleasure. I didn't hold out much hope that we'd find any help in the dark holes we were about to enter. Benny had different expectations: Her face shone like a new penny.

"I'm ever so glad to see you," she said, releasing her hold

on Cormac and standing on her toes to give me an air kiss. "I almost got to do this back when I was seeing that there vampire, Louie, but instead of going out, we got tangled up in the sheets of my bed. It'll be more fun to go with you and Cormac."

I didn't bother saying that this wasn't supposed to be fun.

"Where are we headed?" I asked, looking past Benny at Cormac.

"We're starting at a biker bar. On West Street."

I rolled my eyes. "Lead on, Macduff."

"If'n it's over four blocks we need to catch a cab," Benny said. "Don't know about yours, Daphy, but these boots ain't made for walking." She picked up her foot so that her Manolo Blahnik ankle boots with four-and-a-half-inch heels peeked out from below the pant leg of her tight jeans. I knew how high they were because I was wearing a similar pair, in leopard-print suede.

"I won't argue with taking a cab," I answered. I wasn't dressed for walking—or a pickup. The boots were my only touch of whimsy. Tonight my long, thin body looked like one of those insects called a walking stick: I wore cocoa-colored slacks topped by a Kay Celine dark brown mock turtleneck with crossover detailing under my brown leather jacket.

I chose my drab attire to blend into the woodwork, lessening the chance that a slack-mouthed, half-drunk vampire would hit on me. I shouldn't have worried. All lascivious eyes would be on Benny, with her red, low-cut sweater displaying Dolly Parton boobs in full splendor.

Cormac flagged down a Yellow Cab, and we all climbed into the backseat. Since we couldn't talk business in the taxi, Benny went right where I was hoping she wouldn't. "How's Fitz?" she asked.

"Recovering. He's back at work."

"Well, now, I don't see a ring on your finger yet. He still carrying it around in that little velvet box?"

"I don't know. Don't think so. Can we change the subject?" I said, and leaned close to her ear. "What's with you and 'Macky'?"

She whispered back, "Friends. Just friends. What were you thinking?"

"Never mind," I said, and settled back against the seat, turning my head to look out the window. I hoped we weren't on a wild-goose chase, but we definitely needed two more team members. I reluctantly agreed that the vampire clubs of Manhattan were the best place to find them, because I didn't know where else to look.

I shivered, knowing that in a few minutes I would be among my own kind. I remembered their smell: animal, sensual, not human. I knew I would see a reflection of red light behind the irises of their eyes and a terrible black void in their pupils. I would sense the wariness of the hunted juxtaposed with the look of the predator, sizing up every human as prey. My breath would become shallow, and anxiety would grip me with a bony hand.

I admitted I had a problem. The people I expected to see tonight represented the part of me that I couldn't escape and I couldn't control. And my control lately had been so tenuous. I feared I was losing myself to darkness.

I also felt a disturbing trepidation that I didn't have the clear head I needed to deal with whatever I faced tonight. I had drunk a glass of blood before I left my apartment, heeding the admonition never to go food shopping when you were hungry. But as I hadn't been able to scratch the itch of my sexual frustration, it wasn't my hunger for blood that worried me.

I felt vulnerable to the whims of desire, and I didn't like it. If I behaved like a bitch tonight, it would definitely be because I was crawling the walls. The little devil on my dark side kept whispering, *Find yourself a quick, anonymous fuck and feel better. Who's it going to hurt?* The angel on my good girl side was ordering me to be chaste and true to Fitz. The result was a bad mood straight from hell.

When the cab pulled up in front of the doorway of a run-down tenement next to a rubble-strewn lot, I forgot sex and started wondering what exactly I was getting myself into in this rough neighborhood. The windows on the first floor had been bricked in. Above a door that bore the marks of being kicked more than once hung a clumsily lettered sign: CHAR-LIE'S HARLEY HANGOUT. MEMBERS ONLY.

I glanced over at Benny and saw the disappointment on her face. Once we were out of the cab, she turned to Cormac. "This here is a vampire club? I seen a better class of dumps back in Miz'ora."

Cormac said, "It's a biker bar, not a nightclub, Ben. I have somebody to see in this place. Come on."

Cormac went up to the door and gave it three hard knocks using his elbow. It opened a crack. I couldn't hear what Cormac was saying, but after a few words, a short bald man with twitchy eyes motioned us all in. It was as bad as I feared. The place smelled like beer and cigarettes with a hint of eau de urine.

A jukebox against the back wall was playing Bob Seger's "Night Moves." Men and a scattering of young women sat at small tables in the center of the room and filled the stools at a squat, squared-off, U-shaped bar to my left. A lot of them wore black leather jackets with BLOODS CLUB stenciled across the back. A skull and crossbones was painted beneath the letters.

Two women were bartending. A hard-faced skinny blonde, a cigarette dangling from her lips, was drawing a beer. The other female, a pumpkin on a stick, was setting up shots. Amber bottles of booze lined a counter behind the bar. I didn't see a cash register, but a backlit sign spelled out in magnetic tiles: IN GOD WE TRUST. EVERYBODY ELSE PAYS CASH.

The place was dark, the low light obscuring the 1970s fake-wood paneling on the walls. To my far right was a second room holding a single pool table and maybe a dozen more guys, the majority of them looking more like cowboys than bikers.

Somehow Cormac spotted whomever he was looking for and led us toward a table near a hallway leading to the men's room. Faces turned our way as we walked by. Too many of them had a lean and hungry look. They gave me the creeps. I avoided eye contact and tried not to brush against anybody as we wove our way through the tightly packed space.

A wiry guy who needed a haircut kicked a chair away from the table. I figured it was for Benny, since he was looking at her chest. I pulled over an unoccupied seat I found nearby; Cormac slid into one already at the table.

I had figured out by then that the "theme" of the place had to do with oil wells. Names of offshore rigs in the Gulf were scrawled on the walls, and I could now see that articles about oil drilling were laminated under yellowed plastic on the top of the tables.

While I was wiping off the table in front of me with a tissue, Cormac said, "Daphne, Benny, this is Dog. Dog, these are my partners."

Dog put his cigarette down on the edge of the table and raised himself up a little to stick out his hand, giving each of ours a brief shake. The back of his was tattooed, and D-O-G had been etched out in letters so fancy you had to look twice to see what they spelled.

Dog saw me staring, and said, "Yeah, that's my name. I was dead drunk when I had it done. Stupid, tattooing my name on myself. One time the cops were looking for me.

Two rednecks in uniforms came into a bar in Pasadena, Texas. Told all of us to stick out our hands. Turns out they were stupider than me. They took a look at mine and said, 'Okay, you can go.' I damn near shit a brick."

"Ohh," Benny said. "You're from Texas? I'm from Miz'ora. Branson."

"Houston. The owner of this dive is from up near Louwiz'ana." Bona fides established, Dog didn't waste any more words. He turned to Cormac. "You had Red call me?"

"That's right." Cormac nodded.

"He said you're looking for a man to do a job. Couple o' days. Thousand a day."

"Right."

So we're hiring help, I thought. *Yeah, Cormac, so I "sell us and them short." Looks like my take on the situation was spot-on.* A smirk danced around my lips.

"Talked to two guys. They're on their way down." He looked up. "Pete—he likes to be called Bear—just walked in." Dog stood and took his cigarette out of his mouth long enough to whistle.

A big guy, maybe six-foot-two or -three and weighing two forty or two fifty lumbered over to the table. He didn't sit; he took a quick look at us, let his eyes linger on Benny a long second, then said to Dog, "These the folks?"

"Yeah."

Pete-Bear ignored me and talked to Cormac. "Look, I 'preciate the offer, but I gotta go see a man about a horse. I'll be outta town for a couple of weeks. If you still need a hand, Dog will know where to find me." He nodded at Dog, turned, and went over to the bar, where a red-faced drinker, who saw Pete-Bear coming in his direction, got up in a hurry and scrambled out of the way. The big biker sat down on the vacated stool.

"You want a beer?" Dog asked us. I shook my head no,

Benny said to get her a Coors Light, and Cormac asked for a Bud. Dog ground out his cigarette and went for the beers, or to talk to Pete-Bear in private, which I figured was the real point of his trip.

We never got the beers. I heard somebody behind me snarl, "Hey, shithead, you stepped on my boot." Having nothing else to do, I turned around to see what was going to happen.

A string bean of a cowboy, weaving through the tables, a beer in each hand, had stopped next to the chair of a burly biker all in black. "What the fuck did you say?" he asked in a loud voice.

"I said you stepped on my damned boot, you fucking shithead," the seated guy answered.

Without another word, the cowboy holding the beers hoisted one of the bottles and bashed it against the sitting guy's head. The beefy biker, blood streaming down his face, exploded out of his seat and plowed into the string bean's chest. All of a sudden they were rolling around on the floor and bumping into people at nearby tables. Whoever got bumped jumped up and starting throwing fists. Chairs fell over. The two bartenders and the few women in the room started screaming. I saw Dog dive over the bar and come up with a pipe in his hand. Then he launched himself into the melee. Like a slow wave rolling toward us, I saw trouble coming.

"Time to leave," I shouted, grabbing Benny's arm. I hoped to hell there was a back door, because we'd never get out the front. Cormac did an impressive jeté over the table and headed down the hallway past the men's room door. I shoved Benny in the same direction, and she took off after Cormac.

I never made it.

Something—a chair, I think—hit me across my shoul-

ders, hard. I went down on my hands and knees. Some asshole stepped on my leg before I could scramble up again. I
twisted around, blind with rage. I sprang to my feet and
lashed out at the first face I spotted, feeling my fist connect
with a crack against the side of a guy's nose. I started whal-
ing on him while the guy's girlfriend tried to get between us.
I wasn't aiming to hit her, but she got a fat lip before she decided discretion was the better part of valor.

I started working on the guy with the mashed nose again,
who got in a couple of shots of his own. I felt my cheek
starting to swell. Then I was pulled backward by my hair.
That just made me madder. I went with the motion of the
yank and smashed myself against the body behind me. As
soon as I connected with my attacker, I turned my head and
bit down hard on the hand holding me. I heard a yell and my
hair was free. I turned fast and kneed the guy as hard as I
could in the groin. He went down.

I heard somebody screaming like a banshee, and realized
it was me. I started trading punches with another long-haired
biker who had no qualms about hitting a lady. I was holding
my own until some yahoo hit me from behind with a beer
bottle. The room got dark around the edges, and I figured I
was about to hit the floor, when suddenly I was scooped up,
a beefy arm around my waist, then slung over a leather-clad
shoulder, my head dangling down. I started kicking and tried
to bite whatever body part I could reach.

I heard a deep voice tell me to stop my damn fool struggling and realized I was being carried down the hallway toward a door opening up into the night.

"Put me down!" I yelled.

"With pleasure," the voice said, and let go of my feet. I
barely avoided falling face-first on the gravel of a small
courtyard. I caught myself with my hands and ended up full-
length on the ground. I rolled over and got to a sitting posi-

tion, and as I sat there on my behind, breathing hard, I saw my rescuer climbing a chain link fence. As he pulled himself over the top, he called back to me, "This is the way out."

Feeling dazed, I stayed where I was. My legs had turned to jelly, and I needed a minute to catch my breath. The gravel was hard under my butt, but I was burning up and the cool air felt good. I put my elbows on my knees and just chilled. I heard Benny's and Cormac's low voices talking on the other side of the fence, but I wasn't in any hurry to move—until the door to the bar flew open and the fight inside started spilling out into the courtyard. I hustled to get onto my feet and threw myself at the chain link, hoisting myself up the way my white knight just had.

When I came down on the other side, I saw the guy who had pulled me out of the bar standing with my teammates. Their heads were close together, and they seemed to be having an animated discussion.

I walked over to them. My face was dirty, I had beer in my hair, and my pants had a rip at the knee, but I still looked better than my rescuer did.

The guy was built, as they say, like a brick shithouse. He was big, solid, and not pretty. His face had been hit too many times to be attractive, leaving his nose off center, and, thanks to the latest dustup, one of his eyes was swelling shut. He also had a Fu Manchu mustache and an evil curl to his lip. His hair was long enough to be pulled back into a ponytail. A small silver skull dangled from the lobe of one ear. Wearing his kind's de rigueur jeans, motorcycle jacket, and heavy black motorcycle boots, he could have been a poster boy for Bad Bikers U.S.A.

He gave off vibes that hit me like a bad smell. He looked mean. He looked shifty. I wondered if he had enough brains left in his battered head to carry on a conversation. My gut reaction to him was negative in the extreme. I didn't know why I felt that way. I didn't care.

Benny fished some tissues out of her pocket and handed them to me. I wiped down my face as Cormac said to me, "This is the other guy Dog called about working with us."

I looked up into deep-set, mysterious eyes that were so dark brown they appeared black. They held no warmth. I didn't like what I saw, and it probably showed.

Meanwhile the biker stared back at me with a look of amusement. "So Rambo is with you?" he remarked to Cormac, but kept his gaze on me.

"That's Daphne," Cormac said, sounding almost apologetic. "Daphne, meet Rogue. He's just now agreed to join the Darkwings."

"Like hell," I said.

CHAPTER 5

*All the rivers run into the sea; yet the sea is
not full; unto the place from whence the rivers
come, thither they return again.*

—*Ecclesiastes 1:7*

"The 'lady' doesn't like me. Am I in or am I out?"
Rogue said. He moved his eyes up and down my
body. I felt he was laughing at me.

Angry thoughts whirled like a red haze through my brain.
This guy as a teammate? I couldn't see him as a Darkwing,
fighting for truth, justice, and the American way. He didn't
have the right stuff. This vampire was a barbarian. A marauder.
He brought to mind Attila the Hun. Genghis Khan. I moved
from a negative first impression to hate at second sight.

"Out." I spit the word at the same time Benny said, "In."
I turned my head quickly and glared at her.

"You're in," Cormac reiterated to Rogue while he
grabbed my arm, pulled me a few steps away, and spoke
quickly in a low voice. "We don't have time to waste arguing in the street. I know he seems a little rough around the
edges, but we need Rogue and we need him now. We're still
one team member short. Let's move on."

I shook my arm out of his grip. I had no intention of
"moving on." "I can't go anywhere else looking like this.
My pants are ripped. I'm going home."

An angry blush crept up Cormac's neck. "Look, Daphne,

get over it. We have to find another vampire tonight. That's we, not me, not Benny. The three of us, the team, remember? As for Rogue, we need a street-smart criminal for this job, not one of your Byron-like poets. It's a business arrangement. You don't have to like the guy. Work out your personal issues some other time."

I stared down at my feet. I took a deep breath. I found a quiet place within my mind and pulled myself together. Maybe I was overreacting, but I felt threatened and I wasn't sure why. Finally I looked up, accepting the fait accompli. "All right. What's our next stop?"

"A club on Spring Street. Upstairs." Cormac gave me the address as he stepped out into the street and hailed a taxi. One pulled over. Cormac opened the door and helped Benny into the backseat. When I stepped up to get in next, he blocked me with his body. "No room. You and Rogue take the next one." He jumped in and slammed the door shut before I could protest.

I was steamed. I flagged down the next cab and flung myself into the backseat. Rogue got in behind me. I told the cabbie where to take us and crossed my arms across my chest, sitting as tightly against the far door as I could. I stared straight ahead.

"Don't come near me," I said between clenched teeth.

"Don't flatter yourself," he replied. I could see in my peripheral vision that he had a toothpick between his teeth. He bounced it up and down for a while, then spit it out. It landed on my boot. I kicked it off.

Although he kept his distance, Rogue's massive body loomed over me like a huge shadow covering me with darkness. The mixture of cigarettes and beer that clung to his clothing couldn't erase the distinct male scent that emanated from him. I guessed he had had sex recently.

Rogue reminded me of a rutting stag: a beast balanced

between explosive aggression and a mindless desire to mate. I felt nervous and uncomfortable this close to him. I turned my head toward the window, but I didn't see what was passing by outside. I recognized only that my emotions were burning like dry sticks thrown on a bonfire.

The ornate room upstairs at the Spring Street locale shook me up from the moment I stepped into it. I knew at once that this was the kind of club I desperately wanted to avoid. On one long wall, hand-painted murals depicted sixteenth-century nudes à la Rubens, whose studio I had once visited when he was traveling in Italy. On an adjoining section, beautifully painted couples appeared in various poses of copulation, and idealized humans swooned in the embrace of gorgeous vampires.

Chandeliers cast the room in golden light, and the decor was rich with tapestries and gilt. All the tables were full, and the room reverberated with the sounds of a classical guitar, a loud hum of voices, and champagne glasses clinking. Some patrons had pulled their chairs close as they flirted and exchanged kisses; others lounged on the plush vintage sofas, their bodies pressed close together.

But the elegant facade of the place took on a tawdry air when, surveying the room, I spied an Adonis of a young man sitting with his legs splayed and a look of ecstasy on his face. A woman knelt in front of him performing fellatio. No one seemed to pay any attention to them, or to the two women lying prone on a divan, wrapped in each other's arms.

Just then, from a far corner came a low, long moan. Despite my instinct not to look, I did. A small woman, her hair curly and shorn short, stood naked between two clothed men. From the movements of their bodies, I soon understood that one of the men was entering her from the front. She had her face hidden against his shoulder as he supported her in his arms. Suddenly, as I watched, she lifted her head and arched her back, a sharp cry issuing from her lips. It was clear that the second man had swiftly penetrated her from behind in a classic sex sandwich.

It was her moan, not the men's, that had drawn my attention, and now she began calling out, "Oh-oh-oh." Some of the champagne drinkers turned their heads toward the sounds and began to watch. The woman's *oh*s intensified and reached a crescendo as she climaxed. The lover who held her laughed and thrust hard while the man behind her, a dark, menacing form, leaned tightly against her, gripped her shoulders with big hands, and bit deeply into her neck. She cried out one last time, and then was silent. A murmur rose briefly from the patrons at the tables, then subsided.

Horror overcame me. I wanted to leave this place right then and there. But Rogue was standing behind me, blocking my exit, and there was no going back. My level of discomfort was steadily rising when Benny threaded her way through the tables and arrived at my side. She took my hand. "You just have to come over here," she said, and led me off to the right to the door leading to a second room.

At the entrance to the space within, I could smell the sweet, heavy odor of marijuana. Beyond the doorway, a softy lit interior was blue with smoke. I could make out a tangle of naked bodies on a large, cushioned platform over which stretched a diaphanous canopy of wispy silk. It was decadent yet lushly beautiful. A low, undulating sound rose and fell from the orgy in progress on the platform, punctuated by gasps and groans. I saw delicate fingers encircle a turgid shaft and begin to stroke it. I saw a man with muscular thighs mount the smooth white buttocks of a slender female positioned on all fours. I saw a woman lying spread-eagled while a man performed cunnilingus on her and another sucked on her breasts. Just then another woman shimmied over to the trio and opened her mouth to make it a threesome.

"Do you all believe that?" Benny whispered. Her eyes were wide with wonder. Her hand was warm in mine. "There have to be ten of them going at it. And they don't care if you watch." In fact, voyeurism was very much evident as several vampires sat in chairs surrounding the platform, enjoying the view.

I started to pull away, but Benny's hand held me fast. "Don't go. It's just like Cormac said. You're all pent-up. But you can do this in here and nobody cares, Daphne. You'll feel better."

My heart was racing. I wanted to escape this world, this amorality, these sybarites. "No!" I said too loudly. I tugged hard on her hand and dragged her away from the door into the main dining room.

Hurt washed over Benny's face. I felt heat radiating through my own. I whispered to her, "Benny, it's not my thing, really. I know you mean well, but I couldn't do it." My chest was so tight I could barely breathe.

"I could," she confided. "Don't think less of me, but I want to. It's like something out of a dream. It makes my head just spin, thinking about it." She let out a deep sigh. "Macky says I don't have time tonight, though."

"Where is Cormac?" I asked, hoping to distract her and myself from the heavy atmosphere of erotic excess that was suffocating me. I looked up just then and saw Rogue, who had taken our places in the doorway of the orgy room. In that instant he turned and saw me watching him. He gave me a wicked grin that had nothing to do with desire. I sensed it had to do with conquest. I had a flash of insight that he would one day try to take me, break me, and bend me to his will, my hate goading him on.

I gave him a look of defiance. I stood my ground.

Rogue took a cigarette pack from his jacket pocket. He shook one out and put it between his lips. He never took his eyes from my face.

Benny put her lips next to my ear. "I have three words for our sexy new team member: Dan Ger Ous."

I didn't hesitate another minute. I told Benny I'd wait outside, and fled.

Downstairs and outside once more, I looked up at the strip of sky between the buildings. Even on clear nights, only the brightest stars penetrate the glare of New York City's lights. This evening a murky darkness stretched over Manhattan, any vision of what exists above the earth closed off to those below.

Agitated, I began pacing on the sidewalk. A disheveled middle-aged man with red-rimmed drinker's eyes approached me and asked for a dollar. I pulled out a ten and handed it to him. A Hispanic couple, the woman hugging a baby tightly to her chest, hurried by, giving me a wide berth. A group of college kids huddled together to consult a tourist map. In front of a locked door, a tired-looking woman shifted her packages to one hand and fumbled in her purse for a key. Through a window a few feet above her head, I could see a single lightbulb dangling on a wire like an exposed nerve. A teenage boy appeared in the space. He crossed the room to lean on the sill, smoke a joint, and stare at the street.

Life in its myriad varieties surrounded me, but I was set apart from all humanity, alienated, and cursed by immortality. Without death, I stood outside the circle of life. I belonged to no living generation. My body didn't age. I had no rites of passage. Years passed with a stultifying sameness. Ennui and drifting, a desire for sensation, and a craving for blood had plagued me for centuries. Finally, by an act of will I had defied the fate that had made me into a degenerate, defiled, and defiling creature. Unlike most of my kind, I had chosen to feed my spirit instead of my flesh, first by refusing to hunt humans and then by finding meaningful work: becoming a spy.

Although I knew the truth, I couldn't lecture Benny that pleasure was fleeting and the senses quickly dulled. She had been a vampire for only eighty-odd years. I had walked the earth for over four hundred. And how could I preach to her, when I was no saint? Despite my choice to shape my destiny, the years of my celibacy had left me lonely and nearly mad with suppressed desire. Now I feared that I was slipping down a greased slide to ruin once again.

Did I want to rush over and throw myself into the orgy I had witnessed? Part of me did. I admitted it. I had resisted the impulse. This time. But for how much longer could I keep the gates to my own underworld from opening?

My anxiety started to escalate toward panic. I was seconds away from returning to the upstairs club and losing myself. Suddenly I needed to hold on to something good and decent. Stopping my peregrinations to the corner and back, I pulled out my cell phone and called Fitz. He answered on the first ring.

"Hey, sweetheart," he said.

A sense of relief washed over me. "Hey," I replied.

"What's going on? You at work?" His words were slurred ever so slightly.

"Yeah, I'm working. Taking a break. I needed to hear your voice."

"I like that. But it's not your usual style. How bad is it out there?"

I laughed. "Bad enough." I turned away from the street to face a brick wall in order to concentrate on the sound of Fitz's voice.

"I'll wait up for you if you'll be done even a few hours before dawn," he offered.

I shook my head even though he couldn't see me do it. "Go to bed. I'm in for a long night."

"You're worth waiting for."

"I'm glad you think so." I was the one who didn't think I was. "Talk to me for a minute. Tell me about your day."

He laughed. "Not much to tell."

"Or not much you *can* tell." We both knew that in the spy business, pillow talk could be a security breach.

"That too. I can say I drank a lot of coffee and went to a lot of meetings. I was okay until midafternoon. I started to crap out, but the pain meds got me through until six."

"You need to save your strength. You meet my mother tomorrow night," I teased.

"You sure you can get away? Maybe we should cancel."

"So far *she* hasn't canceled, and she's my boss. If she thinks I can take a couple of hours off, I guess I can. Don't ask me to figure her out. You'll see for yourself. It's going to be an evening from hell."

Now Fitz laughed. "Don't worry about me. I'm used to enduring the torment of a dysfunctional family. I figure that every holiday spent with my family must count as time spent in purgatory, at least."

"Don't say I didn't warn you. Uh-oh, gotta go." I had glanced up the block and spotted Rogue and Cormac standing on the sidewalk, looking in my direction.

"Love you," Fitz said.

"Yeah, me too," I said, and terminated the call, my attention already on the two vampires waiting for me to join them.

"We ready to leave?" I asked as I approached.

Rogue ignored me and moved toward the curb to flag down a cab. Cormac answered. "Yeah. The vampire I'm looking for was here earlier, but she left. She's supposed to have gone to another club on the Lower East Side called Lucifer's Laundromat."

"I can hardly wait to see it. Where's Benny?" I wasn't entirely surprised that my friend still hadn't come out of the club.

"Ummm," Cormac murmured, looking away from me and focusing on something down the block. "She's, um, still upstairs. I told her I'd give her a couple of minutes. You and Rogue head over to Second Avenue. Ask around for Audrey."

"I'll wait here for Benny," I countered. "You go with Rogue."

"Nah. I have to pull her away from something. You don't want to go there. Trust me. Look, we can't risk missing this vampire again. We really need her."

I saw that Rogue had hailed a taxi and was getting in. Without another word to Cormac, I walked over to the cab and followed Rogue into the gloomy interior.

Rogue gave the cabbie the address, and the vehicle lurched forward, starting across town as soon as I had shut the door.

"Welcome to my parlor, said the spider to the fly," Rogue mocked.

"Shut up." I slid lower in the seat, my chin burrowed into my collar, my hands in my pockets.

"I scare you, don't I?" His cigarette-harsh voice grated on my nerves like a file against metal.

"Yeah, right. I'm shaking in my boots." I refused to look in his direction.

"So what's the problem? I didn't graduate from Harvard?"

I decided to be honest for a change. What the hell. I had nothing to lose. "I don't like you, that's all. Maybe there's something about you I don't trust. Or just call it bad chemistry and leave it alone."

"You're real good at fooling yourself, lady."

Okay, he had just pushed one of my buttons. My head whipped around and I spit out, "What the hell is that supposed to mean?"

"Oh, come on. I bet you know exactly what I mean. You don't like me. Why? I'm not up to your high standards? Nah, I don't think that's it. Sure, I was born with bad luck up the ass, but I deal with it. I did hard time a while back. I got quite an education, all right. I don't pretend to be better than I am. But you? Besides thinking your shit smells like roses, you can't admit you liked breaking heads in that bar. It made you feel better, didn't it? And you liked what you saw upstairs in the club. You just can't accept that you liked it—any more than you can accept who or what you are."

"Go fuck yourself," I said.

"Fucking *myself* wasn't what I had in mind," he said.

"What part of 'I don't like you' don't you understand?" I glared at him.

"You don't have to like me to want to fuck me." His obsidian eyes seemed to glitter, a glow behind them burning like hot coals.

"You disgust me," I said, and turned away.

Rogue laughed. "You wouldn't be the first woman to say that." He cracked the window open a few inches and lit a cigarette despite the NO SMOKING warnings. The cabbie didn't say a word. I started counting the blocks we were passing. This was turning out to be the longest cab ride of my life.

At our destination, a bloodred neon sign depicted a grinning devil alongside the words LUCIFER'S LAUNDROMAT, but I could see faded letters spelling out SECOND AVENUE LAUNDERETTE behind it. The club, obviously once a real Laundromat, was sandwiched between a Ukrainian social club and the Veselka café on the corner of Ninth Street.

While Rogue settled up with the cabbie, I didn't bother waiting for him. I went up to the doorman. Upon demand I showed him my sharp incisors, paid him twenty bucks, and got my hand stamped with a cartoon bat in the kind of ink that glows under a blacklight. Then I pushed through a chrome-and-glass front door into the club's interior and quickly decided that Lucifer's Laundromat was the catch drain for the sins of the world that were washed away, like the Christian liturgy says.

In the shadowy room the music was so loud the floor shook. Washers running on their spin cycle added to the din, with scantily clad girls giggling as they sat on the vibrating tops. The crowd looked hipper than at the other two clubs. Orifices were pierced. Limbs were tattooed. Glazed eyes announced that most patrons were stoned out of their minds. And somewhere in there, gyrating to the music or sitting at the bar whose base was made up of front-loading clothes dryers, was Audrey. I couldn't imagine how a grunge-scene groupie was going to help us. What the hell was Cormac thinking?

I pushed my way through the crowd. A notice posted on the wall warned: PATRONS MUST REMAIN IN HUMAN FORM. ANYONE TRANSFORMING ON THE PREMISES WILL BE EJECTED. I shouldered my way up to the bar and called out, "Anybody here named Audrey?"

A guy with a mohawk haircut and safety pins hooked through his eyebrows, nose, and lip appeared at my side. "Audrey said somebody might be looking for her. She's riding on the third washer to your right."

I glanced over. "That can't be the Audrey I'm looking for," I said.

"Why not?" the punker asked.

"She looks like a librarian," I said.

"She is," he said.

CHAPTER 6

Fortune favors the prepared mind.

—Louis Pasteur

"Excuse me. Can I interrupt? Are you Audrey?" I asked. An old Maytag was shaking violently in front of me. On top of it sat an angular dark-haired girl whose face was dominated by a large nose and heavy black Elvis Costello eyeglasses. Her eyes, appearing shrunken in size behind thick lenses, didn't blink. They looked right at me, then slid away and focused on Rogue, who to my dismay was standing behind me, much too close behind me.

The girl's gaze returned to me as she reached over and stopped the machine, then jumped down onto the floor. When she opened her mouth to speak, I noticed that her tongue was pierced. "The answers to your questions are yes, you can interrupt me, and yes, I'm Audrey. I wasn't getting off from sitting on this washer anyway. But hey, dildos don't do it for me either. Who are you? I thought that dancer, Cormac O'Reilly, was supposed to meet me."

"He's coming later. I'm Daphne Urban, and this is Rogue." I glanced over my shoulder at my nemesis. "Do you have a last name?"

"Rogue's good enough," he answered.

"Okay. That's cool. I'm Audrey Greco." She extended to each of us a bony hand with long, thin fingers. "Let's go find a table." Audrey led the way across the dance floor, her skinny ass looking like a boy's in her jeans. The ridge of her spinal column jutted through a pilled blue sweater.

We found an empty "table," a Sears Kenmore washer surrounded by tall stools that was positioned with a row of others along the rear wall. We had no sooner sat down when a waitress appeared. Audrey explained that there was a cover charge and a three-drink minimum per table. "Is one of you buying?" she inquired.

"The lady's picking up the tab." Rogue jerked his thumb in my direction and said to me, "And you owe me fifteen bucks for the cab."

I nodded yes to Audrey and ignored Rogue.

"In that case, I'll have a pomegranate Bellini."

I ordered a mineral water, even though the waitress informed me it would cost seven bucks. Rogue asked for a Boilermaker, and he specifically wanted a shot of Johnnie Walker Black Label (Winston Churchill's favorite) and a glass of Budweiser. It crossed my mind that Rogue ordered the fine Scotch to have with a beer merely to annoy me. I thought of Fitz, whose favorite drink was Jameson served straight up. He would have been appalled at Rogue's crudity.

Everything about Rogue irritated me. I made an effort not to snap out a nasty remark. I turned my attention back to Audrey. Most vampires are physically attractive, a natural consequence of victims being chosen for their beauty, since biting is an erotic as well as a dining experience. Perhaps the vampire who had sunk his teeth into Audrey's neck had been a bibliophile dazzled by her mind. Or, more likely, she had been very young and her terror had been an irresistible turn-on to some unconscionable bat bastard.

In any event, she appeared not to care about her looks.

Contacts would have eliminated the Coke bottle–bottom lenses, and a nose job could have reshaped the beak that dominated her features. As for her anorexic appearance, I suspected she didn't drink enough blood, and that, I mentally filed away for future reference, meant she was hungry most of the time. Despite Audrey's meek appearance, a starving vampire can be both aggressive and unpredictable.

As I studied her, Audrey's attention had been focused on Rogue. She looked as if she thought he was an ice-cream cone that she'd love to lick. She must have felt me staring at her, so she dragged her eyes away from him. "You have a question for me or something?"

Since I had no idea why Cormac had singled out this young woman or how much she had been told about the mission, that was what I asked.

"I heard you needed a research librarian. A vampire research librarian. I'm the only one in New York. There are a few in London, though. It's not the first time I've gotten freelance work." She smiled, revealing an overbite. "I'm very good."

"Good at what specifically?" I pressed. "What do you research?"

"My specialty is the architectural history of New York; that includes infrastructure as well as buildings. You know, the sewer system, subway, water lines. Those kinds of things."

My respect for Cormac rose a notch. It was clear now how Audrey could be helpful in finding the kidnap victims. I assumed Rogue was chosen to provide muscle or insight into the criminal mentality. Maybe he had done time for kidnapping or extortion. I could easily believe it, but I wasn't going to ask.

The waitress arrived with our drinks. I squeezed a wedge of lime into my glass and wiped my fingers on a napkin. Meanwhile Audrey sucked down half her Bellini without coming up for air. Rogue dumped the deluxe Johnnie Walker

Scotch into his beer and chugged it. I might be the only one of the three of us sober by the time we left here.

I delicately sipped my water and asked Audrey, "Were you told anything about the situation? I mean what we need you to research?"

"Oh, yeah," Audrey said, as she twisted a strand of lank hair around her index finger. She had a faint pinkish-orange Bellini mustache on her upper lip. "You're looking for ten kidnap victims stashed somewhere in the city. I'm supposed to figure out where they are."

I choked on the water and started coughing. When I caught my breath, I said, "That's confidential information. Please don't tell anybody, okay?"

I saw Audrey's tiny eyes roll behind her lenses. "Of course I won't tell anybody. I'm supposed to be a spy, right? Top-secret and all that."

Oh, my God, I thought. *I am going to strangle Cormac when I see him.* I also noticed that none of this seemed like news to Rogue. I wondered how many vampires on the island of Manhattan knew about the Darkwings and at least some of the details of our latest mission. The way vampires tended to gossip, I suspected it could be in the hundreds.

"And it's a temp position, right? Unless I get asked to stay on, natch. And the rate is a thousand a night, right?" Audrey asked.

I was quiet for a moment, trying to figure out how to respond. I had no power to pay her anything. I didn't know what Cormac had set up to authorize the money, if anything. Finally I explained that what they each had been promised was strictly in my partner's department and I didn't know anything about it. But I added that I was pretty sure that both Audrey and Rogue would have to meet our boss, J, who would make the final determination about their joining the Darkwings even pro tem.

As I said it, I started to smile. I knew that J wasn't going to give us a pat on the back for our hiring initiative. He was going to have a shit fit. And his boss, my mother, who wanted all the control all the time, would have an f'ing royal shit fit. It could be a highly satisfying evening after all.

While I was smiling, Rogue wasn't. He stood up fast. "I'm getting out of here," he said, his words spilling out fast in a stream colored by bitterness. "You people are all alike. I should know better than to trust the agency. You fucked me before, but you sure as hell aren't going to fuck me again." He stood there with his hands clenched into fists, his head lowered like a bull about to charge.

Whoa! I thought. *What the hell is this all about? So Rogue had dealings with the agency in the past?* I hesitated just a second before I slowly stood up too. I moved close enough to Rogue so we couldn't be easily overheard, but not close enough to invade his space. I kept my voice low, calm, and reasonable. "Look, I honestly don't know what the agency does or doesn't do. But the Darkwings don't screw one another. Whether I like you or don't like you, I won't mess with you. I'll do what I can about you getting paid. But if you want to walk, go. Now's the time."

Rogue looked at me hard, then gave a small nod. "All right. But I need that money." He moved the chair with his foot and sat back down.

Audrey, on the other hand, finished her Bellini and said she felt that meeting the boss didn't sound too unreasonable. She did want to know how fast she'd be told whether she would be accepted as a permanent spy. I didn't have any answers for her either. It was probably a good thing that Cormac and Benny showed up right then.

Rogue immediately got into Cormac's face over the money thing. They moved their chairs close together, but I could hear Rogue telling Cormac he didn't like being jerked around and demanding to know whether Cormac had the authority to pay him or not. Cormac assured him that he would be paid as promised. I raised an eyebrow. I wondered if Cormac had cleared the hiring with J and didn't let Benny and me know. It seemed unlikely.

Cormac asked us all to "get better acquainted" while he stepped outside to make a phone call to the office and get everybody some answers. When he left, I introduced Benny, whose cheeks were flushed and whose eyes were pink, to Audrey.

"Well, what all do you come to this here club for?" Benny asked while she glanced around at the thumping washers and spinning dryers. "Do you all really do your laundry?"

Audrey looked at Benny with a quizzical expression. "You're from out of town, right?"

"Sugar, are you saying that I took the late train and came in on the caboose?"

"Huh?" Audrey replied. "I meant you don't seem too, uh, familiar with what goes on. Around here, I mean."

"That's what I jist say-ed, didn't I?" Benny's accent intensified with her burst of annoyance. She pressed her lips together and looked around her again before turning her attention back to Audrey. "Now, don't y'all take me wrong. I know I'm the country mouse in the big city. I think this place is grits. Just fine and dandy. But I was wonderin', not much seems to be going on besides dancin' and drinkin'. Am I missin' something?"

Audrey nodded vigorously. "Team sports. This is a place for team sports."

"Y'all mean like football?"

"No. What we do is a lot more fun. See those magnetic blackboards over there, behind that row of dryers?"

Benny and I both looked. One board was titled *RACERS*;

the other was CHASERS. A dozen names were listed beneath each title. "Okay, I see them," Benny said.

"Well, this is how it works. Each team is picked by a nightly lottery—it costs ten bucks to enter it, by the way—and they compete. The members go out to find donors, you know, blood donors. They have one hour. Whichever team brings back the most donors wins. Then the winners are awarded the losing team's catches to keep along with their own. If there are more than twelve donors, the winners can invite friends to join them."

"Join them?" I asked, an anxious feeling starting in my stomach.

"For supper," Audrey said, and giggled. "Courtesy of the donors, of course. People in the club who don't get picked for either team usually bet on the results. It makes it more fun. And of course, being on the winning team is incredibly exciting. Some of us come here almost every night to get into the hunt lottery."

Benny was clearly intrigued. I felt increasingly uneasy. Rogue looked bored. He mumbled that he wasn't into team sports. He liked to go out hunting on his own.

"Where do the winners dine?" Benny asked, looking around.

"Oh, not in here. Downstairs. In the lounge." Audrey became excited, eager to give us all the details. "It's a beautiful setup with every amenity. The club management does a stupendous job: six-hundred-thread-count Egyptian-cotton sheets on the beds; the finest wines, all of which have scored over ninety-two in *Wine Spectator*; Jacuzzis with the best bath salts and loofahs; hashish, marijuana, and cocaine—whatever the winning team wants. A doctor is standing by in case there's an 'accident,' you know.

"The club has set up viewing windows if anybody wants to watch. But they charge you an arm and a leg to do it, and watching makes me horny and hungry, so I don't. If I'm not picked in the lottery, I usually head for another club—only on my nights off, of course. I have a full-time job as an independent contractor with the city."

Benny was scrutinizing the librarian across from her. "Don't take offense, sugar, but you don't look like a party girl."

Audrey gave Benny a sly look. "All cats look alike in the dark. Besides . . ." She shrugged and looked away. Her neck was long and graceful; her profile regal. "I work hard, so I play hard."

Benny gave Audrey a second appraisal. "Sugar, I bet you do."

Cormac's face was ashen when he returned. "We have to get over to the office," he announced.

"J wants to meet the newbies?" I deduced, also thinking that Cormac looked more shaken than I thought a tongue-lashing from J could produce. If he didn't physically have to fight, Cormac normally tuned out hostility. Under those circumstances his face became blank, as if he were in a self-induced trance. Broadway directors, some of the best screamers on the planet, threw down their scripts and stomped on them to get his attention. But they soon concluded that if they yelled at Cormac, he wouldn't even hear them. I didn't know whether J had figured that out too.

"Not exactly. He said to bring them along, but he needs to see all of us as fast as we can get there. We have to meet somebody."

"Who?" Benny asked as she stood up.

"The Morrises. You remember it was their daughter Nicoletta who was hosting the party at the Rockefeller estate. Now their other daughter has been snatched too."

CHAPTER 7

Begin at the beginning . . . and go on till you come to the end: then stop.

—Lewis Carroll, *Alice's Adventures in Wonderland*

I could smell fresh coffee when we arrived at the offices of ABC Media, Inc., around ten that night. Unlike earlier, the overhead lights were now on, making the room brighter than normal and exposing its faded paint, grimy windows, and beat-up furniture. This was not a venue to impress visitors, but I didn't think the man and woman sitting near J at the conference table cared about the ambience.

The man rose from his chair when the five of us piled into the room, perplexity and disappointment both evident on his face, which was deeply lined, his skin nearly gray, his eyes darting from one of us to another. I wondered if he had been expecting a SWAT team of uniformed commandos.

"*This* is the crack undercover unit that is going to get our daughters back?" He addressed J in a voice laden with disbelief.

His wife, a big woman whose huge bosom wasn't disguised by her dowdy tan jacket, tugged at his arm. "Marshall, please. He told us they were working undercover, remember?"

J introduced them and revealed that Marshall Morris was

actually Judge Marshall Morris, a member of the federal bench. He referred to Benny, Cormac, and myself by our first names only, then let Cormac do the honors for Audrey and for Rogue, whose size alone made him seem the most military in our group. On the other hand, the little silver skull hanging from his earlobe and the smell of beer and whiskey on his breath probably didn't build a lot of confidence in the Morrises. Neither of them offered to shake our hands.

The five of us vampires sat down on the same side of the table, across from our guests. I was profoundly disturbed by these people being here. Our deep-black status meant no one knew about us. Thanks to Cormac, our cover was being blown among the city's vampires, which was bad enough, but now these outsiders had gotten entrée to us, which meant someone had gotten to my mother. My mother was never "gotten to," and I felt worried and confused.

"Judge Morris asked to meet you," J explained, his tone conveying something—reluctant acquiescence? I knew J well enough to recognize how stiffly he was holding himself and to pick up on the way he was clipping his words, as if speaking took great self-control. Since I had seen him angry many times before, it was clear to me that he was totally pissed off under his polite exterior. The Morrises must have enormous influence in the highest circles of power to have forced this meeting.

J turned to our side of the table. "The Morrises know that your identities are top-secret, and they've been cleared through security. They understand that they cannot make public anything they learn here and that you cannot divulge your . . . your backgrounds."

Okay, I figured that was code-speak that they didn't know we were vampires and we weren't supposed to tell them.

"However," J continued, "the situation is so critical that

Washington felt you should question the Morrises directly, figuring it might help you in finding their daughters, and the other girls, of course."

I didn't believe that for a minute. For one thing, "Washington" didn't even know we existed. The security agencies in Washington were obviously trying to play Cover Your Ass, and whomever my mother reported to must have told her to set this up to placate these VIPs. The Morrises must have been raising holy hell with the president himself.

Nevertheless, I figured since we were here, we might as well use the opportunity to find out what we could. "Judge Morris. Mrs. Morris—" I began.

"Mary," the woman said. The man said nothing.

"Mary," I said in a gentle voice. "Please be assured we are actively looking for your children—"

"So where are they? Why haven't they been rescued?" Judge Morris interrupted.

"Marshall," Mary Morris pleaded, "let the woman talk, please."

The man clasped his hands firmly in front of him and fell silent. I began again. "Describe for us what happened to your second daughter."

The man talked without consulting his wife. She didn't seem surprised. "Deborah goes to Princeton. She's a sophomore there. We had been instructed not to tell her that her sister had been abducted—"

"I didn't agree with that," Mary broke in.

"Quite frankly, I didn't feel comfortable withholding it from her either," Judge Morris went on. "We called the school and said there had been a threat to our family. We needed to put some additional security in place for Deborah, as a precaution. Actually, the school was willing to send her home, but Deborah insisted she couldn't miss class. Maybe if she had known about Nicoletta she would have taken the situation more seriously. Instead, when we spoke to her, she complained that having a bodyguard was embarrassing."

"When was she abducted?" I asked.

"This afternoon. She told her roommate she wanted to go shopping at a mall over on Route One. A Macy's or something is over there. She slipped away from her guard by climbing out the dorm room window. She told her roommate she'd be back within two hours. She never returned. Instead we—actually Mary—got a phone call from a man, the same kidnapper who had called before. Our phone line is tapped, of course, so there is a record of this. He told Mary that they now had Deborah."

I looked at J. "Do we have the transcript of the call?"

"Yes," he said. "And we know the call was placed from a cell phone. At the time the caller was in Hoboken, New Jersey, near the Holland Tunnel. Probably in a vehicle."

"And authorities have been focusing on monitoring vehicles going out of the city, not those coming in, right?"

"All ingress and egress is being monitored. But you're right. Vehicles entering Manhattan are being scrutinized only as much as they would normally be during an elevated security alert, and we are in orange. So that's a fair criticism," J said.

"Okay." I nodded. I turned back to Deborah's parents. "Mary, do you remember anything about the man? Anything unusual about his voice? Were there any other voices in the background?"

"His voice? He spoke very good English, educated, with no accent. He sounded young, and very angry. I burst into tears and pleaded with him to let my girls go. I asked him why he had to take both my children. He said one million innocent children have been killed in Iraq, and your president does not care. But he might care about my two children.

"The young man had no pity. Just anger."

"Do you remember anything else? Background noises?" I asked.

"Yes, yes. I remember I could hear the sounds of traffic. I assumed right away he was calling from a car. He wasn't the driver, though, because he called out to someone else, 'Take this exit,' before his voice became muffled. I think he put his hand over the phone. But I could still hear a woman ask in English, 'Here?' Then he yelled at her in a foreign language, Arabic, I guess. Maybe it's on the transcript."

Rogue cut in gruffly: "So why was it you?"

"What do you mean?" Mary Morris asked.

"Why both *your* daughters? Don't the other kidnapped girls have siblings?"

"Yes, of course they do."

"So what makes you, your family, the terrorists' target?"

"I . . . I . . . don't know," she said. "All the missing girls come from families as wealthy as or even wealthier than we are. I never thought that we're the target. I assumed we all are."

Judge Morris seemed lost in thought. He remained silent.

Rogue said, "You know what I think? The other girls, maybe they're a diversion. A smoke screen. Again I have to ask, why *your* family? What's your importance, or draw, for the kidnappers? They're only calling you, by the way."

"I don't know. I really don't know." Mary Morris was becoming visibly upset. "Marshall?" She turned to her husband.

Judge Morris sat up straighter, puffing out his chest and raising his chin so he looked down his nose at me. I imagined it was a habit that he practiced often when presiding in court. "I'll have to take your question under consideration, but I assume it's because I went to law school with the president. Our families socialize, and I speak with him on a regular basis. Sometimes daily. No one from the other families has that kind of a personal relationship with him.

"That's why these animals have stolen both my children. Both my children! And yes, I did tell the president to give them whatever they want—and we can deal with that after my daughters are safe. What are we waiting for? They've mutilated one of my daughters already."

He looked at each of us in turn, not disguising his feeling of superiority as he did. "I'm not saying you people can't find my children. I hope to God you can. But I'll say to you just what I said to the president: Give them the damn Buffalo; then blow it up. For crissakes! Can't you people think outside the box!" He thumped his fist, gavel-like, on the table with each of these final words.

Judge Morris's face had become dark red, the veins bulging on his temples. Mary Morris had begun weeping quietly. Although I didn't say it, I was inclined to agree with him. The government's one-size-fits-all approach to abductions didn't work.

J pushed a bottle of water over to the judge and indicated that he might want a drink. I gave the judge a minute to regain his composure, then asked, "Judge, somebody close to these kidnappers knew about your younger daughter's birthday party, and they knew about it with enough lead time to set up the abduction. They also knew where your older daughter was and how to get to her. That means it's someone you know. Someone you work with, perhaps? What are your ideas on that?"

The judge hesitated just a second too long, and he didn't maintain eye contact with me when he answered: "No. I can't imagine who it could be. I have no idea."

I looked at J. "What about friends of the daughters?"

He shrugged at me. "I'll get you a list of people associated with the Morrises who've been questioned. I don't know how far investigators have gone in that direction."

"Is the older daughter's roommate on the list?" I queried.

"I believe she is. I'll check."

"I think we need to speak with her ourselves."

Then I turned back to the couple on the other side of the table. "Judge, Mary, is there anything else you can tell us? Anything at all?"

Mary blotted her eyes with a tissue and shook her head. The judge said, "No."

I didn't particularly like the judge, but I couldn't discredit his genuine distress, which had turned, by now, to the desperation that fueled his bursts of temper. His wife's sorrow affected me deeply. I spoke to them both gently. "I can't know what you're feeling—nobody can—but I promise you that somebody is out there searching. Somebody is doing something. But if you have nothing else to tell us, we have a long night ahead of us."

I lifted my hand and gestured toward Audrey. "Our colleague should get to her computer; she's looking for possible places the girls could be hidden in the city. The rest of us need to coordinate our investigation. We won't rest until we find your girls; I promise you that. And I'm sure we'll have more questions for you, perhaps tomorrow."

"My daughters might be dead by tomorrow." The words erupted from Judge Morris as he slammed his fist into the table. "We need something to happen now."

Rogue cut in. "The kidnappers need your daughters alive, Mr. Morris. I can guarantee it. But you have a point. By tomorrow another one of the girls could be dead. They're expendable, and killing one or more of them will increase the pressure on you."

"Oh, how horrible!" Mary Morris had gone paper white. I heard Benny whisper to Rogue, "Hush up. They didn't need to hear that."

Rogue didn't bother to whisper when he answered. "I think they do. The judge needs to figure out his part in this.

He's the linchpin." J started to protest, but Rogue cut him off. "He is." Rogue leaned forward, locking eyes with the judge. "I think you know why, Judge Morris. When you're ready to tell us, we'll be ready to listen."

Judge Morris's face twisted in rage. "I won't be accused of being a part of this. I had nothing to do with my daughters' kidnappings."

J tried to pour oil on the troubled waters. "Judge Morris, nobody's accusing you of anything."

Rogue didn't back off. "I am. You're up to your neck in something, and it's linked to the reason—besides your being a VIP with ties to the White House—that you're the target."

J couldn't let this continue. I'm sure he could see his career being steered right into the rocks. He'd be scrubbing latrines if Rogue didn't shut up. He barked, "That's enough. Judge Morris, I apologize. We're all feeling the pressure."

Judge Marshall Morris had gotten to his feet. His angry face was set in stone. "I didn't come here to shoulder any blame. I bear no responsibility whatsoever in this. But there will be plenty of blame on your shoulders if anything happens to my children. Now we do need to be going. We're supposed to wait by the phone in case the kidnappers call again."

He helped his wife get heavily from her chair. When she stood up, I could see that her bottom was as broad as her bosom. She had to weigh three hundred pounds. She swayed, then steadied herself against the table.

She looked at all of us with anguished eyes. "I want you to know that I do appreciate your help. You're wrong about my husband, Mr. Rogue, but I'm glad to see your passion. It means you care." She stifled a sob. "Find my girls. Find all those poor girls. You're our only hope. I feel that."

We all stood while they exited the room. When the door closed behind them, Rogue said, "I'm not wrong."

Benny looked at him. "How can you be sure? You don't know that man."

"I don't have to know him. Every guy in jail says he's innocent. A few of them are, but damn few. You hear enough people lie, you spot the signs."

"So you've done time?" J asked.

Rogue turned to him. "Yeah. Texas. New Jersey. Rikers. I know criminals, and shit, you want to know? I know how to set up an inside job. And this sure as hell was one."

"You ever set up a kidnapping?" I broke in, my voice snide.

Rogue gave me a hostile stare and stayed silent a moment. When he spoke, his voice was low and angry. "Maybe yes, maybe no. I admit I've done some shit. Why the hell do you think your friends brought me into this? Because I went to Yale? You ever plan a heist? A snatch? That's why I'm on board, ain't it?" Rogue glared at me. I glared back.

J didn't butt in right away. He was quietly appraising the big, crude biker. Finally he stood up and put out his hand. "Welcome to the Darkwings," he said.

CHAPTER 8

*You need to know three things to survive in here.
Life isn't fair. Shit always rolls downhill. And
nobody gets out of this life alive.*

—Dwight Mason, lifer, Trenton State Prison

I had hoped to see J pissed off. I wanted fireworks. I didn't
get them—not right then, anyway.

J turned to Audrey and cordially told her that her services
were needed and welcome. I guess he was a pragmatist first
and a son of a bitch only second. He even had some paper-
work ready for both of our recruits. I offered Audrey the use
of my small office right off the conference room. I hadn't
spent much time there, but there was a desk and a computer.
She said thanks but no thanks. She'd work from her home
office, where she had the right software and e-mail contacts.

At that point J said he needed to speak with me *in his office*. He told the others to formulate a plan of action for the
next twenty-four hours. His foot having been injured a few
weeks earlier, he leaned heavily on a cane as I followed him
into the triangular room that sat in the apex of the Flatiron's
wedge shape. He shut the door behind us.

"Sit," he ordered.

"No, thanks." I intended to remain eye-to-eye with him. I
knew his game of intimidation—at more than six feet tall, he
liked to tower over subordinates—and I wasn't going to play

it. Since I wouldn't sit, J walked over and stopped maybe two feet in front of me. That was too close for my comfort zone. The backs of my legs were against a chair. I couldn't move away; I'd have to stand my ground.

"You went outside of channels and brought these vampires in," he said, his cold blue marble eyes boring into mine.

"Not just me, all three of us did."

"So Cormac tells me. On one level you did the right thing—"

That was a shocking admission, I thought.

"But you know the government doesn't work that way."

I shrugged. "We're not exactly government. We're an extra-government arm, aren't we? Exempt from the law, not governed by rules, not recognized by any agency. So we operated outside of channels." I lifted my chin and stared back at him. "Deal with it."

A muscle twitched in his eyelid. His jaw got tight. J's volcanic temperament was building toward an eruption. I started talking more rapidly. "And you must have provisions for us to use freelance agents and informants. That's part of the spy game, isn't it?"

His voice became very low and menacing. "It's customary, Miss Urban, to clear initiatives and financial promises with your superior officer first. Why didn't any of the three of you come to me?"

I flicked my eyes away and looked toward the ceiling. "We, uh, felt we had to move quickly. The bureaucracy would take too long."

"Or did you believe I'd say no?" J moved a bit closer, invading my personal space.

"We didn't really consider that. Honestly. You seem to have gotten over your aversion to vampires. But we figured it would be easier for *you* to get approval if we had actual candidates. You know, it's easier to beg for forgiveness than ask for permission." I could feel J's breath on my face. I was acutely aware of his proximity. As much as I didn't want to be attracted to J, we had always had chemistry.

Our relationship had been, from first meeting, like the tide going in and out. We felt a pull that brought us toward each other and a camaraderie when we fought together against the enemy. But all too quickly we'd start fighting each other or circumstances would drive us apart.

Bottom line? J was my boss—and I was the boss of me. I resented authority figures. He gave me orders. I defied them. I came on to him once. He rejected me. Much later he kissed me, and I, crazy about Darius della Chiesa, basically told him, *No deal.* Then he played a particularly dirty trick to break up me and Darius, and my fury at him for that still burned.

Now the tide had turned again, flowing in, the silvery waves reaching higher to embrace the land. My voice got softer; my gaze searched his face, implying intimacy and a connection between us. "You wouldn't have let us bring two more vampires into this, now, would you? We're hard to handle. Hard for you to control. Tell the truth, J."

His eyes held mine. His voice became intimate too. "I would have had reservations. But in retrospect, it was a good idea."

"You really think that?" I was surprised.

"Yes, I do. But I have a major problem with what you and your two partners did." J was careful not to touch me, not with his hand, not with his body. Nearly chin-to-chin, our lips inches away from each other, we had somehow moved until we were standing nearly toe to toe.

"What problem?" In truth I was losing the train of con-versation. I was looking first at J's lips; then my attention was being drawn to his neck. He worked out at a gym; his bulky muscles attested to that. His neck was thick and strong.

I stopped listening to his words. His voice was a silky caress. I closed my eyes. "Our per diem rate is three hundred dollars a day. So I have bad news. We don't have the money to pay these folks what you promised—"

My eyes opened. I curtailed my increasingly lascivious thoughts. I knew this conversation was leading somewhere, and it wasn't to a sexual dalliance or a quickie on the desk. "Well, you have to find the money," I cut him off.

"No, Agent Urban, *you* have to find the money. And there is the matter of a missing cashier's check for fifty million dollars from your first mission—and yes, officially you don't have it, but we both know you do. An additional fourteen hundred dollars a day to pay for your recruits shouldn't be a problem. It's chump change for you."

He stepped back from me abruptly, snapping whatever physical bond had been building between us. His tone was snide. "You've demonstrated that you have no scruples about *anything*. Consider the money a donation to a good cause."

I felt as if J, coldly calculating SOB that he was, had played me. "I might be without scruples, but you're a flat-out bastard," I said. He knew very well I wasn't talking about the money.

He took another step away and leaned over to look through some folders on his desk. "I've been called worse. Anyway, I'm surprised you didn't ask Darius della Chiesa in on this. Or did you and he turned you down?"

The color came up into my cheeks. "You really are low; you know that?" My eyes were blazing as I glared at J, and with his head turned away, I couldn't read his expression. A curtain had fallen between us, and he was shutting me out. He'd never forgive me for preferring Darius over him, I guess.

He straightened up and we exchanged one last glance, the gulf between us wider than ever.

"It's time to return to the others," he said, and waited for me to walk out before him.

The plan of operation for the next twenty-four hours seemed straightforward enough. In the nearly seven hours left of the night, before dawn forced vampires indoors to hide and sleep, Audrey would search for potential hideouts where the kidnappers might be keeping the girls. Rogue would make some phone calls or go looking for some former partners in crime who might know something.

Meanwhile Benny, Cormac, and I would review transcripts of phone calls and interviews with individuals connected to the Morrises. We asked to have the roommate available in New York tomorrow evening. Then we'd spend the next night checking out more locations.

What my cohorts had come up with wasn't brilliant. But with Audrey's talent and Rogue's underworld connections—if he was telling the truth—we had a shot. A long shot. Unless the technicians trying to find some electronic connection to a cell phone came up with something better, it was the only shot we had.

"Something else might help us out, though," Rogue observed. "If I can find one."

"What?" I asked.

"A snitch."

It wasn't until we were out on the sidewalk, the hour pushing toward midnight, that I got fireworks, and I no longer wanted them.

Our discussion started off innocently. We agreed to go to Audrey's apartment down on Sullivan at Bleecker Street. She warned us that her second-floor flat was small and funky, but she needed access to her computer, and we needed to be nearby in case she found a location for us to check out.

The street was quiet, no pedestrians in sight and only a few cars cruising down Broadway. We were about to look for a couple of cabs when Rogue announced, "I gotta go do something personal before I get into this thing. I'll meet you at Audrey's in an hour or two."

I had been through a pile of crap already tonight, what with the fight in the biker bar, the scene at the upstairs lounge, and my little tête-a-tête with J.

"You don't have time for anything but this business tonight," I snapped, my words leaving my mouth without passing through my brain.

"I'm not asking you for permission," Rogue countered.

Cormac backed me up. "Sorry, man. You can't take a break. Not now. We need to use every minute left of darkness. Your personal business has to wait."

Rage flickered across Rogue's face, his fingers curling into fists. He took a long look at Cormac, then blew out a hard snort, reminding me of a bull in the ring. "Okay, let me spell this out. I haven't eaten in a couple of days. My energy is in the fucking toilet. I'm not going to function tonight if I don't get some blood in me."

We couldn't physically stop Rogue from taking off, but I had an idea. "Wait a minute, will you? We can take a detour up to my place. I have some bags of blood in the refrigerator. You can take what you need. It will be faster than your going out on a hunt."

"And it won't work," Rogue said. "Not for me. I need to do this my way." Before I could say another word, Rogue had stepped back into the deep shadows of the building. He stripped off his clothes, which he heaved in my direction, saying, "Take these with you. I'll need them later."

For a long second he stood there naked, a big man, his body scarred, dark hair defining his chest and stomach, and his manhood, even in its flaccid state, large and pale below a tangle of dark curls.

"Like what you're staring at?" he asked me, and winked before he was consumed in a vortex of whirling energy and sparkling light. My own long hair was caught up in a rush of wind, and an electric charge ran over my body. I felt a strong urge to join Rogue in his transformation, but I resisted it with all my might.

When the flashes of light died down, a monster now emerged from where a man had stood. The face on the beast was clearly Rogue's, but the disturbing eyes were no longer human: They were large, golden, and glowing with reflected light. Long white incisors gleamed against his lips. His hair had become a streaming mane flowing down his shining ebony pelt. Where there had been fingers, sharp, fearsome claws extended. A wide span of midnight black bat wings stretched out from his back. Those wings dipped and fluttered, and without a sound Rogue leaped upward toward the murky sky, melted into the shadows of the buildings, and was gone.

Rogue had rejected my offer of blood, but the subject having been broached, I realized that common courtesy and plain common sense required me to extend the invitation to the rest of the team. My private stash of blood was large enough to share, and we would all function better after dining. I offered to go back to my apartment and pick up pints for all of us, then bring them to Audrey's. The others greeted the suggestion with enthusiasm.

It didn't take me long to arrive at my apartment, traffic being nonexistent and the cab I hailed making all the lights. But I felt the pressure of fleeting time as I rushed into my apartment. Nevertheless guilt nagged at me. I should walk

Jade, no matter how much in a hurry I was. Jade barked a welcome from her doggy bed in the kitchen, but didn't act as if a potty break was urgent. I soon discovered it wasn't.

A white paper against the dark granite of my kitchen island turned out to be a note from Fitz. He had come by, walked Jade, and fed her and my white rat, Gunther. He wrote that he hoped my night had improved since our phone call, and asked me to call him if I was through with work before dawn. If he didn't hear from me, he'd pick me up at six thirty tomorrow for dinner at Mama's. He signed it with a row of Xs and Os.

Thanks, sweetie, I thought, and then fleetingly wondered how much longer such a nice guy would put up with me. I didn't dwell on that. My mind was soon elsewhere. I grabbed a Coleman cooler and threw in a couple of trays of ice cubes, followed by eight pint bags of blood for the Darkwing version of *Le Déjeuner sur l'herbe,* although I assumed we would keep our clothes on unlike in the famous painting. I lugged the cooler back downstairs, caught another cab, and headed for Sullivan Street. During the ride an image of a huge black bat kept appearing in my mind's eye, its fast descent on a victim, a scream of terror, a bite—and the nightmare scenario of Rogue drinking deep from an unwilling victim's neck. And despite my high moral standards, I realized that the vision excited me and awakened my baser instincts that urged me to go back to hunting and the wild passions of the vampire life.

I was happy to escape such ruminations when the cab pulled up in front of Audrey's prewar walk-up in the heart of Greenwich Village, its stoop worn by generations of feet, its iron railing rusting and in need of paint. Carrying the large cooler, I squeezed with some difficulty up the narrow stairway, a fit so tight that my jacket rubbed the peeling green paint off the walls.

My teammates greeted my arrival by crowding into the long, narrow hall and gathering in the doorway. They toasted me with mismatched glasses as soon as my head appeared in the stairwell. I had barely gotten through the door before Cormac took the cooler out of my hands. Officiating from the softly lit windowless kitchen, with its old bathtub covered by a piece of plywood to make a table, he played sommelier and poured the elixir of life for each of us.

Raising our glasses high, we laughed and drank, Audrey gulping down the deep-red blood too quickly. "Two pints each? That's it?" she asked. Her eyes had a wild look.

I had dined earlier. "You can have one of mine," I offered.

She greedily took the plastic pouch from my hands and filled her glass. She threw her head back and let the blood slide down her throat until the glass was empty, and gave an unladylike burp. Her cheeks flushed with a healthy rose pink, she stood straighter, and the miasma of drabness vanished. Nearly six feet tall and extremely thin, Audrey Greco had a model's bones, and the large features of her face gave her a striking handsomeness that proudly proclaimed her Adriatic ancestry.

Before my eyes, Audrey had changed from being gawky and homely to resembling a supermodel in the rough. That's what blood can do for a hungry bat.

After we'd quenched our thirsts, our lips were encrusted with clotting blood and our teeth were stained with gore. None of us cared. A little water can wash away the stain, and we had been given an instant high and burst of energy.

Audrey excused herself and left to work on her computer, which she kept in her bedroom.

Cormac, Benny, and I went into the living room, 121 cramped square feet given the illusion of more space by a high ceiling and two tall windows. A tattered Oriental rug covered the hardwood floor. Benny and Cormac sat on a low sofa that was modern in the 1950s. A blond wood–and-Formica coffee table from the same era sat in front of it. I lowered myself into a wing chair to the right of the coffee table, the silk upholstery threadbare on the arms. Meanwhile Cormac spread out the transcripts on the coffee table.

I leaned forward with my elbows on my knees as we chose to start with the butler, Clarence Roberts. He had been interviewed at the scene, as had members of the catering staff. No connection to the kidnapping or the victims could be established for any of them, and their testimony consisted only of what they remembered about the crime itself.

We turned to the material on the other persons questioned sometime on Sunday night and Monday; I assumed the FBI did the interviews, but there was nothing to confirm that in our records.

We quickly eliminated the Morrises' cleaning lady as a suspect. She was sixty years old, a devout Catholic of Polish descent, and she had worked her rosary beads throughout the interview. She had been in the employ of Mary Morris since the first year the Morrises had been wed, twenty-five years earlier. She had no criminal record, had never left the country, and lived with her brother, a retired New York police officer, and his wife.

Benny tossed her transcript onto the floor as a definite discard. We all quickly agreed that the gardener and driver, both seemingly employed from cradle to grave by the judge's family, were also off our list.

The personal trainer, however, was a person of interest. Especially provocative was that Hana Rida had been hired by the judge only a year earlier, following his hospitalization for a back problem. A picture scanned into the document showed a dark-haired young woman in a midriff-baring leotard. Her face was average but her body was killer. She had already been questioned twice, so we weren't the only ones who felt she was a possible lead.

On paper she looked squeaky clean, but she had a link to the Middle East. When asked, she responded that she was of Syrian descent, although she had been born in the United States.

"Where exactly was she born?" Cormac asked. "You see it anywhere?"

Benny had picked up the transcript. "Yes, it's here. In Rensselaer, New York. Her father taught at Rensselaer Polytechnic Institute. He died a couple of years ago. Her mother's still alive, still lives there."

"Any siblings?" I asked.

"A half brother. By her father's first wife. It says she has no contact with him. A note says the FBI is trying to find him."

"Aha," I said, leaning back in my chair and putting my feet up on a nearby ottoman.

"Why 'aha'?" Benny asked.

"I've been bothered about what Mary said, about a woman's voice in the background during the phone call." I looked up at the high plaster ceiling, noticing a webbing of cracks and a distinct brown water stain as I spoke. "Al Qaeda doesn't have women members. The Wahhabis, the Muslim sect they all seem affiliated with, keep women in burkhas and essentially slaves to men."

I turned my head to look at Benny. "If a woman is raped, for instance, it's *her* fault; they assume she somehow seduced the rapist. Among the Muslim puritans, like the Wahhabis, the rules or *fatawa* for women are extreme: Chewing gum is forbidden because it is seductive; wearing perfume in a car being driven *by a relative* is forbidden because the driver might be seduced. As for doing the driving—women aren't allowed to operate vehicles in the

Wahhabi stronghold of Saudi Arabia, for example. Having a woman involved with these terrorists didn't seem credible to me."

"But you're figuring if the woman's half brother is in Al Qaeda, it might be a different story?" she asked.

"Exactly. She's not in the group, just being used by them. With ten young women as captives, the abductors need a female to help, to handle personal hygiene matters, for example. These men are misogynists; they fear and hate women. I can't see one of them going into Walgreens to buy tampons."

I gestured toward the transcript. "What's the status on Hana's brother? Has he been found? We need to find out."

"I'll check on it." Cormac fumbled around in his manpurse for his BlackBerry and made a note.

"And what's Hana's relationship with the judge?" I asked.

"According to this, it's strictly professional. They work out every morning at five-thirty a.m."

"Where?"

"Let me see," Benny said, flipping the pages until she found the answer. "Here it is. In the poolhouse on the Morris estate in Tuxedo Park. The judge installed a gym. So what I'm thinking—and I guess you are too—is that their workout is probably sexual."

"All that bending and touching between a young woman and a man with a three-hundred-pound wife and maybe a midlife crisis. I bet he has a healthy glow when he gets done with his reps," I said.

Benny suggested that both Hana and her half brother, if he was located, should be available tomorrow to talk with us. I agreed. I also told Cormac to see if J could bring the judge back, without his wife, and have him around when we questioned Hana. It might be enlightening to see them together.

"Will do. And let's have Rogue look at Hana's transcript and get his take on her testimony," Cormac suggested.

"If he ever shows up," I said, sitting up again. "Maybe he had second thoughts about being a Darkwing. What do you really think of him?"

Cormac gave me a worried look. "It's too soon to tell. Let's see what he comes up with. I don't buy his tough-biker persona completely. I've been in a lot of theater, you know. Sometimes I think it's an act. I'm not saying he's not tough. I just think he's playing the role too. That make sense?"

"I guess," Benny responded. "I don't know how *I* feel, but I don't hold his being in jail against him. Down in Miz'ora some of those boys called the county jail their home away from home. Better than where they came from, for some of them. They could count on three hots and a cot, they said."

She seemed about to rattle on about the boys back home before Cormac cut her off by saying, "I'll give J a call about bringing in Hana." He took out his cell phone and walked out of the living room into the kitchen to make the call.

I turned to Benny. "What's it been since Rogue transformed? Over an hour?"

"He did say an hour or *two*," Benny reminded me.

"I feel he's going to be trouble," I muttered.

"I don't disagree with you, sugar," Benny said, her big brown eyes soft when she looked at me. " 'Cause I think he's going to be trouble for *you*."

"What do you mean? I think he's trouble for all of us. I don't trust him."

"I mean, Miss D, that you not only don't trust him; you don't trust yourself. You know, Rogue is probably bad to the bone. And you're with a really nice guy right now, but you don't think you deserve him. Now don't get all huffy on me. You didn't like Tallmadge either, remember? He wasn't anything like Rogue. He was classy, educated, a hunk and a half, and mmm-mmm, good in bed. But you? It wasn't just that I was having an affair with Tallmadge. You wouldn't give him the time of day."

Benny was dead wrong about that. The truth was that I gave him the time of day, all right, if the hour can be told from my pudenda. Denying I had sex with him because we never had intercourse was like President Bill Clinton protesting that he "never had sex with that woman." I had been tipsy at the time, and I used that as an excuse. It had been a mistake and a betrayal of Benny's trust; I had decided long ago to take my secrets about Tallmadge and me to my grave.

I turned my head away, unable to look at Benny when I thought about my "slip," but she didn't notice. She went on talking. "Vampire men bother you. You don't like any of them. Maybe they remind you of what you are."

I didn't want to hear this old song again. I knew what I was, but I didn't think I had to sink to the lowest levels of behavior common to my kind. I lifted my nose in the air. "You know, unlike most vampires, I do think morality and respectability matter. Those aren't merely human values. But just doing what feels good at the moment doesn't mean we should forget about fidelity and ethical standards."

Benny's face became blank, her eyes glazing over. She didn't want to hear this, obviously.

"Okay, forget it," I said. "But you know, I've personally had enough psychoanalyzing for one night, thank you. So what's really going on, girlfriend? Have you and Cormac been talking about me behind my back?"

Benny jerked her head up, her eyes widening. "Oh, no, Daphne. Not behind your back, really. Not like that. It's just that we care about you. You pick men who light you up like a candle, and you burn so hot we need sunglasses. Hell,

every time you and J are within ten feet of each other I expect him to jump your bones."

"J! Get real! We can't stand each other."

"I didn't say he liked you, or vice versa. But whooeee, I
want to fan myself, there's so much heat coming off you
two."

"Not true," I griped. "What you think is heat is open dislike."

"Whatever! Now, this Rogue feller, he's *hot*. I wouldn't
trust him alone with my purse, and I don't know yet if I like
him much, but he's macho and sexy. I'd have no problem
doing him; that's for sure. But you? You are scared to death
to even think about it. And you know why? Because you're
afraid you might like it, sugar. And then where would you
and your nice human guy be?"

"Shut up, Benny. And butt out. I'm seriously thinking
about marrying Fitz."

"You'll get married when pigs have wings," she muttered
under her breath, and turned her attention back to Hana's
transcript. Then she looked up at me again. "Daphne? Watch
out for yourself around Rogue. He knows you're a-scared of
him. And he's not a nice guy."

Right on cue, I heard Rogue's voice yelling to open up as
he pounded on Audrey's front door.

Chapter 9

Those who know do not talk.
Those who talk do not know.

—Lao Tzu, *Tao Te Ching* (trans. J. H. McDonald)

After fumbling around with three security locks and a floor bar, Benny and I got Audrey's front door open. Rogue stood in the hallway, one hand holding a *New York Times* wrapped around his lower body like a towel. With the other he kept a strong grip on the collar of a young man wearing eye makeup and blush.

Benny let out a laugh. "The *Post* or *Daily News* must have been too small."

"The *Times* makes it a really classy outfit," I said. "Is your friend a fashion accessory?"

"Where are my clothes?" Rogue snarled.

"On the back of the commode, next to the sink. Straight ahead and to your left," I answered.

"Hang on to Jo-Jo here," he said, and released his captive, pushing him roughly through the door. Rogue moved past the young man and I stepped back to let the biker by. His arm brushed me as he passed. I shivered.

The captive stood with his back to the door, trembling, looking wide-eyed first at Benny, then at me. He had curly dark hair and a deep olive complexion. Behind the heavy makeup he looked very young, maybe still in his teens. He was scared, but all things considered, he had a lot of guts. He had probably been abducted from somewhere by a scary-looking naked man and marched over here. He hadn't peed, shit his pants, or fainted, so I gave him a lot of credit.

Benny reached out and grasped Jo-Jo's forearm, tugging him toward the interior of Audrey's apartment. "Come on in and have yourself a sit-down," she said to Jo-Jo. "Don't be scared. We won't bite." Unable to help herself, she giggled and added, "At least, not right now."

I followed behind them, wondering what this was all about.

In a few minutes Rogue joined us in the small living room. Audrey came in behind him to see what was going on. Jo-Jo sat at one end of the tattered couch. Benny had poured him a glass of water, and when Rogue walked back in, his hand shook so much I leaned over from my nearby seat and took the glass from his hand before he spilled it.

"I told you we needed a snitch. So I went and found Jo-Jo here. He might have something for us," Rogue said. "He came in a couple of days ago to see a 'friend' of mine who buys and sells information. It cost me a couple of bucks, but my 'friend' turned me on to him. His name isn't really Jo-Jo. It's Muhammad. Jo-Jo, start talking to these nice folks. Now."

"I don't know what you want me to say," the captive answered in a high, squeaky voice, then cringed at Rogue's angry look. "Okay. Okay. My name is Muhammad Bukhari. Jo-Jo LaBoom is my stage name. I'm a dancer. I do interpretative dance—"

"Oh, for fuck's sake. You're a female impersonator. Cut the crap. Just tell my friends about the men who've been coming into the grocery store."

"What do you want me to tell you about them?" he asked, his voice even higher. His face paled under his makeup.

Benny cut in. "You go on now, honey," she said. "Start at the beginning. What grocery store?"

"My family's. It's a Middle Eastern grocery store. In the East Village. I work there during the day."

"And what men is Rogue talking about?" she coaxed.

"Two men. They've been coming in on and off for a couple of weeks and talking this radical stuff to my father. I'm usually in the back, stocking the shelves. My father's ashamed of me, doesn't want me out where people see me, but I could hear their voices. They were loud, arguing all the time. They want my father to go to their mosque. My father's influential in our community. If he went, others would too. My father told them no. They were saying the most sick stuff. They kept talking about the Crusades and a Zionist conspiracy and how Muslims have to fight back."

Benny looked over at Rogue and shrugged.

"Tell them exactly what you overheard," Rogue ordered. "What you told my friend Jimmy Speed-o."

Jo-Jo nodded. "Okay, sure. Last week they came in. I think it was Friday. They were all excited, talking really fast and boasting. They said my father better listen to them this time, because very soon the world was going to see that the United States was weak and Islam was strong. My father got very nervous and convinced them to go to the back of the store to his office, where I could hear them clearly. They said another September eleventh was coming. They were going to hold the children for ransom and turn the weapons of the infidels against themselves."

"Sounds like it could be our boys," Cormac said. "Did you get the impression they were actually talking about a kidnapping?"

"That's what I thought right away. I didn't know if I

should tell anybody. I mean, I thought maybe I should because that September eleventh talk scared me. I knew Speed-o because . . . because he's a cook . . ." Jo-Jo's voice trailed away and he looked down at his feet. His legs were shaking inside his skinny black jeans.

Rogue broke in. "A *cook,* not a chef. That's the 'friend' I told you about. Speed-o cooks up methamphetamine for some of us—and for Jo-Jo here. Being a snitch keeps him from getting busted by the cops."

"Oh," Benny said. "I'm sure not in Miz'ora anymore."

"Jo-Jo, what do these men look like? Do you have any names?" Cormac asked.

"One man was older, middle-aged, I'd say. He had gray in his hair and beard. Very well dressed, a suit jacket, nice slacks. The other man was maybe in his twenties, you know? He wore hip-hop clothes—baggy jeans and an oversize jacket—which I thought was weird because of his politics. He still looked nerdy, though. He had these cheap knockoff Nikes. And he had pimples. He wasn't a nice person, not at all. He saw me in the back of the store and called me something nasty. His name was Rashid. That's what the older man called him."

"Did either of the men have an accent? Anything else you can tell us?" Cormac pressed.

"Accent? They spoke in Arabic; I don't know about their English. The younger man might be Syrian. The older guy? I don't know. From Yemen? A Saudi? It's hard to tell. They're fanatics, though. My father is a little afraid of them, I think. He didn't throw them out, just listened. He gave them some money, a donation, to get rid of them. I know that."

"Jo-Jo, honey," Benny said, "did you hear them say anything else about the kidnapping?"

"Well, they did say something, but it didn't make any sense," he said.

"Tell us anyway, okay?" she said.

"That Rashid, he said they would put the children under the ground until it was time to bury them—and then they'd bury the Great Satan."

Rogue made Jo-Jo promise to call us if the men came back into the grocery store and then told him he could go. Benny accompanied the young man to the door and Audrey went back to her computer. Rogue sat down heavily on the couch, and I ignored him as much as I could. Cormac handed him Hana's transcript to read.

I leaned back in the wing chair, putting my feet up again. I wanted to think and stared up at the cracked, stained ceiling, my fingers laced together on my chest. I closed my eyes. I had been taken off guard by Rogue's showing up with Jo-Jo. He had come up with some solid information, and the rest of us hadn't. I had to consider that my emotions and my sexual frustration might be affecting my judgment. I had always trusted my intuition. But was it off? I heard Benny come back into the room.

I tried to stop thinking about myself and focus on the kidnapping. I was hoping inspiration would come to me. Nothing did.

Finally Cormac said, "So what do you think?" I opened my eyes and looked over at Rogue.

Rogue sat there hunched over, with his elbows on his knees, a man too tall and bulky for the low couch and clearly unable to get comfortable. "I definitely think this girl is the link between the kidnappers and the Morrises," he said. "She's been going in and out of the house for a year. She's close to the judge. She probably knew about the party. She had to know about the judge's relationship with the president. He would have told her to impress her, to get in her pants. My guess is that she talked about it at home, and her brother heard about it."

He looked around the room at each of us. "That's how it always happens with a big crime. Somebody on the inside. Same thing with robberies. A person's house doesn't get robbed at random. It gets robbed after somebody—a deliveryperson, a repairman, a visitor—somebody's been inside and sees what's there.

"Of course, there had to be an inside person on this kidnapping. No doubt about it. She's the one. Got to be. We should lean on this chick."

"That's what we thought too," Cormac said. "I just talked to J. He's going to request that Hana, the judge, and, if they can locate him, the brother be available to us at the office tomorrow night, around eight thirty."

Audrey walked into the room a few minutes later with a small stack of printed sheets in her long, slender hands. "I've come up with some possibilities working from the information J gave us. Take a look." She handed out the papers. "Each page contains information about a potential hiding place.

"I had specific criteria in mind when I began my search. The hiding place couldn't be a residential space, such as an empty apartment. Several men taking ten girls out of two ambulances would attract the attention of neighbors or passersby. That meant the space had to be isolated enough that there were no prying eyes in the vicinity.

"A few categories of structures fit those parameters. I focused the search on what I consider the city's most isolated, secret, and secure abandoned structures—those would be unused subway stations, platforms, lines, and tracks. What Jo-Jo said about the girls being underground confirms my opinion, by the way. Here they are." She fanned the pages, showing us there had to be more than a dozen sites.

"It's shocking, really, that there are so many. Manhattan

alone contains nine closed stations and eleven unused platforms. Of course, most of those facilities are visible to passing trains on existing subway lines. But six sets of
underground tracks have fallen into disuse and are closed
up. No one goes there. Most people are unaware of them.
Those subterranean tunnels have real possibilities." She
counted off six pages and set them on the coffee table.

"Another area I considered were old trolley stations. The
trolley lines themselves disappeared long ago and the tracks
have been paved over, but many of the buildings remain, and
they're not all aboveground either. Two underground stations are in downtown Newark, New Jersey—one is huge
and sits under a midtown building that used to hold the
Kresge Department Store. That subway line ended at
Newark's Penn Station, where passengers connected to
Manhattan. The two Newark stations are on the other side of
the Hudson, and for that reason alone I don't think we
should focus on them, for now, at least. I included them because no intelligence agency would think to search there."
She slapped down several more sheets in front of us.

"In addition to rail transit facilities that were once in
daily operation but later replaced or eliminated, the city has
a couple of unfinished and abandoned underground projects
that really gave me the creeps." She thumbed through the remaining pages and pulled one out.

"Look at the picture I printed out of this subway station
on Lexington Ave." She pointed with a thin finger. "See that
door just sitting there above the tracks in the wall across
from the uptown platform? Thousands of people look at it
every day and have no idea that it leads to an unfinished station. The door is never used. It's never opened. But behind
it, just feet away from the existing platform, is a huge empty
space that very few people, even the transit workers, know
exists."

She laid the remaining sheets on the table. "See what you think."

We all started looking at Audrey's documents, except Rogue. He turned to Audrey. "Which of these are the strongest candidates?"

"The six underground levels of abandoned tracks."

"Okay, then," he said, and stood up. "Let me make a call. I may be able to get us some information, narrow this down."

"What do you mean?" I said.

"Some of these abandoned places, I know for a fact people are using them. Never mind why. You keep reading." He got up and headed into the kitchen so we wouldn't overhear his conversation. We started looking at Audrey's picks again.

"Oh, that gives me the chills," Benny said as she pointed to one sheet. It was a description of the Hudson Terminal, used by the PATH trains from New Jersey until July 1971, when a new station under the World Trade Center replaced it. The printout said that portions of this original terminal had survived the collapse of the Twin Towers in 2001.

We could see in the scanned photos that the space was enormous. Several tunnels emerged from under the river, and each was big enough to drive a truck through. Portions of train platforms remained, as did a wide mezzanine filled with boarded-up shops, stairs leading upward, and dozens of doors that probably led to rooms used for maintenance, storage, and worker facilities.

Getting to the station, however, seemed difficult. Perhaps the terminal could be accessed from the Jersey side, through one of those old tunnels, but with the collapse of the Towers, it would take some doing to find our way down into the station from ground level. I mentioned this, and Audrey said she'd see what she could find out.

Another location we all found interesting was called the

Queensborough Bridge Railway Terminal. The bridge itself begins at Fifty-ninth Street in Manhattan, crosses the East River past Roosevelt Island, and ends up in Queens. Now it was strictly used for vehicle traffic. No trains crossed it anymore, but portions of track and track-level platforms still existed, as did an entrance to the terminal from beneath the bridge.

Also empty at this location was a trolley stop halfway across the bridge—a kiosk at bridge level, an elevator shaft, and a boarded-up hut where passengers emerged onto Roosevelt Island. A subterranean component housed the elevator works. Back when the trolley was in use, Roosevelt Island had been called Welfare Island, a desolate strand that contained insane asylums, a prison hospital, and a penitentiary that had held Billie Holiday on prostitution charges, Mae West for obscenity, Boss Tweed for corruption, and Emma Goldman for her political views and for providing women with birth control. Now the island sported pricey residential co-ops and bad karma.

But the terminal was our best bet. It existed very near to Midtown on the Manhattan side of the bridge. Unseen by pedestrians and unknown to nearby residents, it was an underground loop of five tracks that sat thirty feet beneath Second Avenue, where it ran under the bridge.

"I like the looks of this one," I said.

"Yeah, and get this." Audrey pointed to the diagram. "The entrance to these abandoned tracks is tucked way under the bridge at the end of a driveway. It's hard to spot. Unloading the girls from ambulances could be done there without being detected."

Rogue came back into the room. We looked up at him.

"You learn anything?" Cormac asked.

"Yeah. Definitely forget about Jersey. Local mobsters are using that station in Newark for a warehouse. And a cook, a friend of Speed-o's, has a lab set up on some old subway tracks down in the financial district. Speed-o's going to call him. See if he's seen anything. He'll call me."

"We think we've got two strong possibilities," Benny said. "Take a look." She handed him the sheets. He remained standing as he scanned them.

"The Queensborough Bridge looks good. The other one, downtown, how do we get in?"

"Audrey's going to research it," Benny said.

"All right then. Yeah, I agree, both of them are possible. Fits Jo-Jo's 'under the ground' real good too. I got a hunch we're onto something."

"Do we honestly think the girls are in either of these underground places?" I looked around at my teammates. "What about the abandoned warehouses? What about unused office space? These girls can be anywhere."

Audrey broke in. "No." Her voice held authority. "I know what I'm doing. I use science, not guesswork. There aren't an infinite number of possible hiding places, not once I factor in all the variables."

Her words were clipped, coming fast as she made her argument. "Office space. Forget it. It's out of the question. Those buildings have security guards even when they're empty. Warehouses? I think they're too risky for the kidnappers. Too visible. Not secret enough. Somebody in the area would have seen suspicious activity.

"Plus I use very sophisticated software, and I know this city in a way few other people do. Statistically it's a ninety percent chance the subway tunnels are exactly where the kidnappers and their victims are."

"Okay," I said, feeling more convinced. "But the two locations are nowhere near each other. One's at Fifty-ninth Street; the Hudson Terminal is way downtown. They're miles apart. What are your thoughts on our next move?"

"I say we check out the bridge," Cormac said.

"Agreed," Rogue said. Audrey and Benny concurred.

"Do we relay the information to J first?" I asked.

"No!" Benny surprised me with her vehemence. "If the girls are in either location and we tell J, he's likely to pass the information on. Then what's going to happen?"

"Some other team could be sent in." I nodded.

"Exactly," Benny said. "We're the girls' best chance. We need to check it out ourselves. Besides, think about it. How can we justify telling J? Audrey may be right, but what proof do we have? None. I say we take a preliminary look tonight at the Queensborough Bridge. Poke around. Tomorrow we see if we get anything from Hana or her brother. Then we spend the rest of that night going after the girls, if we know enough."

"We don't have much time tonight," Cormac said, looking at his watch. "It's after three a.m."

"Even though it's late, let's take five minutes and think this out," Rogue broke in. "How we gonna do this? If the kidnappers are there and spot us, they're either going to bolt or start killing the girls."

He had a point. I immediately had an idea. "Let's pretend we're half-tipsy friends on the way home from somewhere, looking for a private place to have a joint or pass around a bottle. We'll listen for unusual sounds. Check for any signs of entry or activity. We'll keep everything very low-key. It can't hurt."

It can't hurt? Famous last words.

Three a.m. and we needed a bottle of booze. Audrey didn't have a large selection on hand. She didn't entertain much. She thought for a moment: We were the first company she'd had in thirty-five years. Finally, we opted for an unopened bottle of Absolut instead of the sticky-sweet Grand Marnier that had been sitting around since the 1970s. The vodka bottle would function as a prop, but we might have to take a swallow or two, and the Absolut would go down easy.

Rogue pulled out a pack of unfiltered Camels from his shirt pocket and poked around in it. He held up three joints and said we could use them if we wanted to.

With our cover story ready, we decided to take two cabs up to Second Avenue and Fifty-ninth Street. We'd locate the entrance to the abandoned station and look for any signs of recent activity. According to Audrey, there was a stone ramp where the trolleys used to exit right on the north side of the bridge's roadway.

I maneuvered carefully so that I shared a taxi with Benny and Audrey, and the two guys ended up in another cab. They probably communicated in grunts during the ride, if they spoke at all, but on the journey uptown we three females talked nonstop, mostly about ourselves.

I discovered that Audrey was born in New York City in 1813, into a banking family. She remembered brownstones being built to replace the wooden buildings and the last dirt lanes giving way to cobblestones. She'd seen the Brooklyn Bridge being built, and the rising of the skyscrapers to create today's canyons of cement and steel. Being an eyewitness to nearly two hundred years of history gave her a huge advantage in researching the city's architecture and infrastructure.

"I was a bookish child. I particularly loved the library," she said, remembering something and letting loose with a loud bray of laughter. "Oh, yes, I loved the library!" Then she explained that for decades she'd hidden in the stacks of the sprawling neoclassical New York Public Library at Forty-second Street, until a myth began to circulate about a devil hiding down there in the dark. She admitted she had swooped down on a few librarians when she couldn't resist her hungers. None of her victims ever told what had happened to them, of course, because no one would have believed them. But sightings of the tall, shadowy woman scared enough readers that the head librarian capitulated at last and brought in a priest to do an exorcism. Audrey started frequenting the Morgan after that, using her family's banking credentials to gain access and being very careful never to suck anybody by accident or design.

Benny asked Audrey about the club where we found her. Audrey quickly disabused us of the notion that bookish should be equated with prudish. "The club scene is sure not the library!" she said, and laughed loudly again. "This club has been around for only a couple of years, but vampire clubs started back during Prohibition. They were well hidden and very discreet. No more. Now we're hiding in plain sight. Sometimes I wonder how far we can go with that."

She sighed and sat back against the seat. "I love the club scene. I really do. I feel like two people most of the time, and when I'm there, in the clubs, I know exactly who I am." She looked at me as if she felt my disapproval.

"It's decadent, more decadent now than ever. So what? Vampires can't have a family. We aren't made for lasting relationships. The clubs bring me intimate contact. They give me release. You know, in time, everything gets boring. The clubs keep me feeling alive," she said. She sat up in the seat, her voice rising.

"Look at me!" Her voice shook with emotion as she turned to us and gestured to her long, thin body. "I'm an ugly duckling. No breasts. All bones. Believe me, I feel the rejection every time I go to the clubs. I've looked like this for two centuries. But I made up my mind, you know."

"About what?" Benny asked.

"LASIK eye surgery. A nose job. Boobs. My teeth done.

New clothes. I want the works," she confessed. "I need the pay from this job. I'm getting a makeover."

I told her what I had thought earlier about her having great bones. "None of my business, but I think your nose fits your face," I said. "You should get some portfolio photos done if you think you might want to try modeling."

Audrey took this in, considered it a moment, then said, "Modeling? I have to say it's something I never considered. Wouldn't it be tedious? On second thought, I might get to travel more. I could use some decent money if this spy thing doesn't come through. But . . . a model? You really think so?"

"Yes, I really think so," I insisted. Audrey seemed to take in what I said, but she let the subject drop.

Benny told Audrey about her childhood in the Ozarks and the out-of-town bluegrass banjo player who changed her into a vampire back in the 1920s. "Branson is a different world, honey," Benny said. "It's honky-tonk on steroids. You ever been there?"

Audrey confessed she had never been to Branson, Missouri, or just about anyplace else. A train ride to Coney Island in Brooklyn seemed like going to Timbuktu to her. A native New Yorker, she had spent most of her nearly two hundred years on the planet right in Manhattan. New York City was her world. She had even lived in the same narrow brownstone apartment building, the one she currently occupied, since it was built in the 1880s.

Her residence at one address for over a hundred years brought up some of the technical difficulties of immortality that all vampires had to deal with. I asked Audrey how she pulled off keeping the lease; after all, she never died or even aged.

She smiled at my question. "I did the easiest thing: I bought the building. I get a decent rental income every month for the other two apartments; the money pays for maintenance, repairs, and taxes. I leave the building to myself in my will when I decide to 'die' and obtain a new name and birth certificate. I get annoyed paying the inheritance tax over and over; that's the only downside. I've never attracted any attention—a bonus about being plain and unattractive. In my neighborhood nobody notices that I don't age. Most local residents never seem to see me at all."

Then we talked about clothes, shoes, and what Audrey might want to buy for her new look. We decided we all had to go shopping together, and we finally got around to men.

"Men!" Audrey spit out. "Vain creatures. Good for only one thing—and it isn't their conversation. I don't have anything to do with humans, by the way. Only vampire men—and aren't they the most frivolous creatures? I guess I'm used to being alone, but I don't want a relationship with anybody I've met. You know, most vampire men aren't well educated. Until I met Cormac, I never met even one male vampire who had any interests outside of blood and sex. They get boring really, really fast."

"Amen to that." Benny laughed. "But I keep looking and hoping!"

I didn't argue with Audrey. I thought she made an accurate assessment. I looked away from my friends for a moment, thinking about my attraction to humans. Only humans had ever made me love. They might be physically inferior, but they were unpredictable, creative, and fun. Danger and risk increased the excitement. The threat of loss heightened their desires and hopes. The possibility of their death gave drama to their lives—and mine.

Benny interrupted my musings. "I have to say I don't care too much if men are boring, or if they're human or vampire. I care if they have that thingy of theirs in working order and know how to use it. I don't care about nothing too much more than that. If'n I want to talk or go out a-shopping, that's what I got friends for." Her voice dropped into sadness, and she ran her fingers up and down the fabric of her jeans, her eyes cast down. "Of course, my track record with men is jist a tad more miserable than a hound dog tied out in the rain." She paused a second before she looked up and grinned. "But maybe I'll meet somebody in that there upstairs place. I sure do want to go back."

"Benny!" I scolded. "What kind of guy can you possibly meet in a place like that!"

"A real cute one who likes to party! Listen, sugar, I don't want to get hitched any more than I want to get ditched." Her laugh was like silver bells. "You might be almost engaged to Fitz, but as for me, as they say, I need a husband like a fish needs a bicycle."

I felt good with these two women. Audrey turned out to be still water that ran deep. Benny was a merry brook, all on the surface, nothing hidden, a rush of clear freshwater. We covered a lot of emotional geography in the more than sixty blocks from the village to the Queensborough Bridge. I wished Audrey had been willing to tell us how she became a vampire, but she didn't volunteer the information, and it would have been gauche to ask.

Except for the slamming of the taxi doors and the rumble of the two cabs driving off, all sounds under the bridge were muted. Silence blanketed the gray sidewalks and empty street. The five of us stood there close together, exposed to a damp wind coming off the East River, surrounded by shadows and wisps of a ground mist that crawled around the bottom of the bridge's base.

Without discussion, Audrey led us off to the left and up onto a granite block ramp that slanted skyward, hugging the base of the bridge. We scurried up it, and after progressing about a hundred feet we found ourselves on a long cement platform. The place seemed deserted, but in case we were being observed, we took on the roles we had created for ourselves earlier.

"Hey, would you look at this place?" Benny spun around and gawked, peering off the side, trying to see the river, and acting like a ditzy out-of-towner—talk about typecasting. "It was worth the climb. I gotta say, I never know where I'm going to end up when I'm out with you guys."

"Yeah, look up there. That's the roadway to the bridge," Cormac pointed out. As we faced south, we could see glimpses of the traffic moving along about ten feet above our heads. Headlights acted like strobe lights in our cement cavern, and I shook visibly as a wave of cold air rushed past me, generated by a truck passing unseen on the bridge.

To our left, toward the river, loomed a locked gate the size of a huge garage door. Beyond that gate, fading into darkness, a tunnel curved downward.

"Now would you look at that. Where do you suppose that goes?" Audrey said, walking over and peering through the bars. We all knew this was the way to the old subway tracks that ended deep in the earth in a huge underground loop. The five of us walked over to peer through the bars, clandestinely inspecting the area to see if the gate might have been opened recently.

Rogue nudged me and pointed with his foot. Barely discernible in the flickering lights was a tire's skid mark. I nodded and poked Cormac.

While Cormac hunkered down for a closer look, he asked in a clear voice, "Who's got the bottle? This looks like a place we can drink. Isn't that why we came up here?"

"And to have a joint," Rogue said, extracting one from his cigarette pack and lighting up.

"I have the bottle," Audrey replied. We squatted down, huddling close together. Audrey took the Absolut bottle out of her purse, opened the top, and passed it around. I pretended to drink, but I suspected the others really took a swallow or two, maybe to warm their blood or add a sense of cheer. This was a dreary outpost, exposed to the river air and bombarded with exhaust fumes. A stale, acid smell came up from the tunnel as well.

"See anything else?" Benny whispered, "There's a lot of loose papers blowing around."

Rogue stood and sauntered over to one wall, leaning back against it and sucking in smoke from a joint. He held it in his lungs, then exhaled slowly. The sweet smell of ganja was unmistakable above the other odors of this unfriendly place. "Hey, sweetheart," he called out. I looked over at him. "You. Yes, you. C'mere."

I reluctantly straightened up and walked over. "Have a drag," he said, and put the joint between my lips. I sucked in, but kept the smoke in my mouth. In a very quiet voice he added, "There's something glinting, a piece of glass or metal, over by the gate. Let's see if we can get it."

I turned my body around, looked, and spotted something too. Distracted, I wasn't expecting Rogue to slip his arms around my waist and pull my back against him. Then he walked us both over to the gate. I didn't resist, but I stiffened in his embrace, not wanting his hands on me. I felt him against me; he was hard, male, and erotic. I couldn't deny that. Turning my head, I saw the others were watching us. I had to play my part in this, but I wasn't pleased.

He turned me around to face him and positioned my back against the metal bars of the gate, their stiffness pressing into me. He put his hands on my shoulders and pushed me roughly to my knees. "Give me some head, baby," he ordered, and put his hands around the back of my head, tangling in my hair, to jam my face against his crotch. He fumbled around to pull out his stiff member through the fly of his jeans, and it rubbed against my cheek. I had the presence of mind to feel around the ground until my fingers touched a coin. I slipped it into my palm, then used my forehead to butt Rogue as hard as I could.

He grunted in pain and bent over.

"Oops, so sorry! I'm dizzy," I gushed as I stood up. Under my breath I said to Rogue, "You pull a stunt like that again, and I'll bite your damned thing off."

Then I heard footsteps coming up the ramp from the street level. I saw the others turn their heads toward the sound. There was no place to run. We prepared to fight.

The beam of a flashlight swept over us. "Police! Stay where you are," a man's voice ordered.

Shit, I thought. It was too close to morning to get arrested. We had to wriggle out of this with a warning, and we had to do it fast.

"We were just partying, Officer," Benny squealed.

"Put your hands over your heads, turn around, and face the wall," the cop behind the flashlight said.

A second uniformed officer appeared on the platform. "Another car's on the way," he called out to his partner. "What do we got here? We need any more backup?"

The first cop, who had such a baby face he didn't appear to have started shaving yet, said, "Looks like some tourists having a private party. I'll check for weapons." He came over and patted us down. He took the vodka bottle from Audrey. He sniffed the air near Rogue. "Well, well, what have you been smoking?" he asked Rogue's back.

"Camels, unfiltered," Rogue said flatly. I had seen Rogue drop the remaining two joints and kick them over the edge of the platform the minute we heard noises on the ramp.

"Wise guy, huh?" the young cop said.

"No, sir," Rogue said politely.

"No weapons," the officer called back to his partner.

"Ask them for some ID," the second cop said, standing a good ten feet away and keeping us in his flashlight beam.

Just then we heard another set of footsteps approaching up the ramp. I took the opportunity to turn my head around to see who else was arriving.

"*Shee-it!*" a familiar voice said. "Why me, Lord, why me?"

I squinted against the flashlight's beam and recognized the newcomer. "Lieutenant, it's me, Daphne," I yelled.

One of the uniforms asked, "You know her?"

"He knows me too!" Benny called out.

Moses Johnson, a plainclothes detective with the NYPD, had his gun drawn and a sour look on his brown face. When he heard Benny's voice I thought I saw him cringe. He sure didn't look glad to see us. In a voice filled with fatigue and disgust, he said, "Yeah, I know them. You guys get out of here. I'll handle it."

The two young cops did as they were told. While they walked away, Moses Johnson stood there shaking his head. "All right, put your hands down," he finally said.

We did, and I turned around to face the man who had once saved my butt and my dog, but couldn't bring himself to like me.

"Ms. Urban, I could ask you what you're doing here, but I'm not sure I want to know," he said.

"You're right. You don't," I told him.

"Tell me anyway."

Afraid we might blow the whole mission if we kept talking in front of the trolley tunnel, I came over and whispered close to his ear, "You know, Lieutenant, it's cold here and getting near dawn. I'll make you a deal: You drive me and Benny home, and I'll tell you all about it."

Giving his head a little shake, Moses Johnson put away his gun and groaned. "Miss Urban, one day you're going to push me too far; you know that."

CHAPTER 10

White wine with white flesh, red with red.
What goes with spaghetti and meatballs?
Rosé?

Benny and I waved good-bye to the others. They moved off toward Second Avenue and Fifty-ninth Street in search of a couple of cabs to get them home as quickly as possible, before the eastern sky turned light . . . before they were caught in the perilous brightness that would kill us.

For me, this photophobia was a curse hard to bear. Perpetually chilled, shivering even in summer, I remembered what it had been like, when I was human, to feel the warmth of the sun on my face, its radiance bringing heat to my cold bones. But now that could never happen again. A single ray of sunlight would burn my flesh like a laser; total exposure would cause me indescribable agony. In a terrible spontaneous combustion, fire would consume me and my flesh would melt away to dust.

Not by choice but by necessity, I was a creature of the night. The star paths were my roads and the moon my beacon. I had become a denizen among those grotesque and shadowy things that humans feared. I was the predator for whom the darkness provided a hiding place and a stalking ground. For generation after generation my kind created nightmares from which humans woke screaming. My vampire kin were the stuff that bad dreams were made of—

Which made Lt. Moses Johnson dislike me from the moment we first met. Since my vampire state isn't visible unless I transform, at first he didn't know why he shrank from contact with me, except that he had a good cop's instinct that something was fundamentally wrong. But he never considered that I was something other than a human he didn't trust.

Lieutenant Johnson had seen killers, thieves, con men, and every form of human evil. He ridiculed the notion that werewolves, ghosts, vampires, or leprechauns, for that matter, existed. But a few weeks ago I had changed into a giant bat in front of his eyes. He went silent with fury. He blamed me for proving him wrong—that humans weren't the worst of what walked the earth.

I wondered what he knew about the kidnappings. I suspected he had heard something despite its top-secret status. Moses Johnson made it his business to watch over his city. This was his turf, and he resented the federal agencies who periodically, especially since the terrorist attacks of 9/11, marched in and took over. They didn't know their asses from their elbows, as he put it. If New York was now crawling with intelligence agents looking for the kidnappers, I had a gut feeling Moses Johnson knew they were here.

I opened the front passenger side door to Johnson's green unmarked police car. Crumpled-up McDonald's wrappers littered the mats. Two take-out bags from Dunkin' Donuts stuffed with empty coffee cups sat on the front seat. I started to dump them in the gutter.

"Don't litter," Moses Johnson snarled. "Leave 'em on the floor. I'll put them in the trash when I get back to the station."

I rode shotgun and Benny had the backseat all to herself. Johnson stomped on the accelerator and pulled away from the curb, frowning. The streets were empty under the orange glare of the sodium-vapor streetlights. Johnson knew my address, so he didn't ask. His grumpiness was palpable. After a brief silence, he said, "All right, ladies. Now what the fuck were you doing under the bridge?"

I faced a moment of truth or lies. I thought for a moment. I agreed with Johnson that some of the feds were worse than useless, and almost all of them were arrogant, looking down on city cops. I knew Johnson wouldn't fall for any outright bullshit I dished out. I was convinced he hadn't shown up tonight by accident. He was in the vicinity of the bridge for a reason. I decided to hedge. "We're looking for somebody."

"Somebody? Under the Queensborough Bridge? Right. You have to do better than that."

"No, seriously. We're on a case. We had a tip that our quarry might be in that area."

Johnson shook his close-shorn head. "That's maybe true, more likely not. When I spotted you, I figured it was you and your people who were down in those tracks. We had a report come in of suspicious activity around the bridge earlier this week. Vehicles where there shouldn't be vehicles. We've been watching ever since, checking off and on."

"Ummm," I said, deciding whether or not to ask a leading question. "Lieutenant, did you search the old trolley terminal at all?"

"We alerted the transit people. They had other priorities. We had no evidence of criminal intent. We haven't gone in there, no. We've just been keeping an eye on the area. Are you telling me we should go down there?"

"No!" I blurted out. "In fact, order your men away from the bridge for the next couple of days."

"Now, why should I do that?"

I fell silent, trying to reason out what to do. What was more important, keeping our secrets or rescuing the girls? We didn't need the cops showing up and blowing things when we went in there tomorrow night. If the kidnappers had chosen this as their hideout, we didn't want them spooked before we could corner them. If they started shooting, we didn't need the NYPD getting caught in the crossfire.

"Look, Lieutenant, let me be honest with you. We have a touchy situation. Hostages, actually. Maybe they're being held in that underground section of tracks and maybe not. But if you or your people are spotted by the perpetrators, it could get the hostages killed."

It was as if I had taken a stick and poked a bear in the eye. I could see Johnson's whole body react. The air became charged like the sky before a lightning strike.

"Hostages? Why the hell don't I know about this? What's the matter with you people! I could lose good men if they stumbled blind into something because we're being kept out of the loop!"

"Hey, don't shoot the messenger!" I snapped back at him. "I'm not in charge. I'm just following orders. This is supposed to be top-secret. A question of national security."

Johnson turned the wheel suddenly, swerved into the curb, and stopped the car. "Let's get something straight before we go any farther. If this situation is happening in New York and it involves New York, the NYPD should know what the hell is going on. You'd better start talking, or we'll just have to sit here until you do."

I had really put my foot in it this time. It seemed as if we'd caught the lieutenant with his pants down, and he really didn't know about the kidnappings. But we couldn't sit here and chat as dawn edged closer. Benny and I could commandeer the vehicle, only that would be a dumb move for a lot of reasons. For one thing, we needed an ally, not an enemy, and Johnson had good reason to be pissed.

Just then Benny piped up from the backseat, "Why,

sugar, you sure are right to be madder than the snake who married the garden hose. Daphy and I will just have to clear the air. We'll tell you what's going on."

"We will?" I asked.

"Yes, we will. Now, Looie, you didn't hear it from us, understood," she said, and leaned forward from the backseat so that her face was between ours.

"Understood," Lieutenant "Looie" Johnson said. He wasn't born yesterday.

"And y'all need to keep driving, okay?"

I could smell the sweetness of Benny's perfume, and I wondered how the good lieutenant felt with her teeth inches from his neck. He had seen her as a vampire bat too. He seemed a little nervous as he edged the car back out onto the street and started driving uptown again.

"You see, there were these society girls . . . well, they were snatched by terrorists," Benny began.

Johnson hit the brake, jerked the wheel, and almost hit a parked car. "What!" he yelled.

"Hush now and listen," she ordered. She filled Johnson in on the situation, both the abduction at the Rockefeller mansion and the taking of Deborah Morris. Benny jabbered on and told him every last detail of the kidnapping. If J found out, we were toast. I didn't want to even think about it.

Benny, who played the dumb-blonde role but was anything but stupid, deliberately didn't tell Johnson about the suspects we wanted to question, why we were at the bridge, or about the second possible location down near the site of the Twin Towers. She stuck to recounting the crime itself, and that was bad enough, I guess.

By this time we were on West End Avenue and only a couple of blocks from my place. I was anxiously peering out the window and hoping to get out of the car without having to say anything else.

"So you and your friends think these terrorists might have these young women under the bridge?" Johnson asked.

Benny didn't volunteer any answer, so I said, "It's a possibility. That's why the cops can't start poking around."

"Who is going to 'poke around' if we don't?" he asked.

"Ah, well, we are." The police car had turned down my block by this time. "There's my building, remember. You can let me out here," I said. Johnson pulled in front of the awning that stretched over the sidewalk. I put my hand on the door handle, but before I got out, I looked at the sour-faced lieutenant. "This *is* top-secret. A lot's at stake: the girls' lives, yes, and national security. So now you know, but go through channels. Leave us out of it. We don't exist, remember?"

Johnson responded with a guttural "Yeah."

I climbed out of the car and went into my building. I figured the conversation could have been worse. Johnson wouldn't go around talking to any of his colleagues about vampire spies out chasing terrorists. Despite what his eyes had seen and his ears had heard, his bottom line was that he refused to believe in us. Yet we did exist. It put him between a rock and a hard place.

It had been a hell of a night. Limp with fatigue, I dragged myself upstairs and into my apartment. Jade had been asleep but roused at the sound of my entrance; her tail became a metronome beating three-quarter time on the kitchen floor. She was glad to see me. I was glad to be home. I didn't want to think about missing girls, decadent nightclubs, or boorish vampires who wanted to get in a power struggle with me. I didn't want to worry about tomorrow or the next day. I needed to push all my troubles away.

I went over to my CD player and picked out an album by the Baroque composer François Couperin. I held the plastic jewel case in my hand for a few seconds, then put it down on a table, unsure whether I was in the mood to listen to a harpsichord. In the end I selected something very different, a compilation of Beatles songs, the 2006 album *Love*. I was never a big Beatles fan, but the arranger put some interesting twists on the old favorites.

Still dressed, I sank down onto the couch, shucked off my boots, and tucked my feet under me. I knew I should find the energy to go to my secret room and climb into my coffin, where a small packet of Transylvanian earth wrapped in satin was tucked under my pillow. Had I done that, it would have hastened the return of my full energy and powers, but I felt too weary.

I was in no danger of being exposed to daylight within the confines of my living room. The blinds were down and the heavy drapes were drawn across the windows. The music was soothing, and I didn't want to move.

Finally I roused myself enough to shrug out of my jacket. I was about to drop it onto the floor when I remembered the coin I had picked up in front of the gate under the bridge. I reached into my pocket and pulled it out. It was quite small. I turned on the table lamp to get a better look.

Printed on the coin was a palm tree under crossed swords surrounded by Arabic words. On the reverse side was the number 10, a date, and more writing. It was a halala, from Saudi Arabia. I carefully put it down on the end table, switched off the light, laid my head on a throw pillow, closed my eyes, and let myself drift off.

I started to dream. I moaned and turned on my side, dimly aware that my half-conscious mind was being pulled away to another time and place. The feel of the coin in my hand helped to provoke the memories of that time when my life had changed forever. More likely it was the disturbing eroticism of the early part of this past evening in the upstairs club, for whenever I was tormented by my hungers and frightened by my loss of emotional control, I found myself haunted by the worst thing I had ever done—killing my first true love.

That terrible night happened in April of 1824. I wouldn't have left Italy if the man who had stolen my heart had not departed from the country—and my arms—to go to fight in Greece.

Deciding to follow him, I had arrived in Missolonghi, Greece, months earlier, in December. In doing so, I had placed myself in the thick of the Greek rebellion against the Turks. It was a foolish thing to do, but reason completely fled when it came to George Gordon, the poet the world knew as Lord Byron.

We had a long-running affair that began when he was still a youth in England, and had resumed again many years later at my villa in the Italian hilltop town of Montespertoli. There, he had promised me not only his undying love—and truly undying, because he wanted me to transform him into a vampire—but he begged to marry me. Like a fool, I had believed him and said yes.

But one night a coach had drawn up in the courtyard outside the villa's kitchen at Montespertoli. A letter had come from Pietro, the brother of his former mistress, the Countess Teresa Guiccioli. Byron read the missive and told me he had urgent business. He must depart quickly, but swore he would return within a few days. I had to let him leave, innocently believing our separation would be temporary.

He didn't come back. Instead he sailed with his friend Pietro from Genoa to the Greek Isles, caught up in the excitement of still another revolution. He seemed to have forgotten that he had recently been thrown into prison for his part in the Italian fight for freedom. If I hadn't come to his aid, he would have hanged. By leaving me so callously he proved he was an ingrate, but I was a fool for his love; I confess it.

In fact, Lord Byron was a man easily bored, evidently as much by me as by all the women he had loved. He restlessly sought new experiences, new sensations. He had left Italy to become a philhellene, an early supporter of the Greek rebels. He soon had spent thousands of pounds of his own fortune to equip their fleet. The world called him a hero. But I could not forget that he had climbed into his coach and thrown me kisses, vowing he would be back within a fortnight and we would be wed.

At first I pined in the great villa alone. Then I was enraged. I wanted revenge. I wanted him to grovel at my feet and beg my forgiveness. I had to do something or go mad.

Drastic situations call for drastic measures. I did some groveling myself and contacted my mother. I told her I wished to go to Greece and needed a new identity. I had taken on the guises of so many different women since my birth, she didn't ask why. She gave me the name of an innkeeper in Missolonghi. I could claim I was a niece, lately come from Athens to help him. The influx of hundreds of soldiers into the region had increased his business beyond his capacity to handle it. No one would question my sudden arrival in the swampy town.

I disguised my appearance with great cleverness. I arranged my hair with elaborate braids, changed my eye color (using an ancient technique known to alchemists), dyed my white skin to olive, and wore native dress. I spoke an educated Greek, and with a touch of irony did not change my first name, but added the surname of the innkeeper, a long Greek patronymic I can no longer remember.

Oh, yes, the coin. The feel of the Arabic coin helped to send me into this reverie. Going past ten one night at the inn

in Missolonghi, a fire had been lit in the hearth of the public room, this being an especially rainy and damp year. I was
playing at being a barmaid, bringing wine to a group of
English soldiers who had taken to stopping by for drink, and
perhaps to see me. They were lusty young lads, and I didn't
mind a slap and a tickle.

That night Byron had come with them. He looked ill, and
I had heard he had taken sick more than once that dreary
winter. I came over to put a pitcher of wine on the wooden
table. My heart was racing, for this was the first I had seen
him since the previous summer, but I turned my back toward
him and flirted with the other boys, leaning down to receive
a kiss from a blond fellow I fancied.

I felt a powerful hand grasp my arm. I whirled around.
Byron looked at me with those piercing eyes he had, and he
stared directly at my face. No recognition lit his features. He
took my hand and said in his perfect Greek, "You are such a
pretty lass. Fetch me a plate of bread and cheese. I am fair
famished. Here, take this." He dropped a coin in my palm
and folded my fingers over it with his own. My flesh almost
burst into flame where it touched his. He gave me a lazy, seductive smile. "And I should like a room upstairs. Can you
arrange that?"

I could tell by the way he looked at me that he judged me
an easy conquest. I snatched my hand away from his. I lifted
my chin and looked back at him, my eyes blazing with in-
dignation. "You might also ask for a bath, sir. I think you
would benefit."

The other men laughed, and I walked haughtily away. I
had come all the way from my comfortable villa to this
marshy, disease-ridden region to get my revenge. I did not
intend to harm Byron, only to teach him a lesson. I had
planned a seduction and a betrayal, not a murder. Of course,

I did not know that first night when I put my scheme in motion how tragically it would turn out in the end.

But as I walked away from Byron, knowing he watched and guessing he had begun to wonder if he could have me, the coin burned in the palm of my hand.

In midmorning Jade began to bark and I awoke, still on the couch where I had drifted into that troubled dream. I heard a key being turned in the lock. After a flutter of panic, I realized that the dog walker had arrived to provide the massive malamute with some daytime exercise. I stood up groggily, feeling stiff and in need of a shower.

A gray-haired woman holding a dog leash slipped into the apartment and let out a squeal when she saw me standing in the living room.

"Oh, Miss Urban, I'm so sorry. I would have rung the bell if I had known you were home, but you never are, not during the day."

"Don't apologize," I said. "I won't be here when you get back." I didn't reveal, of course, that I would be in my crypt, trying to get a few more hours' rest.

As soon as she left, I went to the refrigerator and got myself a plastic pouch of blood, O positive. Sometimes I ordered A positive. Both are the most plentiful types of blood in the United States. Vampires have no restrictions; any blood will do. These types were simply more available from my source, the rarer ones being sometimes in short supply.

Don't get me wrong; I love all blood. But like wine, its taste and composition reflects its *terroir,* or place of origin, the essence of the person who has produced it.

My blood-bank blood lacks that specificity. It is a blend: bland, filtered, and flat. Fresh blood, ah, it is endless in its variety: thinner or thicker; 98.6 degrees or feverish; filled with antibodies or flush with oxygen.

And fresh blood, taken directly from the vein, can either please or repel a feeding vampire. Fat blood, for example, is an acquired taste. To snatch a gourmand after a heavy cholesterol-laden meal provides blood with a creamy texture, full-bodied with lipids or greasy as a leftover French fry. Such blood is actually good for underweight vampires, although most vampires find the flavor "off," flabby and lingering too long on the palate.

Then there is the booze factor. A donor who has been drinking alcohol provides a vampire with the original Bloody Mary. Barhound vampires occasionally make their victims tipsy not just to keep them docile, but for the dizzying high their blood produces. I suspect some of them add a Tabasco sauce chaser.

And damn the pharmaceutical industry to hell. Their products wreak havoc with the purity of blood. The leading blasphemer? Birth control pills. They adulterate the taste and color of a woman's blood. Should that blood be extracted and allowed to settle, a greenish film would form on the surface. I recoiled from merely thinking about that repulsive concoction. Vampires were always complaining about this "estrogen factor" and claimed they could smell it if a woman was taking the pill.

The flavor of Byron's blood came back to me as vividly as in the moment it had first filled my mouth. It was distinctly male, redolent on the palate, purveying a hint of bitterness that vanished beneath a layered infusion of red cherries, magnificent vanilla, and a core of earthy peat. My lover, my dear, doomed lover, had an ambitious blood with a long finish, rampant with complexity and so sparkling with life that its imperfections had to be forgiven.

My betrayer, Darius della Chiesa, had a different *aqua la vie.* His was a rich port wine, full and round with plenty of oak. It had something special: a vivid acidity and a smoky seductiveness running like a ribbon through it. Yet I could detect a sourish green-wood flavor, a claylike feel, and a bramble aroma that created a dark profile . . . the profile of a dangerous blood, tautly youthful when I drank it, yet with the potential to become poisonous as it matured.

I pushed those thoughts away while I emptied the commercial pouch of blood into a large beer stein. While sitting at my kitchen island, I slowly consumed the entire pint. I might not get a buzz from my blood-bank product, but the quality was consistent. Regular feedings kept my volatile temperament on a more even keel, and, well fed, I had a stronger will to resist temptations of all kinds.

After I had rinsed the glass at the sink and disposed of the plastic pouch, I made a mental note to stay on a strict blood-drinking schedule for Fitz's sake and my own. Sated, my mind at ease, and my conscience clear, I felt grounded in the here and now. I retired to my coffin, setting my alarm clock for five, and tumbled into oblivion. Entombed in a dreamless sleep, I didn't hear the dog walker's return. If I had, I might have known that she did not come back alone.

CHAPTER 11

*"Better is a dinner of herbs where love is
than a fatted ox and hatred with it."*

—Proverbs 15:17

My mother flung open the front door of her Scarsdale home. I had to ring the bell when Fitz and I arrived. She had never offered me, her only daughter, a key. A small woman, she stood there barefoot; silver peace symbol earrings dangled from her ears, her wide-bottom jeans topped by a faux fur–trimmed hoodie. She had combined 1960s retro with Juicy Couture.

"I didn't have time to fuss," she said. "Dinner is takeout. Hope you like sushi. And you must be Fitz." She extended her small hand.

Surprise flickered over my almost-fiancé's features. He returned the handshake and stuttered, "F-F-Fitz. Yes. Actually St. Julien Fitzmaurice, Mrs.? Mrs. Urban?"

Although I had given him the facts—that my mother was born around 890, which made her over a thousand years old; that she was a ruthless, cunning, conniving wielder of enormous power; that she was a businesswoman with a net worth that surpassed Bill Gates's and Warren Buffett's combined, he gaped. He stared. He had to wonder who this eighteen-year-old Lindsay Lohan clone really was. Not my mother, no, she couldn't possibly be—

"Mar-Mar. Nobody calls me Mrs. Urban. I was once Marozia Maria Urbano, Duchess of Tusculani, but that was centuries ago. Come in and let's have drinks." She laughed. "Drink! Drink! 'Malt does more than Milton can to justify God's ways to man.'"

I could see Fitz's mood lighten. I was certain he could use some Dutch courage. We followed Mar-Mar through a hall and entered the living room.

My mother crossed to a side bar and poured amber fluid into a short glass. "You prefer Jameson, neat," she said as she passed it to Fitz.

Of course she knew Fitz's preferred drink. She knew about everything connected to me. She spied, she interfered, she meddled. She stooped to eavesdropping. You'd never guess it by looking at her. Projecting an aura of innocence was her forte. I suspected this carefully crafted image was how she elevated herself from being a prostitute in Rome to becoming the lover of one pope and the mother of another, my half brother, John. But all that had happened before my time, and Mar-Mar did not talk about the past.

"And a martooni for me," she said. She poured straight gin into a tumbler, picked up a bottle of dry vermouth and poured a drop onto an olive skewered with a toothpick, then dropped the olive into the glass. I noticed her fingernails were long and painted bright red.

Fitz raised his Jameson in a toast: "'Drink today, and drown all sorrow; you shall perhaps not do't tomorrow.'" He downed the whiskey in one long swallow.

"Well said." Mar-Mar smiled and took his empty glass. She poured him another, and handed it back.

Then to my surprise, a man came bounding down the stairs from the second floor. "Shalom!" he greeted me. "Are you still practicing kabbalah? Or did you say you had become a Wiccan?"

"Oh, hello," I said to a middle-aged hippie who wore his thinning hair drawn back in a ponytail.

"George was just leaving, weren't you, George?" my mother said, not bothering to look at him as she took a swallow of gin. I remembered George now. He had appeared a few times lately to help Mar-Mar fetch and carry. George—I doubted that was his real name—was a schlep, a gofer, one of the minions Mar-Mar kept close by, but not too close. I didn't know where any of them lived. I suspected she kept some in the basement, chained. I was kidding about that, of course.

He didn't look it, but I figured he was a vampire—and if he was, I knew he could be dangerous.

"Right. I'm on my way out," George said to Mar-Mar. "Nice kicks," he added, looking at my shoes, another pair of Manolo Blahniks, as he exited. He waved good-bye, and I could see that part of his left index finger was missing.

No sooner had the door shut behind him than a high-pitched voice rang out from another room: "Make way for the hors d'oeuvres!"

A young woman wearing cowboy boots and a miniskirt entered from the kitchen, doing a pirouette as she passed through the swinging door. I recognized her as Sage Thyme, a member of my mother's Save the Trees coalition. She placed a silver tray with a lid on the coffee table next to a huge plastic-wrapped platter of sushi that was already there.

"Voilà!" she cried, and removed the cover, revealing an arrangement of steak tartare on crackers and caviar served with fresh toast points and a bowl of crème fraîche. Then she flung herself at me, throwing her skinny arms around me. I stiffened in her embrace.

"Oh, it is so good to see you again," she gushed as she

stood on her tiptoes to greet me with an air kiss as if we were old friends. I had met her only once before. "Are you really engaged? Your mother positively insisted on meat products for you and your beau. No garlic, don't worry. She said you're allergic. Too bad, it's great for lowering your cholesterol. With all that meat, you have to worry. We're all vegans, you know. Your mother was so concerned about getting something you liked. She's such a wonderful person."

Sage Thyme—definitely not a vampire—was so high-strung I felt as if I were watching a squiggle cartoon. She turned to Fitz. "It's hard to believe she's Daphne's mother, isn't it? She looks younger than her daughter. She was a child bride, you see. Well, not exactly a bride. She was a single mother, and such an inspiration, the way she turned her life around. From the ghetto to Scarsdale, it's an amazing story."

She had the *story* part of it right, anyway, I thought.

"Sage, dear," my mother broke in, saluting her with the glass, which now was nearly empty. "You make me blush."

"Oh, I just love her, don't you?" Sage said to me. "Well, I'm not staying. It's my night to deliver Meals on Wheels. Enjoy! Enjoy!" she said as she put on a satin jacket with HOOTERS emblazoned across the back and left via the front door.

"Anyone else here? Is someone about to jump out of the closet? Should I look behind the drapes?" I asked.

"Always the kidder," Mar-Mar replied. "Sit. Have some hors d'oeuvres," she said to Fitz. He lowered himself into an easy chair and did as he was told, spooning some caviar on a piece of toast. My mother took my arm and steered me to the couch to sit beside her. Once seated, she offered me a canapé. I shook my head. My stomach was in knots. I knew my mother was up to something.

She turned to me. "I know you don't have much time;

that you have to work tonight. I'm sure Fitz knows that too; am I right?"

"Of course he does. And I assume your time is limited as well. I'm surprised you wanted us to come. We could have done this some other night." *Some other night in the next century,* I thought.

"*Ma Nishtahnah Ha Lailah Ha Zeh.* Why is this night different from other nights? Because it is a night when decisions must be made." Mar-Mar dramatically reached out and grasped my hand. Alarm bells started clanging in my mind. What was this all about?

She brought her face close to mine. I smelled the gin on her breath. "Decisions for you, Daphne, my dear. My only daughter. And for Fitz. I understand there's talk of a wedding?"

I drew back. "You're jumping the gun. This dinner is just for you two to get acquainted. I've met Fitz's family. It was time he met mine. You're all I have."

"Yes, I've very much wanted to meet you." Fitz nodded his head.

You are the fly, I thought. *Beware the spider weaving her web.* I wished I could have warned him.

"You should feel honored, young Fitz," she said. "Daphne has never brought anyone else home to meet her mother, not in all these years. These over four hundred years. You must be very special."

"I like to think I am." He grinned. "And I know she is. I do want to marry her. She hasn't said yes, but I intend to keep trying to convince her."

"So that means you're willing to convert?" Mar-Mar asked, looking much less like an ingenue than she had when we arrived.

"That's none of your busi—" I began, but Fitz held up his hand and cut in.

"It's okay, sweetheart," he said to me. Then he looked at

Mar-Mar. "If you mean am I willing to become a vampire? No, not right now, anyway. Daphne and I have talked about it, though."

My mother banged down her empty gin glass on the coffee table. "Obviously you haven't talked about it enough. There's no way a human can marry a vampire. Don't you know that?"

"Is that your opinion or a fact?" Fitz asked, showing some backbone. I was glad to see he wasn't about to be pushed around by Mar-Mar. Then again, he had a lot of experience dealing with his own mama: Delores Fitzmaurice the Terrible.

"Fact. It's never happened. Never can happen."

"Well, Mother," I said, "what about my father?"

My mother's face turned an unattractive shade of puce. "Do not bring your father and me into this. It was an entirely different situation."

"How? How was it different? You were a vampire. He wasn't."

"You don't know that," my mother said with ice in her voice.

I stuck my chin out and leaned toward her. "Are you telling me that Pope Urban the Sixth was a vampire?"

"I'm not telling you anything, and I'm not going to discuss it. We are talking about you and Fitz. If he seriously wants to marry you, he has to convert. It's plain and simple." By now her eyes, which had been undergoing subtle changes with each passing moment, had a different shape entirely: They were flattened, almost Asian, and ancient.

"I do not see why we shouldn't marry in our present condition, should we wish to," Fitz said.

"Why shouldn't you marry? Let me count the whys. You will die and she won't. You will age and she won't. You will go out in the daylight, but she can never see the sun. You will want to sail, golf, and ski. You like those things, no? Her only sport is shopping, at night. Oh, don't pull a face, Daphne, it's true.

"You will begin to resent the restrictions on where you two can go, what you can do. Soon, sooner than you might imagine, your family will begin to ask questions about her, questions you can't answer. And it is highly unlikely you will ever have children."

"I am aware of all those things," he said, a frown now drawn between his eyes. "I think we can handle them if we work at it."

I felt left out of this conversation; it was beginning to rankle. "Mother," I broke in, "as I said, this is strictly between Fitz and me. It does not concern you."

"But it does concern me. It concerns me deeply," she shot back. Although her flesh had remained as firm and youthful as when we arrived, her face no longer appeared to be young. My mother's physical self had never aged—it could not age from the moment she had been transformed—but her soul and her mind bore the weight of centuries, and behind the mask she wore that maturity was clearly present—a millennium of life, something to be respected and something to be feared.

When she continued to speak, her commanding voice—the voice of a thousand years—could not be ignored or shut out by me. "On many levels I am both disturbed and worried by this—if I may be blunt—unwise liaison. Fitz, it's not personal. It's what you are—and what we are.

"Let me lay it out for you. We vampires are a race, a people. No outsider can ever understand us. We live by our own rules. And we don't share our secrets with humans. We don't let humans into our world."

My mother turned to me, annoyance and something harder darkening her face. "Surely, Daphne, you can see how dangerous it is for you, for all of us, for Fitz to know we are vampires, without being one himself."

The words burst from Fitz. "My God! I would never betray Daphne. Betray any of you!" He seemed shocked.

"But why not? You are having a love affair with my daughter. It's the most fragile of loyalties. Don't look so insulted by my words. They're true. Right now you can't keep your hands off of each other. But later? After Daphne slips and bites some fine young man, and in biting has sex with him—"

"Mother!" I cried out. "I cannot believe you would say that!"

"Why mince words? Fitz can't understand bloodlust. A vampire would understand your behavior and not be upset by it. But humans feel betrayed by such things. Fitz, you do expect Daphne to be true to you, don't you?"

"I trust Daphne; of course I trust her. She wouldn't—"

"She would. Believe me, she would," my mother said.

"No, she would not—"

"Hold on here, both of you. I can speak for myself, thank you! Mother, you're insulting me. I am perfectly capable of controlling my . . . my vampire behavior. And I'm getting thoroughly pissed off by this whole line of conversation. I said it before, but let me say it better: Butt out!"

My mother stared at me hard for a moment, but didn't speak. When she did, her voice was gentle. "I didn't mean to insult you. I see nothing insulting in remarking that you will—all right, *may*—one day behave like the vampire you are. And if that happens, what then?"

My head was throbbing. I'm sure my blood pressure was going through the roof. I made a great effort not to raise my voice, and the result was that I could barely get the words out. "What then? Nothing—nothing that concerns *you,* anyway. It's something Fitz and I will deal with."

My mother gave me a pitying look. "I know that's how you see it, but that's not reality. Your lover already knows many of our identities, and as your time together lengthens, he'll know many more. And someday, if you provoke him or hurt him or cheat on him, he will become a scorned lover, or even worse, a scorned husband. He very well might send the vampire hunters after us. It's happened before, rather recently, has it not?"

My mother had just landed a low blow. She was referring to my previous lover, Darius. I had made him a vampire, and, resenting it, he began sucking necks all over the Bronx. Then he made things worse by becoming a rock star called Darius DC and the Vampire Project. Vampire hunters had descended on New York in droves to pursue him—and me.

I had had enough of Mar-Mar's lecture. I stood up. "This conversation is over," I announced.

"I think not," Mar-Mar said, and pulled me back down with a grip so hard that her nails pierced my flesh. I could have resisted, but things would have gotten very ugly, very fast. I acquiesced.

"Fitz," she said with a kinder tone. "I realize you are a fine man or you wouldn't be here at all. You are an honorable man. You want to do the right thing. But you are already a grave threat to my daughter and myself. As a human you know too much, you see."

Fitz's face changed. I could see him go from being uncomfortable to being angry to being something else—afraid?

I realized where my mother was going with this and I was horrified. "Mar-Mar," I cried out, my heart beating wildly. "I will not let you harm him. Not now. Not ever. Believe me on that one."

"Are you saying," Fitz cut in, "that if I do not become a vampire, I will be killed?"

"That would be one solution, but *I* am merely saying you put me—and Daphne—in a difficult position. As long as you are human, there will always be doubt. You two might have an argument. You might leave in a moment of anger, not necessarily for long, but long enough for suspicion to replace passion. Perhaps you decide to confide in a friend; perhaps you need a drink and, while satisfying your thirst, you tell someone—a bartender, even the person on the next bar stool—about your troubles with your vampire wife. It could happen. You see, you are only human."

Fitz was quiet. Finally he said, "I don't believe I would ever betray Daphne, but I understand your fear. And to be honest, I do drink, once in a while anyway."

"You see! I am right," she said. "That is why you had to come here tonight, why I needed to meet you. Your conversion can't be delayed, and in fact, from the moment Daphne told you who and what she was, this was, as they say, a done deal. You know that, don't you, Daphne?"

"I hadn't looked at it that way, no," I admitted.

My mother patted my hand as if I were a lapdog. I believe she thought I was immensely stupid. "Sweetheart, you never do. You followed your heart, not your head. I understand that, but you not only have risked your own safety and that of your race, you've put this nice, decent man in danger. In fact, he has no options."

Her voice changed noticeably. Suddenly she was all business. "And we, my dear daughter, if I may be blunt once again, have three. One, you can convert him. Two, someone—not me, I assure you—can take it upon him- or herself to eliminate Fitz as a threat by killing him. Or, three, some other vampire or vampires, if they care about you enough, will bite him and convert him, against his will and your own."

"Who? Who would dare to bite Fitz without my knowledge?" I was stunned.

Mar-Mar didn't answer. "I'm not going to point fingers, but I think you can figure it out."

Benny? I thought. *Or even Cormac? Or both of them? They talk about me; Benny admitted that. Have they discussed this?* I was badly shaken.

"We need to go. Fitz and I have to talk—in private." I shook off my mother's hand and got up, extending my own hand, now cold as ice, to Fitz. He looked at me, his face worried. He grasped my fingers and stood up too.

"Daphne's right. She and I need to talk," he said in a tight voice.

"One minute, please," my mother ordered, and stood abruptly. She grabbed my arm and pulled me to the far side of the room and put her face very close to mine. "Listen. This situation is out of my hands," she said, her whisper like a hiss. "Bite him. Just do it. If you don't, he will be dealt with, in one way or another, before the month is out. And don't even think of telling him to run. He won't get far. Do you understand?"

My face must have reflected my horror. Her voice softened. "I'm sorry. I know it's hard for you." Her hand pushed a strand of hair back from my forehead. "But I'm just the messenger, and this isn't my decision."

I'm sure I looked as if I didn't believe her. "I agree with the decision; don't get me wrong," she added. "You are making this much more difficult than it should be. He'll be fine if you bite him. It's for the best." She stood on her tiptoes and kissed me on the cheek. I stood there like stone.

When I looked over at Fitz, he was watching me intently. He had said he wouldn't betray me. But was he equally convinced I would not betray him?

We hadn't eaten. The plastic wrap still covered the sushi, which looked wilted and unappetizing on the platter. I felt sick, weakened, and emotionally devastated because I could not deny it: My mother was right. I didn't see how it was possible for Fitz to remain human—and remain alive. He already knew too much for us to simply end our affair and go on with his life.

With a great sadness, I concluded he could not escape his inevitable fate. I'm sure he already regretted his involvement with me. Who wouldn't? He had been given a death sentence—or a fate-worse-than-death sentence. And it was all my fault.

We drove back to the city in silence, Fitz staring straight ahead at the wheel of his silver Prius. This fine mess I'd gotten both of us into was my reward for being honest, for spilling my guts and telling Fitz the truth about myself. I always learn the hard way. Hell, even Mafioso know about the code of silence. I had broken the unwritten rules and gotten myself screwed—and gotten Fitz really fucked.

Dumb Daphne. Dumb. Dumb. Dumb. It was a lesson I would never again forget.

Fitz was driving too fast. His face was a rigid mask. He gripped the steering wheel so tightly his knuckles were white. I couldn't say what he was thinking, but it's been said that "the imminent prospect of hanging wonderfully focuses a man's mind."

Fitz and I discussed earlier that he would drop me off in Midtown and I would go on alone to the Flatiron Building. He didn't know where my office was—any more than I knew the location of his.

I didn't have time to go back to my apartment and talk this out with him. I felt bad about that. Fitz must feel unsettled; maybe he was afraid. His immediate future included an experience that few humans would choose of their own free will. In fact, his free will had been taken from him. If he were going to hate me, that hate would begin growing now, when he thought this through and realized he was trapped, completely and utterly boxed in with no avenue of escape.

During the journey back from my mother's house in Scarsdale, a deep depression settled upon me. I had realized that not only had Fitz's fate been sealed, but so had my own. As Julius Caesar had said, *Jacta alea est.* The die is cast. I had put Fitz in this situation. Now I had to face the consequences: Marry or be damned. I was already damned . . . that left marriage.

Whether he realized it yet or not, all Fitz and I had to talk about at this point was not *whether* I would bite him, but *when* I would bite him—and when we would be wed. I would marry him. I owed him that much, if he still wanted to marry me. Knowing Fitz, who prized honor above all else, I assumed he would.

He drove me to Macy's on Thirty-fourth Street. He stopped to drop me off, traffic swerving around him. I began to open the door. He pulled me back, put his hand behind my head, and drew me to him. He kissed me with a fierceness I had never felt from him before.

"This is not your fault," he said. "Listen to me. I love you. We will work this out."

I looked at him—a man I clearly did not deserve—with my vision suddenly blurred by tears. "Okay," I managed to say.

"How long do you think I have before . . . before, you know?" he asked.

I hesitated. "Probably until the end of this mission I'm on. A week? At least a week, I'm pretty sure."

"That's good, then," he said. I climbed out of the Prius and he drove off.

CHAPTER 12

"The credit belongs to the man who is actually in the arena; whose face is marred by dust and sweat and blood . . . and who at the worst, if he fails, at least fails while daring greatly."

—Theodore Roosevelt

A female federal marshal stood behind a red-haired girl wearing a Princeton sweatshirt and a blindfold. The girl was sitting at the conference table in our office at 175 Fifth Avenue. Her hands were folded neatly in her lap. She appeared eager and attentive, as if she had a No. 2 pencil poised and ready, waiting to be told to open her test booklet and begin her SATs.

The rest of the room was pretty much filled with Darkwings: Benny, Cormac, Audrey, Rogue, and J. I had just walked in. Cormac, Audrey, and Benny sat at the table, speaking together in whispers. Someone had put bottles of water and a box of tissues in front of them. J and Rogue stood at one end of the room, no closer than an arm's length of each other. Rogue didn't even look in my direction. He was giving me the deep freeze.

J nodded at me. "Now that we are all here, we can get started. Agent D, do you want to take a seat?"

"No, thanks. I'll stand." I stayed by the door. Benny swiveled around in her chair and passed me a note telling me that Hana's half brother hadn't been found. Judge Morris refused to appear without a subpoena. Hana was being brought in. She, at least, would arrive soon.

"Miss Rhinehart," J began, his voice affable, "we want to thank you for your willingness to talk to us. Your first name is Abigail; is that correct?"

"Yes. Everyone calls me Abby, though."

"Okay, Abby. We apologize for any discomfort you might be having because of the blindfold. You understand why it is necessary?"

"Oooh, yes. You're spies. This is exciting, really. I don't mind the blindfold at all."

"We're glad to hear that. You know that the reason you're here is to talk with us about Deborah Morris?"

"Yes. I'm terribly worried about her. I did try to talk her out of sneaking away. I told that to Judge Morris and to the men who questioned me yesterday. Those men weren't spies, though. I think they were FBI." Her head moved around as she talked, making her shiny hair swing back and forth around the blindfold.

J took a look at a yellow pad he had in front of him, then spoke again. "Can you tell us exactly what happened yesterday? Start from the beginning, please."

"Well, not much really happened. Both Deb and I didn't have any classes in the afternoon. I planned on studying in the library. I asked Deb if she wanted to go. She didn't. She was in a really bad mood. She wanted to go to the mall and she didn't want the bodyguard to know. The bodyguard carried a gun—at least, that's what Deb said—and she sat in a chair right outside the door of our suite until Deborah wanted to go somewhere. Then she went with her. So anyway, Deb wanted to go to Macy's out on the highway, and asked to borrow my car."

"She didn't want the bodyguard to go. Do you know why?"

"Not really. She said more than once that it was embarrassing to have a chaperone. Anyway, I gave her my car key."

"We found a key chain in the form of an orange and black tiger on the floor of your car. Is it yours?"

"No. That would be Deb's key chain. With her dorm key and all."

"Okay. Tell us what Deborah did after you gave her the key."

"She climbed out the window. We're on the second floor, but we have a fire escape. She asked me to keep talking to her for a while. I mean to pretend I was talking to her. So the bodyguard would think she was still there."

"And you did that for how long?" J asked.

Abby had her head tilted up toward the ceiling, even though she couldn't see anything through the blindfold. Then she again began moving her head and shoulders in a gentle swaying so that her hair swished around. She was stalling. She was a smart girl and was fast figuring out honesty might not be the best policy.

"Am I in trouble? For helping Deb? That's all I did. I didn't have anything to do with her disappearance."

"Nobody is accusing you of anything," J said.

"Do I need a lawyer?" she insisted.

"All you need to do is tell us the truth. You're not suspected of doing anything wrong."

Abby didn't answer right away. Finally she said, "I have nothing to hide. I really don't. Do you know who my father is?"

"Yes, we do. Now please help us out here. How much time had passed before the bodyguard knew she was gone?"

"Maybe half an hour," Abby answered. "She finally knocked at the door. She was all upset when she found out Deborah had gone. I felt really dumb for going along with the whole thing. I didn't know why Deb just didn't tell the bodyguard where she was going. I mean, she should have, what with the threat to her family and all. I really didn't think having the bodyguard hanging around was a big deal."

Rogue broke in with his gruff voice. "It was a big deal to Deb, though. Come on. Stop playing games. You have to know why."

Abby stopped bouncing around in her seat. She turned her head toward Rogue's voice. Her clasped hands tightened. "Well, sir, I'm not sure."

"Take a guess. There's no penalty for a wrong answer, Miss Princeton." Rogue sneered.

"All right. You don't have to be rude, you know. I think maybe she wanted to meet somebody. I mean, like, a boy."

"What boy? Stop playing games."

Despite the pressure, Abby didn't answer right away. She seemed to be picking her words carefully. "Somebody new. I don't know his name. He wasn't at Princeton; I know that. I think he was older. Like last week, Abby asked me how long it would take to drive up to Troy, New York. I asked her why. She said she wanted to visit some guy. He went to school up there.

"Then yesterday, just when we were getting out of class—we're both taking this environmental science course—her cell phone rang. I mean, I didn't hear what she was talking about or anything, but right after the phone call she asked to borrow my car. To go to the mall."

And that was all she would say. Even though both Rogue and J kept probing the boyfriend angle, they couldn't find out anything else. Then a beeper on J's belt went off. He looked at it, looked up, and said if nobody else had any questions, Abby could go.

In the back of my mind, what Abby mentioned about Troy, New York, and Deborah Morris wanting to drive up there had been nagging at me. "I have just one more question. Abby, do you happen to know what colleges are in Troy? That this new boyfriend might be attending?"

"Well, yeah. I think so. He's probably at Rensselaer."

Bingo. That was where Hana's father taught. I wondered if her half brother was a student there. It would be easy to find out.

The marshal helped Abby to her feet and led her out. When she was gone, I told the others that I had a hunch that the boy Deborah Morris went to meet was Hana's brother. I explained my reasoning. They all agreed we needed to check it out.

J's beeper went off again, and he glanced at the screen. Hana had arrived, he told us; she was being held in a nearby room.

Two burly federal marshals pushed through the door holding the arms of a trembling, blindfolded young woman.

"Please lead Miss Rida over to that chair. That's the one. Thank you," J said.

Once Hana was seated, J said, "Good evening, Miss Rida. We apologize for the need for you to be blindfolded and for any discomfort you may be feeling. It is for your own safety, as well as a matter of national security, that you not know where you are or who we are."

I inwardly grimaced. What a joke we were. If any other covert team were doing this, they would have had formal facilities complete with a two-way mirror. Since officially we didn't exist, our budget had to be buried in some line item in some bureaucracy somewhere. No wonder I was paying for Rogue and Audrey and we worked out of a shabby hole-in-the-wall.

J continued talking to Hana, who was visibly shaking. "You are in a room with a number of federal agents. You are not going to be harmed in any way. You don't need to be afraid. We simply want to ask you some questions. But you must answer them truthfully. Do you understand?"

Hana Rida nodded. J asked her to make a verbal response and she said yes in a small voice. It wasn't until then that I noticed the tape recorder on the table in front of Benny.

"Miss Rida, do you know why we want to talk to you?" J asked.

Again, in a voice so soft we had to strain to hear it, she said, "No, no, I don't. I told the agents who talked to me before that I don't know anything about the judge's missing daughter."

"All right, Miss Rida. We appreciate your cooperation in coming forward tonight. You must understand how urgent the situation is. You do want to help us find the missing girl, don't you?"

"I don't know anything about it," she said again, her voice pleading.

"Let's talk about something else, then, shall we? If you've been asked this before, please bear with us and answer it again. How long have you worked for Judge Morris?" J's voice was friendly and relaxed.

"About a year."

"How many times a week do you see him?"

"Three or four," she said, her voice more confident now.

"Three or four times a week where?"

"At his home. At his home gym."

"You never see him outside of his home?" J sounded surprised.

There was the slightest pause before she answered, "No."

"You mean you've never had dinner with him? At a restaurant, for example?"

"Well, maybe. Once. For my birthday." Hana's momentary confidence vanished. She seemed to be shrinking back into herself.

"And when is your birthday?"

"In January."

"Well, now, I'm confused, Miss Rida, because you had dinner with the judge last week. He told us that himself." Judge Morris had told us no such thing. I assumed J had seen the judge's credit card records. The esteemed jurist would surely have a shit fit if he knew he was being investigated.

"Oh, that. Yes. I'm sorry. I did see him then. I forgot," Hana said.

"You forgot dinner at Babbo's, a very expensive restaurant in Manhattan, on a Friday night?" J feigned astonishment.

"Yes! I mean no. I remember now. I've just been so upset the past couple of days, I forgot. That's all. I forgot."

"And what have you been upset about?" J probed.

"That Nicoletta is missing and now Deborah too. I've met them. I know the family. It's upsetting. It would be upsetting for anyone," she whined.

"How did you find out Deborah is missing?"

Hana squirmed in her seat. "The judge called me. To cancel his workout, that's all. That's why he called."

"Are you upset because the judge can't see you right now?"

"Of course. It's my job. I'm losing money."

"Are you saying that your relationship with the judge is just business?" J's voice became skeptical.

"Mostly. I mean I've gotten to know him pretty well." Hana shifted in her chair and coughed. "May I have a drink? My throat is dry." Benny pushed a bottle of water across the table. One of the marshals opened it and put the bottle in Hana's hand. She took a long swallow.

J waited until she was finished before he said, "Miss Rida, it's time you told us the truth." His voice had become hard and demanding.

"I am telling you the truth. I am," she said, sounding close to tears.

Rogue touched J's arm, indicating he wanted to speak to Hana.

"Hana? I'm another federal agent." Rogue's voice was rough, harsh from years of cigarette smoking. "You're lying. And I know you're lying. Everybody knows you're lying. You can't get away with it. Believe me, you can't. I want you to listen to me very carefully. I'm going to ask you some specific questions. I want specific answers. If you don't tell me the truth you have plenty of reason to be afraid. You will be going to jail for a long time. Do you understand what I'm saying to you?"

Hana nodded, and J asked her again to please give a verbal response. She whispered yes, and he had to ask her to speak louder.

Rogue went on. "Did you talk to the judge this morning?"

Hana nodded.

"I can't hear you, Hana. Yes or no," Rogue ordered.

"Yes. Yes. I told you, he called me."

"Okay, he called you. Isn't it true that he warned you not to talk about your relationship with him? Yes or no." J was watching Rogue intently. We all were.

Hana clutched the edge of the table and sat up very straight. "How did you know that? Are you tapping my phone?"

I had to give it to Rogue: He was a damned good interrogator. What he asked her was a guess—but it sounded as if he knew about it. I had seen enough Gypsies telling fortunes to know it's a skill, not anything mystical.

"It's true, isn't it?" Rogue asked.

Like a deflated balloon, she collapsed into the chair, her head hanging down. "Yes. Yes, it's true. It's all true. You know anyway."

"So you are having an affair with Judge Morris. Tell the truth. No more lies, Hana," Rogue pressed on with his raspy voice.

"Yes. I'm sorry. I'm sorry. I'm so sorry." She began to cry.

I looked at Benny and shrugged. She looked back at me. I wasn't quite sure what was going on here.

"What are you sorry about?" J, the good cop, said gently. "You can tell us. Get it off your chest. Come on, Hana; we know anyway."

One of the marshals put a tissue in Hana's hand. She blew her nose.

"It wasn't my idea. My brother made me do it. Please believe me. I didn't want to. Poor Mrs. Morris. She's so nice."

"But the judge wanted to divorce her, didn't he? He wanted to marry you. Right?" Rogue jumped into the questioning, his voice demanding. "He thought you really cared about him. But you just wanted to use him. It was a setup, a cruel, terrible scheme you played on two good people."

Hana's olive complexion went pale, turning nearly as white as her blindfold. "No! No! I didn't know about any scheme. It was Rashid! I just did what my brother told me to!" Hana's voice was high and wild. I figured she was about to get hysterical any moment.

J spoke again. "So it was Rashid's idea that you have an intimate relationship with the judge? Why did you do what your brother asked, Hana? You say you didn't know what he was planning. So why?"

"Because he made me! He made me. He beat my mother. He threatened to kill us both. I had to do it. I had to. It was terrible. I felt like a whore. I didn't want to do it. Please believe me."

"It's all right, Hana," J said. "We understand. Tell us about your brother. Is he a member of Al Qaeda?"

Hana's head was still hanging down, defeated. She

clasped her hands tightly together in her lap. "Yes, at least, I think he is. He's very secretive, but I know he went to Afghanistan when I was still in high school. To a camp, to train. I think bin Laden was there. Last year he went to Saudi Arabia for nearly a month. He may have gone back again recently, I'm not sure. I found some Saudi coins in a pocket when he brought his laundry for my mother to do. He didn't talk to me about his politics, about anything, but he was always on the computer or spending hours on his cell phone."

"Do you know who he works with? Have you met anyone?"

She shook her head. "I never met anyone else, never. I don't know anyone; I swear. My mother—" Hana stopped suddenly.

"Your mother? What about your mother?" Rogue demanded.

"Nothing. Never mind. It's nothing," she insisted.

Rogue slammed his fist onto the tabletop. Hana's body jerked back. "Stop bullshitting us! Your mother knows something, doesn't she?"

"Maybe. I'm not sure. I think she might. I heard her on the phone once, begging somebody to leave us alone. I don't know who it was. Don't hurt my mother, please! She's old and so afraid, so afraid!" Hana began sobbing.

J spoke again. "Calm down, Miss Rida. You're helping us a great deal. We appreciate that. You're doing the right thing. Have a drink of water."

One of the marshals put the bottle in her hand again. J waited until she collected herself; then, his voice kind and coaxing, he said, "Tell us now from the beginning exactly what happened."

After that the whole story came out quickly, how Rashid told her what questions to ask Judge Morris. How she had told Rashid about Nicoletta's birthday party. She swore she didn't know what Rashid was planning. If she had known, she insisted, she never would have told him anything. She knew he was very political and very radical in his religion. He never said he was in Al Qaeda, except he did talk about bin Laden a long time ago, after he came back from Afghanistan. But he was just a student. He was still in college. She thought he just liked to feel important. And what about her mother? Could we protect her mother? Rashid was going to be very angry.

J promised that her mother would be taken to a safe location and asked Hana if she would be willing to help us save the girls. She began to tremble in her chair, quivering like a leaf in the wind. "Rashid will beat me if he finds out I spoke to you."

"He won't find out. He won't know. Not if you help us. Do you know where the girls are?" J sounded as if he really cared, as if Hana could trust him.

Hana didn't say anything.

"Hana, this is very serious," J told her sternly. "You say you didn't know what Rashid was going to do, but you acted as an accessory. And you participated in the kidnapping of Deborah Morris just yesterday, didn't you? You drove the car. We know you did that. You are in very serious legal trouble."

"I didn't want to. I didn't want to! Rashid made me do it," she burst out.

"Do you know where the girls are? Do you, Hana?"

She shook her head no.

"I think you do. Tell us. Tell us the truth, Hana. Where are they?"

Hana pressed her lips together hard and shook her head.

"Hana! We don't have much time. We can help you if you cooperate with us. You must tell us. Before someone dies."

Tears leaked out from under Hana's blindfold. Her nose ran. "They are underground. I don't know where. I just know it's in, like, a tunnel or something. I don't know where," she whispered.

Rogue kicked a chair, sending it crashing to the floor. Hana recoiled and tried to stand. A federal marshal put a hand on her shoulder and kept her seated.

"I've had enough of this bullshit," Rogue said. "I'm going out for a smoke." He walked by me without looking at me, but he made sure his body brushed mine, pushing me back a step.

J kept asking questions, the same ones over and over, trying to get more information from Hana and getting nowhere. My suspicion was that Hana was too terrified to say anything else. She insisted that she never knew any girls would be kidnapped and that she was never told where they were being held. She admitted she had helped with buying supplies for the kidnappers' victims, but she said over and over that she gave everything to Rashid.

Then J asked where she had taken Deborah after picking her up at the mall. Hana said she had driven the car into a public Park 'n' Lock garage over on Ninth Avenue. She thought maybe it was on Fifty-fourth Street, but she wasn't sure. Rashid had gotten out with Deborah and they went right into a waiting vehicle. She said Deborah seemed confused about what was going on, but she went with Rashid willingly.

As for the kind of vehicle Rashid had waiting in the garage, Hana said it was a black car. That was all she knew. Yes, it could have been a Lincoln Town Car. It could have been any big black car. Finally she broke down and began sobbing. It was useless to keep questioning her. J nodded at the marshals and they took her away.

"Where are they taking her?" Benny asked.

"The federal detention center downtown."

"Oh. So she's being arrested," Benny said.

"She's being detained. I don't know anything else. Forget her. Cormac filled me in on your activity last night. Your team needs to plan your assault on that trolley loop beneath the bridge, ASAP."

"But what about Hana's mother?" Benny insisted. "Are we going to protect her?"

J looked disgusted as he turned away from Benny. "I don't give a rat's ass about her mother. But somebody will pick her up. She needs to be questioned too."

We had a shot at finding those girls tonight, and we were going to go for it. When Rogue came back in, we talked about what we had to do. Our assault plan wasn't complicated: We'd leave from the roof of the Flatiron Building, five vampires in full flight. We'd come in low toward the bridge from the river. We'd bust through the gate to the tunnel, fly into the depths, and find the hideout. Then, having the element of surprise on our side, we'd swoop down on the terrorists, disarm or disable them. Kill them if we had to. Then we'd phone out to J that all was clear.

Then we'd fly out of there like bats out of hell, carrying any of the girls who were injured and needed medical attention. J would meet us on the surface with vehicles and backup to go in after the rest of the girls. We five would take off. Mission accomplished.

It looked good on paper, anyway. We all knew that the whole thing could go to shit in a New York minute. Contingency plans? We didn't have any. We just knew we would fight as hard as we had to, and we wouldn't leave any of us Darkwings behind.

We hurried up to the roof, where the air was clear and chill. A stubborn cold front moving in from the west refused to let winter be forgotten, although it was officially spring. I shivered as much from excitement as from the temperature.

My hands were trembling. I was hyped as adrenaline rushed through my blood and I prepared to transform into the beast I was within.

The five of us gave one another space and removed our clothes. I couldn't stand Rogue. I disliked him more each time I was with him, but I stole a glance in his direction. His body was worth looking at; I gave him that. Benny and Audrey were looking at him too. And he knew it. For the first time that night he met my eyes, and there was a challenge in his.

I moved my eyes away and focused inward, into my shadow self. I let the change begin. I gasped as a great whirl of energy obliterated my consciousness and wrenched me away from my human form. I lost myself and found myself in the same instant. Amid flashing lights and a vortex of wind, my skin became black fur, shining and slick, iridescent with the rainbows of fractured prisms. My nails extended into razor-sharp claws; my teeth grew into fangs.

Then a fearsome rustling began as wings sprang angel-like from my shoulderblades, but feathered they were not. They were bat wings: dark, deeply veined, and graceful, wings that fluttered, arched, and beat hard as I leaped into the sky.

Once we were all airborne, Benny called out to me that she had along her cell phone and, as was her practice, her purse on a shoulder strap. My golden eyes glittered as I grinned. My friend was a graceful tawny-colored bat; I was a rangy ebony one, as was Rogue, though he was nearly twice my size—a magnificent beast. Cormac was muscle and sinew in sable brown; Audrey, not surprisingly, was thin and long and gray.

Our squadron of Darkwings flew north and east, swooping around the spires of buildings. We skimmed the rooftops, we scratched against windowpanes with our wingtips, and we terrified the inhabitants within, those few souls unlucky enough to glance up and see the image of their worst fears fly by. A woman screamed and let a glass slip through her hands to shatter in a bathroom sink. A man idly scratching his arm suddenly froze, his mouth falling open before his eyes rolled back and he collapsed to the floor in a faint. A tiny Chihuahua barked fearlessly as we passed and flung itself over and over at a balcony door.

Soon we were hugging the river's edge, the snakelike currents of the murky water eddying below us. Within minutes the massive span of the Queensborough Bridge stretched before us. We dove low, coming as close to the river's surface as we dared before careening around a parapet and flying up the ramp where we had walked the evening before.

Rogue, who had led all the way, reached the gate to the tunnel first. The chain and padlock snapped easily as he ripped the bars asunder, the sound of the demolition masked by the bangs and steady roar of the traffic over-head. He swooped into the tunnel and we followed. Gliding silently downward we needed no illumination to see with our bat eyes; we made no sound except the faint whirring of our fluttering wings.

The tunnel descended with a shallow grade, curving under the bridge and continuing down perhaps thirty feet beneath the streets above. Its end was blocked with cement rubble. No vehicle could pass this point. Beyond the makeshift barrier, a huge cavern extended for blocks, containing tracks five abreast, bordered on either side by narrow platforms and surrounded by tiled walls. Riveted steel girders ran like straight rows of trees between the tracks.

A rustling sound made our heads swivel and we got ready to attack. A big river rat ran along the far wall, turning his red eyes toward us. After that I heard nothing but water dripping from somewhere above, making a steady tapping as it fell like tears.

The place appeared to be empty. The five of us began a search, sailing around the perimeter of the abandoned trolley terminal looking for signs of life and hiding places. Nothing moved. All was dank, desolate, and deserted. We concluded quickly that the kidnappers and their victims were not here. We changed our focus from preparing for an assault to looking for any evidence that the kidnappers and their victims had been here at all.

Audrey saw it first, what we hoped might be a sign of the girls: a green plastic garbage bag and a supermarket cart next to a large cardboard box with blankets inside. A closer look revealed it was a street person's hovel, not anything the kidnap victims had left behind.

Seeing nothing from the air, Rogue landed and began to walk the narrow platforms, inspecting the floor and walls, looking for doors to adjoining rooms. We all did the same, spreading out to different sections of the terminal. I walked the tracks for a while, then stepped up on a platform and stopped in the gloom, wondering where to look next. I saw a recess in the tiled wall and went over to inspect a shallow alcove. It was a shelter of sorts, set back from the abandoned tracks, and I detected a different smell, a floral fragrance almost like perfume. I scanned the area from ceiling to floor. I almost missed it, but very low, scratched into the dust and greasy grime were the words:

Help Us Toni Alice Nicci Marty Ann Jem Terry Liz Penny Cat

We were a dollar short and a day late. The girls had been here. They were gone. This was all they had left behind.

I called over the others. Rogue took one look and
punched his fist into the tiled wall. Cormac muttered, "Oh,
shit, shit, shit." Audrey just stared silently. Benny's mouth
trembled, but she paid attention to business, using her cell
phone to take a picture of the message on the wall. Then the
five of us Darkwings huddled together.

"Shake it off," I said. "We gave it our best shot."

"Yeah, but the pieces fit. Goddamn. We should have
busted in last night," Rogue said.

Shoulda, coulda, woulda, but we hadn't. But we had to
look at the bright side: It meant the girls were likely to be in
the old Hudson Terminal near the Twin Towers site. The
problem was, we didn't know how to get in there except
through the tunnel from the Jersey side. Audrey hadn't
found any access from the surface at Cortlandt or Fulton
Street or via any of the nearby subways. We decided to give
the problem to J and raid it tomorrow night. Meanwhile,
maybe Hana could provide some clues to help us hunt down
Rashid. He was key to the whole operation.

Benny phoned the bad news up to J, who waited somewhere on the street above the terminal. To her report of our
mission's failure, he replied in a flat tone, "Roger. I copy."

"And J," Benny said, "y'all need to talk to Hana again.
We need to find that there Rashid and fast."

Only silence came in reply. "J? Did y'all hear me?"
Benny asked.

Finally his voice responded, "We can't question Hana
any further."

"Why not? It's important."

"Hana's dead. She hanged herself tonight."

CHAPTER 13

Life doesn't get better the longer you live. Longevity just gives bad things more time to happen. Maybe that's why churches are filled with old ladies. The young need neither comfort nor forgiveness as much.

Personally I had a lot I needed to be forgiven for. Foremost on my mind tonight was Fitz and the world of pain I had caused him.

I went back to my apartment following the fiasco under the bridge. The five Darkwings had flown back to the Flatiron Building, retrieved our clothes and our human form. Then we parted, each going our separate ways. J said he'd try to get us word on access into the Hudson Terminal so we could raid it tomorrow night. Beyond that, I hadn't a clue what to do.

The one solid link we had to the kidnappers had just killed herself. Now we had none.

Although it was heading for four a.m., very late or very early, depending on how you looked at it, I called Fitz. I doubted he would be getting much sleep tonight, and I had a few hours before dawn signaled my bedtime. Fitz answered the phone, very much awake, but he was slurring his words ever so slightly.

Yes, of course, he said, he'd get a cab and come over.

While I waited for him to arrive, I tidied up the apartment a little, running the lint roller over the couch because I knew from the patina of long white hair that Jade had sneaked up on it while I was gone. I picked up the folder with the information about the kidnapping that I had left on the dining room table and stashed it in my computer desk drawer. I put away the clothes I had left on the floor this morning and spritzed the air with Febreze.

My own toilet was next. I washed my makeup off and brushed my teeth. Then I slipped into something more comfortable: an extra-large T shirt from PETA and a pair of silk boxer shorts. Seduction was not on my priority list; in fact, the less appealing I looked, the better.

I decided to put on some music and went over to the CD rack. I looked for the Couperin album, then remembered I hadn't put it away. I glanced over at the table. It wasn't where I left it. That was odd. Then I saw it on the rug. Jade must have swept it onto the floor with her tail. It'd happened before.

I decided on some Celtic music, in deference to Fitz, mixing Enya with the Irish Tenors. I might not have given the Couperin CD's change of location another thought if I hadn't decided to put it away. But since I was being tidy tonight, I picked it up and something sharp stabbed my finger. I gave the jewel case a closer look and saw that the edge was cracked. It hadn't been broken that way when I opened it yesterday.

A cold chill washed over me. My reasoning mind told me that it must have been Fitz, if he had stopped by while I was gone, or the dog walker returning with Jade who stepped on it. Surely that was the most logical explanation. But then an-

other memory came back to me. I had left the Arabic coin on
the end table next to the lamp when I fell asleep on the
couch. I had completely forgotten about it. Now, with a
building apprehension, I hurried over to retrieve it.

The table was empty. The halala was gone.

Goose bumps ran up and down my arms. Perhaps I
shouldn't jump to conclusions; Fitz could have picked up
the coin. The only other explanation was that someone had
been in my apartment, someone who shouldn't have been
there. With the doorman downstairs, it was unlikely. And
why would anyone steal the coin? No one besides me knew
it existed. It couldn't have been the reason I had an intruder—if I had an intruder. I made a mental note to ask Fitz
about the CD case and coin and to have a talk with Mickey
the doorman.

The buzzer rang, and I flung the door open. Fitz lounged
against the doorjamb. He was wearing a fine tweed sportcoat
with his silk tie undone. His hair tumbled across his forehead and his long lashes made his eyes sultry and dark. He
was tall, patrician, and gorgeous, not the kind of man anyone would guess was about to take a vampire as his bride.

He smiled a boozy smile. "Hi, beautiful. Your prince has
come." His words rolled out fuzzy and indistinct, as if
wrapped in velvet.

There was no doubt in my mind that he had been drinking all night. I'd get blotto too after that visit with Mother, if
alcohol were my drug of choice. But my preferred drink was
obviously blood. I think liquor was the lesser poison.

"Hello, big boy," I said. "You look better than George
Clooney, and that makes you the sexiest man on Earth. Do
you still have that box containing an engagement ring in
your pocket," I asked, "or are you just glad to see me?"

"A Boy Scout always comes prepared," he said, pushing

himself to an upright position and making his way a bit un-
steadily through the door. "I was an Eagle Scout. Did I ever
tell you that?" He headed for the couch.

"No. There's probably a lot you haven't told me," I said,
following him across the living room.

"Have you any libations available? Not type O, please. I
need something from the Old Sod, not from an old sot." He
gave me a lopsided grin filled with charm.

"I have a bottle of Jameson, yes," I said. "But haven't you
reached your limit?"

"Limit? My dear, I have a hollow leg, or so they say. And
I need a drink. I am about to become a married man. No!
Scratch that. I'm about to become a married vampire. Will
the bride be wearing black?"

"Perhaps. I think white would be a bit over the top, don't
you?" I said, and brought him a short tumbler of whiskey. I
handed it to him and joined him on the couch.

He raised the glass in a toast.

"May you never lie, cheat, or drink—
but if you must lie, lie in my arms,
and if you must cheat, cheat death,
and if you must drink, drink with me."

He tipped his head back and took a long swallow. He
drank the last drop, held the empty glass up, turned his wrist
so it swiveled, and carefully observed it before he said,
"God invented liquor so the Irish wouldn't rule the world."

He set the glass down on the coffee table, then reached
out and took my hand. His eyes were on my face. He seemed
to be studying me, or maybe he was just trying to focus. "I
do have the ring. I've carried it around in my jacket for
weeks. Foolish optimism I guess. Are you serious,
Daphne?"

"I'm serious. The whole situation is serious. I've dragged you into a terrible mess." Suddenly I needed to touch him. I stroked his cheek. It was rough with stubble.

"You didn't put me in any situation without my full co-operation. Will it hurt? I'm no wuss about pain, but I'd like to know what to expect."

"Are you talking about the wedding ceremony or me biting you?"

My joke fell flat. He was completely serious when he said, "The process of becoming a vampire. The bite is one thing, but what happens afterward?"

"Do you really want all the details now? Will you even remember them in the morning? You're a little drunk, I think."

He put his arm around me and pulled me close. I felt the roughness of the tweed against my arm. "No, I'm very drunk, and I don't think—I know. But tell me true. How do I become a vampire?"

"There's nothing to it, really. We start to make love. I bite you. I drink your blood. You feel a little weak. You don't remember much except that you had the best sex of your life."

"Really? The best sex? Hmmm, now that I like." He looked over at me. He turned my face toward his and kissed me lightly on the mouth.

"Cross my heart," I murmured, my lips still against his.

He pulled back and asked, "Then what?"

"We wait a couple of days, so you can recoup your blood loss, and do it again. Once is not enough to make you a vampire. Lots of people get bitten and never remember it. It doesn't affect them at all except for the little puncture wound in their neck."

He put his forehead against mine. "How many times does it take? Maybe we need to get started, with the best-sex part, anyway."

"I'm not sure you're capable of arousal, dear Fitz. But how many times will I bite you? Probably three. Maybe four to be sure. After that you'll need to have daily blood yourself, to live. And you'll be able to transform, pretty much at will, when you get the knack of it, into a vampire bat. You saw me do that. You know what it is."

Okay, I edited the truth. I left out a lot. I omitted the detail that I could drink just enough blood to make Fitz a zombielike creature, like Dracula's Renfield. Afterward he would exist indefinitely as a sex slave or servant, reduced to eating flies and rats and spiders to stay alive.

I didn't mention that after the first sanguinary kiss from my lips, his libido would increase. After the second bite he would care nothing for work or food, hungering only for a reunion with the vampire and sex. After the third or sometimes the fourth bite, he would turn feverish, collapse, and hallucinate. From his bed, he would cry out in anguish and sink toward death—calling out for me to come to him and bite him again. And if I did, it would kill him.

"And that's it?" he said, believing my every word.

"That's it. But once you change, you can't go back. You can never be human again." His arm was still around my shoulders. I turned my head and kissed his hand.

"Reach into my inside jacket pocket," he said.

I did. My fingers touched a velvet box. I took it out.

"If you're willing to become Mrs. Fitzmaurice, you can put it on," he said.

I opened the box; it was from Cartier. A three-carat diamond was set simply in a platinum band. "It's pink," I said.

"I thought you'd want to be different," he said, searching my face.

I took the ring out of the box and held it in my hand. For such a small item it felt uncommonly heavy. My heart was beating wildly. I had so many doubts about doing this, including doubting the depths of my feelings for Fitz. But love wasn't always the best reason for marriage. Keeping Fitz from being killed by one of my mother's henchmen had to count as a more important motive for me to say, "I do."

"Will you marry me, Daphne Urban? Will you be my wife?" Fitz asked.

"Yes," I said without hesitation.

Fitz took the ring from me and slipped it on my finger. Then he kissed me slowly, thoroughly, his mouth tasting of whiskey, his lips devouring mine before he drew back. The kiss had been a prelude to what Fitz wanted.

The table lamp was lit. He stood up and turned it off. He walked over to an open spot of carpet and took off his jacket, folding it and setting it on the floor. I saw him take a small bag out of one pocket and lay it on the rug. Then he faced me and undid his trousers, let them fall, and carefully stepped out of them. "Are you watching me, you with your cat's eyes that see in the dark?" he asked.

"They're bat's eyes, and yes, I'm watching," I said. I liked to look at him. I didn't plan on sex tonight, but I just had gotten engaged. It was a very good reason to let myself surrender, and I had been denying myself any carnal satisfaction for too long because I was afraid I would bite him. I didn't have to worry about that anymore.

Naked, Fitz stood in front of me, and it was obvious alcohol had not impaired his capacity for erection.

"Come here," I coaxed. He did, standing before me as I sat on the couch. I pulled my T-shirt over my head and shimmied out of my boxer shorts. I leaned forward and licked his shaft. He moaned. He grasped my head in his large hands. I took him in my mouth, and, using the techniques I'd learned a century earlier in a caliph's seraglio, I let him plunge deep into my throat, encasing him with my lips and sucking hard.

He threw his head back and moaned again. He rocked

back and forth. As he did he grew harder, until his shaft was like iron. I would have let him come—he was on the verge of orgasm—but he stopped and withdrew.

He pulled me to a standing position and pressed his body against mine. His arms were powerful; his shoulders were broad. He was a magnificent male, fully aroused, and he picked me up with ease. He turned around and went to the open area of the room. There he gently laid me down so that I could feel the Oriental rug beneath my back.

Kneeling over me and using significant force, Fitz took both my wrists in one of his wide hands. He raised my arms over my head and pinned me down, dominating me and controlling me. It was only a game. I had more than human strength and could have resisted if I'd wished to, but I found this exciting. I began to pant, to hunger, to want, as my own arousal began to build.

"Can I do what I wish with you, Lady D?" he said in a hoarse voice, looking down at me and tightening his hold on my wrists, letting me feel the pressure.

"Anything you wish, St. Fitz," I said in a soft whisper. We had played this game a few times before. Fitz had surprised me with his ingenuity. He liked a little twist with his lovemaking. Somehow I knew tonight would be very different from any other time, and only partly because of how I knew it would end.

"Anything," I said again. "You can do anything at all."

He took his free hand and put it between my legs, probing between my lips for the dark center within. He inserted a finger in me and pressed deep. "Anything, Lady D? Anything?" he asked again, and my yes ended with a moan.

"Do it," I whispered then. "Do it hard. Make me scream." My eyes sparkled, and my legs quivered in anticipation.

Fitz's fingers were long and thick. Suddenly he plunged three of them inside me and pushed upward. I made a sharp cry and closed my eyes. The ride had begun and the journey would take me far from this land of sensual darkness to the land of blood.

"Spread your legs wider," he demanded.

I bent my knees and splayed them as Fitz pushed four of his fingers, tightly held together, inside me. I opened wide for them. I flung my head back and forth, overwhelmed with the sensation of it, the fullness it imparted to me.

Liking to tease me, Fitz moved his inserted hand slowly, out and in. I began to make mewing sounds and pushed against him. I was enjoying myself a great deal. Then he pulled his hand free and a flash of anger welled up in me. "Don't stop," I demanded, and tried to sit up.

He held my wrists tighter and pressed me back down. "Play the game," he snapped. "You said I can do what I want."

I felt a push, then gasped, for I was suddenly impaled on his turgid shaft. He had surged into me and propelled his member upward, guided by his entire weight. He smacked into me hard with a slick slap, then thrust again and again. He went so deep it touched me in a way that sent rings of pleasure radiating through me.

"Anything, Lady D?" he demanded again, looking down on me, his mouth a devilish grin. "I can do anything?"

"Yes, yes," I whispered.

He took his free hand and pushed each of my legs upward so they pressed into my chest. Then he moved his body, probing and searching with his shaft, looking for a certain angle before he moved forward. I cried out as he drove himself deeper.

By now a delicious tension was building in me, suffusing me with a wild passion. I moved my body from side to side, rocking against him in an ancient rhythm. I was lulled into thinking this was all there was, sensual but not erotic, not a foray into the regions of the forbidden.

But after a few moments, keeping his shaft tight against my pubic bone, Fitz stilled. He ran his hand up my ribs until he found my left breast. He teased the nipple erect. He did the same to the right.

Then I heard rustling. He was reaching for the little paper bag he had set down earlier near where we lay now.

"What are you doing?" I asked.

"What I want to," he said in a ragged voice. "You need a surprise."

Something cold and metallic touched my breast. My flesh jumped. "*Oh!*" I cried out as a clamp pinched my nipple. I tried to lower my arms to push Fitz back. Yet he held my wrists firmly, keeping me restrained. Ignoring my struggles, he took a second clamp and let its coldness trail over my flesh. I knew what was going to happen. I tensed as another hard pinch applied a steady pressure to my right nipple. And the mild pain was like an electric charge—and my arousal had intensified. It took me unawares. "Oh, no!" I cried when I realized I was climaxing. But Fitz wasn't through.

"Lady!" he said sternly. "You said anything. I ask you again. I will go no further until you allow it. You just had a taste of the unexpected. Now can I do anything? Anything I want to do to you? Tell me."

I was riding a wave of pleasure. "Yes," I breathed softly. "Yes."

"Yes what?" he insisted.

"You can do anything you want. I give you permission." My breath began coming in little pants. My stomach was fluttering. I knew he was about to do something perhaps naughtier than the nipple clamps. I shivered, a little fear building as I waited for whatever was to come.

Then I felt the silk of his tie being wrapped around my

wrists. He took the free end and secured it to the leg of a heavy chair. I was tethered like a lamb, bound into immobility.

With both his hands now free, he slipped his palms behind my buttocks, cupping my cheeks. Gently, kindly, he stroked the division between my cheeks with his fingers. I stilled. I let myself be petted. It felt wonderful, but I wasn't sure I would like what I suspected was coming. I felt a moment of terrible apprehension.

"No, no!" I called out when with a quick movement he cruelly pushed a finger into my ass. He thrust against me with his member from the front at the same time, sandwiching me between the pressures. I made a long moan that became, "Oh, oh, oh." In another moment, though, I began to relax and enjoy feeling so filled. But in the midst of my comfort, Fitz worked a second finger into me, and the sudden pain made the pleasure wild. I arched my back, then bore down on him, grinding against him.

I was totally in his power, held fast and impaled from two directions so that I could not move. Faster and faster his fingers slipped in and out behind; then he would pause while he buried his shaft inside me from the front.

The sensation was almost too much to bear. I was whimpering, not wanting it to ever stop. I wanted more. "Harder. In me harder," I demanded.

Fitz pressed down with enormous strength, pushing his member up toward my belly. Then he pulled me forward with the hand that cradled my buttocks, lifting me up for access as his other hand attempted to insert a third finger into me. I screamed out, my mouth falling open and my head falling back. The silk tie embraced my wrists. He tried again, slowly working the finger inside me.

"Say my name," he demanded.

"Fitz," I replied.

"Say, 'Put it in. Do it, Fitz,' " he persisted, not to be denied.

"Do it, do it," I moaned as he had his way with me, and the erotic combination of dominance and penetration swept me away. I swooned, nearly unconscious, carried by sensation into a dark, dark place.

Then Fitz thrust once, twice, three times with his member, stopped, remaining deep inside me but not moving. I could feel him throbbing. In that hiatus he concentrated on slipping his fingers, now slick and smooth, in and out of my backside. I could barely contain myself.

Then I couldn't hold back. Lights exploded in my head. I heard myself moan. I was climaxing again in long, steady waves. I heard Fitz's voice, hoarse and guttural with a primitive sound. His fingers pulled out of me. His hands grasped my shoulders and as he bucked atop me like a pony, I felt his shaft give a mighty throb inside me.

When I felt his hot semen flood into me, I knew it was time.

My eyes snapped open. At the moment of his orgasm, Fitz's head was arched back; his face was beatific.

"Release my wrists," I ordered. "Release my breasts."

He did both. It was my turn now.

Fitz became motionless, lying still atop my prone body. His shaft slipped away from me. His body began to tremble in fear. I raised myself up and pulled myself toward his neck. My teeth had grown long and razor-sharp. I felt his warm flesh under my lips, and then with a terrible snarl I bit down hard. And when I did I turned into a beast, stronger than any human.

Releasing his neck, I slipped out from beneath his weight and flipped him easily onto his back. Then, crouching next to him, I had become the predator and he the prey. I leaned

down, fastened my mouth on his neck once again, and began
to suck.

Sliding down my throat, Fitz's blood was a dizzying
brew: thin with alcohol and potent in its effect. Its taste was
peaty, like a fine single-malt Scotch, with a hint of winter-
green and the salt of the Irish sea. His blood was vibrant,
filled with life, and young. My head began to spin as I drank
greedily.

Fitz groaned. I moved so I was lying atop him. Then I
reached down and guided his member back into me.
Encased by my velvet, it grew hard and broad, infusing with
blood even as I was stealing it from him. I pulsed around
him, my pleasure building.

His breath quickened. He sighed my name. And as all my
victims did, he begged me not to stop. And then he exploded
once more, crying out as I climaxed too—not for a fast second of intense pleasure, but with a violent spasm that made
my body rock with an orgasm that lasted for a minute or
more.

Only when I was sated did I stop. Blood dripping from
my lips, I raised my mouth off his neck. My body was wet
with sweat and semen. Fitz turned his head. He looked at
me, appearing dazed. Then he closed his eyes and slipped
away into sleep, or unconsciousness. The deed I had so long
dreaded had been done.

I stood up on wobbly legs and picked up a woolen throw
from a chair. Fitz was snoring when I draped it over him.
Then I went into the bathroom. I focused on unwrapping a
new bar of soap; I counted the remaining clean towels; I
looked in a magnifying hand mirror.

I got into the shower humming "Here Comes the Bride."
I let the hottest water I could tolerate wash away all physical traces of the macabre union just past. I shampooed and
loofahed, keeping my mind on mundane things such as what

clothes needed to go to the cleaners and how much dog food I had to order—except for that brief moment when I assured myself that my behavior had been necessary, and the sooner Fitz became a vampire, the better.

Yet after I had turned off the spigots, wrung the excess water from my long black hair, and toweled off, I was slipping on a lacy thong—aware there was a good chance Fitz might be around to admire it—when an insistent voice crept by my carefully guarded consciousness. The voice said that I didn't care about Fitz at all. I had just found an excuse to get what I wanted: to drink human blood from a lusty young man, one I did not love, but who I had been wanting for weeks to use for my own needs. Now having done so at last, I had damned us both.

I pushed the thought away. Fresh and clean, I put on jeans and a warm sweater. Dawn was coming, and I wanted to go out. The blood had brought a blush to my cheeks and put a spring in my step. I put Jade's leash on and strolled along the empty predawn streets, leaving behind the man and the memories I wanted to now forget.

When I returned to my apartment, Fitz was still on the floor, deep in slumber. His arm was thrown over his eyes; the wool throw had bunched up between his legs. He looked none the worse for my attack; in fact, he was smiling in his sleep. I gave Jade and Gunther a snack before I retired to my secret room, shutting out the world as I entombed myself in darkness.

But after I climbed into my coffin and pulled the pink satin quilt over me, sleep wouldn't come. I tossed and turned. I questioned my morality. I questioned my sanity. I had gotten engaged. I had a ring on my finger. I had committed myself to a wedding, and I imagined it would not be a small, intimate ceremony. Fitz would want an expensive, catered extravaganza attended by hundreds of guests. He would expect me, if not dressed in white, to be in ivory. It was sure to be a couture gown. Fitz would wear a tux. His cousins would be groomsmen.

Then I imagined Mar-Mar making her entrance; the mother of the bride would cause a stir. *She looks so young,* they would whisper. Fitz's mother, the regal and thoroughly mad Delores, would be out of the asylum for the day, sedated by Thorazine. *Lock up the knives,* some guest would whisper. *The groom's mother looks as if she'd like to kill the bride.*

The thoughts tumbled through my brain. We would need a photographer, a videographer, invitations, flowers, a buffet or sit-down meal. Where would the happy couple honeymoon? Transylvania? *Ha, ha.* The locale had better have an exciting nightlife. A beach holiday was out. Wedding planning was something I never envisioned myself doing. Suddenly I felt as if I'd go mad.

I forced myself to stop thinking about the whole insane mess and to concentrate on the Darkwings' mission and the kidnappers. To put my overstimulated cortex to some good use, I went through the details of the case again, from the first moment we were told about it. Something in there was being overlooked that could lead us to the abducted girls.

Wait a minute, I thought. *What if we can't find the girls? We* think *they're in the old Hudson Terminal. We have no proof. Why not go after their captors instead?* As I lay there in my coffin unable to sleep, lightning struck. I had an idea. I pulled myself out of the satin depths, walked across the floor, and pushed open the secret door. Tiptoeing around the snoring Irishman, I went into the kitchen to use the phone. I hit the speed dial and called J.

CHAPTER 14

In skating over thin ice our safety is in our speed.

—Ralph Waldo Emerson in "Prudence"

Passion when fresh is insatiable. It grows stronger the more it is fed.

I left my secret room in the late afternoon, the sun still low in the sky. I didn't know if Fitz would be waiting for me. Just to be prepared, I wore only my tiny white lace thong. It was a smart move. He was there.

St. Julien Fitzmaurice, that scion of an influential Irish-American family, was soon to become one of the race of the damned. But right now, dressed in well-tailored gabardine slacks and a Brooks Brothers blue broadcloth shirt that emphasized his wide shoulders and narrow waist, he was still human, red-blooded, and wholesome. Good enough to eat—or bite.

I rubbed sleepily at my eyes and asked for coffee. Fitz had made a fresh batch and it was on the kitchen counter. I padded my way over to it and poured myself a mug, drinking it black. Fitz explained that he had gone to the office for most of the day, but he'd left early enough to be sure he'd see me before I left for my night's work. Jade had been walked. Her food and water bowls were filled. And I should know, he said, that he did it all to get on my good side. This was a nooky call, he added with a grin.

I looked at him, wondering how much he remembered of last night. A small red mark was visible at the base of his neck.

"You smell good," he added, and pulled me into his arms, burrowing his face in the crook of my neck.

"I don't have much time," I protested, though not too loudly.

"Then a quick one," he insisted, kissing me.

"I have coffee breath. I didn't brush my teeth yet," I objected as he backed me against the kitchen island.

"Then I will kiss you again after you do," he murmured, his eyes sultry and half-closed. He looped his thumbs into my thong and tore it off me. My eyes got wide. He loosened his jeans. He pressed against me, lifting me up on the island by holding behind my thighs, and I wrapped my legs around him.

The entry was quick, the invasion brief, but the results satisfactory. I did not bite him, of course. I was sated from this morning, and it was far too soon to drink again. I planned to make Fitz a vampire, not a corpse.

I purred in contentment before I left his arms to dress for the night ahead. Despite my misgivings about marriage, Fitz was a catch, a steady mate who insisted fast sex was a good way to greet the night. Slow sex would be even better, I thought, but I had urgent business to attend to.

A woman was talking on her cell phone when I arrived at the Flatiron Building. She ended the call when I walked in. J introduced her as B and said she had flown up from Charleston, South Carolina, that afternoon.

After my dalliance with Fitz, I had dressed quickly in black pants, a black sweater, an ivory bouclé jacket, and a pair of Bettye Muller peep-toe pumps, really cute, with a bit of a platform and a three-and-three-quarter-inch heel. Thanks to a new shine-mist hair product, my dark hair was as glossy as patent leather. Sex and new clothes gave me a positive attitude, even though I knew I had to spend an hour or two with J.

I had walked into our Twenty-third Street headquarters soon after darkness fell, having taken the subway to avoid venturing outside as much as possible. It was only about six p.m., still not quite dark, but the day had been cloudy, and the lingering twilight was a nonlethal if somewhat uncomfortable misty gray. The rest of the team was due around six thirty. I was the only Darkwing present besides J. I didn't know if my idea was within the realm of possibility, but J had agreed to let me find out. He had gotten a representative of Force Protection Industries to come to talk with me.

I looked at the woman called B. If she were a rock, she'd be granite: smooth, beautiful, and unbreakable. Sitting erect in the chair, she commanded her space. Her body language clearly telegraphed that she didn't move before she was ready.

"Okay, Captain, let's get the ball rolling now that the troops have arrived," she said to J, who, as always, wore his Ranger uniform.

After I crossed the room to join them, B reached across the table to take my extended hand. Hers was firm and businesslike. She looked at me but didn't stare. She didn't ask who I was. She asked only, "What do you want to know about the Buffalo? I bought every piece of metal on the vehicle. There's not a bolt that I don't know about. Same with the Cougar and Cheetah, the other models. As we say, 'They're bred from the same beast.' Y'all know what I'm talking about?" She raised one carefully shaped eyebrow.

I hadn't a clue. "I guess the Buffalo is some kind of armored car, sort of like a Hummer."

B laughed. "Yeah, like a lion is some kind of kittycat. The Buffalo is what is called 'a ballistic- and blast-protected vehicle.' Here, I brought you some photos." She slid a file across the table to me.

A tan steel fortress on wheels, the Buffalo looked like it could take down a house. A wicked-looking mechanical arm, extending from its roof, reached out to scoop up land mines. The tires were nearly as tall as I was. The front and side windows looked down from a good ten feet above the road; dark green and impenetrable, they appeared three inches thick. I whistled. "My God, I never saw anything like this."

"Most people react like that. It's certainly not a Hummer. Nobody would ever drive one to the mall! Our vehicles have tons more substance than style. They're designed to be the solution to the problem of the three-hundred-and-sixty-degree battlefield, where the front line is on all sides. They eat improvised explosive devices, or IEDs, for lunch. Roadside bombs, land mines, rocket-propelled grenades. Bring 'em on. And bullets bounce off these babies like spitballs. They protect our boys, keep 'em safe, and that's what I care about."

I looked at J. "How much can I say about our problem?"

He nodded toward our visitor. "B has the highest security clearance possible. She went to Baghdad with Rumsfeld in 2006. She knows about the kidnappers' demands."

"Yeah, I know about the kidnapping," B said, her voice hard with anger. "The company president knows. We're backed into a corner here. Under no circumstances can we give those dumbass terrorists our new model—or even the old one. I can imagine what they could use it for. They could drive right up the White House steps before they could be stopped—and that's only if the air force dropped a bomb on them."

I nodded. "I understand that. I'm not proposing that we give them one. I'm proposing that we make them *think* we're giving them one. That we use it as bait." I turned to J. "Don't get me wrong. I'm not suggesting we give up on rescuing the girls. We keep the search going. But we have the dynamic of this situation going only one way. We're doing the pursuing. We're going to them. We need to turn it around. Make the kidnappers come to us."

"You realize the weakness to your idea is that we might apprehend the terrorists, but not get the girls back," J said.

"That's the risk. It's better than a dead end," I said belligerently. "Right now we have nothing. What's the latest on the kidnappers' demands anyway? I only know about the original one, the day the girls were taken, and you said that officially the government turned them down."

"The Morrises had a call today. The kidnappers are giving the government forty-eight hours before they start killing the girls. They told the Morrises that Deborah would be the first to die."

"That's not unexpected. Have they revealed any specifics about how they want the diamonds and the vehicle delivered?" I asked.

"Some. We're supposed to drop off the diamonds and the Buffalo at an as yet undisclosed location. We leave. They make sure we leave. They retrieve the ransom and the vehicle—and drive off unimpeded. If they're given the chance to get away, we get the girls. If not, we don't."

"We didn't agree to that, did we?" I said, tapping a pen on the table.

"Hell, no," J said. "We asked for another phone call to negotiate the details of the exchange. But that's just a stall tactic. The government won't give them the Buffalo at all. It's an impasse."

I sat there thinking for a minute. B and J just watched me. I turned to B. "The terrorists don't know anything about this new advanced Buffalo—the interior, I mean."

"No way they could," she said.

"And you can't see into it from the outside, right?"

"Sure can't," she affirmed.

"So we could deliver it with a surprise inside."

B laughed. "Yeah, like the biggest Cracker Jack box in the whole wide world."

I smiled at her. "That's going to be the easy part, I bet." I looked at J. "Consider this. Judge Morris convinces the terrorists that he pressured the president to deliver the Buffalo. Al Qaeda has said they think the president is both corrupt and stupid. Morris needs to make them believe the president has given in—without telling his advisers. But Morris tells them he needs assurance he will get his daughters back alive. He needs to be in closer contact with these people. That should buy us some time."

"That's doable. How do we trap the kidnappers and get the girls at the same time?"

"I don't know yet. Find out where they want the drop to be. Once we get a location, we have something to work with. There's something about their demand for the vehicle that's not sitting right. I have this gut feeling I'm missing something."

"My gut feeling is that the whole thing can blow up in our faces," J said. "We were ordered to do a rescue of the girls, that's all."

"Look, J, what choice do we have? The president's big idea was to send us out to get the girls back. That makes it easy for him, doesn't it? No hostages, no problem. But we haven't found them, and if dead girls start being left on the streets of New York, this is going to be at the very least a media circus—"

Something occurred to me in a flash. "Shit! J, these terrorists are not going to let it go at killing the girls. There's more to their mission than an abduction and an opportunity to get the Buffalo. No, I don't know what, but they've been planning this for years." The bad feeling I had was worse. If we didn't get proactive and make a move, the terrorists were going to make theirs—and I had a feeling it was going to make a car bomb going off in Baghdad look like a firecracker in comparison.

J stared at me hard. I had gotten the wheels turning in his

head too. "I'll get them to give us a Buffalo. B, can we fly one up from South Carolina?"

"You get us the go-ahead; we'll get a Buffalo to you. Just tell us where and when," she said.

B had left the premises by the time the rest of the Darkwings arrived. Wearing a snug-fitting denim jacket and crisply pressed jeans, Benny walked in smiling, her eyes bright. Audrey followed, wearing a shabby raincoat that was frayed at the cuffs. Her lips were blue and her white skin almost transparent. Rogue had a couple of days' growth of beard. A dark cloud seemed to be hanging over Cormac's head.

Once everyone was there, J said he wanted to start the evening's briefing with the plan concerning the Buffalo. I was riding on a rush of my own adrenaline, yet after J conveyed my brilliant suggestion about trapping the kidnappers, nobody else as much as gave me a high five.

"That's a backup plan at best, isn't it?" Audrey said. "It can't happen for, what, one day? Two days? The girls could all be dead by then. They were taken *five* days ago. Maybe they're dead already."

I felt defensive. "But not one of the kidnappers has been found. We don't know where the girls are being hidden. We need to come at this from a different direction."

"It's a distraction from our search for the victims," Audrey added. "It's a terrible risk."

"J," Rogue cut in. "Audrey had a point. Morris has to demand that the kidnappers prove the girls are still alive. Daphne's right too. The kidnappers have been controlling this situation. We also need to shift the locus of power. Right now they have it all. Morris wants a new video, with tomorrow morning's newspaper in it. If they harm the girls, no Buffalo, no diamonds. Who's talking with these yo-yos, anyway?" His voice got louder and louder as he spoke.

J looked like he was sucking on a lemon, the words sour in his mouth. "Everything has been going through Judge Morris. He's the liaison between the president and the kidnappers. Professional negotiators are listening in on the calls and helping him respond."

"That's jist about the worst news I ever did hear," Benny said. "He's nothing but a puffed-up bullfrog."

A muscle in J's jaw twitched. "It's not good. But we've got to work with what we've got."

"When are the kidnappers calling again? Do we know?" Rogue pressed his point.

"Tonight. In about an hour. I'll see that the judge makes the request."

Cormac, dark circles under his eyes, tapped his fingers on the table. "The girls' best chance is still for us to find them and rescue them. Did you find us a way into the old Hudson Terminal?"

J looked down as if studying his legal pad. "That's a no go. The terminal still exists but the entrances collapsed when the Twin Towers went down. We can't access the terminal without doing a major excavation from the street. Even if we had the manpower, we don't have the time. If we can't get down there, neither could the kidnappers. Audrey will have to do another computer search. The girls can't be down there."

Audrey shook her head. "It's the most likely place. There must be a way in. Look, I printed this out." She took a folded sheet of paper out of her jacket pocket. She opened it up and spread it horizontally on the table.

The paper showed a diagram: five sets of double tracks running parallel across the sheet and curving up toward the edge of the page and both ends in a wide U. At the top of the sheet were five squares of different sizes.

"Here." She pointed to the squares one at a time. "This one I think was a ticket kiosk. This big box? That's the double set of stairs going up to Church Street. It's this third box that interests me. It must have been a maintenance room and workers' locker room, I'm pretty sure. It had ventilation, and probably still does—fresh air not just there, but in this whole area." She dragged her finger across the tracks. "And there's a tunnel going in. Tunnel going out. At worst, we come in from Jersey, but those collapsed entrances weren't the only openings into this area."

"Where is it? The opening?" J said flatly.

"I have to look at some other databases," she said.

"Time's running out," Rogue broke in, sounding irritated.

"Do you have a better idea?" I said.

"Maybe," he snapped at me.

Frustration overwhelmed me. The emotions from meeting with my mother and committing to marriage still churned around in me. Looking at Rogue my personal problems collided with my professional ones. Suddenly I felt a burst of anger and took it out on Rogue. That was not one of my brightest moves. "Maybe?" I said too loudly. "I thought you were supposed to talk to your criminal friend, Speed-o. What happened?" My eyes blazed when I looked at him.

So quickly I almost didn't see it come out of the sleeve of his leather club jacket, a knife flew through the air, and its blade quivered as it struck the paper, pinning it to the table. It vibrated for a moment. Rogue leaned over and pulled it out. Then he looked at me, a warning in his eyes. "It was no deal. Somebody had already cut the cook's throat."

A shiver ran through me. I thought that I'd better watch my back. On second thought, we'd all better watch our backs.

The briefing deteriorated after that. J told Audrey to come up with some other options where the girls might be. She insisted she was going to find out how to get into the Hudson Street Terminal.

"What are the rest of us supposed to be doing tonight? Sitting around on our asses? The clock's ticking," Cormac burst out. I'd been thinking the same thing.

"I'm not here to hold your hands," J said. "You figure it out. I need to coordinate getting the Buffalo up here. All of a sudden, I don't think grabbing the terrorists is our best shot. I think it's our only shot. See you here tomorrow, six thirty." He stood up, grabbed his cane, and limped out of the room.

Rogue gave him the finger behind his back.

"Let's get the fuck out of here," Rogue said, and pushed his chair back.

"Where to?"

"I don't know about any of you, but I'm going to make some more calls. See if I can talk to anybody else. If that cook was using those tunnels as a lab, he got killed because of it."

"Hold up on that a minute," Cormac said. "Let's talk out in the street. This place is probably wired."

We gathered out on the sidewalk and stood close to the building. People passed by, minding their own business, and generally in a hurry. This was New York City. Most of them didn't even give us a glance.

Cormac turned to Audrey. "First off, I think you're right about where the girls are. But it won't hurt to take another look at possibles, even if it's just a CYA move—"

"Fuck that," Rogue said. "Let's not waste our time. We've had two outside sources—Jo-Jo and Hana—say the girls are in the tunnels."

Cormac looked at me and Benny. "How do you two feel?"

I shrugged. "Maybe we should go to Jersey. Come across under the river."

Benny nodded. "I'm with Daphne. We have to check out that underground hidey-hole."

Just then Audrey swayed and put her hand against the building. Then her eyes rolled back and she started to faint. Rogue grabbed her.

"What's wrong?" Benny said.

"It's pretty obvious, isn't it?" I said. "She needs blood and fast."

"Let's get some raw steak into her. It will revive her for a couple of hours anyway," Rogue said. "Where's the nearest butcher?"

I bit off a wiseass remark and said, "There's a Whole Foods Market at Twenty-fourth and Seventh. It's close. A couple of blocks."

Cormac was the best runner among us. He headed for the store immediately. Rogue got Audrey to come around by gently slapping her face. When she had recovered enough to talk, she said, "Sorry about that. Except for the blood two nights ago, I haven't been eating."

"That's got to change. I'll set you up with blood-bank deliveries starting tomorrow," I offered.

Rogue made a face. I turned on him, snapping, "She can't rely on hunting. Can't you see that?"

Audrey nodded. "I know you're right. But look, don't get mad at me. After Cormac gets back and I get some meat in my stomach, I want to go back to the Laundromat. The first team goes out around ten. I need to get in the lottery."

"Can I go along with you?" Benny asked with her eyes dancing. "I want to try it."

"This isn't the time—" I started to say.

"Hold up," Rogue broke in. "I think we should all go."

"What? Why!" I felt totally confused. Was everybody just going to forget about the mission and go hunting for blood? Were we that irresponsible?

"Let me think this out," Rogue said. "These are vampires who compete in hunting on a regular basis, right?"

Audrey, who was still being held up in his arms and didn't seem inclined to disengage herself, said yes, that some of the Laundromat's regulars scored every time they went out. They

ranked as grand champions, which meant they'd caught a hundred donors in a single year, she explained.

"I think we need to meet them," Rogue said. "I think we need
to recruit them."

"Are you out of your mind?" I blurted out.

Rogue gave me an impatient look. "No, I'm not. I'm just
'thinking outside the box,' using my brain. So listen up, sweet-
cakes, and see if you can keep your mouth shut for two minutes—"

"Excuse me!" My face grew hot. I wanted to slap the son
of a bitch. But I shut up. I had a bias against doing anything
with these underworld vampires. I worried that it clouded my
thinking.

"Look, we're up against the wall here. These are top ama-
teur hunting teams. We're understaffed. A challenge like this—
hunting down these kidnappers and terminating them—could be
a tremendous turn-on for them. As for getting in and out of subterranean caves in Manhattan, who better to know about that
than vampire bats? It's worth trying."

"You know, it sounds like a great idea," Benny gushed. I shot
her a dirty look.

"Let's see what Cormac has to say," I groused.

Cormac got back with Audrey's "snack." He had purchased
two pounds of hamburger, figuring a woman eating a piece of
raw steak on the sidewalk might draw attention. She delicately
began to pop this finger food into her mouth while Rogue ran
down his idea.

I folded my arms across my chest and waited for Cormac's
response.

Cormac didn't react at first. He seemed to be considering the
matter. I didn't think it would take more than an instant to give
Rogue a big fat *no*. I knew I was in trouble. "We haven't got anything to lose," Cormac said. "Let's go."

My world began to spin out of control from that point on.

CHAPTER 15

Let us have wine and women, mirth and laughter,
Sermons and soda-water the day after.

         —Lord Byron, *Don Juan*

"Can I ask you for a big favor?" I said to Benny as we sat together in the cab en route downtown to Lucifer's Laundromat.

Benny was jammed into the middle of the backseat, me on one side and Cormac on the other. We were tight as sardines. It was a good thing we liked one another enough not to mind this forced intimacy. Audrey, not surprisingly, had opted to ride in a separate cab with Rogue. She certainly did like being close to his body.

"Why, sugar," Benny said, taking my hand in hers, "anything you want, you know that."

"Be my maid of honor."

Her eyes practically fell out of her head. "Cormac, did y'all hear that? Daphne's getting hitched."

Cormac rolled his eyes. "Yeah, right," he said.

I pulled my engagement ring out of an inner pocket in my jacket and handed it to Benny, who immediately put it on her own finger to admire it. "No, she really is. Look! Ain't it purty. Oh, my, what it must have cost. Daphne's going to be a bride, and I'm going to be the maid of honor."

"You want to be a bridesmaid, Cormac?" I asked. "You used to like to go around in drag. I think that was your transvestite period, remember? You were doing that showgirl number with RuPaul."

"You think you're funny, right?" Cormac said. "You know what, Daphne, how would you feel if I took you up on that offer? A vampire bride and a bridesmaid in drag; it would make Page Six in the *Post*. Benny and I can shop for a dress together. Fuchsia is my color, darling; remember that."

I laughed. I had virtually no family and only a handful of friends. Why not make Cormac a bridesmaid? It would give the guests on Fitz's side of the aisle something else to talk about. "Cormac, you're on."

Benny dropped the ring back in my hand. "So when's your big day?"

"I'm not sure yet. Sometime in June, maybe? It's traditional, right? A June bride, why not? I'll run it by Fitz and let you know."

"So you're marrying the Fitzmaurice guy," Cormac said. "I wasn't sure."

"Touché," I said, and we all laughed. Only your oldest friends can really bust you. It said something, too, that I'd rather deal with the instant anxiety of thinking about my wedding than contemplate what might happen once we arrived at the underground club. . . . Once I was again among my own kind.

"Hey, Joey," Audrey yelled out to the bartender over the punishing din of Metallica. "Who are the team leaders tonight?"

"Martin and Gerry. Should be going up on the board in a minute," he said while he dried some wineglasses on a towel.

"You know where they're hanging?"

"Check downstairs. They should be there until after the lottery."

"Right!" she called out, waved to us, and led us down a hallway to a flight of descending steps. I hung back, reluctant to go, but finally forced myself to follow them into the depths of the club.

Seated at a table in a plush lounge where the dominant color was—what else?—red, Martin was doing today's sudoku puzzle in the *Daily News*. Gerry, who turned out to be female, had one bare foot up on a wooden chair, polishing her toenails. She took a long, slow look at Rogue with the brush poised in her hand, forgotten, dripping scarlet polish on a the floor. I disliked her on sight.

As for the first vampire, Martin, he was just what I expected: thin but muscular in a T-shirt artfully torn at the neck, his narrow hips poured into skintight jeans, and his features fine, regular, and too perfect to be human. He was probably used to being gawked at—just as Benny was gawking at him now. He looked up and saw her staring. She smiled at him, and he gave her a smile in return that said he was interested.

Cormac seemed oblivious to this subtle exchange as he walked up to Martin and introduced himself.

"Oh, the dancer who's a spy. That's you, right?" Martin said, and put his newspaper and pencil aside.

Cormac nodded yes. He had to feel me giving him the evil eye right through the back of his idiot head, because he looked over his shoulder to see if I heard what Martin said. I glared at him to let him know I had.

Martin pushed his chair back and stood up to get a good look at the five of us. "Are you all spies? Well, hey, that's cool. What's going on?"

"We need your help. Both you and Gerry."

"Hey, Ger," Martin called out. "Come over here."

The slender redhead put the top back on her nail polish and joined us.

"Here's the deal," Cormac began while I sat down at the table and put my head in my hands. As far as I was concerned, this was a crazy scheme, our cover was blown, and we were so fucked.

I listened to Cormac telling Martin and Gerry nearly everything, except for the details of the ransom demand. He explained that we had to track down the terrorists and rescue the girls, and that we thought they were being held underground, at Cortlandt between Church and Fulton, in an abandoned PATH terminal.

"So what can we do, man?" Martin asked. Gerry, meanwhile, had positioned herself close to Rogue and kept looking him up and down.

"First off, you've got maybe, what? Forty regulars who are out on the streets hunting a couple of times a week?" Cormac asked. I reached across the table to pull the newspaper over to me and picked up the pencil. I couldn't bear to listen to much more of this. I started to do the crossword.

Despite focusing on the clues, I couldn't shut out the conversation.

"Yeah, that's about it, forty hunters more or less," Martin said.

Cormac put a hand to his chin and thought a moment. "Okay. We need to talk to them, find out if anybody's seen any two specific men, Middle Eastern–looking, down near the Twin Towers site, sneaking around maybe. We also want to know if anybody has gotten down in that old terminal since nine-eleven."

"Sure, we can ask around. No problem. What else? So far it's not too interesting, you know?" Martin commented.

Saving the lives of eleven girls obviously didn't move

Martin. Cormac had to hook Martin with something that he'd really get excited about doing. "Here's the bottom line," Cormac said. "We need you to help us nail these terrorists. Find them. Hunt them. Snatch them. If you get your hands on them, you can terminate them if you want to."

"You mean suck them dry? What a hoot. We never get to do that. Whooooee!"

I didn't even want to acknowledge that I was hearing this exchange. It was worse than I thought. I twiddled the pencil between my fingers.

"Do you know how we operate?" Martin asked. At that point, I heard an annoying whispering. I looked over to see Gerry with her lips near Rogue's ear. I swear to God she was tonguing him.

Meanwhile Cormac was responding to Martin. "Audrey gave us an overview of the team competition."

"But we'd sure like to see you in action," Benny chirped.

"No, *we* wouldn't," I spoke up as I watched that hussy Gerry take Rogue by the hand.

"We'll be right back," she said to Martin. "Give us a couple of minutes anyway." She giggled as she pulled Rogue off into an adjoining room. Rogue looked at me and winked as he left. The pencil snapped in my hand. *He is such a degenerate,* I thought.

Benny sat down next to me and whispered, "You're jealous. It's written all over your face."

"Are you nuts! I am not. I think he's a jerk for walking away in the middle of this," I hissed back at her.

"I sure do like this Martin feller," she whispered to me. "I think he's the one."

"The one what?" I said, totally annoyed.

"Oh, Daphy, you know. I think I could really fall for him."

I let out a deep sigh. "Benny, look at him. He's a heart-

breaker." Then I saw that her face was so hopeful. "Oh,
hell," I said softly. "I wish you luck, but don't say I didn't
warn you."

"Oh, don't worry about me, sugar. I'll be my-t-fine."

The game began at two a.m. It was no statistical miracle that
all five of us won the lottery that night. It was rigged, and
Audrey was appalled to find out it usually was.

I shrugged. "It's being run by vampires. What did you
expect?"

We had already spent maybe an hour talking with some
of the regular hunters. Cormac and I had teamed up and
were interviewing a guy who called himself Handy Andy.
He was a stockbroker of sorts, maybe more of a speculator
or day trader. He hung around Wall Street, he said, because
he thought he made better stock picks when he sucked bro-
kers' blood. It was nice to turn the tables, score a little payback for the customers, he added.

Handy Andy thought he had seen a couple of men, maybe
foreigners by the way they were dressed, out on Church
Street at three or four in the morning. He noticed them again
on Tuesday night and last night too. He figured they were
restaurant workers, but one was dressed pretty well to be
doing menial work. I looked at Cormac. He nodded. We
needed to check it out.

A half dozen vampires promised to look for a way into
the terminal. We set up a communication center at the club.
Joey the bartender would coordinate. As soon as access to
the Hudson Terminal was found, we'd rendezvous here.
Then, in surely one of the strangest rescue attempts ever envisioned, this squadron of vampires would depart for lower
Manhattan, get into the tunnels, and free the girls. Everybody
wanted in on the raid.

I didn't believe for a minute that it would actually happen, but the room buzzed and club members were stoked about it. When our questioning of members was done, the other four Darkwings had stayed upstairs to dance and drink. Despite Benny's pleading, I refused to join them. I went back downstairs to sulk in the lounge, the thudding bass of the speakers becoming a dull throb to match the migraine I was getting.

I had been steadily sliding into misery, unhappy at my proximity to this crowd of mostly drunk, groping, and increasingly wild vampires. I wanted to be away from this place, these creatures. I longed for my comfortable apartment, my animals, and yes, I wanted Fitz.

Finally, when it got late enough that any pedestrians left on the nearly empty streets were more likely than not to be young and stoned, the two teams were called together. I rose from my chair and reluctantly joined them. Within minutes, we had all left the club to hit the streets and begin the competition.

Benny, Audrey, and I were on the Chasers, headed by Martin. Cormac and Rogue joined the Racers, with Gerry as the captain. I was bound to be a liability to my team. I had no intention of scaring humans that night, and I certainly wasn't going to capture anyone. I agreed to join the hunt to see these so-called experts in action.

The hunting vampires invariably worked in human form, although transforming into a bat was not forbidden by the rules. Also their quarry didn't have to be gender-specific. But when the game started most of the male vampires seemed to prefer to hunt women and the female vampires went after men. Later in the night, when time was running out, they grabbed any young human they could. The only common denominator was that the captives were all young.

And the hunters were good. They moved swiftly and with a practiced technique. I watched Martin take his first victim. He had skulked across Second Avenue and slipped like a dark shadow into the little graveyard by St. Marks Church-in-the-Bowery. A wrought-iron fence topped by vicious spikes ran around the perimeter of this historic cemetery except at one place near the Second Avenue sidewalk, where it was separated into two lengths by a wide marble post.

At that very spot, Martin crouched unseen, a shadow among shadows, his lurking in a cemetery a touch of irony that didn't go unappreciated by me. A twenty-something girl, her spiky hair dyed pink and her eyebrows pierced, crossed St. Marks Place. She looked around nervously and walked with hurried steps. Then she stopped and fished a lighter and a pack of Winston Lights out of her shoulder purse. She paused to light a cigarette, the Bic's flame illuminating her face. At that moment, Martin's hand slid over the top of the marble post and quick as a snake grabbed her shoulder.

She looked up in terror to see him, his fangs long and sharp, leaping out of the graveyard. With a deft, practiced movement he silenced her scream with a kiss as he embraced her body, pinning down her flailing arms. Her eyes were wide with horror. I could hardly bear to watch.

But no human can resist a vampire's lure. The girl stopped struggling. Her face became blank while she slipped into a trance. As if from some ancient instinct, she turned her head to expose her neck to her attacker and moaned. Martin didn't hesitate. He sank his teeth into her neck, not to drink deeply, but to ensure she stayed in a hypnotic state. She sagged into his arms, her gaze now enraptured, as he continued his tender and terrible caress.

At that moment another teammate, in a practiced move, appeared at Martin's side. The feeding vampire looked up, lifted his mouth from the girl's neck, and handed his victim over. The second vampire whisked her off to the Laundromat, where this first unfortunate victim would await the deeper feeding given to the winner's team.

If she survived the night without incident—and accidents did occasionally happen—this girl would remember nothing when she awoke tomorrow; humans never did. But she would feel dizzy and a little strange. She might look into the mirror and wonder where she had gotten those two small marks on her neck. She would run her fingertips over the wound and feel a chill. Without knowing why, she would feel embarrassed and conceal them until they healed. Then she would forget that they had ever been.

As the hour wore on, I saw how carefully choreographed the hunt became. The vampires worked in teams. They emerged from dark doorways or from between parked cars. Once they chose a victim, they struck without hesitation. They never chose a human with a dog. They never tackled groups or couples. They targeted the most vulnerable, the most easily victimized, and not one human they attacked was able to escape.

Since it was a mild night, many hapless humans walked the streets of the Lower East Side alone. More fools they. I counted twenty snatches by the Chasers before the hour was up.

At the end of the hunting period, the two teams gathered downstairs at the Laundromat club. Since the Racers had brought in only seventeen captives to the Chasers' twenty, according to the rules they must give them to the winners. But as there were more than enough humans for all twenty-four members of the two teams, the Chasers were invited to stay for the orgy to follow. Other club members, waiting around upstairs, were also brought in for the fun.

I had caught no quarry; I wanted no part in what was to come. Now that the hunt was over, I removed myself from the lounge, but hesitated, curious in spite of myself. I walked into the viewing room, whose wide plate glass let voyeurs witness the feeding—and the sex.

Should I stay? My better part said to leave before the first bite began. I needed to go home. But even as I stood there I saw Martin enfolding the girl he had captured in his arms. She looked at him with a lover's eyes and swayed toward him. Her will gone, she docilely let him lead her to a nearby bed, where he laid her down.

He looked over at me, then, as I stood on the other side of the glass. His eyes glowed with a hellish fire. His perfect mouth was now a cruel slash; his teeth were pointed fangs. He liked me watching; I could tell. He turned away and leaped atop the girl, sinking down on her neck. I saw a rivulet of red trickle across the snowy white sheets.

I looked away. It was not that I feared for the girl or hated what Martin had done. I was disturbed because my own hunger was becoming a raging desire. I knew if I stayed I would go back into those rooms, find a captive, and surrender to the very urges I fought.

With a growing fear, I hurried out of the viewing room and rushed toward the steps. I had put my foot on the first riser when a hand roughly grasped my arm. I spun around. It was Rogue.

"What do you want?" I cried.

"What do *you* want?" he echoed as he pulled me from the stairs and close to him.

"I'm not in the mood to play games," I said, drawing back. "I'm going home."

"No, you're not," he said firmly.

"Who do you think—" I started to say when his mouth came down on mine.

He knew all along what would happen. Perhaps I did too, and that was why I disliked him so much. When our lips met, the world exploded in sparks as if two electric wires touched. My resistance melted. My whole body burst into flame.

A part of me still wanted to run away from him, from this. I was about to be married to Fitz. I owed him my loyalty. But in that moment, it didn't matter. That's not an excuse for what I did. It was just that I couldn't have stopped Rogue—or myself—once our bodies touched.

We sank down onto the floor. He pulled off my coat and sweater; I unzipped his jeans. With urgent movements our clothes fell away until there was only our bodies, skin to skin, as we knelt before each other there on the hallway floor. He ground his mouth into mine again as he pushed me down.

There was nothing poetic about our joining. There was no foreplay, no finesse, no games, no kisses. Rogue rammed himself into me. I was nearly mad with passion, driven over the edge of reason by sex and desire and something more: the way we fit. We came together as if we had been designed to mesh, as if we were pieces of a puzzle made to join. I didn't know where his body stopped and mine began. We stopped being two and became one.

He stroked hard. I rode him with every thrust. We gave and took, going "Uh, uh, uh," until Rogue cried out and came in great, long shudders. I began to quiver then, climaxing in his arms.

We said nothing when it was over. I picked up my clothes and put them on. He dressed and went to walk away. I had reached the stairs when he spoke.

"Daphne," he called to me.

I stopped.

"Take it for what it was," he said. "We're two of a kind. I knew it from the minute I saw you busting heads in that bar. You knew it too. You just didn't want to admit it. No matter how much you pretend, you can't change what you are."

Then he turned back toward the darkened lounge and was gone.

CHAPTER 16

Were it not better to forget
Than but remember and regret?

— Letitia Elizabeth Landon, *Despondency*

The night offered no comfort. I hurried out of the club onto the cracked sidewalks of Second Avenue. A damp wind was blowing from the East River. I glanced back at the garish red neon sign of Lucifer's Laundromat blinking on and off. The words came out of my mouth with something between a scream and a sob: *"I am not like you!"*

But perhaps I was. I had tried to cut the sexual hungers out of me and cauterize my desire for blood. I had failed, even knowing those carnal passions were not the way to happiness; they led only to tears.

"Daphne?" A familiar voice spoke to me. I turned to see Cormac. "It's not my scene either," he said.

I nodded and gave my oldest friend a trembling smile. We had met in Regency England two centuries ago. We were rivals then, often competing for the same lover. A dilettante and a denizen of gambling hells and brothels, he dressed in silks and velvets and frittered away his time. I, calling myself Lady Daphne, was in search of a poetic heart to feed upon and had found Byron.

Both Cormac and I had had our season in purgatory;

neither of us really wished to go back again. I felt better seeing him now, knowing I didn't have to explain myself to someone who had known me so long.

"I was thinking," he said, "we should go down to see if we can spot those guys around Church and Cortlandt streets. It's about the right time of night."

"And if we see them, what then? We can't capture them without endangering the girls' lives." I put my hands in my pockets and considered his suggestion.

"We just watch them. See what rabbit hole they tumble into. I borrowed Benny's camera phone. We might get a photo opportunity."

"Okay, let's go." I walked into the street and flagged down a Yellow Cab.

The streets were filled with ghosts. We climbed out of the cab on Church Street, near the viewing area for the World Trade Center site. Here, in proximity to where the Twin Towers fell, I felt as if the spirits of the dead wandered about, so crowding the sidewalks that I hesitated to move. But when I started forward, they vanished.

I imagined that Cormac saw them too. His face was solemn and filled with grief. He melted away from the streetlights and drew into the shadows of a building. I followed him. We glanced over at the entrance to the R line of the subway. The station, closed since the terrorist attack on 9/11, had only recently reopened.

Surely, down there in the vast connecting caverns, behind a hastily repaired wall or a forgotten door, was the way to the Hudson Terminal. Tonight we had little time and too much territory to cover to begin to search. Perhaps some of the marauding vampires from Lucifer's Laudromat were already combing the area . . . those who were not mindlessly pursuing pleasure in the orgy at the club.

Having both of us conduct this surveillance was a smart move, even if it was unplanned. A man and woman attracted less suspicion than a single person of either sex. Now I clung to Cormac's arm as if we were a couple out late, perhaps stopping for some final kisses before we headed home.

Only amateurs stand around in doorways or sit in parked cars; they're not places people wait around. Choosing a position near a subway entrance with a clear view in both directions, Cormac and I stayed in plain sight like the purloined letter, too commonplace to be noticed. We talked in whispers and played the role of lovers reluctant to part as we waited and watched on this street haunted by souls far more lost than myself.

We didn't have to wait long.

Two men turned the corner onto Church Street and walked in our direction. They were laden down with white plastic grocery bags and almost staggering under the weight. One looked like a college kid, dressed in jeans that were falling off his ass, the crotch down to his knees. He had on an over-size jacket, and the bling around his neck glinted every now and then in the streetlights. The other man was older, bearded, and dressed carefully in a nice sport jacket and well-tailored slacks.

My heart speeded up. They fit the description that Jo-Jo had provided perfectly. Cormac feigned making a call on Benny's mobile phone.

The men approached our position near the subway steps. I could see the younger man clearly. His nose had a high bridge and flaring nostrils; his mouth was petulant and drawn down in a frown. He definitely could be Middle Eastern. The other man held his chin up and kept his thin lips pursed. His face was elongated and dominated by a broad nose that made him look like a camel with a bad attitude.

Nevertheless, his skin was pale, his hair blondish, and he was clearly Caucasian. That was a surprise.

"That's got to be them," I whispered to Cormac. He shrugged and captured them on the screen as they passed. We stepped out onto the sidewalk to follow them using a loose tail; in other words, we hung back as far as necessary to avoid detection. We ran some risk of losing them by letting them get a full block ahead of us, but if they spotted us, they might relocate the girls again or retaliate by harming their captives.

Cormac stayed on one side of the street, and I crossed over to the other. We stayed close to the buildings as we walked, trying to remain inconspicuous. I kept expecting the two men to descend into one of the subway entrances. They didn't. They walked up Church, past Fulton, past Vesey, and turned left onto Barclay Street. When they disappeared around the corner, I made sure Cormac went ahead of me. There was always a risk of ambush. If I hung back, I wouldn't be caught in it. Instead I could provide backup. But when I too turned onto Barclay Street the men were still hurrying along in the distance, and they were not paying much attention to their surroundings.

These two men had no street sense at all, and they clearly weren't New Yorkers. Here they were, out very late on city streets with their hands full of groceries. They were not prepared to defend themselves if attacked. They were easy prey for muggers, and even easier targets for us. That was further proof we were dealing with amateurs, political idealists who were cruel and clumsy, but didn't know a lot about hiding their tracks. Having a professional criminal like Rogue on our team gave us an advantage, as did the skills of deception, disguise, and evasion that all vampires have to develop to survive.

Now the men walked past the entrance to the Eighth

Avenue subway line. They crossed the street in midblock and went straight into the entrance of an old office building. Had we been wrong all along and the girls were being held in a vacant office?

Cormac walked past the building and took up a position where he could see the doorway. I did the same on the approach. Minutes passed slowly. The street stayed completely empty except for Cormac and me; not a single pedestrian passed by and only two vehicles, both taxis.

After fifteen minutes, my feet started to ache in my peep-toe pumps, which were not made for spies doing a stakeout. I signaled to Cormac that I wanted to leave and noticed he took several pictures of the building before rejoining me. He caught up with me, and we went straight to a subway entrance, stopping to talk only when we were halfway down the stairs. Had we stopped on the street and those men reappeared, even amateurs would figure out we had been tailing them.

"What do you think?" he asked as we stood on the stairs, leaning on the railing.

"I think they had to be our guys. The only thing that doesn't fit is why they didn't go into the subways. But maybe we were wrong that the girls are in the tunnels," I said.

Cormac shook his head. "No, the hostages have to be down there. Why else would those guys, assuming they're the terrorists, be in this neighborhood at all? Either they have a supply depot set up in the building or they went through it and out the back. That's what I think, anyway."

"You're probably right, but we can't risk going into the building. There's nothing else we can do tonight. Let's call it quits for now," I replied. With that Cormac headed for his Village apartment. I found a cab on the nearly deserted streets and began the long ride home.

*   *   *

Except for my animals, the apartment was empty. I had entered cautiously, looking around before I came in. No one was hiding behind the door. Nothing was out of place.

And I was relieved Fitz wasn't there. I didn't want to face him tonight. My head said I shouldn't have had that quick fuck with Rogue, but the fact that I wasn't eaten up with guilt bothered me. If I were honest with myself, I'd have to admit I wasn't feeling comfortable about being answerable to anybody about what I did. And worse for someone about to make a lifelong—and a very long lifelong—commitment to another person, if I were honest with myself, I'd have to say something had happened in the encounter with Rogue that didn't when Fitz touched me.

In the empty apartment, I felt like my own person again. And I felt safe. I had left a note for Mickey, the doorman, asking him if I had any unusual callers yesterday. But by now, I was positive the whole intruder thing had been my imagination. Both the dog walker and Fitz had been in my apartment, and either of them could have trodden on the CD. Jade could have knocked the coin on the floor. I'd have to take another look around for it. It could have been knocked under the couch. I was being paranoid. Just the same, I planned to set the alarm so I could talk to the dog walker when she showed up later this morning.

I didn't stay alive over four centuries as a fugitive by being careless.

I glanced over at the telephone and noticed the message light was not blinking. I was a little surprised that Fitz hadn't called, but when I walked into the kitchen, a dozen dark red roses sat in a vase on the counter. Another velvet box from Cartier and a card propped against it sat next to them. My chest felt tight and filled with a dull pain.

Jade, whose bed was next to the refrigerator, thumped her tail hopefully. I said, "We'll go out in a minute," as I went for the box. I lifted the lid. A ruby ring set in platinum with two round diamonds on either side glittered against the satin. I opened the card and read, *To the future Mrs. Fitzmaurice. With my undying love, Fitz.*

I picked up the vase of roses and Fitz's card. I carried them out of my apartment into the hall. I opened the trash chute and dropped them in. Then I went back into my apartment and put the Cartier box with the ruby ring in my computer drawer.

The pain inside me lessened.

"Come on, Jade," I said. "Let's enjoy what's left of the night."

After Jade's walk, I took a shower so hot that my skin was deep pink when I toweled off. I put on a pair of cowboy-print pajamas and stretched out on the couch. I made sure the drapes were drawn tight and set a travel alarm for ten. I decided to read for a while and thumbed through the latest Neiman Marcus catalog, dog-earing a few pages to order from at a later time. I picked up a catalog from the J. Peterman Company next and found a *dévoré* Victorian blouse that I just had to have.

My emotions thus soothed by shopping therapy, I turned out the light and drifted into a light sleep.

The buzzing alarm jarred me into wakefulness. I resisted the urge to hit the snooze button. My body ached. My mind was foggy with the need to sleep. I felt foolish for sacrificing my rest to question the dog walker. But as I was awake, or at least partially awake, I might as well wait for her to appear.

I propped myself up to a semiprone position and felt around for the TV remote. I wanted to see the Weather Channel. I needed to know what to wear tonight when, I hoped, we would be swooping down on the abandoned terminals in the rescue mission. I hoped, but wasn't going to count on it.

The forecast called for clouds, then thunderstorms, starting tonight and extending into tomorrow. "April showers bring May flowers," the meteorologist quipped. "But flowers may be blooming late in the metropolitan area. Once the rain stops, a cold front will drop down from Canada, bringing a threat of a frost."

If I believed in omens, I'd say the cold and damp did not bode well. I don't know of one good thing that ever happened on a rainy night.

I heard the key turning in the lock a short time after ten a.m., same as yesterday. I clicked off the TV. "Hello? Anybody here?" a young man's voice called out. The sound hit Jade's "on" switch, and she started barking and leaping around in a frenzy.

"Yes, I'm here in the living room. Hang on a minute," I yelled over the noise, instantly regretting not having at least thrown on a robe over my PJ's, with their pattern of rodeo cowboys lassoing broncos. I headed for the kitchen to get Jade on a lead. She was usually friendly to people as long as I was present, but I didn't want to take a chance.

"Okay, come on in," I called out.

A long-haired punker wearing black corduroy golf knickers and high-top sneakers peeked his head in from the hallway. "Hi," he said. He had tattoos on every inch of exposed flesh, including his neck.

"Who are you? Where's the regular woman?" I asked.

"I'm Jamie. Marva quit. Okay to come in?"

"Sure, Jade's tied. About the gray-haired lady, though—I just saw her yesterday."

"Yeah, well, it was sudden-like. She came back from her daily runs and announced it was her last day. Left us shorthanded. Don't worry; I'll be able to fit your dog in. I've got another client in this building."

"Did Marva give a reason? She's the only dog walker I've ever used. She never missed." Suddenly my paranoia about someone having been in my apartment was back, stronger than ever.

"She said she came into some money. She was going to the West Coast. Seattle, I think. But really, you don't have to worry. I get along good with dogs. See, your malamute has stopped barking. If she didn't trust me, I probably wouldn't get past the door."

He was right about that. The intruder would have had to get past Jade, and a stranger couldn't do that. If a stranger had been in here, that person had to be with somebody Jade knew. I didn't know what to think except that I'd better make time to talk to Mickey the doorman.

I asked Jamie to wait while I called the dog-walking service. I spoke to the owner, and she confirmed what Jamie had said. She said he was great with dogs and not to be put off by how he looked. His clients—owners and dogs—loved him, but she'd send someone else if I preferred.

I told her all I cared about was that he was reliable. She said he'd been with them for five years, longer than anyone, and had never lost a dog.

"Okay, Jamie, you're hired," I said after I hung up. Jade sniffed Jamie and checked him out. He must have a good scent, because she went with him without hesitation. I went over to the intercom and called down to the lobby.

"Mickey? Daphne Urban in ten-B."

"Yeah, Ms. Urban?"

"I left you a note. Did you get it?"

"Yeah."

"Who did you let up to my apartment yesterday?"

"Just the usual people."

"Which ones?"

There was a long silence.

"Mickey, I'm not accusing you of anything; I just need to know," I said into the wall unit. Other tenants had complained that Mickey sometimes dozed off at his desk, especially if he stayed for a double shift. It was a touchy subject with him.

"Well, your boyfriend—the newest one, the tall Irish guy. He was here a couple of times."

"Anybody else?"

"Let me think. The dog walker, of course, and come to think of it, she had her helper with her. Said he was some kind of trainee. He was here yesterday, yeah."

"This guy. Was he young? Punk type?"

"Nah. This was a way older dude. Long hair in a ponytail. I think his name was George."

George! I thought. *Goddamn. My mother must have sent him.* "Tell me something, Mickey. Did you happen to notice his hands?" I asked.

"Come to think of it, yeah. When he pushed the button for the elevator. Only had half a finger."

CHAPTER 17

Who ran to help me when I fell,
And would some pretty story tell,
Or kiss the place to make it well?
My mother.

—Ann Taylor, *Original Poems for Infant Minds*

I knew why my mother had sent her favorite gofer to enter my apartment. She intended to know if and when I bit Fitz. I understood her methods all too well. I went looking for surveillance cameras.

A tiny audio device had been hidden in the lamp on the end table in the living room. I pulled it out and threw it. It bounced off the wall and ended up on the rug, unharmed. I picked it up and shoved it into the garbage disposal. I found a tiny and very sophisticated camera in the bedroom up near the ceiling—aimed at my bed. I tore it down. Using the stacked heel of one of my Manolo Blahnik boots as a hammer, I smashed it to dust.

I was seeing the world through a red haze. Blood throbbed in my temples. I tore off my stupid cowboy pajamas and put on jeans, a black cotton turtleneck, and my Frye boots. I pulled my hair back into a knot and scrubbed my face. Then I went to the refrigerator and pulled some steaks out of the meat drawer to mix into Jade's dinner. I was chopping the hell out of them with a butcher knife when the dog walker came back.

"Any of your people named George? Anybody new?" I snapped as I snatched Jade's leash from him.

The kid edged back toward the door, his eyes bugging out of his head. "George?" he bleated. "No Georges. We have a Harold, a semiretired guy. Why? You want him to come tomorrow?" he asked hopefully.

I realized I was waving the butcher knife around wildly. "Sorry about that," I said, and put it down on the kitchen counter. In a calm, soft voice I said, "I heard you had somebody named George working for you, that's all. Jade seems to like you. Come back same time tomorrow, okay?"

He started to rush for the door. "Hold up a minute," I yelled after him. He stopped.

I went to my purse and got out a twenty-dollar bill. The dog walker shrank back a bit as I stuffed it in his breast pocket.

"Thanks, but I gotta go," he said, and beat a hasty retreat into the hall. "I have a rottie in eight-C. If I'm late, he pees on the rug." He hurried toward the elevator. I didn't know what he thought about my mood swings. Maybe he figured I had a bad case of PMS.

I had a bad case of MMS—Meddling Mother Syndrome. I was so frigging pissed off I knew I couldn't go back to sleep, but I couldn't get hold of Mar-Mar until after sundown. It would be a waste of time even to try.

I was pacing back and forth in the living room like a caged animal when Fitz showed up around five. He was carrying takeout from La Rosita, a Cuban restaurant over on Broadway. He paused to give me a kiss on his way to the dining room.

"Filet mignon *salteado very* rare for you. The Friday special, *bacalao guisado,* for me. I feel guilty if I don't eat fish on Friday, despite Vatican Two. What's the matter?" I had turned my face so he kissed my cheek, not my lips.

"You don't want to know," I said.

"Must be your mother," he said, setting the take-out bag down on the table. "I recognize the look. Delores always brings it out in me. What did Mar-Mar do? Tap your phone?"

I raised an eyebrow. "You're close. She sneaked a surveillance camera in here."

"No kidding," he said, and proceeded into the kitchen to get us some plates, utensils, and a couple of glasses. "I think she's got Delores beat. Worst thing my mother ever did was hire a private detective to see if I was dating this Jewish girl. That was back when I went to Harvard."

"So you think I shouldn't be so upset?" I asked.

"I didn't say that," he called in from the kitchen. "You should be. She invaded your privacy—and mine, I guess. But you told me she had actually staked out your building, back when you were seeing Darius. I figured she might pull something like this."

He came back in and arranged two place settings, took my hand, and pulled me over to a chair. "Come on, eat something. You'll feel better if you go to work with something in your stomach. I know, I know—blood is your thing, but you do enjoy meat now and then."

I sat while Fitz plated my steak. From another bag he pulled out a bottle of red wine from Montepulciano.

"None for me. I've got to work tonight," I said, and put my hand over my glass.

"Actually, the Pellegrino is for you." He pulled a green bottle of mineral water out of the bag. "It's chilled. I bought the wine because it seemed appropriate. I have a suggestion."

"About what?"

"I don't know if you remember, but the first time we met, at the Kevin St. James, I told you I was going to Ireland this spring and might want to take a side trip down to Tuscany. You said you had a villa there, in Montespertoli."

"I remember. Of course I remember. I remember everything about that night."

"Well, I'm still going to Ireland. In two weeks, as a matter of fact. Why don't you fly over and meet me? If it's something you'd like to do, we can honeymoon at your villa."

My fork stopped in midair. "What are you saying?"

"I'm saying we get married simply. No big wedding—for a lot of reasons, our respective mothers topping the list of why it would be a nightmare. We just get a priest—you are Catholic, right?—and do it." He looked at me. "Are you disappointed?"

"Hell, no! I'm relieved. But you're talking about a honeymoon in two weeks?"

"Three. I'll have business in Dublin for a week. We can get married before I leave, say, a week from Friday. Ask Benny if you'd like to. Cormac too. I'd like my cousin Mike to be there. But that's it, no major production."

His eyes were shining. He reached out and took my hand. "You're trembling," he said.

"To tell the truth, I'm scared to death," I said.

"I think that's normal. I pretty much sprang this on you. We don't have to rush into it, but—"

"No. No, we do. I mean, it's for the best, the sooner we're married. And the sooner you're . . . you're—"

"A vampire. Yes. Then maybe your mother won't feel the need to spy on us."

"Yeah, she's not really a voyeur, just thorough. She doesn't take anyone at their word, even me."

"It stands to reason. She needs to make sure you actually go through with biting me. Not that we would fake it, but we could." He uncorked the Montepulciano, poured it into his glass, and drank it fast.

"I think she'd know if we tried that," I said. "But you're probably right. To change the subject for a minute, did you take a small silver coin from Saudi Arabia off the end table yesterday?"

"No, why? Have you lost one?"

"I didn't lose it. I think my mother's Sancho Panza stole it when he set up the cameras. But it wasn't worth anything. Why would he do it?"

Fitz was pouring himself a second glass of wine. "A crime of opportunity, I guess. He saw it. He picked it up. Some people are naturally thieves. Or was it something your mother might want?"

It was true I hadn't told J or Mar-Mar about the coin, and it did have to do with the mission. "Maybe," I said. "I'll ask her anyway—after I tell her what I think about her latest stunt."

Fitz downed the second glass of wine and started on the third. He wasn't looking at me when he asked, "So when do you want to . . . I mean, when should we work on the . . . the . . ."

I knew what he was trying to ask. I stood up, my steak untouched. "Oh, not for a couple of days. In fact, I've got to hustle. I have a briefing at six thirty. I'm pretty sure I'm working all weekend. Maybe Monday, okay? You'll have all your strength back by then. And we'll have plenty of time before you leave for Ireland to finish it up."

"Right." He looked up at me. "But I'd like to be married before the last time, okay? I need that commitment. Do you understand?"

I leaned down and kissed him, first on the forehead; then, when he shut his eyes, I kissed each eyelid. "I know. And thank you. For the ruby ring. I understood what it meant."

I started for the bathroom to put on makeup before I left for the office. "But I'm not sure about getting a priest to perform the wedding. My baptismal record is about four hundred years old, and I'm not really comfortable in a church."

"Is the church absolutely out?" he called after me. "It can't be a Catholic ceremony if we hold it anywhere else."

I peeked my head out of the bathroom, a mascara wand in my hand. "I can probably handle it as long as it's not a Mass. Is a Catholic wedding that important to you?"

Fitz paused a moment. "Yes. It is. One of my cousins is a monsignor. He already said he'd do it. He's at St. Patrick's, okay?"

Fitz's family had enormous political power. Evidently they had pull in the Church too. "Well, as long as we're going to do it, why not go first-class?" I said lightly. In truth my head was spinning, and I felt downright nauseous at the very thought.

A breakthrough of sorts had occurred by the time I showed up at the evening's briefing at the Flatiron Building. Cormac was so excited he must have been watching the door to tell me the second I walked in.

"Guess what!" he said before I even sat down. "Guess who that guy is!"

"Huh? What guy? Back up a minute, okay?" I made sure I noticed where Rogue was seated and headed for the other end of the table.

"The guy we spotted last night. Down on Church Street. The older man. I e-mailed the photo to J, and you'll never guess who it is."

"That's true," I said, folding myself into a seat. "I haven't a clue. Should I?"

"None of us guessed," Benny broke in.

"Okay, tell me," I said. "Who's the older man?"

"Tell her, J," Cormac said, looking over at our boss, who had a manila folder in his hands.

He glanced down at his notes, then said, "The younger man in the photo is Rashid Rida. The older man is his uncle, his deceased mother's brother, a British subject of mixed Yemeni and English ancestry who's been in this country for a decade. His name is Clarence Roberts."

"Clarence Roberts? Wasn't he the butler at the Rockefeller estate? You're kidding me," I said.

"No, I'm not. We've made positive identification, then ran a background check. We found the connection to Rashid."

"How could the FBI miss that? I mean, they had that guy right there." I shook my head. I'd heard of screwups, but this one stunned me.

"To cut them some slack, this guy had been hurt, and pretty badly hurt, during the abduction. There were no red flags. He was white, middle-class, and had worked for the Rockefeller estate management company for years. No criminal record. Nothing to tie him to the terrorists. He wasn't an American, true, but he was British. He came highly recommended. He had gone to medical school but dropped out before he did his residency. Then he went to butler school. Now that we've taken a closer look it's a different story, of course."

"What did you find? Anything helpful?" I queried.

"Very. So congratulations to you and Cormac. Roberts belongs to a mosque up in Buffalo, a radical Islamic sect. He was affiliated with the same group in London. We obtained a list of other members and, showing photos to the catering staff, we've pretty much nailed down the identities of the kidnappers, all of them."

"So where does that leave us? Any closer to getting the girls back?" I asked.

"Maybe. Thanks to Rogue's suggestion, a videotape was delivered to the Morrises this afternoon. All the girls were on there, holding last night's edition of the *Post*."

"How did they look?" Rogue asked. I tried to look at him without being obvious. It's funny how a fuck changes one's opinion of a person. I sort of liked him, I thought. I liked his body, anyway, even if his manners weren't my style.

"Tired. Pretty upset. Nicoletta, the girl who lost the ear, had her head bandaged. She looked ill. It looked as if someone were holding her up."

Rogue nodded. "At least she's still alive. Like I said to Judge Morris, I have believed all along that these men intend to kill the girls if they think the government is stalling them. I think we've got to move faster than we have been. Time's running out."

"We're moving as quickly as we can. The Morrises are raising hell; all the families are. Several of the parents are staying at the Morrises', waiting for the next call from the kidnappers. We're going to try to set up the delivery of the diamonds and the Buffalo for tomorrow night. The kidnappers want it dropped out in Hempstead at Mitchel Field," J said.

"Tell me about the location," I said.

"It's an abandoned air force base a little south of LaGuardia International Airport. It's been shut down for years, officially, anyway. The CIA has used it from time to time. There are several massive hangars still out there."

Audrey had been silent throughout the discussion so far. In the dim light, shadows played across her face, emphasizing her cheekbones. She took off her thick eyeglasses, revealing doelike eyes, their lashes long, their irises a golden brown. For a moment she was beautiful. Then she slipped the glasses back on and spoke. "I know something about the field. It's an old air base, and not much of it is left. Most of it was taken over by Nassau County Community College. I can get a diagram of the access roads and where the remaining hangars are."

Rogue was shaking his head. "Why do they want the vehicle out there? Something doesn't add up. I don't see how the terrorists can get the vehicle out of the U.S. So where are they going to go with it once they get it? Where are they going to keep it?"

I was listening and trying to make the scenario make sense. I kept thinking about J's description of it being a little south of LaGuardia Airport. "Audrey, how close is it to LaGuardia?"

"Next door, really. What's left of the Mitchel Field runways are adjacent to the commercial airfield. I have to check it out, but I think there's a road linking the two fields."

"Shit," I burst out. "I have a hunch what the terrorists are going to do with the Buffalo once they get it."

"What are you thinking?" Benny said.

"I'm thinking they don't care about hiding the Buffalo or trying to escape in it. They know we're going to try to stop them. They're not stupid. They just want it for a short period of time, a window of opportunity—fifteen or twenty minutes while we scramble around trying to get to the girls—because they've planned a suicide mission. I think—no, I'm nearly positive—they're going to drive the Buffalo onto LaGuardia's runway and crash an airliner during takeoff." Suddenly it all made sense to me. Everything clicked into place.

"Why LaGuardia and not a bigger airport?" I said, my voice excited. "Because it's doable. Terrorists would never get onto a runway at JFK, but from Mitchel Field, they *can* get access to LaGuardia. Nobody would think of an attack coming from there. The plane will be filled with fuel. It will kill everybody on board and maybe some people on the ground. It has all the earmarks of an Al Qaeda operation."

Cormac's face was long and drawn. He was aimlessly doodling on the yellow pad in front of him. "We're not going to have any room for error on whatever we do." He looked up. "How is this ransom-for-prisoner exchange supposed to be handled?"

"Morris and the kidnappers are still going back and forth on that," J said. "The terrorists' terms are that we leave the Buffalo and the diamonds at Mitchel Field. Then they'll release the girls. Morris says no deal until we get a guarantee they will be unharmed. The terrorists say we have no choice but to do it their way. Right now we're throwing out the idea of a videophone situation, where we have live observation of the girls as the terrorists pick up the ransom. But I don't know how it's going to work yet," J answered.

"However it plays out, we need to be in the Buffalo. The hard part will be making sure the hostages aren't put in jeopardy," I said.

Everybody nodded in agreement.

"I think we need to spend tonight trying to locate the girls. That's our priority," Audrey said. "I came up with some more information on the Hudson Terminal. I think it will help us. Listen. The old platforms are under the Cortlandt Street Station, the one that just reopened. What used to be the one-train line—those tracks at Cortlandt Street are twenty feet beneath the street level. The old IRT tracks are at forty feet. The PATH trains running now are at sixty feet. The old terminal is *eighty* feet down, right in the bedrock."

"And that's where they've got the girls," Rogue said, smacking the table with his fist. "All the goddamn way down there."

We agreed to head downtown and try to find a way into the old PATH station. Audrey offered to stop at the Laundromat and see where other vampires had been looking to try to save us time.

We left the conference room and crowded into the elevator car. Rogue hadn't so much as spoken directly to me the entire night. I didn't know what I expected. But after you've fucked your brains out with somebody less than a day earlier, maybe "hello."

Now I squeezed between Benny and Audrey to get to the other side of the car from where he stood. Two could play his game. I ignored him, refusing even to look in his direction. Instead, I tried to focus on the mission ahead. There must be some way to narrow our search and save us some time. A thought occurred to me.

"Audrey," I said. "We saw these two guys go into a commercial building. I know you can get into the subway system from inside dozens of office buildings in Midtown. Were there any entrances to the PATH terminal from inside a building?"

"Sure. Had to be." She nodded. "The original Hudson Terminal had a huge skyscraper over it. They tore that down when they built the World Trade Center. I bet there are plenty of other buildings that connect to all the subway lines that converge right there."

"Then we have to start at that building where Cormac and I saw Rashid and his uncle go." By that time the elevator had stopped at the dark and empty lobby. "But I have to go home first and get something. I have an idea."

"What?" Cormac asked as we all got off.

"Think about it. What creatures live down in those subway tunnels? Rats. If there's a way into those old tunnels from that building, my rat, Gunther, might find it. And I'm bringing Jade too."

I turned to my dancer friend. "You're in the best shape of all of us. Take the stairs—it will be faster—and catch J before he leaves the office. See if he has anything from either Morris girl. Something with their scent."

"Sure," Cormac said, and took off running. The rest of us stood around in the lobby. Rogue started to walk toward me, so I deliberately turned my back on him and went over to the glass doors, the ones on the Fifth Avenue side. I stood there staring out at the street, but in truth I wasn't seeing anything.

Rogue spoke from somewhere close behind me. "What's wrong with you tonight?"

I looked over my shoulder at him. "What makes you think anything's wrong?"

"I could hear you grinding your teeth in the elevator all the way down to the lobby. You're not pissed off, are you? Just because we had sex last night?"

"You mean am I pissed off because you act as if it never happened?" I said, and looked away.

He took my arm and turned me around to face him. His hand felt good where it touched my flesh. His face was very close to mine. I could feel the heat from his body. I couldn't help but look into his eyes.

Then he said, "I told you to take it for what it was. I was trying to make a point."

"What!" I shook my arm free and glared at him. "You had sex with me *to make a point*?"

"Hey, it was good sex. I'm not knocking it. But you didn't think it was because I was attracted to you, did you? You act like you're better than the rest of us. I just wanted to prove that if I was willing, you'd fuck me."

My whole body began to shake. Blood drained from my face. "You are a jerk, you know that? I must have been out of my mind. Well, fool me once. It will never happen again; believe me."

Rogue laughed. "Honey, one thing I've learned in life: Never say never."

"You conceited . . . asshole! I don't even want to be around you."

He laughed again. "You'd better get over it, because we're going to be seeing a lot of each other for a while."

I stalked away and went to rejoin Benny and Audrey, who naturally had been watching.

"What?" I said in response to Benny's questioning look.

"Well, don't be mad at me because Rogue's pulling your chain," she said. Then she leaned toward me and put her mouth close to my ear. "Beat him at his own game, sugar; that's my advice," she whispered.

"What are you saying?" I asked quietly.

"I mean he's a *man,* sugar. He doesn't think with the head that's got brains in it. Get him going; then leave him hanging, you know," she said sotto voce.

I smiled. "That's a damned good idea, my friend."

Just then Cormac burst from the door to the stairs, holding up a glassine envelope. It was Deborah's Princeton tiger key chain, the one she had taken when she borrowed Abby's car key. He handed it to me.

"Perfect!" I said. "Where should I meet you all?"

Rogue said, "I'd like to walk around the area between Church and Chambers."

Cormac nodded. "Okay. We all stay in the vicinity of the new Cortlandt Street subway entrance. We don't want to be just hanging around the office building until you get there."

"Okay. Give me an hour. I've got to call a car service that will let me transport Jade."

We started for the lobby door on the Broadway side when Benny's cell phone rang. She flipped it open. "Hold up a minute," she said to us. "It's J."

She listened silently for a minute. Then I heard her say, "Are you sure? I understand. I'll tell them." She flipped the phone shut. Her face looked pale.

"A body's been found. Dumped on the viewing platform for the Twin Towers. It's a girl. They think it's Toni Duke, the youngest kidnap victim. But they're not sure. She's been beheaded."

CHAPTER 18

Great blunders are often made, like large ropes,
of a multitude of fibers.

—Victor Hugo, *Les Misérables*

A heavy downpour swept across the blue-and-white police cars that blocked the streets around the World
Trade Center site. I could see them in front of me as I
climbed out of the car service's black Lincoln on Church
Street. I had Jade on a lead and Gunther in my backpack
when I dashed for a doorway.

Pedestrians without umbrellas were hurrying along hugging the buildings, trying to avoid getting soaked. Space
was tight, people bumped shoulders, tempers were short. I
couldn't stay in this cramped alcove for long; I was getting
a lot of dirty looks for taking up so much space with my
huge dog.

I pulled my cell phone out of my backpack without disturbing Gunther and hunched over with my back to the street
to call Benny and locate the team. She answered, telling me
she was hanging out near the stairs to the uptown subway
about a block away. The other team members were with
Rogue while he wandered around. I said I'd be right down
and clicked off.

As Ben Franklin aptly said, " 'Tis many a slip twixt cup

and lip." I was soon unavoidably delayed. When I turned around to leave the doorway, my exit was blocked by an angry-looking man. Not just any man: Lt. Moses Johnson was scowling at me. Rain dripped off his hat and ran down the shoulders of his raincoat.

"Hello, Lieutenant," I said.

"Fancy meeting you here," he said. "You want to tell me what you know about the killing?"

"Why should I know anything about it?" I asked him, keeping Jade close to my side, although she wanted to rub her big head against his hand.

"You're here, aren't you? What is that, a coincidence? Not in my book. I have some questions to ask you. My car's over there. Let's go."

We ran though the rain, which was being swept sideways by the wind. Johnson pulled the back door open, and I put Jade in before racing around the car to get in the front seat.

Johnson was already in the driver's side. He had taken off his sodden hat and put it on the dashboard. He pulled a napkin from a McDonald's bag and blotted his face. Then he looked at me. "Let's not play games. We have a dead girl, beheaded, tentatively identified as Antoinette Duke. She was a debutante from up near Tuxedo Park. Now, I know and you know that ten society girls got snatched last Sunday from that same county. Since then, you and some other spooks have been running all over the city trying to find them.

"But you didn't find them. You had some harebrained notion they were under the Queensborough Bridge, so you searched it. Turns out it wasn't such a bad idea. We went in too. You think we didn't see what was scratched on the wall?"

"I figured you'd see it," I conceded.

"Luckily I knew enough to get the brass to call Washington. I caught hell, though. And we're still being shut out. So tell me, what happened? Why was one of the girls dumped down here?"

I stared at the raindrops running down the windshield. "Because these animals have a sick sense of humor. They're pushing our noses in it—that we didn't stop them after nine-eleven."

"So this girl is definitely one of the kidnapped kids?" he asked.

"She is if she's Toni Duke."

"And the perps are increasing the pressure to get the ransom, right?"

"Right."

"So what are you doing here tonight? You knew the place would be crawling with cops." He looked at me hard.

I finally turned my head and met his dark, sad eyes. "Same thing you are. Looking around."

He stared at me. His face changed and got hard. "I don't think so. Not with your dog."

"Believe what you want to, Lieutenant," I said.

"Look, lady, let's face facts. You have a problem. Your people have been able to keep this whole deal out of the papers. How, I don't know. But that's over. How long do you think it's going to take a good reporter to get to that girl's family?"

"I don't know. A day?" I said. I had to give it to Johnson— I always had to give it to Johnson—he was smart.

"Okay, you have maybe a day, max, before it's blown. Your whole mission. Why waste any more time cutting me out of this?"

I didn't answer. I was trying to think. I might as well take some time to cogitate; I wasn't going anyplace. I was stuck in this car for pretty much as long as Johnson wanted me here. "What's your offer?" I finally said.

"Level with me. Cut me in. And if I need to bring in my people, let me."

"I'm not authorized—"

"Miss Urban, don't bullshit me. You're a loose cannon. You don't get clearance from anybody. Neither do your friends. You're rogues, all of you."

That was why, when Benny spotted me from her position at the bottom of the subway entrance stairwell at the southeast corner of Cortlandt and Church, I wasn't alone. I had made my decision. I told Johnson everything, including the story about Cormac and me trailing the two men to the building on Barclay Street and how the whole team had come down to check it out. Now the lieutenant walked down the stairs right behind me.

"I thought you got lost, sugar, but I see you just picked up some company. Hi, Looie," she said, and smiled.

Johnson nodded, barely moving his head.

"You've come to help us out, I guess. It was terrible about that girl. Just terrible. Did Daph tell you why we're here?"

"Yeah. Wild-goose chase, probably," he said, looking around impatiently.

I explained to Benny, "The lieutenant wants to bring in forensics to that building on Barclay Street. I told him we can't risk tipping off the kidnappers that we know where they are. We need twenty-four hours; then he can do what he wants."

"And what did you say to that, Lieutenant Johnson?" she asked, mischief in her big brown eyes.

"I said I need hard evidence. I need reasonable cause to enter that building on Barclay Street. I need that picture of Clarence Roberts. Your partner here says I get it all . . . if I wait."

"Sounds like a deal, then. Oh, here come the others." She waved at the three vampires about a hundred yards away.

Cormac, Rogue, and Audrey approached from the direction of the uptown trains.

"We've got backup, I see," Cormac said when he reached us.

Rogue stopped short as the others came closer. He stared at Moses Johnson. Johnson stared back. They were like two bulldogs getting ready to fight.

"What's he doing with you?" Johnson asked, his voice almost shaking with rage.

"He's our new team member, Looie. You two know each other?" Benny asked, looking back and forth between the two of them.

"We know each other," Rogue said, keeping his distance.

"Steve's dead because of you," Johnson barked. "You're lucky you ended up in jail. It's all that saved you from me killing you."

"What are you talking about?" Cormac turned his head to the left and right between the two men.

"He's the fed who got my partner caught in a cross fire. He was working undercover, only we didn't know that. We had him tagged as a biker running drugs from the Colombians back to Texas. Steve, me, and my people were trying to close down the pipeline. His people had set up a sting operation and were planning a bust. The arrogant bastards just didn't bother to tell the NYPD about it."

"Rogue? A fed?" I said. "What are you talking about?"

"Ancient history," Rogue said.

"Look. I'm leaving," Johnson growled, and abruptly moved to go up the stairs.

"Johnson, wait," Rogue called out. "You got it wrong. Your partner knew what he was walking into. I told him who I was. Somebody set me up too. Double-crossed us both."

Johnson paused midstep. "What do you mean?"

"I didn't get your partner killed. Somebody in the agency was setting me up. I leveled with Steve earlier that day before we went in. He wanted those Colombian dealers. So did I. He knew. He said he'd go in with me and help make the bust."

Johnson's face became dark and furious. "Don't be gaming with me. You led him in there. He didn't know."

"No, listen. I can prove it. We talked. He told me he should have believed you. You didn't trust the girl, that mule. She was up to something. If he didn't tell me, how would I know that? Steve said he should have listened to you. His being there that day wasn't your fault."

"You got that right. It sure as shit wasn't my fault. It was you and the other goddamn asshole feds that got him killed."

Rogue had started to walk closer. The two men were nearly face-to-face, emotions making the air thick. Rogue's voice was solemn, and he had lost his drawl and bad grammar. "Somebody got Steve killed, but it wasn't me. I swear to you. I'm back with the agency to set it right. To find out who did it."

They weren't paying any attention to the rest of us, but I had been thrown off balance. Rogue had been a spy before? Was he a biker or not? Who gave Cormac his name as a recruit? Was my mother involved in this? I felt as if I had been hit by a brick.

Meanwhile Moses Johnson didn't move. He didn't let his anger go. His hands were balled into fists. The words poured from him. "How can I believe you? Those fuckers of yours might as well have pulled the trigger. Nobody told us shit. I would never have let him go down there that day if I knew. He went in blind."

Rogue persisted with his story. "I told you he didn't. He knew the deal, but he still wanted to try to make the bust. I didn't know I was being set up. But both of us knew it was going to be dangerous. I can prove it to you—that we talked, that I had cut him in on everything. He told me if I made it and he didn't to tell you something."

"So why didn't you? It's been four years," Johnson mocked.

"I was unavoidably detained, remember? In the shitholes of New Jersey's state prison system. What did you think, I was going to call you collect from Trenton? And frankly, since I've been out, I've been a little busy."

"Okay, what do you have? It had better be good," Johnson growled.

"Steve said if you want the Maglite he borrowed off of you, to ask Sergeant Wilson about it. He was supposed to give it back to you. Then he laughed. That make sense?"

Johnson stared at Rogue. I thought he was trying to get something straight in his head. Finally the anger seemed to leave him; his hands relaxed, and he gave his head just the slightest shake in Rogue's direction. "Son of a bitch. I always thought that was my Maglite Wilson had. Son of a bitch." Then he looked at us. "What are you staring at? Are we going to find these girls or stand here all night?"

Back up at ground level, we turned the corner to walk up Church Street. The rain was lighter now. Water ran swiftly through the gutters. Cars splashed through puddles as they passed. The crowds had thinned out. Evening morphed into night. I barely noticed, intent as I was on returning to the old office building on Barclay Street. I walked with Benny and Cormac. Rogue was hanging mostly with Audrey. Johnson kept his distance from all of us, bringing up the rear.

We had gotten as far as Vesey Street where the pavement widens into a plaza and there's plenty of open space. No longer bucking a sidewalk filled with hurrying pedestrians, we huddled together to come up with a quick plan. We couldn't go storming into the entrance of the office building like gangbusters without knowing if the terrorists were close by or not.

Since I had brought an umbrella and had been using it, I was pretty dry, but Jade was soaked. We decided I'd duck into the building with her, pretending to check out her paws or something. It was a pretty feeble ruse, but a woman with a dog wouldn't arouse suspicion.

A few minutes later, everybody walked past the Barclay Street building except me. I turned into the alcove and paused. It was going to get tricky if the outer glass doors were locked, but they weren't. I pushed one open and entered a poorly lit lobby about twelve feet square, lined by black granite walls. It was as charming as a mine shaft. A board listing tenants hung to my right. Two elevators sat to my left. A tattered, faded sign on one said, NO SELF-SERVICE AFTER SIX P.M. RING BELL FOR THE NIGHT GUARD.

I wasn't about to ring the bell, but I suspected there hadn't been any night guard in this run-down building for years. Next to the elevators was a heavy door marked STAIRS. That was it. No other doors. No hallways. It made my choice really simple.

Leaving my wet umbrella dripping by the defunct elevators, I held Jade's lead in one hand and pushed open the stairway door into the shadows and darkness beyond. Enough light from the lobby seeped in to illuminate a staircase going up and one going down. I didn't hesitate. Grasping the banister, I coaxed Jade to come with me and we went down.

I descended one flight, then reached a landing. The stairs switched back there, and kept leading downward. I could see nothing in the dark void ahead, even with my bat eyes. This interior space had no light at all.

I took a penlight from an outer pocket of my backpack. I aimed it down the flight of stairs. I started descending and had gone about six steps before the small flashlight's narrow beam picked out the rusted metal of an accordian gate that had been stretched across the bottom step. At one end the gate canted crazily where it had been bent back far enough to let a person pass through.

I flicked off the penlight and listened. I heard nothing except a low rumble, then a screech of brakes as a distant subway pulled into one of the nearby stations. I waited a minute; Jade was obediently still behind me. From inside my backpack I detected some muffled squeaks from Gunther. Then from that dark void ahead I heard other squeaks, and they weren't his.

Not bothering to flick the light back on, I got my cell phone out and flipped it open. Its screen lit up the stairwell enough for me to return to the landing above, where I had better reception. I called Benny and explained about the stairs to the subway tunnels. I told her I was going down. She said it would be better if I waited, and they'd be right there. I terminated the call and made sure I turned the cell phone off—a sudden call at the wrong time could alert the kidnappers.

I put my light on again and fished around in the back-pack's pocket for the glassine envelope Cormac had retrieved from J. Being careful not to touch the orange-and-black tiger key chain inside, I pinched it open and put it by Jade. She snuffed, snorted, and stuck her wet nose into the opening.

"Go find her, Jade," I said, not knowing if Jade would track the girl. My dog was highly intelligent. Some people even thought she possessed some of the magical powers of her former owner, a South American shaman. I reserved judgment on that, but I knew she had an uncanny under-standing of everything I said to her.

She didn't disappoint me. She began pulling me down the stairs. She squeezed by the broken gate. I had to stoop down and twist my body to get through. On the other side of that rusty barrier, I found myself in a large space. Using my light, I figured out that I was standing in a sprawling mezzanine, a remnant of a dead city below the teeming streets above.

Boarded-up shops lined one side of a wide concourse, a newspaper kiosk with its shutters drawn sat in the middle of the space, and an ironwork fence stretched from floor to ceiling about twenty feet from me, its original purpose to separate paid passengers from people who ducked into the underground to buy a Nathan's hot dog or get a shoeshine.

Jade was straining at the leash to go forward. I heard noises above me and knew the others had arrived and would be coming down the stairs in a moment. Feeling Jade's urgency, I decided not to wait. My teammates would easily spot my light and follow.

I had no idea where the concourse led, but I followed Jade's tugging. I felt we were headed south, and the floor was sloping downward. When I drew even with the ruins of a token booth, Jade darted to the right and trotted under a turnstile. I opted to climb over the top.

Once I was on the other side of it, and now behind the iron fence that stretched endlessly in either direction, I glanced behind me to see if the others were catching up. Sure enough, circles of light glimmered a few hundred feet behind me. I flicked my light on and off using a short, short, short, long pattern; one of them repeated the sequence, so I knew they spotted me.

Jade pulled me on, still going in what I believed was a southern direction. We were crossing a space so huge my narrow beam just petered out in the distance without showing me a wall or structure. I stumbled once where the floor was cracked. I felt as if I were in a cave, but I felt a cold breeze, fresh, not stale, so I knew there had to be access to the maze of Manhattan subway tunnels that converged here.

Again I stopped to check on the whereabouts of my teammates. Their lights seemed farther away than before, but I decided to keep going forward. Jade was on the scent and pulling hard. Finally a tiled wall loomed up before me, and I realized I had reached a place where several corridors branched off in different directions.

I aimed my light at the wall. Set in old mosaic tiles of sienna brown and cream were the words HUDSON TUBES & DOWNTOWN, with an arrow pointing to the right. My heart raced with excitement. Another sign said VESEY STREET EXIT and pointed straight ahead. The old Hudson Terminal should be only a block away.

I again looked behind me. This time I didn't see the lights of my cohorts, but I assumed they would spot the same directional arrow I had just seen. I wasn't concerned about them, and Jade was impatient to continue, so we trotted off in the direction that the arrow indicated. My hopes were rising. If we could locate where the girls were being held, we could rescue them—right now, tonight.

Darkness consumed the space around me as I pressed forward, focused on the idea of finding the girls. Then Jade halted. The corridor ended in a plywood wall. She started scratching at it, trying to get her paw in the narrow space left at the bottom. I shone my light around the edges of the wooden sheets and noticed that the screws had been removed along the one side nearest to the tile wall.

I stooped down at that corner and, like Jade, paid attention to the space at the bottom of the sheet. I hooked my fingers under the wood and tugged. It moved slightly. By applying as much force as I could, the plywood came away from the wall just enough to allow a person to squeeze by. I figured it would be easier on the way back, when all I'd have to do was push.

Now I gripped it tightly and held it open for Jade to pass by; then I worked my way through the opening. The rough edge of the plywood sheet scraped my shoulder and snagged

my sleeve. When I turned the light in that direction in order
to pull it free, I saw another piece of fabric hung there. I
never doubted the kidnappers had taken this route, but that
was proof.

The corridor beyond the plywood was strewn with rubble, and I could see the steel support beams in the ceiling
above my head. The debris-covered floor turned into a ramp
that slanted downward. I had to walk carefully to avoid a
nasty fall as I descended into a huge space, black emptiness
around me on all sides. The sound of my footsteps against
the cement floor resonated sharply. I could hear Jade's
breathing and occasionally the squeals of subway trains
braking as they came and went.

The ramp switched back and kept descending until it
ended on a platform. I suspected that I had arrived inside the
five-track terminal loop, which lay somewhere in the darkness before me. I pulled Jade to a halt.

I had to make a decision whether to keep going or return
to find the others. My dilemma was that if I kept going I'd
have to proceed in total darkness. Even my small light could
be easily spotted, like a soldier who lights a match and gives
a sniper an easy target.

But Jade, following the scent, could lead me. I switched
off the light and decided to go on. I walked as quietly as I
could. Periodically I stopped and listened. I could still hear
the trains rumbling and squealing; but now the sounds came
from somewhere above me. Once when I stopped I thought
I heard a voice.

Cool air kept flowing past me, probably from the old
tubes under the Hudson River. I worried about tumbling off
the edge of a platform to my right. Just then my shoulder
rubbed against the corner of a building. I stopped Jade and
ran my hands up the wall until I felt a countertop, then a
glass window. This could be the ticket kiosk on Rogue's

drawing. That meant the double set of stairs would be a short distance ahead, and beyond that the freestanding room where Rogue felt the girls were being held.

I peered into the inky blackness and spotted a dim glow about forty feet before me, down near the ground. Light was escaping from under a door. I had found them. I could scarcely breathe. I moved slowly forward, nervous because I could hear Jade's nails clicking as she walked. I kept my left hand outstretched until my fingers touched another wall and then a doorjamb.

I took a huge gamble that this led to the double bank of stairs. I tugged Jade over to it, passed beyond the doorway, then crouched low. I risked flicking on the pen light, keeping it cupped in my hands, and carefully inched it along the floor. I saw a stair. I assumed the exit above was blocked off on another level, but once these stairs had led straight up to Chambers Street.

I told Jade to stay and tied her to the stair railing. I crept back out onto the platform and cautiously moved toward the glow in the darkness. As I got closer, I saw the outline of a doorway. I reached it and put my ear against the door. I heard men's voices inside. Where the light escaped from under the door was an opening at least two inches wide. I lay down on my stomach and angled my head to try to see something. I saw feet.

To be more exact, I saw the shoes of four men, eight feet in all. The butt of a semiautomatic rifle sat in a corner. I was looking at the floor of what I guessed had once been a small employee day room. Beyond it I identified a closed door of a dark wood. One set of shoes walked over to it and the door opened a crack. "I said shut up back there!" he yelled. "Fucking women."

I slowly got to my knees and stood. My chest was tight, my shoulders tense. I wanted to act, but there was nothing I could do alone. Two of them I could have handled, but four posed too much risk for the hostages. I had to retrace my route and find the rest of the team. I drew back from the door and started moving toward the double stairs where I had left Jade. But going back was more difficult. I no longer had the door's light in front of me. I could see dimly with my sensitive eyes, but the way was filled with shadows. Something furry ran by me and I jerked sideways, my shoulder hitting a metal post.

I stumbled, stretched my hands out to catch myself, and clutched the pole before I hit the ground. The noise wasn't especially loud, but in the empty terminal it was clearly audible. I knew the men inside would hear.

I froze as the door I had just left suddenly opened, throwing a narrow slice of light into the darkness. Not more than eight feet from me, I could see a short, stocky figure silhouetted against the brightness. I stayed unseen in the shadows, not daring to breathe.

"You hear that?" he said to someone behind him.

"It was probably a rat," another voice answered. "The place is crawling with them."

"I think we'd better take a look. Get your flashlight."

I was certain to be spotted if they used the light. I did the only thing I could: I reached into my backpack and grabbed Gunther. I had a terrible moment of regret about what I had to do, but I didn't hesitate. I tossed my pet rat toward the open door. He landed in the slice of light almost at the guy's feet.

"*Aiiiiieeee!*" the guy yelled, and jerked backward. He slammed the door shut.

I heard a muffled voice ask, "What happened?"

"A rat. Ran right at me. A huge white son of a bitch. I'm not opening that door again. Let's go back."

I didn't know where Gunther had run off to, and there was no way to search for him. I slunk back into the stairwell and found Jade. Even in the darkness, it wasn't hard. I could smell her and hear her breathing. I hugged her tightly and whispered, "Let's go home."

Instead of returning to the platform, she started tugging me upward. I tried pulling her back. She resisted. She clearly wanted to continue up the stairs. I could drag her back down, but then what? She had led the way here. I didn't know if I could find the route back to the Barclay Street building without her help. Suddenly the thought of being lost among the dozens of abandoned corridors and miles of abandoned tunnels sent panic fluttering through me.

I tried to quell my fear. I reasoned with myself. The worst that could happen if we took the stairs was that we'd hit a dead end and I'd coax her back down. I climbed upward after her. The flight stopped at a landing, then turned and led upward to another set of stairs. After I counted four flights, I turned on my penlight.

Surrounded by gloom and the intermittent rumbling of trains, Jade and I stepped onto a broad concourse at the top of the fourth flight. I swung my light around me. Part of a wall to my left was caved in, and rubble stretched out across a marble floor. In front of me, wide steps ran around a raised platform. Huge tiled columns connected with a ceiling fifteen feet above my head.

Jade tugged me into the rubble, and I picked my way around pieces of cement and broken tile. We entered a hallway, the ceiling lowered so that it was just a few feet above my head. I didn't like it here. I felt like a mouse in a trap. Jade looked back at me, then continued forward. She stopped in front of a green door. I reached out and grabbed the knob. It turned, but when I pulled the door stuck. I used both hands and tugged with all my strength until the door started to move. I edged it open to let in a weak light. The stench of urine wafted toward me. I put my head through the opening and peered out.

To my left, people were standing on a subway platform. A sign hanging above the tracks read, CHAMBERS STREET. Old newspapers and coffee cups lay in the corners; the tiles of the walls were stained by dripping water; the benches were too grimy to sit on; the floor was a dull black. I switched off my penlight and stepped through the doorway onto the platform. Jade jumped down behind me. I pulled the door firmly shut behind me.

A few people waiting for the uptown subway had looked my way. Nobody said anything, even though a woman and a dog had emerged from a mysterious door that hadn't opened in decades. It was New York City. Bizarre things happened all the time. Nobody cared.

Jade and I rushed up another set of stairs and crossed a dismal mezzanine. I finally spotted the exit to the street and ran for it, feeling desperate to get back into the air, into the night. When we emerged from a stairwell, the rain had stopped and the night was clear. I looked around.

We had surfaced far from Barclay Street, all the way down near City Hall at Centre and Duane. I carefully noted where I was. I had to remember the exact location of the platform and the door at its end. It was important. That old green door led straight to the kidnappers and their victims— and they didn't know it existed.

CHAPTER 19

He that lives upon hope will die fasting.

—Benjamin Franklin, *Courteous Reader*

The lieutenant had broken his arm. I discovered this when I turned on my cell phone. Three messages were waiting for me, and each one gave me a case of agita.

First came Benny's voice, accusatory, a little shrill. She explained that after the rest of the team and the lieutenant had followed me into the underground concourse, Audrey saw something glittering in the beam of a flashlight. They all ran over and discovered it was a woman's watch. Naturally they figured one of the girls had dropped it on purpose. The lieutenant put it in an envelope and everyone was pretty excited—until they looked around for me.

I had vanished from sight, and they were lost. Did I realize it took them over an hour to find their way back to Barclay Street? And the poor lieutenant, who didn't have a flashlight with him, didn't have bat eyes, and was behind everybody else, tripped over a toppled florist's display. They had to take him straight to the emergency room once they finally got out of that "hellhole."

"Now, sugar," she continued, her voice softening, "I told you to wait up for us. But no, you took off like a hound dog after a scairt coon. Look what went and happened. Far as I knew you were lost in there too. I shouldn't be a-yelling at you when I might be crying at your funeral. I'm just a little upset; that's all. Call me when you get this message; we're all going back to the Laundromat. Maybe I'll see that Martin feller. And one more thing," she added. "J wants you to call him."

I'll be sure to put that on the top of my priority list, I thought.

The next message was from Fitz. I could see from the "missed calls" record on my cell phone that he had tried to get me six times in all. "Hi," he said. "I know you're working, but I need to get an answer ASAP. My cousin, the monsignor, says the only date that a side altar is open at St. Patrick's is this coming Thursday. It means moving our wedding date up a week. Does it really matter? I gave him a tentative yes. Let me know, okay? Hope I can see you later. Bye."

I turned cold all over. The cell phone shook in my hand. I couldn't understand why I was reacting this way. Fitz was a terrific guy. Instead of throwing myself at a total bastard like Rogue, I should be counting my blessings. The sooner we were married the better. Right?

Going from bad to worse, the third message was from Mar-Mar. "Daphne, this is your mother," she said. *Like I didn't recognize your voice,* I thought. "I suppose you are annoyed at me. What I did was for your own good. You should know that. I'd like to see you on Sunday. And Fitz, of course. By the way, who is this Jessica or Jessie person he's been meeting in the afternoon? Someone he works with? Well, I know you're busy. I won't keep you. Love you."

I felt as if she had just smacked me on the head with a hammer. Jessica! That was Fitz's ex, the love of his life who ran off with his best friend. I couldn't believe this. He'd said he was at work. Was there no honest man in the whole goddamn world! I stood there on Centre Street and the tall buildings seemed to spin around me.

Tears came unbidden, and I blinked them away. I bit down

hard on my lip. I squeezed my eyes shut and I tried to think. Maybe I deserved this. After all, I *had* just cheated on Fitz, hadn't I?

From somewhere deep inside me, the answer burst forth like a shout in the night. No! My slip, my sin, wasn't anything like what Fitz had done. I was an amoral creature desperately struggling to be moral. In my blood, in the very marrow of my bones, I was a vampire. I might be good some of the time, perhaps even most of the time, yet I could never be a paragon of virtue. It was not in my nature.

Not so for Fitz. He was proud of his principles. Being virtuous was the rock upon which he built his character.

Besides, I rationalized, as my emotions ricocheted and pain shot through me, it had been just a physical thing between Rogue and me. An impulsive mistake. A weak moment.

Not so with Fitz. His behavior was premeditated. It was sneaky. It was . . . it was breaking my heart.

Everything turned black, then red. I started pacing back and forth on Centre Street, dragging Jade along in a figure-eight pattern as I wore down the sidewalk. It occurred to me that my mother must be having Fitz followed after I destroyed her ability to play Peeping Tom. Were there no depths too low for that woman to go? See her on Sunday? When hell froze over I'd see her. As for Fitz, the double-crossing, lying rat, I would see him later. He wanted a wedding? He'd better get ready for a funeral.

Just then my cell phone rang. I figured it was Fitz and flipped it open without looking at the caller ID. "*You bastard!*" I screamed into the receiver.

"No doubt I am, but I am also your boss."

Oh, shit. It was J.

"Sorry," I muttered. "I thought you were somebody else."

I heard a muffled laugh. "Agent Urban, we need to talk about tomorrow. Can you get up here to the office?"

"Okay. I have something you need to know too. But I have

Jade with me. It might take some time until I find a car service that will pick us up."

"Where are you?"

"At the entrance to the Chambers Street subway stop at Centre and Duane," I said.

"I'll come get you. Give me twenty minutes."

I spent the waiting time circling the block with Jade, trying to walk off my anger. This far downtown, the streets were desolate after midnight. I almost hoped for some mugger to take a crack at me. It would feel good to smack somebody. I was having crazy thoughts, like maybe I should have J drop me off at that biker bar, where I could start a fight.

Along about then, a little red flag started waving in my consciousness, warning me to watch out. I wasn't in the best frame of mind to see J. He had a knack for pissing me off even when I was in a good mood. Tonight we could be in for World War III.

J drove up in his personal vehicle—not a company Hummer, but a pickup truck complete with a gun rack and an homage to Dale Earnhardt on the fender. Fortunately, his truck had a crew cab, and Jade could ride comfortably in the backseat. She woofed and jumped in happily, her red tongue lolling out of her mouth. She was always excited to take a car ride.

J glanced over at me, looking amused.

"What?" I snapped at him.

"You look as if you were rode hard and put away wet," he said.

"Why? What are you talking about?" I flipped down the visor to look in the vanity mirror. *Oh, crap.* Black grime streaked across one cheek. I had cobwebs in my hair. My turtleneck had cement powder or some kind of white dust all over it. My makeup was completely gone. I couldn't look much worse.

"I was in the subway tunnels," I began to explain. "I found the girls. And . . . and . . ." At that point my voice became a wail and I burst into tears. "I lost Gunther!"

*   *   *

It took me six blocks to regain control of myself. J drove without saying a word while I carried on with big gulping sobs. At one point he opened the center console, pulled out a box of tissues, and offered them to me. Finally, I stopped, hiccupped, and took a deep breath.

"Sorry about that," I said, and dried my eyes.

"It happens. Soldiers react different ways after a mission. Get drunk. Have sex. You cried. It was a release. Sorry about your pet rat. Now tell me what happened."

I gave J a narrative of the events from the time I'd entered the office building on Barclay Street to the minute I'd popped out of the door on the uptown subway platform, including finding the terrorists' hideout in the old Hudson Terminal and how I'd lost Gunther. I described in detail the area where the girls were being held and told him I had started thinking about a way to get them out. But my plan had a lot of holes in it, and I needed to talk it through.

"My concern is coordinating the rescue with capturing the kidnappers during the ransom delivery at Mitchel Field," I said. "The whole operation looks like it can go south really fast."

"Could you determine how many people were guarding the girls?" J asked as he drove north toward Midtown.

"I saw four."

"That makes sense. We're certain that Clarence Roberts is the leader of this group, and Rashid is his number two man. Rashid has been the negotiator talking with the Morrises, although our belief is that Roberts is telling him what to say. The other four men probably watch the girls. I believe Roberts, who has a medical school background, severed the ear and beheaded the Duke girl. She was strangled first, by the way."

Those bastards had killed a fifteen-year-old girl without mercy, without conscience. I wanted—I needed—to get them all. In a hard voice I said, "What about the rest of the group? There were fourteen during the kidnapping."

"We are executing a manhunt for all of them. We think they're waiting for the mission in a motel or hotel, wherever Clarence and Rashid have been holed up. Just like nine-eleven, they'll all gather for the grand finale, when they get to be martyrs."

It sounded good, but I figured that J was guessing, the same as I was. "Let's review the facts as we know them," I said. "Rashid and his uncle Clarence went into the tunnel with the supplies last night. Then there are the four men I spotted who are already in the underground hideout in the Hudson Terminal. As far as we know, no other terrorists have gone in or out. Did Rashid call the Morrises tonight?"

"Yes. That's what I wanted to tell you. The ransom delivery is set for nine p.m. tomorrow at Mitchel Field."

"How are they guaranteeing that the girls are alive and will be released?"

"They are FedExing us a videophone. It will ring at ten minutes to nine. We will watch the girls during the ransom pickup. If we screw up, we'll see them executed. If we withdraw our people and disperse, at nine fifteen the girls will be set free. Of course, if you're right, that's enough time for the terrorists to get to LaGuardia and bring down an airliner."

"We have time to go back in tonight and get the girls, J. Let's do it; let's not screw around. I can show you where they are."

J didn't answer. He stared through the windshield at the street ahead. "There's been an executive decision. Despite the risk to the girls, the priority is now to capture or kill the terrorists."

"What? We've got a chance to get them out now!" I protested, my voice a screech.

"And if we get them out now, Clarence Roberts, Rashid, and the others in the Al Qaeda cell will get away. They'll be free to

plan another operation. Instead of eleven deaths, we would looking at hundreds, maybe thousands in another terrorist attack."

"But what about the girls' families?"

J let out a long, deep breath. "The president has decided he
will handle the fallout for the families if the remaining girls die.
He will probably take the position that they died to win the War
on Terror. I was told he will posthumously award each of them
the Congressional Medal of Honor, for valor in battle—even
though they were civilians."

"This all sucks," I said, feeling defeated.

"It's a tough call. I can't say it's the wrong one. From a military standpoint, he's right. And he signed off on sending in a
team of crack commandos for the baited-Buffalo scenario. He
doesn't know who the Darkwings are, but he assumes you are
army Rangers."

I looked over at him. His jaw was tight. He wouldn't look
back at me, just kept staring straight ahead. I got it then. "So
you're saying . . . what you're telling me is that the girls have already been written off. They're dead heroes as far as the president is concerned?"

J didn't answer right away. "The best we can do is to try to
pull them out once we've lured the terrorists to the Buffalo. I'll
make sure we have Rangers ready to go into the tunnel and get
them while the Darkwings engage out at Mitchel Field." He
looked at me with sad eyes. "Daphne, the terrorists will execute
them no matter what we do. I believe that. And they'll do it
while we watch it on the videophone. It's their mentality. We do
need to get them, stop them. I'll do everything I can to rescue the
girls, but the Darkwings have been pulled off that part of the
mission."

I was furious. I had to come up with a better plan. "Can we
at least get surveillance on the Barclay Street office—in case
they bring the girls there? I don't know if they can get a cell
phone connection from the hiding place in the old terminal."

"It's already been done. As soon as Benny called in, I put some people on a stakeout outside the building. Night-vision cameras have been installed both on the concourse and in the stairwell. No one can enter or leave without us spotting them, and they can't move the girls out without us being right there to grab them."

"But your thinking is that they won't. The guards will wait until the Buffalo is rolling toward LaGuardia, then begin the executions. They will be figuring it will buy the suicide mission more time, divert our attention."

"That's a roger," J said. The pickup truck reached Eighth Avenue. "You want to go back to your apartment?" he asked.

"Yeah, I'm tired," I answered, my voice laden with sadness.

The pickup hit potholes and bumped over the uneven pavement as we rode up the avenue in silence. I tried to keep my mind from going back to the darkness of the dungeon where the young women waited for death. I focused on the here and now: the sounds of the moving traffic and tooting horns. The siren of an emergency vehicle whooped nearby, then faded away. We were maybe ten blocks from my apartment when J said without looking at me, "I hear you're getting married."

"I suppose my mother told you that," I said.

"Doesn't matter. Actually Benny mentioned it. Look, you didn't ask for my advice—"

"So don't give it." I crossed my arms across my chest.

"As your commanding officer and your friend—"

I almost choked on that. "My *friend*?" My voice was incredulous.

I could see a muscle in J's jaw twitch. His hands tightened on the steering wheel. "I know you don't think that. But I'm going to say this in plain English: You're making a mistake."

"What?"

"A mistake. It's obvious, isn't it? A few months ago—what was it, December? January?—you were involved with Darius della Chiesa. You almost got yourself and your teammates killed because of your infatuation—"

"Infatuation!" I blurted out.

"Yes, your infatuation. Now you're getting married? I think you're trying to get back at Darius." J looked smug.

"That is so not right," I replied. I shifted around, feeling uncomfortable in the seat.

"It's what I think. I also think you're not—I don't know how to say this—*mature* enough to make that kind of commitment."

Anger boiled up inside me. "Mature enough! I'm over four hundred years old!"

J snorted. "You are as stupid as a teenager when it comes to men, if you don't mind my saying so."

"Mind?" I yelled at him, twisting in the seat and straining against the seat belt. "Mind? I do mind. My relationships are none of your business."

"Yes, they are," he yelled back, turning his head toward me, his face twisted with rage. "You're a spy. Your relationships make you vulnerable. Marriage is out. And that's a direct order." He looked away then, his lips pressed together. His eyes were on the traffic ahead of him, and the muscle in his jaw was doing a veritable tap dance.

I didn't say another word. When I got out of the truck and opened the back door to get Jade, J said, "We rendezvous at the office at eight o'clock. We need to be at Mitchel Field to get into the Buffalo no later than eight forty. This is one time, Agent Urban, that you cannot be late."

I didn't answer. As soon as Jade was on the sidewalk, I slammed the truck's door—hard.

By the time I had gone up to the tenth floor in the elevator and reached my apartment, I had come up with an idea. Maybe the adrenaline rush of my anger gave me some mental clarity, but

I had decided to finesse J, the kidnappers, and the president himself.

Could I screw everything up? Maybe. But I didn't think so. I mentally reviewed what I knew about the modus operandi of the hijackers during the terrorist attacks of September 11, 2001. Once they left for the airports on that morning they didn't communicate with anyone. To the best of my recollection, most had ceased all contact with others the night before.

After that they were mentally preparing themselves to die, to be martyrs.

I believed Roberts and Rashid, along with the others involved in the kidnapping, were planning to be martyrs too. It was for them the highest form of glory. And once they left for Mitchel Field, the whole mission was in its final phase. I was positive there would be no contact after that with the women's guards below the streets. Why should there be? Whatever those guards were going to do—and I too believed they would execute the girls—would have been decided from the start. *When* Rashid, Roberts, and the others left for Mitchel Field, however, was key, because at that point what I was planning would be successful . . . or I'd blow the whole mission. I was willing to risk it, and take the weight if I had to.

As soon as I got inside my apartment, I called Benny.

She answered, sounding a little out of breath. "What's going on, sugar? You okay?"

"I'll explain everything later. Listen carefully, though. Are you at the Laundromat?"

"Yes, we're waiting to leave for tonight's hunt. I'm on Martin's team," she said.

"I'm not surprised at that. But pay attention for a minute. Here's what we're going to do. Tell everyone who wants to be in on the rescue mission to meet on the uptown platform at the Chambers Street stop tomorrow. Enter through the stairs at

Centre and Duane streets. Be there by seven fifteen sharp. Not a minute later. You have that?"

"I do. Anything else?"

"Yes. Can you get hold of Lieutenant Johnson?" I asked.

"I'm pretty sure I can, sugar. But why? He's pretty mad at us right now."

"Tell him we're going to make it up to him. Tell him to have ambulances, enough to carry ten young women, at the corner of Centre and Duane at seven twenty and not a minute earlier."

"Really?" she asked.

"Yes, and Benny—this is strictly a vampire thing. J is not to know until it's all over. It's important to me."

"If that's how you want it, you got it. It sounds like a hoot!" She laughed.

"Oh, it will be," I said.

The die had been cast.

Now I turned my attention to other things. I fed Jade and thanked her for all she had done tonight. I think she understood.

Then I saw Gunther's empty cage. I walked over to shut the small wire door, my legs feeling heavy, my heart aching. I knew he was gone. It was no comfort that he was free with his own kind. I didn't know if he would enjoy their company any more than I did when mingling with mine.

Finally I stood up straight and made another call, to Fitz. He answered immediately. I kept my voice light. I asked him if he'd mind coming over. We had several hours until morning. He said he was on his way.

Fitz showed up on my doorstep looking maybe two out of three sheets to the wind. He could have used his key. Out of politeness, I think, he rang the buzzer. I opened the door, my heart thudding as my eyes took him in from head to toe. I felt confused that I wasn't angrier with him. I didn't know why, but my initial outrage had disappeared and had been replaced by something else, as if some kind of pressure on me had been relieved.

And to tell the truth, the way Fitz looked tonight delighted my eyes and excited my senses. He had on a heather blue crew neck with a rim of white T-shirt visible around the collar. His jeans were just tight enough to be sexy, and rode low on his hips. His jaw was square, his brown hair brushing his forehead. He wore a silver watch and a claddagh ring; they gleamed against his skin. Hanging from his index finger, a light sport coat dangled over his shoulder. He could have landed a job modeling for Calvin Klein.

"Hello, dollface," he said, and smiled.

I managed a smile in return and ushered him in. I didn't ask him if he wanted a drink. I needed him somewhat sober for what I had to say. He crossed the room and sat.

I followed him. He stretched out his hand and took mine, pulling me down next to him on the couch. He smelled nice, like an expensive cologne, citrus and patchouli maybe. He draped his arm around my shoulder. "I'm sorry to have bugged you so much today," he said, "but I have to give Tim an answer in the morning. Is Thursday okay?"

"Let's get back to that in a minute," I said. "I have to discuss something with you first."

"What's on your mind? You look glum," he said, and put his finger under my chin to turn my head toward him. Then he planted a kiss on my nose.

"Did you know my mother is having you followed?" I asked.

"No, is she?"

"That's what she said. She called me today . . ." I paused.

"And she told you I saw Jess," he said, understanding coming into his eyes.

"*You* didn't tell me." My words were brittle.

"I didn't want to upset you. It was nothing. She wanted to talk to me. She and Billy are having some problems."

I moved out from under his arm and faced him. "So she went running to you? Out of the blue?"

"No, not exactly. She heard you and I were getting married—Delores called Billy's mother or something. Jess called to say she wishes us well."

"Oh, I bet she does," I said.

"No, I think she really does. She loves Billy, but there are some things going on between them. That's all. She had nobody else who would understand; that's what she said, anyway."

I shook my head. "You can't be that naive."

Fitz reached over and picked up my hand. "You're cold again. Your hands are like ice. You don't need to be upset over this. Believe me—"

"Why? Why should I believe you?"

"Because I love you. Because I am willing to become a vampire for you. Because we're getting married in a few days—and we're going to spend eternity together."

All of a sudden I felt as if I couldn't breathe. I pulled my hand free and jumped up. "Maybe I need a drink," I said quickly. "Do you want one?"

Of course he did. I poured him a Jameson and then splashed some into a glass for myself. I handed him the whiskey. "I hear what you're saying, Fitz. But this is kind of a shotgun marriage, isn't it? For both of us? Are you sure you want to go through with it?" I stood there watching his face carefully.

"I'd be lying if I didn't admit that becoming a vampire is a hard thing for me," he said, not meeting my eyes. "But that's how the cards were dealt. That's the hand I got. There are many worse things that can happen."

"Like being killed," I said softly.

"Oh, I don't know," he said, looking up. "I wouldn't go looking for death, but life is a more difficult thing to face sometimes. But to get back to your question." He searched my face with his eyes, which were as gray as the mists of Ireland. "I do want to marry you. I love you. If it means I have to become a vampire, so be it." He raised his glass. "*Sláinte chuig na fir, agus go mairfidh na mn go deo.* And that means in Irish, my love, 'Health to the men, and may the women live forever.'" He drained his glass.

Then he smiled, an honest, good-man's smile. "Daphne, my one true love, if we are done with arguing for tonight—and we need to remember that both our mothers are more devils than angels and seem determined to cause us troubles—can we go to bed?"

I looked at his long, handsome face. A great affection for him welled up in me like tears. What did I care what J said? I had a fine man wanting to share my life. A better man than I deserved. We both had a past, and it was sure to rise up to surprise us now and then. I was in no position to cast stones. No doubt my mother would tell Fitz about my slip with Rogue—if she ever knew.

"Okay, dear St. Fitz, to bed it is," I said.

We lay down together and kissed. Then we made love with more familiarity and tenderness than passion. When we had finished, I wished him sweet dreams. Then I lay awake in his arms until shortly before dawn. When I finally slipped from beneath the covers, St. Julien Fitzmaurice was soundly snoring. Jade was asleep in the kitchen. Gunther's cage sat forlornly on my computer desk. And I entered my secret room to sink into my coffin, realizing I had not bitten Fitz this night, knowing that neither of us was ready for me to take that second drink of his blood quite yet.

CHAPTER 20

My heart is a lonely hunter that hunts on a lonely hill.

—William Sharp (Fiona MacLeod)

Sixteen vampires from the Laundromat, all young and mostly male, met on the subway platform at seven fifteen on Sunday night. Martin and Gerry, the team leaders of the Chasers and Racers, both showed up.

I had taken on the role of mission commander. My skin was clammy with a cold sweat. The rescue we were about to attempt was my baby, my brilliant idea. I had decided not to reveal to my teammates what J had told me on the way home. This preemptive raid was a totally ad hoc mission and my responsibility alone. What my teammates didn't know couldn't be used against them.

I took a deep breath and squared my shoulders. I called the group, along with the four Darkwings, over to the end of the platform near the green door.

"Everybody ready?" I asked.

They raised their fists and shouted, "Yes!"

I quickly explained the plan and assigned specific tasks to other Darkwings and the Laundromat people. We joined hands briefly. Benny, Cormac, and I repeated the one unbreakable rule the Darkwings followed from the Ranger creed: "I will never leave a fallen comrade to fall into the hands of the enemy." We had adopted the creed during our second mission, and this had become a ritual for us.

I noticed Audrey's face, intense yet filled with joy, her body fairly trembling with excitement. This was her first mission, her first taste of battle, so to speak, and she was pumped. Rogue gave me a wink. I wanted to hate the guy, really I did, but he was a brave son of a bitch—that I knew—and I was glad he was along for this.

Then, ready for action, the entire group of New York vampires went forth. We all climbed through the strange little green door in the tile wall at the end of the platform. Behind it, in the darkness, we all shed our clothes and transformed, producing a light show of dazzling flashes and kaleidoscopic colors, which, in the vast, hollow emptiness of that abandoned space, no one from the outside world could see.

I took the time to fasten my backpack across my chest like a bandolier. I carried my cell phone in it but not much else. Beating my great wings, I took to the air, leading the way, fluttering above the rubble, heading for the stairs that led down to the Hudson Terminal. Behind me I heard the whirring of wings and the cheeps of sonar as this armada of great vampire bats found its way through the utter darkness.

We needed to travel at most five hundred feet from the subway station to the terrorists' den in the bedrock below. As I swooped down the stairs, I forced my mind to empty. I knew that in a few seconds, the girls would either live or die—but I had to push the thought from my mind or I would be frozen with anxiety. Instead I smelled the mustiness, felt the beating of my huge dark wings, heard the thumping of my own heart.

I reached the platform. The door I had peered under was directly ahead. Time stopped. I gathered all the power of my vampire being, pulling it into a tight, hard ball of determination. I paused in midflight, then dove downward so fast I heated the air around me.

At the last possible second I did part of a half gainer in midair, twisting backward, and hit the door with my feet, smashing it from its hinges. I somersaulted into the first guard I saw before he had time to reach for his gun, so hard that I caved in his breast-bone and probably collapsed a lung. Blood spewed from his mouth. I looked away from that and just happened to see a cell phone lying on an old battered coffee table. I grabbed it and dropped it in my backpack.

Rogue came flying in directly behind me and rammed into another guard, grabbing him, and I heard a snap. Somewhere in the back of my consciousness I realized that Rogue had broken the guard's neck. "I'll search the area. You go on!" I did, glancing back just once to see him take the terrorist I had struck and throw him onto the platform.

I didn't slow down as I rushed over to a dark four-panel door at the back of the room, the one I had seen opened by the guard as I lay on the platform last night. I grasped the knob and it wouldn't turn. Drawing my foot back, I kicked hard, splitting the wood and sending the door flying inward. I grabbed its edges and tore it from its hinges, tossing it aside as I heard humans scream-ing behind me.

Rogue and the Laundromat team had no doubt seized the re-maining guards and dragged them into the gloomy depths of the terminal. There they would do with them whatever they wished. I didn't care to know.

I squeezed my huge body down a short hall and into what had once been an employee locker room. It was a foul place of no light and little air. The girls, listless and perhaps drugged, were sitting or lying on the floor, barely raising their heads as I appeared.

"Special Squad U.S. Rescue," I yelled, hoping the phony label would help explain my terrifying appearance. "Don't be frightened!" Even so, my fearsome shape penetrated through their drugged haze. Their eyes went wide with terror, and a few of them tried to struggle to their feet.

"Relax! Relax! We're getting you out of here," I tried to assure the captives as Benny, the golden bat, came up behind me. I heard her say, "Oh, thank you, Lord! They're alive."

I kept talking softly as I went from woman to woman, hoping to stop any panic. I told each of them, "We're going to carry you upstairs. Don't be alarmed at our appearance. Ambulances are waiting. Please, please just relax."

I don't know how much they heard or understood of my words, but I spoke slowly and in a gentle tone as I went deeper into the room, counting heads and making sure all the girls were there. They were, except for Toni Duke, the girl we had failed, the girl we had let die.

I looked back over my shoulder to see Benny, followed by Audrey and Cormac, pick up a young woman in her arms. Before we transformed, I had designated members of the Laundromat crew to help us carry them out. I was relieved to see that they crowded in behind me now.

"My sister, my sister!" one girl cried. "Over there. She's very sick."

"I'll get her," I said as Gerry from the Laundromat scooped up the crying girl, who, I guessed, was Deborah Morris.

I moved carefully over to a form huddled under a blanket against the back wall. I stooped down and cautiously turned her over. "Nicoletta?" I asked.

"Are you an angel?" she murmured. Her head was wrapped in a dirty bandage and her eyes looked feverish.

"Something like that," I said, trying to smile. "I'm going to take you to your parents, okay?"

"Okay." She said and closed her eyes. As I gathered her into my arms, her eyes fluttered open again and she whispered, "Please, can we take my friend?"

"What friend?" I asked, thinking she was hallucinating.

"Mickey." She sighed. "He tried to keep me warm."

I heard a squeak. A tiny white head peeked out of the blanket. A surge of joy rushed through me like a flash of light. "Gunther!" I cried. "Come on!" He squeaked again and ran up my arm to perch on my shoulder, his little claws firmly gripping my fur as he chattered in my ear.

"His name is Mickey Mouse," she whispered. "Not Gunther." Then she closed her eyes again.

I was the last one to leave the women's dark prison on the terminal platform. I could detect sounds, bestial and deep, not far away, but I shut them out of my mind. Justice had come in the form of a bat to these cruel men who had used innocent people— children, really—as pawns. I had no pity for them.

With Nicoletta cradled in my arms, I leaped into the air, my wings arcing, lifting me upward. Our plan had been to bring them as far as the inner side of the green door, where Benny—the first to return—would have changed back into human form. She'd lead the girls out onto the platform. The other team members and the Laundromat crew—those who had returned from the gruesome hunt below, at any rate—would retrieve their clothes and melt away into the night.

Cormac's job was to convert back to human form and sprint up to the street level to alert Lieutenant Johnson and bring the EMS people back to the girls waiting on the subway platform below.

When I saw the green door ahead, I landed, walking carefully across the rubble-strewn floor. When I put my head through the opening, Benny stretched out her arms to take Nicoletta from me. But by that time I sensed the slight young woman's fragile life slipping away. I shook my head at Benny and didn't hesitate. Without transforming, I ducked my entire body through the door with Nicoletta in my arms and bounded onto the subway platform. Then, with a powerful beat of my bat wings, I took to the air and zoomed up the stairs.

I had begun traversing the mezzanine by air when I saw a familiar face below. Lt. Moses Johnson, one arm in a sling, the other holding a radio, had stopped in his tracks as he spotted me. His face appeared to be frozen somewhere between anger and surprise.

I landed directly in front of him. "She's critical," I said. "Hurry." I gently put Nicoletta down, tenderly touching her cheek before I went airborne again, hoping no other eyes had seen me flying through the mezzanine, the stuff of their nightmares made real.

I returned to the green door and squeezed back into the abandoned section of the station. Safely inside, I took Gunther carefully off my shoulder. I put him into the backpack where I had left my clothes. I felt at home in my bat body. More than that, I felt whole and unconflicted, my true self no longer hidden. But I could not remain in that form. With a whirling vortex of light and wind, I returned to human shape once more.

By the time I had dressed and stepped back onto the subway platform, it was after seven thirty. I looked around. The rest of the team was nowhere to be found. That was a good thing. It meant they were already on their way to the office. But if I didn't find a way up to Twenty-third Street fast, I was going to be late. My adrenaline had drained away; I felt limp. I could think of only one thing to do.

I went in search of Lieutenant Johnson.

I found him at street level, speaking into his radio set. All the ambulances had gone. A few blue-and-white squad cars remained at the curb. He looked up. I couldn't read his gaze.

"I need a favor," I said.

He looked at me. "I guess I owe you one."

"I need to get to the Flatiron Building, fast. Can you take me?"

"I can't leave, but hang on a minute." He walked over to one of the blue-and-whites and stuck his head in the open window. Then he came back. "Sergeant Wilson is over in that squad car," he said, and I thought I saw a twinkle in his eyes. "He'll give you a lift. I told him to put the sirens on. You'll get there on time."

"Thanks," I said. "One other thing, Lieutenant."

"What's that?"

I had already started for the squad car as I talked. "The four terrorists who were guarding the girls? You'll find their bodies down in the terminal. And you'll discover they'll have been drained of blood."

"How the hell am I supposed to explain that?" he exploded.

"You'll figure out something," I said as I opened the door to the police car. "And here." I tossed him the cell phone I found down in the terrorists' hiding place. He caught it and looked at me with a puzzled expression.

"What's this?"

"It's something very important; trust me. It's probably going to ring around nine o'clock. Do me a favor and answer it, will you?"

Two camouflage-painted military Hummers were idling at the curb on the Fifth Avenue side of the Flatiron Building. Sergeant Wilson's squad car, siren wailing, careened around the corner from Twenty-third Street. It screeched to a halt. The time was seven thirty on the dot. I murmured thanks, jumped out, and ran to join my team members.

Benny hooked her arm through mine. She put her lips close to my ear. "J still doesn't know," she whispered.

"Exactly how I wanted it," I whispered back.

"We made Looie's night, didn't we?" She grinned.

I nodded. "And I hope Nicoletta pulls through. The only other thing I could have asked would be to've had Rashid and his uncle there too. That would have ended it. Then this second event would be canceled tonight."

"Sugar, don't ask for the moon," Benny gently chided me. Then she beamed. "We sure did have some kick-ass fun—and the night is still young!"

A feeling of foreboding passed over me like a shadow.

Whether by plan or accident, Benny, Audrey, and I sat together in one vehicle, while J, Rogue, and Cormac got into the other. An army Ranger, who didn't speak to us, was driving. Another Ranger, who didn't talk either, rode shotgun on the passenger side. They didn't know who we were. They obviously didn't think three women had any business going after armed and dangerous terrorists.

The journey out to Mitchel Field would take less than a half hour, and our adrenaline from the rescue had drained away, sending us into an emotional crash. I noticed Benny and Audrey shutting down, getting tense, picking up the grimness of the army Rangers in the front seats. We had the second phase ahead and we needed to get ourselves ready. I made it my business to start talking, making an effort to put energy into my words. I reminded them that the women were safe, but an airliner filled with people was in jeopardy. We could and would save them. We were the Darkwings.

"And I brought along a mascot," I said with a grin. I opened up my backback to show them Gunther comfortably nestled up inside.

"A rat is a rat is a rat," Benny said, shrinking back.

Audrey smiled. "*Rattus novegicus.* An albino too. They're unbelievably smart."

That they are, I thought. I stroked his head, and he rubbed his cheek along my finger. He had been through a lot in his little life, from witnessing the ax murder of his first owner, the art dealer Herr Schneibel, to my hurling him onto the platform and abandoning him. Yet he was one of the sweetest, most intelligent animals I had ever met. I didn't doubt he knew what he was doing when he had given comfort to an ill, perhaps dying child.

I carefully hung my backpack in the rear of the Hummer. "Hey, soldiers," I called out, leaning forward and tapping the one in the passenger seat on the shoulder. "I've got explosives in that backpack. Don't touch it. Don't move it. Don't crush it, understand?"

"Yes, ma'am," he said.

"He's cute," Benny said in a low voice. "What do you think, Audrey?"

"I think you have a one-track mind," she answered.

"I do! I surely do!" Benny laughed, our tension broken now. I decided to take the opportunity to drop a small emotional bomb.

"Benny—and you too, Audrey," I said in a serious voice. "I have something to ask you."

"What's on your mind, sugar?" Benny asked.

"Are you two free on Thursday night?"

Both said they were and asked why.

"My June wedding is off," I said. "Fitz and I are getting married this Thursday. I still want you to be my maid of honor, Benny, even though we won't have much time to get a dress. And Audrey, if you're into it, I really want you there too—as a bridesmaid, if you'd like it."

Audrey looked a little stunned, then nodded. "I've never been a bridesmaid. I've never been close enough to anyone to be asked. Come to think of it, I've never been to a wedding—of one of us, I mean."

"You couldn't keep me away," Benny said. "I'm gonna cry buckets; I surely am."

"There's one small problem, though." I braced myself for their reaction.

"What's that?" Benny asked.

"It's at St. Patrick's Cathedral."

"Well, butter my butt and call me a biscuit." Benny whooped. "How did you pull that off?"

"Fitz's family has connections. But can you handle it? The crucifixes and all. It won't be pleasant. And we have never been welcome guests of the pope—any of them. The Church has been trying to hunt us down for centuries."

"Well, sugar, that's what makes this such a hoot. You in white—you are wearing white, aren't you? A vampire bride, with an all-vampire wedding party, and held in New York's most famous church. I hope the building doesn't fall down on our heads." She clapped her hands. "I just love stuff like this!"

Audrey was humming "Here Comes the Bride." She stopped and smiled. "Listen, you two. I've got something I need to say. I've felt isolated most of my life. Now I find I'm on the A list at the Laundromat and having more fun than I've had in over a hundred years. So, Miss Daphne Urban, I'd go to your wedding even if it was at the Vatican itself."

"Amen!" Benny said with a grin, and grabbed me in a bear hug. She just couldn't help herself.

And that was why, instead of preparing for battle, as the men were probably doing, we spent the next few minutes of the ride scheduling a shopping trip at Bloomie's for Monday night and planning a quick party after the wedding ceremony for a reception. I told them the postwedding prandial feast had to be quick.

They giggled at that.

I didn't tell them the real reason for the rush—I had to transform Fitz into a vampire on his wedding night.

Old, unused, and largely forgotten, Mitchel Field sat in gloom and mist like a ghost town. Above our heads the roar of a plane taking off from LaGuardia impressed upon us why we were here. The three of us got quiet, pulling our thoughts inward, preparing ourselves to face the terrorists.

The men's Hummer had stopped in front of hangar one. Ours

pulled up next to it. Two more massive blue-painted hangars
were positioned beyond the first. In one of them sat the Buffalo,
waiting for us to get on board. In front of this one, next to our
Hummer, a black BMW 700 series was idling.

At that moment, a man dressed in combat fatigues and wearing a Kevlar vest stepped out of the Beemer carrying a FedEx
box. I gaped. It was Judge Marshall Morris.

"What's *he* doing here?" Benny asked. I assumed he had
come to deliver the camera phone that he was supposed to speed-
dial when we got the Buffalo out on the access road. The guards
were supposed to answer and show him that the hostages were
still alive.

The three of us climbed out of the Hummer and started to approach J, who stood talking to the judge. J waved us away and
gestured toward the second hangar. So we went on, catching up
with Rogue and Cormac.

Inside hangar two, the sight of the sand-colored Buffalo left
me awestruck. More impressive than its photo, it seemed unstoppable and impenetrable. On top of the vehicle, an army Ranger
was opening the top hatches and gestured for us to come on
board.

The plan developed earlier was for Rogue to be the team
leader for the assault. When we reached the rendezvous point
with the terrorists, the army Rangers—a team of three—would
climb out of the vehicle. They were supposed to stand aside,
keeping their hands up while the terrorists took over the Buffalo.

We'd be waiting. We were told to take the men alive if possible, but if we didn't, *c'est la vie.* I suppose *c'est la morte* would
be more accurate.

The judge entered the hangar with J and walked to where we
Darkwings had paused, preparing to climb onto the Buffalo. J,
stiff with repressed fury, asked us to listen up. He told us that he
had been ordered by the president himself to allow Judge Morris

to join us on this mission. He finished by saying that the judge had asked to say something to us personally. J stepped back.

The judge's face was puffy. His eyes had swollen so much they were mere slits. Perhaps he had been suffering greatly—he looked as if he had—but when he spoke, flashes of his old arrogance remained.

He stood up straight and looked at each of us. "I know that I once told you that I bore no responsibility for the crime that was committed by these men. But I was wrong. As it turns out, I do. My daughters have suffered and innocent people have died because of my mistakes. Now, I need to do what I can to right the wrong. I ask you to understand that I need to be there to fight with you to capture these men—and if you do not, to die in the attempt."

"So now he'll be a hero," Benny hissed in my ear.

I shook my head, thinking, *Oh, holy hell. This is just terrific.* J had no choice but to let the judge join us. The president didn't know his "special commandos" were vampires. But having the judge along wasn't going to fly. It was one thing for other vampires to know who we were. It was not going to be a good thing if a federal judge got an eyeful of giant vampire bat.

Rogue was already on top of the Buffalo. He turned his back on the judge and slid through an open hatch. One of the four Rangers accompanying us in the Buffalo reached down and offered a hand to Judge Morris. The rest of us managed on our own. We seated ourselves inside the spacious interior, which could hold fourteen people. Then we were ready to roll.

With Audrey acting as navigator, we headed toward an access road that led into the field from the far side of the compound. Cormac operated a night scope to reconnoiter as we moved. After a few minutes he called out, "I can see three cars. And one, two, three, four—ten men. All armed."

Rogue called Cormac over to him, where they spoke together in low tones. Then Cormac came back to the three of us

Darkwings and pulled us aside to tell the others what I had already figured out.

"The judge is a problem," he said quietly. "We can't risk the judge seeing us transform. So here's the deal. If you all concur, Audrey has volunteered to make him a meal."

Benny laughed. I thought it was pretty funny too. Audrey said she'd close her eyes and think of England, but she'd never turn down a free pint.

I watched Audrey only to the point where she slid into the backseat and positioned herself behind Judge Morris. After that, I joined Cormac at the night-vision viewer. When we were about a hundred feet from the terrorists, a young man whom I recognized as Rashid stepped forward, a semiautomatic rifle cradled in his arm. He gestured for us to stop.

We did.

Rashid made motions that the occupants of the vehicle were to exit. The four young Rangers climbed out of the Buffalo through the top hatch, leaving it open—hoping to ensure that was the route the terrorists would use to enter the vehicle.

We watched on the TV viewscreen as the soldiers put their hands behind their heads and walked toward the group of terrorists. Rashid shouted something at them and they lined up maybe twenty feet in front of him.

Suddenly Rogue cried out, "Those fuckers!" and jumped into the driver's seat. We all saw what he did. Rashid had swung his rifle up and started shooting at the Rangers, who went down like bowling pins.

"See you in hell, motherfucker!" Rogue roared, and put the pedal to the metal. Rashid leaped to the side, rolled, and came up firing. The bullets bounced harmlessly off the heavily armored vehicle. The other terrorists took cover behind their cars and started shooting too.

The Buffalo crashed into the first car, an older blue Ford

Taurus, sending it tumbling while the terrorists behind it ran. He then drove over the top of a white minivan, crushing it, before he swung the Buffalo around and lowered the massive teeth of the great beast's minesweeping arm, which skewered a green sedan.

Meanwhile the rest of us—with the exception of Cormac, who'd volunteered to man the machine gun mounted to the roof of the vehicle—stripped off our clothes and took our positions by the rear door. Rogue faced the exit away from the location of the terrorists, and as soon as the vehicle stopped, we dropped down one at a time. Almost before we hit the ground, we spun in a phantasmagoria of light and quickly shed our human shape to emerge as the fearsome monsters we truly were.

Benny led the charge against the panicked and fleeing terrorists. I came up close behind her.

We spotted two men running down the access road, and together we swooped down above them, each of us grasping one man in our talons and lifting him into the air. Gliding back toward the Buffalo, Benny called out, "Bombs away!" and we dropped our captives from a height guaranteed to break some bones but probably not kill them. Cormac, aiming the machine gun at the fallen men, immediately screamed at them to stay where they were and not move.

When we got back to the fight, Audrey had knocked out three more of the men who had been firing their rifles at the Buffalo. One of them, his throat slashed by her sharp claws, was definitely dead. The other two lay groaning on the ground. Cormac swung his gun around and fired at two more men who had more guts than brains and were rushing at the armored vehicle. That left one terrorist for each of us.

I spotted an older man standing quietly some fifty feet away, watching the melee. I flew at him, at the last minute seeing the gun in one of his hands. I didn't stop. I attacked.

Clarence Roberts took careful aim at me and fired, but I swooped down low, and the bullet—which might have hurt like hell and knocked me down, although it couldn't kill me—went harmlessly over my head.

I barreled into the former butler with my shoulder. I got my clawed fingers around his throat, so enraged that I had no compunctions about squeezing the life out of him, when I saw a golden figure land next to me.

"J wants him alive," Benny yelled, and I momentarily loosened my grip on Clarence Roberts's throat. As I did, I saw his hand with the gun move. "Look out," I screamed at Benny.

I was too late. I heard her say something like, "Ouffff," and fall to her knees.

I looked at Roberts, still in my hands, who dared to give me a self-satisfied grin. With a cry of rage, I tightened my grip on his throat and crushed his windpipe. I heard his death rattle as I ran to my friend.

"Benny!" I yelled. She moved, lifted her head, and shook it. "I'm okay," she said. "I'm okay. I got the wind knocked out of me; that's all." She groaned as she rolled into a sitting position. I squatted next to her and hastily looked for a wound. I found one. It was dead center in the middle of the pink Prada purse she had carried with her.

"That was my new Prada," she said sadly, and unclasped the bag to peek inside. She reached in and pulled out her camera phone, which was nearly cracked in two. "I guess he killed my Nokia." She chuckled.

"C'mon," I yelled, grinning with relief. "We've all got to get out of here."

Just then we heard the roar of a jetliner. We looked up and the blinking wing lights passed above us. *Safe journey,* I wished them silently.

Benny stood. She and I glanced about at the wrecked cars, the dead bodies, and the five terrorists still alive, but stayed motionless as Cormac aimed his machine gun at them.

"Uhh, uhh. J is going to be busier than a blind hound dog in a meat house," she said.

We didn't get back to hangar two for another half hour. We had to wait until J sent out a team to pick up the captured terrorists and the fallen Rangers. Rogue had rushed over to them, grabbing the medic bag out of the Buffalo. All of the men were alive, although one of them was bleeding badly. Their lives had been saved by their Kevlar vests. Once everything was squared away and we rumbled into the parking area, we could see even from our seats behind the dark-smoked windows of the Buffalo that J was, in Benny's words, "about to pitch a hissy fit."

"I guess he talked to Lieutenant Johnson," I said.

He certainly had. "The NYPD found the remaining ten girls," he informed us as soon as we climbed out of the Buffalo and stood on the asphalt parking lot.

"What happened?" Cormac asked, all innocence.

"How the hell do I know? I hit the speed dial to reach the guards, as we had been told to do. A New York cop answered." He looked around at us, searching our faces. "And you five had better have not had anything to do with this!" he said through gritted teeth.

"Who, us?" Rogue said, leaping from a tire onto the ground. "First we're hearing about it."

J sputtered, but before he could get another word out, Benny spoke up: "Y'all need to get somebody to take the judge home. He's still in the Buffalo. He's unconscious."

"What!" J said, alarmed. "Does he need a medic? Don't tell me you let the damned fool get shot!" J had worked himself up so much his complexion was brick red.

"Oh, no, sugar," Benny said. "He fainted soon as the fighting started. He never got out of the Buffalo."

That was our story, and we were sticking to it.

CHAPTER 21

The Vampire Bride

Fitz folded me into his arms when I staggered into my apartment after four a.m. on Monday morning. His body felt warm and good next to mine. He kissed the top of my head and asked me if I was okay.

I shook my head yes. "I'm just beat. Long night, but a good one. I'm glad you got my message and came over," I said, separating myself from his embrace and going over to Gunther's cage. The little guy popped out of my backpack and ran straight for his food bowl. My white rat was back home, and all was right with the world.

Mostly. The light on my answering machine was blinking. I hit the blue play button and my mother's voice began, "Daphne! Call me right—" I hit the delete button. I turned to Fitz and smiled. "I'll call her later. Maybe."

I was getting a warm and fuzzy feeling looking at him. He was looking back at me in the same way.

"We have a side chapel reserved for Thursday at eight," he said. "You still okay with it?"

"The idea is growing on me." I laughed. "I invited Audrey to the wedding," I said. "All of us girls are going shopping tomorrow, but you and I have to get to City Hall for the license first."

"It's a date," he said, and walked over to me. "You know, we have a lot of practical things to talk about. The apartments. A bank account. Breaking the news to our mothers—"

"After the ceremony!" I said. "I know she'll be furious, but I'll tell her we eloped. I don't trust her not to speak up during that part about, 'Does anyone know why these two should not be wed.'"

Fitz chuckled, because he knew I was only half kidding.

"Are you thinking about having Delores there, though? I really wouldn't mind," I said, crossing my fingers behind my back.

"Absolutely not. First of all, I'd have to pull all kinds of strings to get her out of the institution on a travel pass and up here from Florida. Technically she's still serving time for killing my uncle. Besides," he said, and came over to put his arms around me again, "I want to be able to concentrate on my beautiful bride, not be wondering if my mother is about to pull a gun from her purse to stop the ceremony."

We didn't talk for a while after that. We just stood there and kissed until my head began to spin. "We'd better take a break," I said. "I'm a little dizzy. I probably need to get some blood into me." I went to pull away.

"I have some if you want it," he said, looking at me with serious eyes. "Tonight might be a good time."

It would be the second biting. Fitz still wouldn't be one of my race, but he would be in transition, very close to crossing forever over the line. I scanned his face. Each day I appreciated him more. True, I had nearly lost my faith in him when my mother told me about his seeing Jessie, but I should have known that was just Mar-Mar making trouble.

Fitz's character was transparent. He did what he promised. He didn't disguise his feelings. He gave me his whole heart and sincerely wanted to stay with me, just me, for the rest of his days. Although he didn't say it, I had a feeling he had been given a desk job at the Secret Service. He had the guts to be a secret agent, but not the deceptive nature. It struck me that he'd make a terrible vampire. He wasn't suited to a life of duplicity and lies.

A good man does not a great vampire make.

Troubled by this realization, I sighed. Fitz was still waiting for my answer about having him for dinner. "Not tonight, my love," I said. "I'm really much too tired. Let's pour me a glass of type O and go to bed."

Emotions chased across his face—first confusion, then relief, then naked desire. "As long as we don't just 'go to bed,'" he said in a hoarse voice as he nuzzled my neck, "you're on."

Sated with the refrigerated blood and no longer worried about controlling my urges, I let Fitz lead me into my bedroom.

"Since you're tired," he said, "let me help you." One by one, he removed each piece of my clothing for me as I watched him with glowing eyes. His lovemaking was always full of surprises, and I wondered if he had anything special in store for me tonight.

When I was naked, he asked me to please lie down, for he was my servant and existed only to bring me pleasure. I watched him as he removed his clothes, my eyes feasting on his beautifully muscled body.

Then, unexpectedly, he reached down and removed something from his jeans. He put on a watch cap and a pair of gloves, which he must have been carrying around in his back pocket.

He reached out and fondled my breasts. He ran his gloved fingers down my body and between my legs. The texture of the gloves was erotic, almost electric. As for the watch cap, it changed his looks. It made him look more rugged, different, almost a stranger. Surprisingly, that was erotic too.

Then Fitz turned me on my stomach, and with the rough wool of his gloved hands he massaged me from head to toe. Sometimes he used almost too much force; other times he stroked with an amazing gentleness. My body became languid and liquid.

Then Fitz got off the bed and knelt on the floor, turning me again and swinging my long legs over his broad shoulders. Cupping me under my buttocks, he drew me forward until he licked the dark, warm place that now so longed for his touch.

I moaned softly and let him pleasure me with his tongue until I was nearly mewing like a cat. After I climaxed, Fitz came to lie next to me and took me in his arms. A slow, lazy coupling followed, leaving us both satisfied and ready to rest.

During the afternoon, I stirred enough to realize that Fitz had departed. I thought, *Let him enjoy the sunlight while he can,* and I slipped into my secret room to finish my long day's slumber into night.

On Monday I awoke at dusk, dressed quickly and hurried down to Bloomingdale's to meet Benny and Audrey for a shop-until-we-dropped evening. The moment we entered the store we began arguing over the colors for their bridesmaids' gowns. My one nonnegotiable demand was that they *not* wear black, and I said I would prefer it if they avoided red as well.

They balked at any pastel, and I didn't blame them. We threw out ideas until we agreed on a color scheme we laughingly called "deeper shades of pale."

Benny's off-the-rack dress, in ecru, was tight, cocktail length, and strapless. Audrey's dress, also a sheath but with a sheer "illusion" bodice and a high neckline, was a honey champagne. Nothing about their choices screamed "bridesmaid," and the dresses would later be perfect for any evening out. Benny wanted very high heels; Audrey went for the kitten type. The only matching items were the adorable retro beige satin hats we found, and their bouquets, which would be made of creamy calla lilies nestled among graceful wheat sheaves, an ancient symbol of prosperity.

When they modeled their outfits, Benny evoked Marilyn Monroe; Audrey recalled Audrey Hepburn. Both of them looked drop-undead gorgeous.

We finished up at an earlier hour than we expected, but I begged off joining them for a drink, and returned to my apartment, my arms laden with bags filled with my own purchases. A wave of sadness hit me as I opened the front door to the darkened rooms. All night my feelings had seesawed between exhilaration and a vague, gnawing anxiety. Now, barely acknowledging my animals, I walked into my bedroom and shut the door behind me. I put down my packages on the floor and opened the largest of the shopping bags.

My wedding dress was white—off-white, but white. It was a flowing ivory silk crepe gown with a back that plunged nearly to my waist. Its bodice had delicate beading and spaghetti straps; its hem spread out in a small puddle train. It had been astronomically expensive. But it was a magnificent dress, a designer's sample, and it hadn't even needed alterations. I laid it out on the bed and stared at it, my eyes misty.

I had never been married in all these centuries. I had never even been formally engaged. Despite my many love affairs and passionate flings, no vampire man and only one human—and his promise to wed me had been quickly broken—had ever wanted me as his bride. Maybe this kind of commitment was what I needed. I could relax and just be happy. Be happy? I couldn't imagine not feeling discontent, unsatisfied, or totally miserable about something for long.

I was also excited about returning to Italy. I hadn't been back to the villa in years. I needed to call the estate management and get it ready for our arrival. I remembered the smell of the rosemary bushes that grew outside the kitchen door. I recalled the sound of the wind through the tall pines next to the Tuscan-pink walls of the main villa. How I loved that house! I had decorated every room, picked out every painting. I wished I had never left it, and I knew once I returned how wrenching it would be to depart from it again.

I sat down on the floor of my bedroom and stroked my hand over the silk of my wedding dress. Memories of Montespertoli danced through my brain. I could hear the maid, the round and cheerful Estella, calling out as she came to my bedroom with a tray, "*Signora Urbano! Buon notte. Come stai? Bene, bene!*"

I smiled at the memory. Estella had died long ago, but her daughter would be waiting for me when my classic white Maserati, the one I kept in storage in Florence, pulled up to the electronic gates, bringing me home at last, this time with my groom. Lulled into contentment by that thought, I put my head down on the bed, and I must have fallen asleep, because the dream came to me then, more vivid, more real than it had ever been before.

I was walking in the garden of the inn at Missolonghi. Byron's arm encircled my waist. The night was still warm; the stars were like diamonds spilled across black velvet. The air smelled of roses—and of roast beef cooking in the kitchen.

A damp wind blew in from the sea. I shivered, and suddenly Byron stopped and bent double with a cry.

"What's wrong?" I asked. "Are you dizzy from drink? Are you ill?"

"Give me just a moment." He gasped. "I haven't been well lately. All the physicians seem to know is to bleed me. It's made me weak."

"You must not let them do that," I said with alarm. I feared Byron had been bled too much, and any further blood loss might be fatal.

He didn't answer, but after a time he steadied his breathing and straightened up. With his usual bravado, he gave me a wink and smiled, putting his arms about me again as if the incident had never happened. "I'll not let a damned surgeon kill me, my love. Don't you worry."

"Perhaps we should go inside," I urged.

"No," he insisted as he pulled a flask from his jacket and drank deeply of some strong spirits before putting it away. He looked deeply into my eyes. "I wish to be out here; I need the air. I'm stronger already. Let me prove it to you." He grabbed my hair with some force and pulled back my head, exposing my neck, which he kissed and gave little nips. Then he whispered in my ear, " 'She walks in beauty, like the night' "—he quoted himself, as he often did—" 'of cloudless climes and starry skies. And all that's best of dark and bright meet in her aspect and her eyes.' "

He led me over to the garden wall, positioned me against it, and planted his arms on either side of me. The stucco was rough against my back. He moved close, rubbing himself crudely against me. I could feel his stiffness through the silk of my skirt. I pretended I didn't like it and squirmed away.

"Oh, George," I said, "tell me of England, please. Do you miss it?"

His eyes dimmed and looked downward, his mouth trembled for just a second, and I felt instantly sorry that I had mentioned the land that had banished him forever.

After a pause, he shook off the sadness. "I prefer Greece," he answered. "Let's not talk about England.

Talking bores me. I am much more interested in this." He pulled my face toward his and kissed me with a hard, brutal kiss. He tasted of wine, and he had drunk too much. Yet my blood raced as his tongue plunged into my mouth and he pressed his hard body against mine.

But I playfully pushed him away again. I did not wish to make love in a garden. I preferred the soft bed in the upstairs room.

"Daphy," he said, looking annoyed, "come on, sweet thing, give me a little. You know you want to."

I knew what he wanted, and that his lust had nothing to do with wanting me. He wanted his way with a woman. That was his reputation, and it was true. But I didn't care. He grabbed me again and pulled me close. He moaned and brought his face to my breasts, pushing down my camisole with his long fingers and using his teeth to tease my nipples erect. I held his head in my hands, his hair coarse against my skin. I let him suckle as I fell into a swoon, wanting him so much.

He raised his head and looked into my eyes. I could have been anyone; there was no special recognition in them. "Daphy," he said. "You make me wild with longing. If I cannot have you now, my girl, you are going to be the death of me."

"Let's go inside, George," I whispered. "We will be so much more comfortable in bed."

But he was beyond reason, and he was also a little drunk. He held me fast in his arms. "It's been a long time since I've wanted a woman this much. There's something about you. Something."

Then he grabbed my hand hard. His cold signet ring bit deeply into my flesh, and I tingled from the pain, feeling a building excitement about what I knew was to come.

Byron dragged me over to a bench and pulled me down

on top of him. He slipped his hand up under my skirts. He made a low growl deep in his throat. He kissed me again, his lips like satin, wet and smooth. I closed my eyes. I was being carried away by sensation, wanting this man with a hunger that was building into an unstoppable desire. He lowered his mouth again to my breasts and bit me hard. My eyes flew open with the pain. Clouds chased across the rising moon, and as they cleared it, its pearly brightness lit up the landscape . . . and Byron's pale white neck.

I had no excuse for what I did except that I could not stop what fate had decreed to happen in that garden in Greece on April 19, 1824. My incisors grew long and sharp. A red glow flickered behind my eyes. I bent my head down—just as Byron himself, startled by my sudden movement, looked up.

Only then did recognition light his eyes. "You!" he cried, stunned, suddenly understanding. "My lady," he moaned as my teeth bit into his neck. And I, foolishly, forgetting he had been recently bled by idiot physicians, drank too much, too quickly. Lord Byron slipped into unconsciousness. Although his actual death would happen days later, I knew I had killed a great man, and my own one great love.

I began to cry and looked down at his face. But suddenly I felt confused: The face I saw wasn't Byron's; it was Fitz's. Why was he in Missolonghi?

"Daphne, wake up!" Someone was shaking my shoulder. "Wake up; you're having a dream."

"What? Oh. Oh, I was," I said, realizing I was in my bedroom and Fitz had found me sleeping.

"You were crying, I think," he said, and knelt down beside me on the floor. "Are you all right?"

"It was just a bad dream," I said, wiping my eyes on the back of my hand.

"I'm afraid I've seen your wedding dress," he said quietly. "I'm sorry. I hope it's not bad luck." He pushed the hair back from my face and kissed me lightly on the forehead. Then he sat beside me and gathered me into his arms.

"I'm not superstitious," I said, then fell silent. I laid my head on his shoulder. I was trying to clear my mind, which was foggy and confused. I felt sorely troubled by what I had dreamed. The memories of Byron had been so vivid. Killing him had been the worst thing I had ever done in my life. But why had a dream about that awful night come to me now?

"What's the date on Thursday, our wedding day?" I finally said to Fitz.

"April nineteenth," he said.

The epiphany came with a terrible flood of understanding. If I bit Fitz tonight, then bit him again for the third time on our wedding night, he would not survive. How could I have forgotten that he had almost died less than two months ago? He had lost so much blood when he was wounded. With a crystalline vision of his death before me, I knew I could not risk it.

Even if Fitz did not die—and now I was sure he would— I knew he lacked the darkness within that a vampire must have. In my heart I knew the truth: Making him someone like me would be the wrong thing to do.

We sat there together on the floor of my bedroom for a while without speaking. I let myself feel comforted by the solidity of his body beside me. I allowed myself the luxury of being held safe and secure by his arms. From my centuries on this earth I knew *tristesse*. I felt it now. The last experience of this wonderful thing needed to be savored, for it would be only a memory soon.

"Fitz," I said at last. "We need to talk, and what I have to tell you won't be easy."

He kissed me lightly on the top of my head and tightened his arms around me. "You sound so serious, Daphne. Whatever you tell me, it will be okay. We've both done things we regret. But that's in the past. We have each other now."

"No," I said, twisting around in his embrace so I could look at him. "No, that's not what I mean. Listen; please hear me out."

"All right," he said solemnly, and watched my face.

"Fitz, I want to marry you. I realized tonight how much I really do, and what an honor it would be to become your wife. But I also realized that I want to be with you and that I care about you *because* you're the man that you are. What I cherish most about you is your character—your goodness, honor, honesty, loyalty, and selflessness."

"You'll make me blush," he said, and grinned, kissing my forehead once more.

I pulled back, putting my hands on either side of his long face. "Fitz, listen to me. Those are human qualities. A vampire cannot possess them and still survive. And if I make you into a vampire—and I'm not sure even my biting you would succeed in doing that—then I will have lost you forever. I will have lost the man, the *human,* whom I want to spend forever with, and you'll lose yourself."

"What are you trying to tell me?" Fitz asked.

"I cannot make you a vampire," I said. "And if you don't become a vampire, I can't marry you."

He stared at me, confusion evident in his eyes. "Can't we just fake it? We'll pretend I'm a vampire. We can still get married," he suggested.

I shook my head sadly. "No. It wouldn't work. My mother would know." I had put his engagement ring on when I went shopping. Now I slipped it off and put it in his hand. "Fitz, I cannot be your wife."

"No!" he cried out, putting it back in my hand and closing my fingers over it. "That ring belongs to you. If you don't want to wear it, I understand. But my heart hasn't changed. In it, I will be always married to you," he said in a strangled voice.

"Oh, Fitz, please. You are making this so hard." I could barely talk, my throat was so tight with pain.

"Daphne, Daphne," he moaned, letting me go and putting his face in his hands. "You should go ahead and bite me. I have nowhere to turn. Don't you see that? If you don't, another vampire will—or I will be killed."

"Fitz, I won't let that happen, but you have to leave—quickly, tonight. I want you to run," I said.

"Run?" He raised his head and looked at me, not understanding.

"Yes, get out of here. Take off. I can tell you how to escape them. I can tell you what you need to do. If you're careful, no vampire will ever be able to get to you."

Then I took his hands and held them in my own. I kissed his cheek. I talked to him long past midnight, telling him all I knew about living life on the run, as I had done for hundreds of years. As I had escaped the vampire hunters, I explained how he could elude the vampires hunting him. I urged him to go to Ireland, where he was connected by blood and soul to the land. I told him about the "thin places" in that lush, green magical land that were alive with invisible spirits and protected by fairy rings. No vampire ever dared tread in those sacred places. I promised him that if he followed carefully my instructions and remembered all my secrets, his days would always be safe, and even in the dark of night, when monsters like me roamed the land, he could sleep in peace.

"You won't be able to come back here, though," I admonished him at the end of my long instructions. "New York City is a vampire playground. There is no more dangerous place on earth for you to go, except maybe Los Angeles."

Fitz had listened quietly throughout my recitation.

Occasionally he had asked for clarification. He took out a pen and wrote down the locations, like the Hill of Tara, where he could find sanctuary. "Will I ever see you again?" he asked at last.

I shook my head, and in a voice laden with tears I said, "I don't know. But I don't think so."

It was close to the hour of the wolf, and dawn would be breaking all too soon. We had to go.

We went together to Fitz's apartment, where he retrieved his passport and packed his bags. He gave me the house keys and explained what needed to be done to put his finances in order and transport his belongings into storage. I promised him I would do everything that needed to be done. Then he told me, when I helped him pack his suitcases, to keep whatever I wished from what he was leaving behind.

"What could I possibly want when you are gone?" I sighed.

He thought for a moment before he took off his claddagh ring and put it on my hand. "Then take this. Do you know about its meaning?"

"No. Something about friendship, I think," I said.

"Look here. In the center of the ring is a heart. The band of the ring is two hands that hold it. Atop the heart sits a crown. The ring itself symbolizes the love between two hearts that are oceans apart. The heart is for love, the hands for friendship or togetherness, and the crown is for loyalty." He held my hands tightly. "My darling—and you will always be 'my darling'—no one symbolizes all those things better than you." He closed my fingers over the ring and brought my hand to his lips. He held it there until it was wet from his tears.

Fitz drove his silver Prius to Kennedy airport and stopped at the international departure gate. He climbed out of the driver's side. I emerged from the passenger's seat. We met at the back of the car. Tears were streaming down my face. He looked on the verge of breaking down. But there was nothing left to say. He pulled his luggage out of the trunk and handed me the car keys.

"Stay safe," I whispered.

"I love you," he said, and searched my face with those eyes as gray as the Irish sea.

I never wanted to forget how they looked. I never wanted to forget him. And I had never told him I loved him, not even once. "Fitz, I—"

"Hush," he said, in a voice that was almost a whisper. "I know. You don't have to say the words 'I love you.' Everything you did tonight showed me how much you do."

I couldn't bear to look at him. I turned my head. "You'd better hurry," I said, the cold metal of the car keys cutting into my clenched hand. "Remember everything I told you."

He didn't answer, but I realized he had picked up his luggage and stepped onto the curb. I looked at him beginning to walk away. Suddenly he stopped and turned around. "Daphne?"

I waited for the last words I might ever hear him say.

"Remember me," he said. Then St. Julien Fitzmaurice joined the stream of passengers hurrying into the terminal and disappeared from view.

And I let the best man I had ever loved walk away.

CHAPTER 22

Being entirely honest with oneself is a good exercise.

—Sigmund Freud, *Letter to Fliess*

Dry your tears, straighten your shoulders, and go on. That's what I've learned in over four hundred years on this planet. Moaning about disappointments, railing against fate, or sitting around bitching about how unfair life is— that's the behavior of quitters and losers. The only antidote to getting smacked down is to get back up.

Having good friends helps. After a day's rest and nonstop weeping, I found myself out of tears. I called Benny. She called Audrey. They both came over with some Ben & Jerry's ice cream and a DVD of *Casablanca.* We made some popcorn and watched the film. In unison we recited the lines everybody knows. Then, at the end of the movie, when Rick makes Ilsa get on the plane with her husband, we all called out the line where he tells her if she stayed she'd regret it, not today or tomorrow, but soon and for the rest of her life.

Of course I started bawling my eyes out again, and all three of us hugged and I had a last good cry.

Afterward, we finished off the ice cream, sat around, and talked about the mission we'd just finished. We laughed about deceiving J. Of course we thought our dirty trick was amusing. We're vampires, after all.

Then I asked them what I should do about telling Mar-Mar the wedding was off, and we got serious. The consensus was I had to stall as long as I could. Then all I would say was that Fitz didn't show up one night and when I went looking for him, his phone was disconnected, his apartment was sublet, and he had disappeared. We considered faking his death, but that scheme got vetoed. Mar-Mar would never fall for it.

In the end we realized it was up to Fitz to escape her. I really didn't think my mother would try too hard to find him, now that he was out of her daughter's life and out of New York. Anyway, it wouldn't help to worry. Accept the things you cannot change, as the twelve-steppers say.

But I did have one more thing I needed to do to make myself feel better. With a little help from my girlfriends, I intended to get even with Rogue.

The vampire-only victory party began at midnight. Originally, the gathering was to have been my wedding reception, and emotionally I was still dealing with a lot of pain. At the same time I was a pragmatist. It would have been a shame to waste the liquor and food, including the special treat of three dozen pints of rare AB-negative blood that were tastefully displayed on a bed of ice.

A glowing Benny showed up on the arm of Chaser chief Martin. Cormac escorted the Racers' Gerry, although I thought it more a courteous act than a romantic one. Audrey, sleek, tall, and fitted with contact lenses, looked like a runway model when she arrived with the other Laundromat regulars who had helped in the rescue.

Rogue came alone, as planned and manipulated by the Darkwing females; Benny and Audrey had both twisted his arm to be my escort for the evening. He strode in the door filled with arrogance: a big, bold biker, holding a bottle of beer. Coors Light. It wasn't even an imported brand. He also looked damned good. You had to wonder how a man with that big a chest could be blessed with such a cute little tush.

Wearing his black leather club jacket (I suspected he slept in it) and black leather pants, Rogue had completed his outfit with a tight black T-shirt and motorcycle boots. The master key for a motorcycle chain dangled from the right boot's cross-strap. He wore a heavy silver bracelet, and nearly every finger sported a silver ring. His Fu Manchu mustache was trimmed, his head was freshly shaved, and I detected the spice and wood scents of Brut aftershave. He had gone all-out for the evening.

I had also dressed carefully for the occasion. Correctly predicting Rogue's sartorial splendor, I had chosen my clothes to mirror his tastes. I too wore black leather pants along with a plunging black halter top, and I had put on black boots with four-inch heels. I accessorized with a spiked leather choker around my neck and shoulder-length dangling earrings. My makeup relied heavily on kohl eyeliner. The look, a mixture of punk and S and M, was a bit outré for me, but tonight was all about my "theater of the payback," not fashion.

As Rogue approached me, I greeted him with a sad smile and a sweet kiss. I took his hand and led him over to the booze-and-blood table. I heard one woman whisper, "He's hot," when we passed. Another one remarked, "When she's done with him, I want a turn."

I had instructed Benny, who offered to act as the deejay, to pick out music that allowed for conversation. I didn't want to be yelling over the top of Seven Mary Three or Jane's Addiction. As soon as Rogue made his appearance, she had put on Billie Holiday singing "Love for Sale."

"So you got dumped," Rogue said as he put down his empty bottle and grabbed another beer from an open cooler. Then, picking up a bottle of Jameson from the bar, he set up a shot glass to make himself a boilermaker.

"I guess it was not to be." I sighed. I paused for effect before I continued. "It was really your fault, though."

"How's that?" he said as he chugged the beer straight from the bottle.

"It was the comparison. You know what I mean. After you and I . . . well, got it on that night, Fitz kept coming up short."

Rogue laughed.

"I just couldn't get excited by him anymore, to tell the truth. Plus he was too white-bread." I looked shyly down toward the floor, letting my silky hair hide my face. Then I flipped it back and moved closer to Rogue, my mouth very close to his. "How do I put it without seeming crude? Let's just say he preferred the missionary position."

"And you like to be on top, don't you?" Rogue said, openly leering at me and leaning forward as if to kiss.

I moved away and smacked him playfully on the arm. "Now, come on; that's not true. And *you* of all people should know it's not true. You were definitely in control when we . . . when we . . . you know. I guess I like a man who's . . . umm . . . a little more 'adventurous,' if you know what I mean."

Rogue raised an eyebrow. "I might."

I handed him another beer and poured him another shot of whiskey. "Of course, I wouldn't know for sure about you. You were pretty rushed that night. Is that normal with you? Maybe you're one of those premature ejaculators." I looked at him with limpid doe eyes and sighed.

Rogue looked insulted. "Hey, I was in a hurry. We were out there in public, in the hall, remember? But I ain't one of those guys who produces the juice before he puts it in the caboose."

"You have to have some kind of flaw," I simpered, "or why would you still be single?"

"Why?" he said. "'Cause I'm not the kind of guy who likes

to settle down." I stifled a groan. Byron at least quoted himself. Rogue paraphrased Golden Oldies.

"Oh, I can see that. So many women, so little time, right?" I batted my eyelashes shamelessly.

"Yeah, that's right." He grinned.

"Are you ready for some blood?" I asked. "I know you prefer yours live, but this is rather special."

"I'll try it," he said. "Why not?"

I decanted a pint and led him off to a corner of the large living room to a table. I made small talk as he drank.

"So what do you really like?" I asked. "For sex, I mean."

"I'm not big on talking about it," he said as he sipped, clearly enjoying the drink.

I ran my finger over the tablecloth and kept my eyes cast down. My other hand went under the tablecloth, and my fingers worked their way up his thigh to stroke his crotch. "I should tell you something. A secret," I whispered conspiratorially. "Not that I like to brag about it, but I spent some time in a caliph's seraglio. I was, well, *forced* to learn some interesting techniques."

Through the leather of his pants, I felt Rogue get harder.

"I've seen it all," he said dismissively.

"Really? I bet I could teach you something." I looked at him all wide-eyed. I had grabbed his attention while I was grabbing his crotch. I could almost see what was going through his brain. But I didn't want to make this too easy. I removed my hand from beneath the table.

"You know, I think I'd better mingle. I'm the hostess," I said brightly, and stood up. "You just enjoy yourself for a while. Have another drink if you'd like," I suggested.

As I passed by him I leaned down and whispered in his ear, "Did you ever try Maithuna? It gives an orgasm that lasts . . . well, for a very, very long time." I turned his face toward mine, kissed him, and gave him some tongue before I walked away.

Audrey and Benny both did their part, spending time with Rogue and keeping him downing alcohol. They told him how I really needed something to make me forget losing Fitz, and they'd just bet nobody could make me forget faster than he could. I don't know what else they said to feed his ego, but they could shovel it with the best of them.

After a while, Rogue didn't take his eyes off me as I flirted with every unattached male vampire in the room.

As the evening rolled toward a close with the guests leaving one by one, I did get into another conversation with my target for the evening. I was stroking Rogue's ego this time. Although the subject was not sexual, it was very enlightening. I asked him about the exchange he'd had with Lieutenant Johnson.

"What's the story, Rogue? I've been totally convinced you are really a biker. Is it all an act?" I asked. I said it lightly, but the whole issue bothered me deeply. I wondered if he had been planted in the Darkwings by my mother. I wouldn't put it past her, and the conversation she'd had with Fitz that night in Scarsdale, about me "cheating on him" because of bloodlust, suddenly seemed part of a setup, with Rogue doing his part.

Rogue didn't answer right away. He took a swig of beer, then put his bottle down. "I'm a biker. Shit, yes. I was living in Texas during the 1980s, down near Kemah when I started running with the Bandidos. But shit happens. I had my reasons for working for the government. I'm not a rat bastard. Call me patriotic maybe." He looked at me. I was sure he wasn't totally sober anymore. "Ah, sweetheart, you didn't think I got picked for the Darkwings out of a hat, did you? I was on a list or something. As for the stuff with Johnson, that's between him and me. It's nobody else's business. Let's talk about something else."

So that was as much as I was going to find out, I guessed. Rogue was a spook in the world of smoke and mirrors I now called my own, but how he ended up in prison and why, I didn't know. And I didn't know how deeply he was entangled with my mother, if at all.

When the last guests finally left, I turned to Rogue and said, "You don't have to leave, you know?"

"Yeah, I know," he said.

I took his hand. He was unsteady on his feet as I led him into my bedroom. Earlier I had set up everything I'd need to make the night a success. I started to undress him. He sat down on the bed and stretched out a foot for me to take off his boots.

"You know," he said in a lazy voice, "when I was in Texas, I never once took off my own boots."

"A man like you shouldn't have to," I cooed, almost choking on my cloying tone.

When he was naked, I shimmied out of my clothes. He was half sitting, propped up by pillows. I knelt between his legs and took his stiff shaft into my mouth. It really wasn't a hardship. I might be angry at Rogue, but he was—no lie—a very sexy guy.

And I knew that no man will refuse fellatio, anytime, anywhere. I soon had Rogue groaning and thoroughly enjoying himself. He was so relaxed and inebriated, my only worry was that he'd fall asleep.

"Now for a taste of the Maithuna I promised you," I said in a breathy voice.

"Anything you say, babe," he moaned. "But it doesn't get much better than this."

"Oh, yes, it will. It's going to make you scream and squirm like nothing you've ever felt before. That is, if you're *adventurous* enough."

"Bring it on," he groaned, "and stop talking about it."

I trailed kisses up his stomach, and rubbed my body over his. Then I lifted his hand, and with a fast, efficient motion, I cuffed his wrist with a pair of the NYPD's finest steel handcuffs. The other end of the cuff was fastened around a post in the headboard of my brass bed.

"Huh?" Rogue said, and looked around, seeming a little dazed.

"Oh, come on, don't be a party pooper," I said as I reached in the bed-table drawer and took out a special leather ring. I slipped it on his turgid member. It keeps a man up when he might want to go down if a woman gets it on him right. It felt good, I'm sure, because Rogue moaned in pleasure and didn't pull away when I slipped a second handcuff on his other wrist.

Then, using some of the techniques I really did learn in the seraglio, I used my fingers to manipulate and probe Rogue into a state of near ecstasy. He kept saying, "Oh baby, that's good, that's so good."

When he was close to climaxing, I stopped. He started to protest, but I whispered, "Give me just a minute. I've got to get something I bought just for tonight. It's got these special little silver balls . . . well, you'll see; it'll take you higher than you've ever been before," I breathed into his ear.

Then I slipped off the bed and quickly gathered up Rogue's clothes in my arms. I hurried out of the bedroom and rushed into my secret room. I dumped Rogue's clothes on the floor. When I climbed into my coffin feeling nearly happy, I thought I could hear some muffled curses. Or maybe they were cries for help.

Of course, I knew Rogue could free his hands eventually, although I'd probably have to buy a new bed after his struggle damaged the old one. But by the time he escaped his tether, he would be very uncomfortable from having to wear the cock ring so long.

I had been considerate enough to leave Rogue a bath towel to wear on his cab ride home. He was welcome to use it—unless, of course, he borrowed something from that young dog walker—if he was still here when the guy arrived to pick up Jade in another four or five hours.

All in all, I had a very good night.

EPILOGUE

Naturally, I wasn't over Fitz, not after I got even with Rogue, not as the days rolled past through the rest of the spring, which remained free of any Code Reds and left me bored, with nothing official for the Darkwings to do.

Audrey, Benny, and I met frequently and shopped. I had my teary moments, but I have to admit, I moped about thinking of Fitz less and less. I decided I needed to take a break from men—all of them, Rogue included.

But I confess, whenever I thought back on the girls' rescue, I got a glow. A lot of good things had happened that night.

Feeling immensely pleased with myself topped the list.

The Sunday morning following our successful wrap-up of the mission, the rescue of the "debutante prisoners" was all over the newspapers. None of the reporters got the facts anywhere near correct, but that was a good thing. The press release from the city's police commissioner talked about an anonymous tip from members of a private "social club" on the Lower East Side, who heard cries for help when they were waiting on the subway platform early Saturday evening.

A full-color picture of Lt. Moses Johnson giving a thumbs-up was emblazoned across the front page of the *Daily News* under the headline TERROR UNDERGROUND. On Sunday night Johnson had a whole hour with Larry King on CNN and on Monday morning Matt Lauer interviewed him for the *Today* show. When Al Roker let him do the weather from Rockefeller Center, I think it was the first time I ever saw the man smile.

J could never prove that I, or any of us Darkwings, were involved with getting the girls out of the old Hudson Terminal, but he was sure we'd been behind the whole thing. His suspicions were fed by one sentence in an early edition of the *New York Times*. It read: "Several of the girls insisted they had been carried out of their underground prison by a special federal rescue team wearing bat suits. It was later determined that they had been heavily drugged by the terrorists and were probably suffering from a mass hallucination." The sentence disappeared from later editions.

Nicoletta survived and was recovering. Judge Marshall Morris was never called a hero. We discovered his fate when Mrs. Mary Morris messengered a lovely thank-you note to the office. She told us that Nicoletta would be fine and was having an ear reconstructed by a top plastic surgeon from cartilage taken from her ribs. Her appearance would be normal, but she owed her life to us. In a P.S. Mrs. Morris added that she had filed for divorce. Later we heard that the judge retired from the federal bench and had gone to live in Costa Rica.

In early June, the weather having turned unseasonably hot, I sat at my kitchen island with the apartment's air conditioner turned up full-blast, more for Jade's comfort than my own. I was reading the *New York Times* and getting a chuckle from a Metro Briefing story about a man in Connecticut who pleaded guilty to blowing up portable toilets in three towns.

He blamed his vendetta against the innocent privies on a prescription drug he had been taking that made him think the privies were spying on him.

I also laughed at a stupid criminal in Alabama who had donned a ski mask before carrying out a home invasion and yelling at an elderly man, "Give me all your money and valuables. And Paw-Paw, I mean it!" His grandfather called the police to tell them his grandson had robbed him of fifty bucks.

I was about to turn to a different section to start the cross-word puzzle when I noticed another news story buried in the back pages of the first section:

> As of Monday, June 5, the Intrepid Sea, Air, & Space Museum will be closed. The ship has been towed off for repairs and the pier will also be renovated. No date has been set for the ship to return or the museum to reopen.

I would have forgotten about it, I'm sure, since I had no plans to visit the popular tourist attraction, if the phone hadn't started ringing right at that moment. I let it ring while I located the crossword puzzle; then I lazily reached over and answered it. I figured it was Audrey or Benny calling with news of a sample sale or something equally as urgent.

To my surprise, J's voice barked into my ear, "Agent Urban, get to the office ASAP. Code Red. Do you copy? Code Red."

I yelped out "Yes!" hung up, and ran to the bedroom to throw on some clothes. After our long hiatus, the Darkwings were being called to another mission: I was about to find out that the *Intrepid,* that grand old World War II aircraft carrier, had not been sent out for repairs. It had vanished, as if into thin air. . . .

ACKNOWLEDGMENTS

Books don't get written and published without a great deal of collaboration and serendipity. As always I owe a debt to many people during the creation of this fourth in the Darkwing series. My editor at NAL, Liz Scheier, has been the leading light and biggest help in the writing of this tale. If I haven't said thank-you loudly enough, I hope she hears me now: Thank you, Liz!

But fate also had a hand in this one. In the summer of 2006, I was on a plane flying from Cincinnati to Atlanta, en route to the Romance Writers of America annual conference. By chance I was sitting next to a woman named Brynda J. Huntley, at that time a senior buyer for a company called Force Protection Industries. We talked about Charleston (her destination and a favorite city of mine), food, antiques, and business flying.

Finally, during our conversation, Brynda told me what Force Protection Industries made: the Buffalo, the leading armored vehicle in use by American forces in Afghanistan and Iraq. I said I had heard of a Hummer, but not a Buffalo. She laughed. She also told me about Al Qaeda's and other terrorists' attempts to capture one, and why it was so important that they never do.

I mentally shouted, "Eureka," and the plot for *In the Blood* was born. More impressive than my words can convey, the Buffalo is a beast of a machine. I encourage everyone to get a glimpse of this aspect of the real war in the Middle East by accessing the company's Web site, www.forceprotectioninc.com. You will discover a fascinating inside story that isn't on the nightly news.

And readers should know, without a doubt, that this book is completely fictional, entirely made up. But the techniques I describe on surveillance, specifically that done by Daphne and Cormac on Church Street, can be found in *Shadowing and Surveillance: A Complete Guidebook* by Burt Rapp. Really, it's common sense, but you might pick up a few pointers, as I did. Be aware that the book, originally published in 1986, could use a technological update.

Similarly, Mitchel Field, where I locate the ransom drop, no longer exists, but it once did, south of today's LaGuardia Airport. Charles A. Lindbergh used it as a base during his tours (but his famous transatlantic flight began at nearby Roosevelt Field). Mitchel Field was also used as headquarters for the Continental Air Command from 1947 through 1949. After some devastating plane crashes into the residential area that was built up around it—the most notable was when a P-47 smashed into Hofstra University's Bernard Hall—the field was closed in 1961. Nassau County Community College has since been built over the site of this historic airfield. Several hangars, including Mitchel Field's hangar three, now a museum, do remain, but the Mitchel Field I describe is real only in my imagination.

As for the real-life underworld of New York, the Internet holds a wealth of information on the unused and abandoned subway, trolley, and train tracks, terminals, and stations that truly do exist under the streets of Manhattan—including the old Hudson Terminal. The New York transit system (www.nycsubway.org) is one such site. Another excellent resource is the site "Abandoned Stations" by Joseph Brennan (www.columbia.edu/~brennan/abandoned). Publications on this fascinating subject include *Rails Under the Mighty Hudson: The Story of the Hudson Tubes, the Pennsy Tunnels, and Manhattan Transfer* by Brian J. Cudahy and *The City Beneath Us: Building the New York Subway* by the New York Transit Museum with Vivian Heller.

My descriptions of this vast underground labyrinth, however, are fictionalized, partially drawn from childhood memories of riding the PATH trains from Newark to Manhattan and from spending countless hours on subways in Manhattan and Brooklyn during my hippie youth. Mostly, however, they were created from my nightmares and the phantasmagoria of my imagination.

Last, regarding the clubs of the vampire underworld, alas (or thank goodness), none of them are real, nor are they based on any actual clubs in Manhattan. The only association— and it's a very loose one—between reality and my fictional night spots concerns the biker bar. Charlie's Harley Hangout was modeled after an actual Harley hangout on Wednesday Street in Houston, Texas. The fight that I describe, in which Daphne meets Rogue, was based on one that truly happened . . . and that I happened to know about. 'Nuff said.

Hugs and love,
Savannah Russe

Read on for an excerpt from the next book
in the *Darkwing Chronicles*

UNDER DARKNESS

Coming from Signet Eclipse in May 2008

Hope is the thing with feathers
That perches in the soul.

—Emily Dickinson

The footsteps—slow and measured, heavy and determined—hit the pavement behind me with the steady rhythm of a funeral drum. The sound alone told me that they belonged to a man of considerable size and consequence. I didn't have to look back. I knew he meant trouble.

At half past three a.m., night covered Manhattan like a shroud. A fast, hard June shower had just ended, leaving the stone buildings black with rain. As I passed, their windows stared at me with blank, empty eyes. Until the arrival of the man, only the occasional swish of a yellow cab's tires on the wet streets had broken the hush of the late hour. The cool air felt as sharp as a knife blade when I inhaled deeply and kept walking, my dog, Jade, on a leash at my side.

Glancing down, I saw Jade's body tense, her tail going straight, her ears up. The footsteps became quicker, got closer. To anyone watching, I appeared to be an ordinary young woman, taller than most and thin as death. Perhaps, as I strolled alone on the empty city streets, a mugger or a rapist had targeted me as easy prey.

That thought fled as quickly as it came. Who was I kidding? Sane people invariably drew back from me, giving me a wide berth. Some ancient instinct struck dread in their very bones, telling them that I was someone—no, not some*one*, but some*thing*—to avoid. As for the crazies of New York City, even they weren't stupid: my huge malamute, looking more like a wolf than a dog, kept them away.

That meant the odds were 101 out of 99 that my stalker was a vampire hunter. If I didn't do something quickly, I was about to die.

West End Avenue intersected with my block about two hundred feet ahead of me. I broke into a run, Jade keeping up with my stride. I reached the corner, turned sharply, hugged the granite wall of an apartment building, and stopped. I turned, crouched, and quickly released Jade's chain. I readied myself to attack.

I never got the chance. The moment the man passed the wall of the building and appeared, Jade sprang so fast that her body became a blur of snarling rage. With a growl that made my blood run cold, she knocked him flat, her teeth sinking deeply into his forearm. He screamed. The polished wooden stake he clutched in his ham hock of a hand arced up, catching the light of a streetlamp before spinning and falling into the street with a clatter.

My mind became a haze of red anger and no thought. Irrational and reacting, I raced after the lethally sharp implement, meaning to use it as a weapon of my own. I grabbed it from the asphalt. My long fingers tightened around its smoothness. I raised it high above my head and charged toward my assailant, seeing him clearly for the first time.

Fighting to push Jade off and struggling to stand, the hunter was a fearsome sight. Clad entirely in black, he was broad and solid. With no visible neck, his head appeared to sit directly on his body, so thick were the muscles of his shoulders. He had a wrestler's build and an assassin's face, flat and dull and cruel. A thick silver chain wrapped diagonally like a bandolier across his wide chest. Three more stakes hung from it.

The sight of the stakes drove me toward madness. Throughout my centuries on this earth, too many of my friends had felt the piercing agony such an instrument delivered. And as a stake drove into a vampire's heart, from the vampire's lips came a last terrible scream—a heartrending animal cry of pure terror. Then came the fierce, horrible burning: the withering of flesh and bones crumbling to dust until nothing but a fine dry ash remained.

These memories fueled my rage. My own animal nature took control of my soul. My mouth widened to show the terrible whiteness of my pointed incisors. I think I was screaming as I leapt forward, intending to drive the glistening point into the hunter's slab-like face. But as I struck, he twisted away and the stake grazed his cheek, leaving an angry streak of red. Shaking Jade from his arm at last, he gained his feet. My dog flew at his legs, her barks and snarls wild with fury. He ran then, but in the moment before he moved, his dark eyes sought mine and I felt their hatred.

I did not give chase. My chest heaving, my brain spinning, I stopped. I called Jade back and she returned to me, her mouth smeared with blood. I found her leash on the sidewalk and snapped it on. I still held the long, smooth wooden stake in my hand as my dog and I retraced my steps and headed home.

As I pushed my way through the glass doors into the lobby of my apartment building, I spotted Mickey, the doorman, asleep in a wooden chair. The *New York Post* lay spread on his lap; his hanging head bobbed up and down with his snores like a davening Jew at temple.

So much for security. Annoyed, I walked over and gave a leg of his chair a kick.

"Huh?" he said, lifting his head, his eyelids fluttering. "Wah?" he muttered as his gaze fastened at knee level on my faded jeans. He tipped up his chin for his barely open eyes to take in my black tank top until he focused on my face and my eyes, which held no warmth. "Miss Urban? Wah you want? Your dry cleaning?" His breath smelled of beer.

"You were asleep again, Mickey!" I gave the chair another kick out of pique. My voice sounded shrill even to my own ears.

Giving his head a shake, he stuck out a rubbery lower lip and said, "No way, Miss Urban. No way. Just resting my eyes."

I snorted. "Yeah, right. Listen, this is important. Has anybody been around asking about me? A big guy? Maybe earlier tonight?"

Mickey's bleary eyes got wider, and he stared at the stake in my hand. Suddenly he got it. "No," he said and lumbered to his feet. "The Brits after you again, Miss Urban?"

Mickey's brain was scrambled eggs from drink, but he was a tough old guy. After taking a beating on my behalf a few months back, he had made up his mind that I was working undercover for the IRA. He wasn't that far off. I was a spy, but for a top secret American intelligence organization, a deep-black operation called the Darkwings that was so hush-hush, even I didn't know which agency hired me. I was one of the original three Darkwings; now there were five of us in this antiterrorist group, vampires one and all.

My completely nocturnal existence alone would have been enough to raise questions about my identity. I also received deliveries from a blood bank every week. And strange men and women showed up to find me at all hours of the night. They were furtive visitors who ran the gamut from a New York City police detective to a Mafia hit man.

Privy to some of the shadiest aspects of my life, the world-weary doorman had come up with an explanation for me that sat a lot better in his scheme of things than the truth would have. He could envision me as a spy, but as a blood-drinking vampire who looked to be in her midtwenties but was over four hundred years old? No way. So if my recent love affair with the proudly Irish St. Julien Fitzmaurice, who had often taken the time to listen to the doorman's stories and to discuss the troubles of Northern Ireland, convinced Mickey I was a Provo, that was cool.

I also would never forget that Mickey had put himself in harm's way for me. My voice was softer when I answered his question about whether I was in deep doo-doo once again. "To tell the truth, I don't know," I said. "Watch your back, okay?"

Fully awake now and ready for action, he shot out his words like bullets. "Don't you worry about me. I'm from Ulster, y'know."

"I know, Mick, and a fine young lad you must have been," I said with a gentle smile. "Who's on days this week?"

"McDougal. I'll fill him in. We got you covered, Miss Urban," he assured me.

"Thanks. I appreciate it." I tugged on Jade's leash and moved toward the elevator, my step lively but a heaviness weighing down my heart. I hoped my double life didn't get Mickey or somebody else in my building killed one day. I pushed the number for my floor, and as the door slid shut, I thought, *Evil thwarted doesn't go away. It just waits for a more opportune time.*